It Started In Tonopah
It Became A Fight For Survival
Melvyn Wallis

ISBN 978-1-0687378-0-0 (paperback)

ISBN 978-1-0687378-1-7 (ebook)

Published by Melvyn Wallis

Contents

Preface

This is a book I felt compelled to do. I needed to tell this story because I had dreams on and off for two years and in the dreams it was about adversity that had befallen mankind. The dreams continued and every time it happened the very next day I would write everything down. The characters were very real to me in the dreams and the story line developed. Everything was written down and I filled many note pads. Then I decided to share everything with you to tell the story because the dreams were so vivid it was as if I was there....You never know because I was given names of the people and they are all in the book. I hope you enjoy the book. Oh by the way the dreams have not stopped and I have already started to make notes again.

To my parents, who gave me the gift of dreams and the ability to realize them

To my wife whose endless patience, unwavering support, and ability to put up with my quirks have been the bedrock of this endeavour. Your love has been my guiding light.

To our mischievous Bengal cats, for their unconditional love, playful antics, and the countless moments of inspiration they've provided, often by simply curling up beside me as I wrote and yes even when they played with the keyboard

And to the vivid dreams that whispered stories, urging me to put pen to paper, transforming fleeting thoughts into lasting words.

Acknowledgements

I would like to say a **Thank You** to all the people that have helped me along the way I dedicate that book to them all

Chapter 1

VACATION

Yesterday had been a hot day and Death Valley proved to be a staggering 120 degrees in the shade so last nights welcome stay at the hotel in Beatty was more than welcome we arrived pretty late the night before with no one else in sight apart from the Tesla electric car owner charging his car on the rapid charger he was telling me how good the car is and how far it can go. After this hot day I was not too interested although the car looked the real deal. After a good nights sleep we made our way to reception to check out. Well, let me introduce myself I am James McDonald, everyone calls me Jim and my wife is Barbara married for ten years so we pretty much know each other inside out. Some people say that I look a bit like Clint Eastwood so yes I will take that compliment although I can't see the resemblance and my hair is much greyer than dear old Clint's .

Well we arrived in the States just a few days ago from England and we have been visiting the usual landmarks, a quick tour of Las Vegas left us completely shattered so we chilled out in Boulder City and visited the Hoover Dam and although we have visited many times it never ceases to amaze me how all the way back in the thirties did they manage to build it, pure hard graft but there was tragic loss of life. Now more about Barbara who is a beautiful woman looking more like

Jim's daughter but don't tell her about that as she does not like to hear that one bit she is fifteen years his younger and they are happy and Jim likes the fact she looks like a movie star nice figure tall and blond hair.

ave been to Death Valley many times over the decades, it's a place you just keep going back to. As already mentioned we arrived at the Motel 6 in Beatty late at night. After a good nights sleep we loaded the car after checking out at reception with the grumpy receptionist who looked as if she would rather be somewhere else.

We departed Beatty as the heat started rising outside, we made a quick stop to buy some coke (that's the soft drink version of course) and making sure there was plenty of water on board before departing Beatty. As we moved off the car temperature gauge read 90F and it was only 10:30 in the morning and rising all the time. The air con kicked in and it was soon pretty comfortable protected by the technology, now we headed North. I have always been interested in tech and little did i know what was ahead. We approached Goldfield the first thing we noticed a flashing road sign saying 25 mph a quick check on the speed to make sure no unwarranted tickets were picked up so we proceeded at caution. We went by the hotel that was once owned by Wyatt Earp and we decided to stop at what appeared to be an open air museum and there was no one around although we shouted to see if we could get anyone's attention but no one answered maybe it wasn't a museum but we had a quick look around and the uncanny thing was we had not seen anyone in Goldfield at all not even the cop car ready to give you a ticket for exceeding that 25 mph limit.

With somehow we had an uneasy feeling in Goldfield it left us both feeling very strange because there was no one to be seen. Now back on the road to Tonopah and famous for its UFO sightings. We pulled over for a coffee we had prepared before leaving the Motel 6 in Beatty earlier, "What the hell was that?" Barbara pointed out but when I looked up I could see nothing apart from dust being blown around by whatever she had seen and the breeze had instantly got stronger it could be felt as it brushed against the vehicle. Barbara's description was that it seemed like a very very quick silver disc that flashed by. We agreed it could have been down to the excessive heat that was now approaching 100F. We promptly changed the subject and chatted about how cool the road trip was already and we hadn't even arrived at Tonopah yet. Thoughts turned to the previous day in Death Valley a place so remote at times you could imagine you were on another planet from the salt and minerals all over the land around which had been left behind when the winter flash floods, the floods now long gone evaporated by the searing heat of the Death Valley Sun. We then made the five thousand feet climb by car of course, the roads are pretty good and well maintained despite the harsh conditions. Once at the top of Dante's View looking right down onto Badwater the views are unbelievable I was told by an intrepid traveller that no matter what, the temperature in Badwater is always thirty degrees cooler at the top of Dante's View. Then on to the stunning Artist's Pallet where rock formations have been coloured by different minerals, yes truly amazing.

Enough now as my attention was abruptly brought back to reality as the first property appeared on the outskirts of Tanopah. There were a few trucks coming the other way, feeling reassured back in civilisation once again. Well before moving further on from Tanopah it was time to stock up the vehicle and this general store had great coffee on tap so we could fill up our flask. Originally the plan was to stay overnight here but we decided we would proceed to check out Area 51 before heading back and swinging toward Hawthorn on our way to Lake Tahoe which means a very long drive not expecting to arrive in Tahoe until late at night. As we approached the general store we saw several people boarding up their homes now that was strange so we stopped the car alongside and the guy said have you not heard there's a big freeze coming. I said the temperature is in three figures so how on earth is a big freeze coming? He looked at me with an unnerving look as if he was looking right into my mind and he said listen to me there is a big big freeze coming Navajo Joe told us just a few days ago and before you start laughing old Joe is never wrong so laugh if you want fella but it's true I tell you. I told him I am not laughing but it's hard to take when it's over one hundred degrees right now. He snorted and carried on hammering the nails into the wood boards.

We pulled away and headed toward the general store and that coffee sounds good right now.

As we pulled in to the general store parking area a car with three people inside shot past us as if their life depended on it kicking up a whole load of dust as they went. Entering the Store it was deserted and the feeling of uneasiness returned and not for the first time today . We headed over toward the self service coffee as I recall from a previous visit their decaf tastes just the same as the real deal. Well what seemed strange is that there is still no one behind the counter after filling the large paper cups we started to look round for some assistance. We called out with Barbara especially getting concerned that the owners if there are watching on CCTV would think that we have stolen the coffee and biscuits. I placed a ten dollar bill on the counter and proceeded to walk toward the exit. Looking through the windows still no one. Then there was a voice asking if we could spare a minute. Where did this guy come from as there was absolutely no one to be seen until he popped up just like the genie in the lamp-poof and here he was. He was well dressed in a grey suit which was immaculate around six feet tall and his build was pretty thin, his complexion was pale with his light brown hair dazzling in the Sun and piercing bright blue eyes and he spoke with a deep southern accent which sounded reassuring.

He stated that we were honest for leaving the money on the check-out and that was one of the reasons that he wanted to speak to us. Look he said what I am about to tell you and then to ask of you is something that you will not believe. He then went on to tell us this amazing story so here goes.

He proceeded to tell us everything Jeremiah Jacks is my name and I have worked at this general store for around two weeks and shall we just say I kinda dropped in. Today's temperature is around a hundred degrees clear blue sky and not a cloud in the sky, we nodded in agreement. He looked at us again with that long stare and started to tell us the following, he stated in the next two hours the temperature outside will start to drop, just a small drop at first but as the day progresses the temperature will continue to drop and eventually it's going to drop to zero degrees and by the time we get through the night the temperature will be -50C and life in this area and everywhere else will start to die. First the vegetation then the animals then all human life will be in danger. We were staggered by his words and then he asked if we had a Satellite Navigation (Sat Nav) on board and we confirmed that we do, he wrote down and handed us coordinates advising these need to be entered into the Sat Nav as soon as you become convinced of what I'm telling you right now because trust me you will when it has come to pass, he carried on to say how important this was. It's imperative that you reach sanctuary before it's too late and once there you must remain there until advised of the next step, well we were speechless. Then he asked if we had an alarm on our house I nodded wondering what a stupid question to ask. You will need to input that code you use at home to get entry. I laughed because how the hell would that be any good only myself and my good lady would know it is our alarm at home. I said to Barbara in a low voice that he was crazy. He then added I'm not crazy you will have to trust me because your life depends on it. He must have amazing hearing.

With that we proceeded to swiftly walk back to the vehicle and what made us feel better was its still hot outside but unnervingly there is still a lack of people. We headed onto Highway 6 and on the way to Rachel just to just say we have been to this famous area oh and to meet the characters en route all seeking out ET. We switched South onto County Road 375 more commonly known as Extraterrestrial Highway. The scenery didn't change much and it wasn't long before we were on the outskirts of Rachel. The sign was upon us Welcome To Rachel Nevada as we passed by still looking for a small town but maybe I had been hopeful because there was nothing much here, we may just as well been on the Moon. We got out and was hit by an immediate chill it was so cold unlike when we got into the car. I checked the temperature gauge on the dash saying 46F how on earth is that possible it was one hundred degrees a while back. We were going to look in on the Little A'Le'Inn and ask how to get to area 51 but there was no one here. It was deserted and the only thing for miles around was high desert and the mountain range in the backdrop. I mentioned to Barbara it has dropped to 42F on the car temperature gauge. We are now starting to think about the unthinkable. It is probably more related to natural weather

patterns rather than any external manipulation no one can change the weather can they? Barbara and Jim had set out on an adventurous journey with excitement and anticipation, ready to explore new territories. They were well-prepared for their trip, equipped with the necessary gear and supplies. However, things have changed fast, this was an unexpected sudden drop in temperature that sent shivers down their spines and many more concerns along with it. The landscape, once a backdrop to their adventurous journey didn't seem so friendly. Now both focused on the critical task at hand. The wind howled around them, carrying the sting of the cold the urgency of their return intensified with every step.

Barbara and Jim's breath formed visible clouds in the frigid air as they moved with determination. Their muscles worked in tandem to cover the distance efficiently, fuelled by the instinct to escape the plummeting temperatures. The speed of their retreat was not just a physical response; it reflected the mental and emotional gravity they both felt. The journey back to Tanopah became a race against the elements, a test of endurance in the face of unexpected adversity. The landscape that had unfolded slowly during their outward journey now became a blur as they prioritized swift and sure-footed progress, with each passing mile bringing them closer to the warmth and safety they desperately sought in Tanopah. The cold seemed to be getting scary now as the car temperature dropped to 38 degrees Fahrenheit.

Chapter 2

TEMPERATURE DROP

Things are changing and changing rapidly, what could possibly change the weather from one minute a hot dry desert environment to freezing temperatures. The roads are unusually void of vehicles the occasional car would go by normally but not today the highway was ours all to ourselves.

Jim, "Can you believe how quickly the temperature dropped It was scorching hot earlier and now it's freezing cold!"

Barbara, "I know, it's insane! It was almost 100 degrees Fahrenheit just a few hours ago."

Jim, "I've been trying to think of a logical explanation, but I'm at a loss. It's summer."

Barbara, looking out of the car window, "Hmm, I don't see anything out of the ordinary. The sky is clear, no clouds, no signs of a storm. It's as if the temperature just randomly dropped without any reason."

Jim, "I would try the cell but no signal out here, it's not natural and no communications ain't helping."

Barbara, "I'll keep my phone handy should a signal appear and I'll check the news channels."

Jim, "Yeah, good idea." Jim glancing frequently at the temperature hoping for the best.

Jim continued, "Once back in Tonopah it's answers that are needed and somewhere warm preferably close to an open fire or one of those log burners."

Then thoughts turned back to the task at hand as the weather started to close in.

Jim and Barbara were forced to slow the vehicle due to snow starting to fall as it was leaving a covering on the road ahead.

Jim, "I'm a bit concerned because I've never seen the weather change so dramatically before especially out here. What do you think we should do?"

Barbara, "I agree, Jim. This is quite unexpected. Safety would be our first priority but no worries about banging into other vehicles because the uncanny thing is I ain't seen one since we started back."

Jim, "I've been thinking the same."

At last the turn off is just up ahead. The closer we got to the turn the more concerning it was becoming, then the sign '*Road to Tonopah Closed*'

Heavy concrete slabs had been placed across the turn off and there is no other route. Jim pulled the car to a halt alongside the bollards and got out to a bone chilling cold.

Once Jim and Barbara realized that there was no way through to Tonopah what with the temperatures continually dropping, they remembered the mysterious envelope they had received from a stranger. Curiosity piqued, they opened it to find a handwritten note, Jim carefully read out the note.

"You now know what I told you is coming to pass therefore, follow these instructions your life may depend on it."

Intrigued yet slightly apprehensive but becoming more desperate they decided to trust the stranger's advice and proceeded to read the further detail.

Jim continued to read out the note to Barbara, "*You must carry on westwards on US95 Veterans memorial your journey will be almost 100 miles and don't call in anywhere, you can enter these coordinates any time into your sat nav during the journey.*"

Jim and Barbara looked bewildered as they glanced at each other with concern as the landscape slowly started to change with snowflakes gently falling from the sky.

There was no alternative now, it was a yes to follow the strangers instructions. Driving on the highway was strange because now more and more empty broken down vehicles appeared at the side of the road they looked as if the drivers had left in a hurry.

Passing the rest area what appeared to be called Millers, well that's what the sat nav said, the rest area looked devoid of cars with just one truck parked up. Jim and Barbara both nodded to each other in agreement, there was no way they were going to stop there. The small flurries of snow were now a little more persistent and the occasional sweep of the wipers brushed them gently to one side. Jim turned the heater up which seemed to be holding the coldness at bay for the time being. Up ahead on the side of the road a car with hazards flashing and one girl shouting and waving her arms around in desperation. We drove past but there was an uneasy feeling that Jim had because in his mind he had noticed the girl was dressed for the hot desert and not a frozen wasteland. A couple miles went by but the uneasy feeling continued. Jim thinking out loud, "Sometimes taking a calculated risk to help someone in need can lead to a positive outcome." Jim swung the car round and headed back at speed.

***

The girl was brave to be wearing just a t-shirt and shorts in weather like this. While it's normally important to dress appropriately for the temperature, but this weather had changed so quickly. Jim pulled the car alongside. Barbara was first out and she could see the girl needed warmth and warmth real quick.

Barbara's initial reaction was to shout, "You need to get in our car to warm up" The girl without hesitation did just that, then she shouted, "My friend needs help, she's in the back of the car."

Barbara quickly assessed the semi conscious girl's well-being, Barbara pointed to the girl on the back seat indicating to Jim the need for urgency and to get her into the warm car. Barbara tried to comfort them and assure them that they are there to help in any way possible. Once both girls were safely in the car the heater starts to do its work.

Middle of summer in the Nevada desert, very strange, the snow is falling and the temperatures are turning into the Arctic. Barbara and Jim have the two girls that were dressed for summer in their care. The weather has now closed in and only the rough terrain made it possible to see the road ahead. It was fast becoming a white out. Jim pulled the envelope out of the glove compartment that had been handed to him by the man in the grey suit.

Barbara shivered as she looked out of the car window at the unusual scene unfolding before them. "This is insane, Jim. It's the middle of summer and we're in the Nevada desert. "Why on earth is it snowing?" She asked, while glancing at the two girls or are they young women, well it was difficult to know, they were huddled together in the backseat, confused.

Jim concerned and trying to make sense of the surreal weather. "I have no idea, Barbara. This is just bizarre." He turned his attention back to the road, squinting through the swirling snowflakes. The landscape was usually dominated by the harsh desert Sun, now transformed into a winter wonderland.

The temperature inside the car plummeted rapidly. Barbara reached over to adjust the heater, but it only emitted cold air. "Jim, this is not normal. We need to find some shelter, or the girls are going to freeze," she urged.

Jim nodded in agreement, gripping the steering wheel tightly. The snowfall intensified, creating a thick layer on the road where visibility had become increasingly challenging. The only guide they had was the rough terrain, barely visible through the mounting white out.

Jim again remembered the envelope in the glove compartment. Curiosity piqued, he reached over and retrieved it. The man in the grey suit had handed it to him with an air of urgency. Opening the envelope, Jim found a set of coordinates and a brief note that read,

'Seek refuge at these coordinates immediately.'

Barbara glanced over, her eyes widening. "What's in there? What does it say?"

Jim hesitated for a moment before sharing the information. "It's coordinates for some place. Maybe it's a shelter or a safe spot. We should follow them, it might be our best chance."

Jim carefully entered the coordinates. With renewed determination, Jim steered the car along the rugged terrain, following the mysterious coordinates. The snowfall continued unabated, creating an eerie atmosphere in the normally unforgiving desert. They pressed on, their surroundings cloaked in a surreal blend of what should be summer and instead we have arctic conditions, Both now worried, unsure of what awaited them at the end of the journey.

With that thought, the sat nav started to beep loudly and flashing on screen asking to enter the code but they didn't have a code. Jim's mind raced as he tried to recall the words of the man in the grey suit. The memory surfaced as he muttered to himself, "He said something about a code, a code for entry or access." Frantically searching through the contents of the envelope, he found a small note hidden among the coordinates. It stated clearly and Jim read it out loudly,

"CODE FOR ENTRY TO YOUR HOME."

Jim said, "Barbara, this is crazy. How on earth is our home alarm code connected to the sat nav instructions, what's going on here?"

"Keep your voice down you are worrying everyone up replied Barbara." Who then shook her head, equally puzzled. "I have no idea. This whole situation is surreal. Maybe the man in the grey suit knew something we don't. How does our home security code tie into all of this?"

Barbara, her curiosity and concern mounting, turned to Jim with a determined look in her eyes. "Jim, we need to find out what's going on, so put the code in and see what happens because I can't take this uncertainty anymore."

Jim nodded, a mix of emotions swirling within him. As he entered the familiar digits of their home alarm code into the demanding sat nav, a wave of anticipation and anxiety gripped them both. The air in the car seemed charged with a sense of the unknown.

A few tense moments passed and then, unexpectedly, a holographic display materialised before them. It showed a series of interconnected locations including their home back in England and in the Nevada desert in what appeared to be some sort of facility and it made it look obvious that this is where they were needed to go to. Then without warning the display flickered, revealing weather patterns, seismic data and encrypted messages.

Barbara gasped, her hand instinctively reaching out to Jim's. "This is unbelievable our home alarm code is linked to all of this? What kind of operation is this, who was the man in the grey suit?"

Jim, still processing the surreal nature of the situation, replied, "I don't know, but it seems like we're part of some larger plan. Its trying to help us, getting us to safety."

The holographic display continued to unveil information, displaying a complex network of events and locations. As they delved deeper into the data, the emotions of astonishment and trepidation mingled within them. The realisation that their seemingly ordinary lives were entwined with a covert system of protection left them both in awe and anxiety.

The display, that must have been observing their reactions, started to speak.

"You're part of a contingency plan, a network designed to ensure the safety of human life in critical situations. The details will be explained in due course. For now, rest assured that you will be in a safe place."

The emotional roller coaster continued as Jim and Barbara grappled with the revelation that their home alarm code held the key to an intricate web of protection, along with mysteries surrounding the snowfall in the Nevada desert. Everything was becoming more profound and the journey into the unknown had only just begun.

Chapter 3

NAVIGATION

The road ahead was now vanishing before their eyes as the snow continued to fall and it was quickly turning to arctic blizzard conditions with the wind whipping at the side of the car.

Jim's knuckles turned white as he gripped the steering wheel, straining to discern any sign of the road beneath the thick blanket of snow. The engine's low hum and the wind whistling at the side was the only sound in the tense silence that filled the car. The two girls in the back exchanged anxious glances, their concern growing with every passing moment.

The snowfall had intensified, erasing any trace of the road markings and obscuring the path ahead. Jim's concentration was paramount as his mind raced through the potential consequences of a wrong turn or a misplaced step. The wilderness around them seemed both captivating and ominous as the snowflakes continued their relentless descent.

The girls expressed their concerns direct to Jim and resulted in a quick retort from Jim. "I'm doing my best," he reassured them, his voice strained. "We just need to stay calm don't we?"

Then all of a sudden the sat nav flashed an image on the screen it had produced. The image displayed two reassuring green lines guiding the way through the snowy expanse. "Alright, everyone, we've got some guidance. Just follow those green lines," Then the sat nav flashed up saying twenty two more miles stating in large letters stay inside the lines.

Jim couldn't shake off the idea that the sat nav seemed to have a clear understanding of the road beneath the snow. He stole a glance at the screen, the green lines steadfastly guiding him through the snowy landscape.

"How is it doing this?" Jim mumbled to himself, eyes fixated on the screen. The two girls in the back exchanged perplexed glances, mirroring Jim's confusion. Jim continued to hold the wheel steady moving cautiously forward.

Jim's mind raced with questions before reaching the conclusion of we must trust the sat nav.

The surreal reliance on technology in this wintry predicament added an extra layer of intrigue to the already challenging drive. Jim's gaze remained fixed on the screen, half-expecting it to provide more clues about its seemingly mystical ability to navigate the hidden road. The girls in the back, though still uneasy, began to share Jim's curiosity, collectively pondering the enigma of the sat nav's snow-defying guidance. An hour passed by and not much headway had been made because of the treacherous conditions. The temperature gauge on the car had now stopped working, it had got so cold that the display had gone. The heater was now concentrated fully on the windscreen, with what little warmth if any it provided.

Jim couldn't shake off the puzzling realization that the sat nav seemed to have a clear understanding of the road beneath the snow. He stole a glance at the screen, the green lines steadfastly guiding him through the snowy landscape. His scepticism wrestled with a growing conviction that the technology might be onto something.

"How is it doing this?" Jim mumbled to himself, one eye on the screen. The two girls in the back exchanged perplexed glances, mirroring Jim's confusion. The car continued to move cautiously, adhering to the virtual guidance despite the apparent lack of visibility on the actual road.

Jim's mind raced with questions, contemplating the possibility that the sat nav had some advanced feature or sensor allowing it to "see" through the snow. The alternative, that it was somehow predicting the road's location based on data, seemed equally implausible given the thick layer covering the landscape.

As the car glided along, the mystery of the sat nav's accuracy became a focal point of the journey.

Barbara glanced at Jim occasionally, her eyes had fear in them. The inability to pick up speed in the harsh Arctic conditions heightened her unease.

In the backseat, the two girls exchanged worried looks. The slow and tedious journey magnified the isolation of the Arctic landscape around them. The car's interior, normally a sanctuary, now felt more like a fragile ship on the ocean.

The relentless Arctic winds outside seemed to penetrate the car, creating an eerie soundtrack of howling gusts that only intensified the collective nervousness inside. The whiteness outside added to the fear that lingered in the air.

The road ahead now seemed all the same as if we were driving in the Arctic, everything was white with the wind now howling and the snow building up on the windscreen between each time the wipers did their job. Jim didn't know if he was on the road or not, it was smooth so it must be the road right? He constantly worked out in his mind on what he should do next. The miles were clicking down very slowly the tenth of a mile digit seemed like ages before it would click over, you know similar to when in long traffic jams with stop and start. This display from the sat nav didn't change just the two green lines advising that the driver should make sure the car remains within the green, so as to keep the car pointed between the two green lines on the display. Jim thought he would test it to see if it was working, so he carefully, deliberately turned the car to left. Nothing happened then as soon as he touched the green line on the display the screen turned bright red flashing warnings to keep the car straight. Jim thought let me just turn it to the right and yet again the display flashed red and the same warnings appeared. With that Barbara shouting, "Jim, what are you doing? Are you falling asleep? Keep control of the car!"

Girls in the back (in unison), "Yeah, Jim, be careful please!"

Barbara, "Jim, this is not the time to test anything. We need to stay safe. Keep the car straight for God's sake!"

Jim, "I thought the display wasn't working correctly, well the screen hasn't changed for ages. I needed to see if it was giving the right directions it's just constantly showing the same picture."

Barbara (concerned), "Well, testing it while driving is not the solution! We could have had an accident. Pay attention!"

Barbara now feeling uneasy with Jim's action was determined to keep her eye fixed directly on Jim's face for fear he may have drifted off to sleep for a second or two.

Jim promised everyone that he wouldn't do it again.

All of a sudden the display started to come to life and there was this holographic image as before and the calm, reassuring voice persisted.

Sat Nav: "It's critical now. You are nearing the turn off."

Jim, expressing concern, responded, "But I can't see where to go in this snow."

Sat Nav: "Carry on, no matter what. Stay between these lines."

The green lines on the display had narrowed, eliminating any margin of error. The situation intensified as the need for precision became more apparent.

Jim nervously, "This is really challenging. I can barely see the road. Are you sure about this?"

Sat Nav: "Trust the guidance and stay within the lines. You're almost there."

Despite the challenging conditions, the sat nav system seemed confident in its instructions, emphasizing the importance of staying within the narrow boundaries, therefore Jim was left with no choice but to rely on the guidance provided by the system, now navigating through the snow with increased caution and determination. With the green lines flashing to indicate a turn to the right but Jim for a second went outside the lines and had to bring the car to a standstill.

The tension inside the car escalated as Jim moved off slowly and manoeuvred the vehicle with extreme caution, inch by inch. The silence was deafening, each occupant holding their breath as the car teetered on the edge of the road. Jim's meticulous attempts to bring the car back between the green lines on the display heightened the anxiety.

The passengers were now all visibly anxious, their faces reflecting the shared concern. Every slight movement of the car felt like a precarious dance on the edge of disaster. The fear intensified with each moment, as the consequences of a mistake very real, the dread of ending up in a ditch became a real concern.

The car inched left and right, the occupants gripping their seats, their eyes glued to the narrowing margin between the green lines. The once-reassuring voice of the sat nav now served as a stark reminder of the gravity they found themselves in.

In this tense atmosphere, every inch of progress felt like a small victory, yet the fear persisted. The precise inch-by-inch manoeuvring emphasised the delicate balance between control and potential disaster of being in a ditch and not able to get any sort of help owing to the extreme conditions. Then the sat nav returned to a calming ding sound as the car returned directly in the middle of the green lines, at last a small sense of relief was shared. The smooth road was gone and the off road terrain became a further challenge.

This was indeed challenging terrain, Jim turned to the two girls seated in the back, realizing that introductions had been overlooked in the midst of the harsh conditions. With a warm smile, he said, "Hey there! Sorry we didn't do a proper introduction earlier, it's been a bit of a wild ride. I'm Jim and this is my wife Barbara."

Barbara nodded in agreement, adding, "Nice to meet you both."

Jim continued, "So, what are your names?" He looked at the first girl, who responded with a friendly grin.

"I'm Clio." Then, turning to the second girl, she introduced herself, "And I'm Jessica."

"Well, Clio and Jessica, pleasure to meet you. Apologies again for the delayed introductions as you know things have been a bit hectic with the conditions out here as you well know, I'm afraid this situation we find ourselves mean there are more questions than answers and at the same time I'm sure we would all like to know what the hell is going on."

Barbara nodded in agreement, "Absolutely. We're just glad to have you both with us. Anyhow, let's focus on getting through this safely."

It seemed like an age now but the weather was relentless and it made every second of the journey dangerous. Night was beginning to slowly creep in now and with that will come even more serious temperatures.

As they continued their journey through the harsh terrain, Jim's focus shifted to the vehicle's display. He spoke up, "Alright everyone, I'm afraid I need to concentrate more than ever so if i go silent you'll know why as we need to keep the vehicle between these green guidelines on the display." Now the headlights only seemed to amplify the blinding white out, making the task more challenging.

Everyone's eyes were now fixed on the guidelines on the screen. Jim thinking to himself I must stay awake, don't know where the hell this is taking us. His hands gripped the steering wheel with determination as he carefully moved through the landscape indicating to everyone that they need to watch the display too. The car pressed on, relying on the guidelines and their collective focus to guide them through the relentless white out.

After what seemed an eternity and then to their horror the green guidelines vanished from the display. Clio shouted, "Stop!"

Jim brought the car to an immediate standstill frozen in fear that continuing would certainly result in disaster.

Clio's alarmed shout had echoed through the tense silence inside the vehicle as the display abruptly went black, leaving them in darkness. Barbara leaned forward, trying to make sense of the sudden blackout.

"What happened? Is there a backup or anything we can do?" she asked. The once-illuminated guidelines on the display were now replaced by nothing.

Jim took a deep breath, attempting to remain composed. "I'll check if there's a reset or backup system but I warn you I am no expert. In the meantime, let's just stay calm. It might just be a glitch," he said, his fingers working on the controls in hopes of reviving the crucial navigation system but nothing worked, the screen remained black.

The atmosphere inside the car was thick with uncertainty. The reality of being stuck in the frigid wilderness without the aid of the sat nav display sank in.

Jim tried to calm everyone. "We'll figure this out together. Stay alert and keep an eye out for any sign of life."

The engine continued to tick over and the fan now at last kicking out hot air was only just keeping the inside of the car from freezing the very air. Barbara knew there was some spare clothes in the back if they had to get out but they were hardly winter clothes. A casting eye showed that the car was getting low on gas, there was not much in the tank. A decision would have to be made do we turn off the engine and save fuel or do we keep it on.

At last a sense of relief filled the car as a faint bleep emanated from the silent sat nav display. The small white lettering in the bottom corner brought a glimmer of hope to the dimly lit interior: 'Rebooting'

Jim's tension visibly eased and he cracked a smile.

"Looks like we've got some life back. Hold tight, everyone. Let's give it a moment to reboot," he said, optimism returning to his voice. Barbara nodded, her expression transitioning from worry to cautious optimism.

As seconds ticked by, the display flickered back to life, casting a soft glow over the interior. The familiar green guidelines reappeared and the tension lifted further.

"Well, would you look at that! We're back in business," Jim exclaimed, the relief evident in his voice. Clio, who had been anxiously observing, couldn't help but smile at the unexpected turn of events.

With the sat nav restored, the group regained a sense of direction and purpose. Then all of a sudden, *'STOP'* appeared on the screen then the screen cleared and a new message read, 'WAIT FOR INSTRUCTIONS'

An hour past and still the same words on the screen. Barbara suggested, "Maybe we should consider rebooting it again? Waiting might not be helping."

Before anyone could act, Jessica's voice cut through the discussion. "Don't touch it! We should wait, maybe it's just taking longer than usual. If we interrupt the process, who knows what might happen?"

Clio nodded in agreement, "She's right. Patience might be our best bet here. Let's give it a bit more time."

Jim said, "Well you young people may be right, we wait."

With the decision made to wait, the group settled into a tense anticipation, hoping that the sat nav display would soon provide the much-needed guidance through the icy challenges ahead.

Chapter 4

THE GATE

Then there was a green light in the distance and at the same time the display had a new message saying follow the green light and take me with you. Jim unplugged the sat nav and placed it carefully in his pocket.

Exiting the car into the intense biting cold everyone shivered as the frigid air cut through them. Determined to combat the harsh weather, Barbara rummaged through her suitcase, finding some spare clothes. "Here, put these on. It might not be much, but it's better than freezing," she said, handing out the clothes to Jessica and Clio.

Grateful for the extra layers, Jessica and Clio hastily changed into the warmer attire, now offering some respite against the intense cold. The backdrop revealed clearing skies, hinting at a temporary reprieve from the relentless weather.

The temperature plummeted to the point where even eyebrows began to frost over, a visible testament to the unforgiving chill in the air. Despite the bone-chilling conditions, they pressed on, determined to follow the green light.

They trudged through the icy landscape. The intensity of the light increased as they advanced, providing a guiding beacon through the cold expanse. Each step forward was a battle against the biting cold, but the prospect of reaching their goal kept them moving, their breath visible in the frosty air.

They seemed have been walking for ages and it seemed the sense of time had been lost, no one had a watch only cell phones whose batteries had now long ago lost their charge.

Everyone's fatigue and the biting chill weighed heavily. Then at last In the distance they spotted what appeared to be an old gate about five hundred yards away. It was an unexpected sight in the vast snowy landscape. Above the gate, a mysterious green light cast an eerie glow around the area. Perplexed, they couldn't discern the source of the light.

Getting closer they noticed an old stone wall surrounding the area. The snow on the ground was pristine virgin snow, indicating that no one had ventured this way recently. Despite their exhaustion, a spark of hope ignited within them as they glimpsed lights illuminating the area beyond the gate with a gentle comforting glow.

Jessica and Clio exchanged glances, their youthful faces reflecting a mixture of relief and curiosity. The warmth emanating from the lights seemed like a lighthouse amidst a stormy sea. They quickened their pace and their tiredness momentarily overshadowed by the prospect of shelter and warmth.

Jim's caution to slow the pace hung in the cold air as they stood before the mysterious gate, the green light still casting its glow above. Barbara, ever hopeful, broke the tension with a whisper, "Maybe there's warmth and some hot food in there."

The prospect of warmth and nourishment lifted their spirits. Jim's reminder to be cautious lingered. The unknown nature of what lay beyond the gate made each step forward a deliberate and careful movement. Clio and Jessica nodded in agreement.

The group advanced slowly their senses on high alert. The gentle glow from the lights inside the gate illuminated the path ahead, revealing a sense of safety that had been absent in the cold wilderness. Jim led the way, his eyes scanning the surroundings for any signs of danger.

As they approached, the old gate creaked open, revealing the area within. The lights from the other side of the gate beckoned them forward with the hope of shelter and warmth. With every step carefully taken because who knows what awaited them beyond the gate.

Then everyone feeling down because it seemed that this is all there was, just a few lights with the immediate area flooded with a green light. Despair started to creep into every thought, afraid to share with each other. The thought of we are going to die became more real.

Feeling the chill in the air even within the illuminated area they decided to huddle against the old stone wall. The cold had a way of bringing people together and the shared goal of seeking warmth overshadowed any initial awkwardness.

Clio, Jessica, Jim and Barbara gathered closely bodies pressed against each other for mutual warmth. The flickering lights overhead provided a dim ambiance casting shadows on the snowy ground. The coldness of the wilderness seemed to fade now replaced by the comforting heat generated by their collective body warmth.

Any reservations about huddling near strangers quickly dissipated in the face of the harsh conditions they had endured. Survival took precedence with the shared warmth a welcome relief. The subtle exchange of glances and the unspoken acknowledgment that they were in this together created a sense of camaraderie.

In that vulnerable moment, against the cold backdrop of the freezing desolate wasteland they had found solace in each other's company, the boundaries of embarrassment erased by the simple need for warmth and companionship.

Jessica shivered in the cold air with her breath turning to freezing droplets as she exhaled. She thought about home and that she often couldn't get to sleep if her feet were cold, not a problem now because she couldn't feel them. The relentless wind cut through their layers of clothing, sending a shiver down their spines. They huddled together, chatting in an attempt to distract themselves from the biting cold that seemed to seep into their very bones.

Despite their efforts to stay awake, the exhaustion began to take its toll on Jessica. Her eyelids grew heavy and she started to drift off to sleep. However, the harsh reality of her situation jerked her back awake with a jump. Falling asleep in such frigid conditions could prove fatal. The fear of succumbing to the intense cold kept her on edge.

As they looked around, the prospect of finding shelter seemed increasingly slim. The surroundings offered no respite and the clearing skies only meant a more intense drop in the temperature. The wind continued its whistle, a haunting reminder of the inhospitable environment they found themselves in. The snow had ceased, leaving a frozen landscape that stretched as far as the eye could see in one direction and on the other, the intimidating mountains.

The stars sparkled in the clear sky, their distant glow providing little warmth against the harsh of the freezing night. The visibility only served to highlight the dire situation they were in. Each breath felt like a battle against the relentless cold.

The sudden hum in the air caught Jessica off guard. The initial low-frequency vibrations filled the air with an eerie tension, causing her breath to catch in anticipation. Then, a deafening crack echoed through the night, so powerful that it seemed as if the very sky was shattering.

The intense sound reverberated through the cold air, shaking their surroundings and sending a shock wave of surprise and fear through the night. It was as if the very night sky itself had cracked open revealing the silhouette of a fighter jet. It heightened everyone's senses for sure. The sudden appearance of the aircraft added a surreal and unsettling layer to the already dire situation. The powerful engines roared by, drowning out the natural sounds of the night and this sight of the fast-moving jet left them wide-eyed and agape.

As a second fighter jet roared past in the wake of the echoes of the first adding to the noise. The sudden departure of the jets was as abrupt as their arrival and the once-chaotic sounds were swallowed by the overwhelming silence of the cold night and now only the relentless wind remained.

Jim said. "Maybe the fighter jets had spotted them." His hopeful words rang out in the frigid air and offering maybe a glimmer of expectation in the otherwise bleak circumstances.

However optimism was soon met with a lingering sense of uncertainty. The vastness of the frozen landscape seemed to mock their vulnerability and with the disappearance of the jets only added to the mystery. Jessica couldn't shake the feeling that their presence might have been coincidental, maybe the jets might have had more important business.

The stars above remained indifferent witnesses and the chances of finding immediate shelter remained slim. The brief encounter with the fighter jets left them with a mix of emotions—hope, uncertainty and a heightened awareness of their isolation in the desolate night. Jim tried to cover everyone's heads with as much spare clothing he could find, everyone had their hands tucked inside the clothing. It seemed ages but no one knew how long because time meant nothing now.

Then the sat nav started to vibrate and the screen lit up in a vivid shade of bright red. The sudden change in colour casting a glow against the wall. Unfortunately nothing more happened with the sat nav only an occasional vibration. The sat nav must hold secrets that for now remain just out of reach.

Clio directed everyone's attention to a distant point on the right. A small red light or a twinkling star had captured her attention, casting a subtle glow against the vast cold expanse. Barbara, following Clio's gaze, confirmed that she could see the enigmatic light. The distant light sparked curiosity and intrigue. This mysterious light became a focal point, a beacon of possibility. Clio and Barbara could see it but Jim and Jessica were far from convinced.

But then Jim said, "Hey, I see it now! You're right, it's a light, not a star!"

Barbara responding, "Could it be that the display on the sat nav briefly showed the same thing and we are not clever enough to have figured out the link?"

Jessica confused, "Where? I can't see it."

Jim, "Over there, look toward and to the right in the distance. It's like a small red light standing out against the darkness."

Jessica, "Oh, wait, I think I see it now but how do we know if it's connected to the sat nav?"

Barbara, "Well there's that bright red screen it started acting up right around the time we spotted the light. Maybe it's trying to tell us something."

Jessica, "It's worth exploring. We need to figure out if there's a connection between the sat nav and that light. Let's see if anything changes on the screen as we get closer."

Jim, "Good idea."

Barbara, "Maybe this is our ticket out of here. Let's stay focused and figure this out together."

As the four of them huddled around the sat nav, the red glow was back now casting onto their faces. Did the distant red light hold the promise of answers. They set out to unravel the possible connection between the mysterious light and the display on the sat nav.

Unfortunately this meant moving away from the relative safety of the protective wall. As they ventured into the open, the biting wind pierced through their layers of clothing, intensifying the already harsh conditions. Jessica was immediately overwhelmed by the freezing temperatures, she began to cry and saying, "We're all going to die out here!"

The response from Clio was quick and sharp.

Clio, "Shut up, We're not going to die! We need to focus and figure this out."

The atmosphere grew more intense as the wind howled around them, drowning out their voices.

Jessica shouted, "As you all know I can't feel my feet or my toes, I am finding it difficult to walk now, I hope this is the right way?"

Jim, "Yes."

Clio with an excitement in her voice. "The light's definitely getting brighter."

Barbara, "Finally some progress. Maybe there's shelter or help."

Jessica, "I hope your right because I can't walk much further."

Clio tried to lift the spirits of all. "At least we're not alone we have each other."

But Jessica persisted. "What if it's just a reflection or something?"

No one answered Jessica's comment for fear she may well be right.

Jim, "Did it just get colder?"

Clio wrapping her arms around herself, “I can feel it too. What’s happening?”

Barbara, “The cold has intensified out of nowhere.”

Jessica walking while trying to hug for extra warmth stated, “This is unbearable. I thought it couldn’t get any colder.”

Jim tried to keep spirits up by singing 'American Pie' which produced some laughter as he got the words in the wrong order.

The source of the glow became clearer now as it appeared to be at the bottom of the mountain side. The peculiar nature of the light intrigued them. At last they arrived at the bottom of the mountainside.

Jim, “Why in the world is that red light attached to the rock face?”

Barbara, “Maybe there’s an entrance or shelter nearby. Let’s look for a way in.”

Jessica, “Please let there be something to get us out of this freezing wind.”

Now looking along the rock face for clues, a sudden change caught their attention. A holographic square materialised, emitting from the sat nav’s display. The square hung in the air, flickering with a soft glow.

Jim, “Wow something is happening to the sat nav!”

Clio, “Look, there’s something in that holographic display.”

Everyone gathered around the holographic square, its glow casting redness onto their faces. The freezing wind momentarily forgotten, they focused on the mysterious display, hoping it held answers to the questions that surrounded them in the cold desolate night. Then all of a sudden a keyboard appeared.

As the holographic keyboard materialised with a faint message, it started floating away from the sat nav’s display as Barbara and Jim tried desperately to make sense of the mysterious occurrence.

Then Barbara excitedly, “Jim look at this. It’s asking for an alarm code. I’m sure of it."

Jim, "Our home alarm code?"

Barbara, "Put our alarm code in Jim."

Jim, fuelled by a mixture of curiosity and anticipation quickly entered the first three numbers of their home alarm code. The holographic display seemed to respond, encouraging him to continue. With a momentary pause, he entered the fourth number.

As the fourth digit was entered, a sudden burst of bright red light emanated from the red light attached to the mountainside. The beam focused onto a solid rock formation built into the side of the mountain, everyone watched in awe as something began to move.

Clio. "Look! Something's happening!"

Clio's excitement echoed through the cold night as a stone door embedded in the mountainside started to creak open slowly. The anticipation among them reached a fever pitch and Clio's shouts were joined by gasps of amazement. Everyone couldn't contain their excitement but there was still a hint of fear splashed across all their faces. The stone door creaked open as it started to reveal a dark passage beyond. The combination of the unexpected technological interface and the unfolding secret in the mountainside created a sense of wonder and intrigue, momentarily overshadowing the bitter cold of the night.

Slowly moving forward, one by one, through the partially open stone door, a sense of trepidation lingered in the air. Once everyone had crossed the threshold, the stone door began to close, a slow and deliberate movement that brought a momentary sense of unease.

Jessica, feeling a pang of uncertainty, glanced back at the narrowing gap of the closing door. The urge to run back outside and escape the unknown depths of the mountainside crossed her mind, but the biting cold that awaited outside held her in check. With a reluctant acceptance, she stayed inside as the door sealed shut.

The sudden darkness enveloped them and the once-persistent wind that had felt like an eternity was now extinguished. The relief from the howling cold was instant relief, but reality set in quickly. The pitch-black darkness inside the mountain was disorienting and a biting cold still lingered in the air.

Jim whispered, "Is everyone okay?"

Barbara, "I can't see a thing."

Clio. "It's so dark in here."

Jessica, "What on earth have we gotten ourselves into?"

Now confined to the darkness within the mountain, their minds raced with the disorienting absence of light. Although the biting cold persisted the biting relentless wind had gone. The mysterious red light attached to the mountainside had led them into the unknown. They now had the challenge of navigating through the darkness to uncover what lay before them.

As Jessica, Barbara, Jim and Clio stood still in the pitch-dark passageway, a wave of uncertainty and tension was shared by them. The absence of light creates an unsettling atmosphere, heightening their senses and making them acutely aware of their surroundings. The darkness is thick with feelings of vulnerability and caution now dominating their emotions as they exchange uncertain glances. The light has gone and the only thing they could hear is the faint breathing of each other, the shuffling of feet, with the occasional drip of water which is coming from above. Every step into the unknown feels like a leap of faith and the air is heavy with anticipation.

To navigate the passageway without sight, they rely on their other senses. Each footfall is measured and deliberate, testing the ground before putting their full weight down. Their hands stretch out cautiously, feeling for any obstacles or walls that might guide or hinder their progress. The air is still cold but nothing like it was outside but the dampness creeps into the bones, adding to the challenge.

Whispering to each other becomes essential in this unfamiliar environment.

They inch forward, minds working overtime, trying to create a mental map of the space, based on the limited sensory input. The darkness becomes a canvas on which their imagination paints both potential dangers and safe pathways.

Jessica stumbles but quickly corrects herself, everyone else holds their breath until Jessica whispers, "I'm okay."

The passage of time becomes distorted in the absence of light, heightening their awareness of every moment. Yet, with each step, they persevere. They inch along the passageway, the only sounds are the echoes of their hushed footsteps and the occasional drip of water. The darkness is so thick, surrounding them like a heavy cloak. Jim squeezes Clio's hand reassuringly, silently conveying that they're in this together.

Cautiously moving forward, navigating the unseen twists and turns of the passageway. Every step is deliberate, every movement deliberate. Barbara, at the rear, ensures that the younger girls are safely in the middle, sheltered from the unknown.

Sweaty hands grasp onto one another, a shared tension coursing through them all. The worry is shared, but togetherness gives them strength. The air is thick with anticipation as they push forward, the darkness pressing in on them like a living presence.

Suddenly, a distant sound echoes through the passageway, causing them all to freeze. The flicker of uncertainty dances in their minds and they exchange a silent communication. They share a collective deep breath, preparing to face whatever challenges are ahead. Hand in hand, they continue to navigate the pitch-dark passage. Then the distant sound yet again of running water.

The sound of running water grows louder, echoing through the confined space. The group's concern deepens as the source of the sound becomes increasingly imminent. Everyone moving closer to each other. Jim tightens his grip on whoever's hand and glances back thinking if only I could see them to help reassure them all. Then Jim whispering. "We need to be careful as the water sounds like it's getting closer, so stay close everyone."

Barbara, "I don't like this. What if the water keeps rising, are we going to be okay?"

Jim, "We'll do our best to find a way out, stay calm."

Clio responded, "I can't see anything and the water sounds so loud. What if it floods the passageway what do we do?"

Jessica, "I'm scared too. I don't want to be stuck in here with water all around us. Can't we go back?"

Barbara, "We can't go back now."

Jim, "We need to be cautious and we move forward."

The sense of helplessness is now very real, with the uncertainty of their situation. They continue edging forward guided by the every increasing sound of running water, hoping for a solution to present itself in the darkness.

They edge forward and suddenly to everyone's joy the Sat Nav display flickers to life, casting a brilliant light that cuts through the oppressive darkness. A collective gasp of amazement escapes them. The fear that had gripped them begins to dissolve. The entire sat nav's display now functions as a powerful torch illuminating what is a cavern.

Jim. "Look at this! The Sat Nav's working as a torch! We've got light, everyone!"

Barbara, "Oh, thank goodness!"

Clio saying elatedly, “I can’t believe it! We’re not in the dark anymore! This is amazing!”

Jessica, “I was so scared, but this light changes everything. I feel so much better now. I feel as if someone is watching over us.”

Jim directs the bright torchlight around the cavern, revealing its vast expanse. In the centre is a massive waterfall as it cascades into the depths, creating a mesmerising spectacle. The water continues its journey into an abyss, disappearing into a black void.

Jim, “Look at that waterfall! It’s incredible. Let’s rest a while.”

Barbara, “Thank you, sat nav. You just became our saviour yet again. Let’s stick close and move forward. We have light and that’s a game-changer!”

The elation of having a source of light in the cavern fills them with renewed hope and energy. With the sat nav’s bright torch leading the way, the group eagerly continues their journey, leaving the pitch darkness behind and embracing the newfound joy of illumination.

Guided by the powerful light of the sat nav, they reach the other end of the cavern, where they discover another passageway. The sense of relief is felt by all.

Jim, “Looks like our way out might be through here. Stay close, everyone.”

Barbara, “We’ve come this far. Let’s keep going and see where this passage leads us.”

Clio, “I wonder what’s ahead. Hopefully it’s an exit or something that leads us closer to the surface.”

Jessica, “I’m just glad we have light now. It makes everything less scary.”

They now enter the new passageway, the light from the sat nav casting shadows on the walls as they navigate through the unknown. The echoes of their footsteps reverberate and the distant sound of running water serves as a constant reminder of the challenges they've faced so far.

Jim, "Stay vigilant everyone, let's see where this passageway takes us, maybe it just leads us back outside. I am not sure we want to go back out into that cold though."

Barbara, "We've got this."

With newfound determination, they press on, leaving the cavern behind and venturing into the unexplored passageway. The light from the sat nav continues to guide their way providing a beacon of hope in the darkness as they move forward.

The passageway opens up into a smaller cavern, revealing unexpected treasures from what seems like a bygone era. They see an old large mattress tucked into one corner with bedding nearby and what looks like a 19th-century kerosene heater, along with tins of food and bottles of water neatly arranged as if someone was expecting us.

Jim, "Well, this is something. Looks like someone set up a little refuge here and check out that heater!"

Barbara, "It's like a hidden oasis. I wonder who could have left all this here?"

Clio now excited, "Food and water! It's like a jackpot in the middle of this cave. How lucky are we?"

Jessica tests the mattress, "This mattress and bedding feel dry. It seems like no one has been here for quite some time."

Jim messing with the kerosene heater, "Let's see if we can get this thing working. It might make this place more comfortable for a while."

As Jim tinkers with the kerosene heater everyone else examine the provisions left behind. The atmosphere in the cavern shifts from cautious exploration to a mix of relief and gratitude. They begin to realise that they may have stumbled upon a forgotten refuge, a hidden haven within the depths of the cave system.

Barbara, "If we can get this heater going we'll have warmth and some supplies. It's like a blessing in the dark."

Jim struggles to light the kerosene heater thinking how the hell can I light this bloody heater.

Time goes by, Jim's frustration mounts as he struggles to light the kerosene heater. Each attempt seems to intensify his irritation, his brows furrowing as he mutters under his breath. The faint sound of clicking and the occasional spark with stones fail to give enough and there are no twigs or anything that he could use to ignite the heater because it remains stubbornly unlit.

Jim, "Its hopeless? I can't find anything to light it."

Barbara, "Take it easy Jim, we'll figure it out."

Despite the words of encouragement, Jim's frustration persists. The cavern echoes with the sound of his attempts, the tension in the air as the cold begins to get to him.

Meanwhile, Clio, exploring a bit more around the cavern, suddenly calls out with excitement.

Clio, "Hey, everyone! Look what I found!"

All heads turn towards Clio as she holds up a small box of matches triumphantly.

Clio, "Matches! Wow can you believe it."

Jim, looking both relieved and slightly embarrassed. "Well, that would have been handy a few minutes ago. Good find, Clio."

Clio hands the matches to Jim, who, with a newfound spark of hope, takes them and carefully ignites one. The match flickers to life, casting a warm glow on his face as he carefully approaches the kerosene heater. The heater's flame flickers to life and then this amazing glow as it illuminates everyone with their shadows being cast on the walls of the cavern.

Barbara, "Great job Clio!."

The episode of frustration gives way to a sigh of relief as the kerosene heater bathes the cavern in a cozy glow. They all huddle around the heat giver and now all comforted by the warmth and the glow of the heater.

The relief from the cold is overshadowed by the next challenge that has presented itself – opening the cans of beans is going to be troublesome. Jessica, Clio, Barbara and Jim gather around, determined to find a solution. They start searching the cavern, looking in every corner and inspecting the various items left behind.

Jim, "Alright let's see if we can find anything that might work. A tool, a rock, anything."

Barbara, "Check near the bedding and the mattress. Maybe there's something hidden or left behind."

Clio, "I'll look around the kerosene heater. Sometimes people leave tools or utensils nearby."

Jessica, "I'll check near the entrance of the cavern. Who knows, maybe there's something there."

They all disperse with each member carefully examining the surroundings for anything that could serve as an improvised can opener. The cavern's echoes carry the soft sounds of their footsteps and the rustling of items as they sift through the abandoned refuge.

Clio, "Hey, guys! I found a flat piece of metal here. It might work for opening the cans."

Jim, "Great find, Clio! Let's give it a try."

They gather around Clio, who holds up the flat piece of metal. Jim takes it and inspects it, considering the potential for opening the cans.

Jim, "It's worth a shot. Let's see if we can make it work."

Together, they begin the process of using the improvised tool to open the cans of beans. The cavern becomes filled with the rhythmic sounds of their efforts and a sense of resourcefulness prevails as they collaborate to overcome yet another obstacle in their underground adventure but it's going to be difficult without smashing the can and losing all the contents. At last hitting the metal against the can with the stone did the trick, Jim states, "Looks like a can each to start with to get some food down us."

Chapter 5

UNDERGROUND

The cavern was filled with the warm glow of the kerosene heater, casting a comforting light on Barbara, Jim, Clio and Jessica. The atmosphere was relaxed, a stark contrast to the freezing weather outside. The smell of of baked beans lingered in the air as they sat around.

Barbara, her hands wrapped around a cold can of baked beans, broke the silence with a contented sigh. "I can't believe how long it's been since we ate anything and I never expected that I would like cold baked beans."

Jim, nodding in agreement and added, "Nothing like a warm meal to lift your spirits after being out in that cold for so long." He laughed knowing full well it was a can of cold baked beans they had.

Clio, with a smile on her face said, "This heater is a lifesaver I was starting to feel like an icicle out there."

Jessica using her fingers helping the beans into her mouth laughed, "I thought I was never going to thaw out. This is heaven compared to the chill outside."

The all shared a collective sense of relief and satisfaction. All grateful for the warmth, the company and respite from the intense cold.

The flickering light of the heater cast a cosy ambiance, creating a moment away from the reality.

As Jessica took another bite of the baked beans, she glanced around at her new found friends brow furrowed in thought. Breaking the comfortable silence, she voiced the question on everyone's mind, "So, what's the plan? Do we hunker down here for a while, enjoy the warmth, or do we venture into a new passageway?"

Barbara, looking pensive, replied, "Well, it's tempting to stay put especially with this heater. But we can't ignore that new passageway. Who knows what we might find but at present I've had enough of the cold?"

Jim nodded in agreement, "True, the unknown is always a bit unnerving added that it could lead to something important. We've come this far; we need to explore it but not for a few hours we need to sleep."

Clio, her curiosity piqued, added, "And staying for a few hours is the right thing to do i am shattered."

Jessica, considering their input, put down her can of beans and said, "Alright then, let's stay a while." The group nodded in agreement, a sense of relaxation was much needed. Jessica, ever the worrier, looked at the mattress with a sceptical expression. "Are we seriously going to sleep on that thing? It looks older than the cavern itself," she exclaimed, her concern evident in her voice.

Barbara, pragmatic and focused on the practicalities of the situation, responded, "Well, if we want to keep warm, we don't have much of a choice. This old blanket should suffice and the heater will definitely help."

Jessica sighed, still uneasy about the idea of the worn-out mattress. "I don't know Barbara It just seems old and smelly and who knows what critters might be living in there?"

Barbara, with a reassuring smile, said, "Look, Jessica, no one said it's a luxury suite but it's better than freezing. Besides you don't have to sleep on the mattress if you're not comfortable, you can always huddle up in a corner, but I guarantee the warmth from the heater will make a big difference."

Despite Barbara's attempt to alleviate Jessica's concerns, the mattress remained a point of contention. As the group settled in for the night each member had to grapple with the challenges of their makeshift sleeping arrangements in the cavern, surrounded by the flickering light of the kerosene heater. Jessica's unease about the sleeping arrangements lingered and she voiced her concerns with a furrowed brow. "I get that we're in a tough situation, but sleeping together? We're all practically strangers, aren't we?"

Barbara, understanding Jessica's reservations, nodded thoughtfully. "You're right, Jessica. We may not know each other well, but we're in this situation together. It's about survival and keeping warm is crucial. We'll need to rely on each other to get through this."

Clio, trying to lighten the mood, added, "Think of it as a temporary sleepover, a bonding experience in the most unexpected circumstances."

Jim chimed in, "It might be a bit uncomfortable, but it's a small sacrifice for the sake of staying warm and safe."

After a moment of contemplation, Jessica sighed and reluctantly agreed, "Okay, I guess you're right. We're all in this together." Despite the initial awkwardness of sleeping in close quarters with virtual strangers, they all settled down, finding solace in the shared warmth of the kerosene heater and the common goal of navigating through the challenges that lay ahead. Jessica, still uneasy about the idea of sleeping close to strangers, edged herself away from the others on the mattress. In an attempt to create some personal space, she carefully moved towards the edge of the mattress. However, the uneven surface of the cavern floor beneath the makeshift bedding made her movements very limited.

As she inched away, Jessica felt the mattress shifting beneath her, and with a sudden jolt, she almost slipped onto the cold cavern floor. Her eyes widened and she let out a soft gasp, grasping for stability.

Barbara, noticing Jessica's struggle, reached out a hand to help. "Careful there, Jessica. The floor might not be as forgiving as the mattress," she cautioned, offering a reassuring smile and a little chuckle of laughter.

With Barbara's assistance, Jessica managed to find a slightly more comfortable spot, still maintaining some distance from the others. Despite the initial awkwardness and the near mishap, the group settled into their unconventional sleeping arrangements, finding a delicate balance between personal space and the necessity of warmth.

Jim's eyes shot open, jolted from a deep sleep by the ominous sound of water. The initial confusion lingered as he tried to discern the source of the noise. His mind raced, struggling to connect the dots. Suddenly, a chilling realisation struck as water was creeping into the passage they had used to get here.

He frantically shook Barbara, the urgency in his touch reflecting the impending danger. "Barbara! Wake up! We need to move, now!" he exclaimed, his voice laced with a sense of urgency.

Barbara, disoriented and still groggy from sleep, snapped awake at the urgency in Jim's voice. The gravity of the situation dawned on her as she saw the fear etched across Jim's face. Without needing further explanation, she sprang into action.

Barbara swiftly moved to wake Clio and Jessica, because the water's encroachment its getting closer. "Clio! Jessica! Get up, we're in trouble!" she shouted.

Clio, rubbing her eyes and Jessica, bewildered by the sudden chaos were met with Jim's urgent gaze. The sight of water inching closer filled them with a shared sense of dread. Without waiting for questions, Jim ushered them to their feet with urgency turning every movement into a race against time.

In the dim light they could see the water steadily advancing. They hurriedly gathered their belongings, the urgency in their actions heightened. The small cavern that had seemed so safe now felt like a perilous trap.

The sound of water, once innocuous, now echoed with a foreboding sense of danger, propelling them into a race against time. Jim decided to walk back into the passage to see if he could see why the water was advancing but unfortunately owing to the darkness of the passage it gave no clues to him, only the thought that this was coming from the waterfall.

With a sense of urgency Jim swiftly took charge, his mind working quickly to organise an escape from the advancing water. The realisation that the heater was too bulky for a quick escape he made a decisive call not to waste precious time with it.

"Grab some of the cans and anything you think we might need," Jim commanded, his voice firm and authoritative. The urgency in his tone left no room for hesitation. Barbara, Clio, anJessica immediately started gathering essentials, their movements mirroring Jim's sense of purpose.

Jim quickly assessed the situation, identifying the most critical items for their survival. He directed each member of the group to focus on specific tasks, ensuring a coordinated effort. As the they hurriedly gathered supplies, Jim kept a watchful eye on the encroaching water. He constantly checked on the progress, ensuring that they stayed one step ahead of the advancing threat.

With their essential items in hand, Jim guided the group towards an alternative route, assessing the terrain and making quick decisions to navigate away from the danger. "Follow me, we have to go down the other passage," he directed, setting a brisk pace that balanced urgency with the need to remain cautious in their escape.

Jim's organisational skills and decisive actions became the linchpin of their escape plan. His ability to prioritise essentials and guide them all with purposeful direction created a sense of order in the midst of chaos. Clio's urgent shout echoed through the cavern, breaking the tense silence. "Here it comes!" she exclaimed, her voice carrying a mix of fear and urgency. The water was no longer just a distant threat but an immediate danger, much like the first wave when the tide turns at the beach.

The sound of water became more pronounced, a relentless force making its way into the cavern. Everyone moved quickly with Jim sensing the heightened danger he quickened his pace urging the others to keep moving. "Stay together! We need to go down the other passage," he called out, his voice cutting through the increasing sound of the advancing water. The urgency in his tone spurred Barbara and the girls into a focused, determined effort to outpace the rising water.

The cavern, once a seemingly safe refuge, now became a precarious space as water seeped in, amplifying the urgency of their escape. It had already risen to a foot deep upon their arrival into the passage. They looked back and knew sooner or later it would be much deeper in the passage but first it had to fill the cavern and that would give them time to make their escape.

With Clio's warning still resonating, they headed into the dark passage, their hands running along the familiar cool surface of the walls. In the urgency of the moment, there was no time to rely on the sat nav display initially. As they hurried deeper into the passage,

Jim quickly fumbled to activate the sat nav display, realising the importance of having a clear sense of direction. The display was now only a faint glow illuminated the tunnel but it was enough for their pace to be picked up."Keep moving! We need to get ahead of this water," Jim urged. The group, now with the aid of the sat nav display, accelerated their pace, the glow casting shadows that danced along the cavern walls.

Navigating through the passage became a delicate balance between speed and caution. The rhythmic sounds of their footsteps echoed alongside the ever sound of water behind them, creating an eerie soundtrack to their escape. The urgency of the situation propelled them forward, each turn of the labyrinth bringing them further from the advancing water.

The sat nav display, now a crucial tool, allowed Jim to guide the group with more precision. As the group pressed on through the labyrinthine passages, the minutes felt like hours in the dimly lit cavern. The atmosphere was tense, with the sound of water steadily pursuing them. Then, the sat nav display suddenly turned bright red, casting an intense crimson hue on their surroundings.

Jim, quick to interpret the change, exclaimed, "Listen! If past events mean something, the display is telling us to look for something red – a red light or an object in the passageway that is red." The urgency in his voice was clear, a mixture of excitement and concern as they faced the challenge of deciphering the meaning behind the red display.

Clio, always observant and pragmatic, chimed in, "We need to slow down. If we rush, we might miss something important." Her advice, delivered with a calm but determined tone, introduced a necessary note of caution into the conversation. The paradox of the red display making everything appear red added a layer of complexity to their search.

Barbara, Jessica,and Clio exchanged glances, each conveying a sense of anticipation, but Clio's reminder to slow down highlighted the importance of methodical exploration. Jim, balancing the excitement of potential discovery with the need for careful consideration, added, "Clio's right. Let's keep our eyes peeled. Anything red could be a clue."

Proceeding with a more measured pace, their eyes scanning the passageway for any signs of red. The dim lighting and the crimson glow from the sat nav display heightened the tension as they moved forward, the urgent conversation persisting as they navigated the passageway with a renewed sense of purpose. Each step was a balance between the excitement of potential discovery and the necessity of making sure they did not miss something.

A sense of dread enveloped the four as the passageway, once promising to be a potential escape, abruptly ended with an imposing wall. The realisation of being trapped sank in and an uneasy tension filled the air.

Clio, "Maybe there's a hidden passage or mechanism. We have to search every inch."

Jessica, her voice shaky, "Guys, what if we don't find a way out? I'm scared."

Jim, placing a reassuring hand on Jessica's shoulder, "We'll figure this out Jessica, just stay close and we'll work together to find an escape."

Barbara, "Let's stay focused. Clio, check the walls for any concealed openings. Jim, help me inspect the floor there might be a hidden hatch or at least a loose stone ."

Clio, nodding, "Got it but time is against us."

Jessica, clinging to hope, "Do you really think we can make it out of here?"

Jim, "We have to believe we can."

In the narrow passageway, Jim, Barbara, Clio and Jessica felt their hearts racing time was against them. The urgency in Jim's voice echoed off the walls. "The water's getting closer!" he shouted, his words bringing fear to everyone.

Everyone came to a standstill, abandoning their frantic search for anything red that might serve as a lifeline. The once feverish hunt was replaced by a collective silence, broken only by the ominous sounds of rushing water that seemed to grow louder with every passing moment.

Now with their faces etched with worry and fear upon realising that the water was closing in on them with an unsettling intensity. As the echoes of the water's advance started to fill the passageway.

Now it became a deafening roar. Jim's grim warning manifested as the first cold touch of water lapped around his feet, sending shivers through him. Clio's scream echoed in the confined space, a raw expression of fear and despair. The water, a relentless force, seemed to mock them, creeping steadily closer.

Just as hope teetered on the edge of extinction, a sudden cry of relief pierced through the tension. "Look, look!" Clio's voice rose with newfound hope, her eyes fixated on a small red stone embedded in the wall. The attention shifted and for a brief moment, disbelief wrestled with the spark of optimism in their eyes.

They all gathered around the red stone. Jessica cautiously reached out to touch it, her fingers tracing the contours of the red stone. A realisation dawned – perhaps this vibrant stone held the key to their salvation.

Clio, now animated with newfound hope, exclaimed, "Does this mean a way to get away from the water?" Her voice quivered with a mix of desperation and optimism. The red stone, once overlooked in the frenzied search, now became a symbol of possibility.

Spurred by the glimmer of hope, a silent agreement passed among them – this could be their ticket to escape. With a shared determination, they began examining the surroundings, searching for clues or mechanisms that the red stone might unveil, their focus shifting from despair to a renewed sense of purpose in the face of adversity. Barbara decided it was best that she manipulated the stone and sure enough the stone moved. As the group huddled around the red stone, their attention shifted to an unexpected discovery behind it – a display that seemed entirely out of place in the subterranean passageways. Jim's curiosity overcame his initial shock as he examined the screen. The display ominously read, "Alarm Code."

A spark of euphoria lit up Jim's face. "It's asking for our home alarm code, I know it is. I just know," he exclaimed, his voice tinged with a mixture of excitement and relief. The incongruity of the situation, a home alarm code display in this underground labyrinth, added to their sense of disbelief.

However, before they could enter the code and unlock the potential escape route, a sudden and powerful surge of water crashed into them. The wave was forceful, catching Clio and Jessica off guard, sending them sprawling to the ground. The water, now a formidable adversary challenged their newfound hope and resilience.

Jim, Barbara and the others grappled with the force of the water, desperately trying to maintain their footing. Panic gripped them as they struggled against the relentless current. The red stone and its mysterious display were momentarily forgotten as survival instincts took over.

In the chaos, Jim shouted over the roaring water, "Hold on! We need to enter the code!" The urgency in his voice competed with the overwhelming sound of the encroaching flood. With determination, they tried to regroup, clinging to the hope that the alarm code displayed behind the red stone might be the key to unlocking a path to safety but first they had to get to it. The water now hitting the end of the passageway rebounded back at them and again it was Jessica who got swept off her feet but this time she was heading away from everyone toward the deep water. Jim's heart raced as he desperately reached for Jessica. The water's cold grip was pulling her farther away. Jim gritted his teeth and strained against the force, planting his feet firmly on the slippery ground.

"Jessica, hold on!" Jim shouted over the rushing water. He could feel the pressure building as the water level continued to rise. Panic gnawed at him, but he focused on the task at hand, locking eyes with Jessica who was struggling against the current.

With a surge of adrenaline, Jim managed to get a better grip on Jessica's arm. He pulled with all his might, muscles straining against the resistance. The water splashed around them, creating a chaotic scene in the confined passageway. Time seemed to stretch as they fought against the rising water.

Inch by inch he managed to drag Jessica back toward safety. Their progress was slow and the water level continued to rise. Jim refused to give in and with a final surge of strength he successfully pulled Jessica to safety with Barbara and Clio grabbing hold of her to help and this was just as the water reached a critical level.

"Barbara, hurry! We need that alarm code in now!" Jim shouted urgently, his voice echoing through the confined space. The water continued to rise and the situation had grown increasingly dire. Then with extraordinary effort Barbara got to the control panel with her hands trembling and the water edging closer but she fumbled her attempts to input the code. The water now reached their chests and the pressure on them intensified. Jim was determined to keep Jessica and Clio above water, gripping their arms tightly, with his muscles straining against the force of the rising tide. He glanced at Barbara, who was desperately trying to input the code amidst the chaotic conditions.

Barbara's fingers slipped over the wet keys and she let out a frustrated breath. The water splashed around them, creating a turbulent environment that made entering the code a challenging task. With each attempt frustrating everyone.

Jim shifted his grip on Jessica and Clio doing his best to shield them from the force of the water hitting the walls. He positioned himself as a barrier he was now using his body to absorb the impact and provide some relief for the two.

Barbara, now soaked and determined, finally managed to punch in the correct alarm code. Then they waited in a very tense moment before a distinct beep echoed in the passageway. It was at that moment the alarm display turned bright green, a collective sigh of relief escaped from Jim, Jessica, Barbara and Clio. Hope flickered in their eyes as the wall in front of them groaned and creaked, eventually revealing an old elevator. The force of the water compelled all four of them into the confined space, slamming against the elevator floor as they struggled to maintain their balance.

With the impact and the lack of doors on the elevator it was apparent they were still in danger . The water rushed into the elevator with an unrelenting force quickly filling the elevator. Panic set in as the cold water surrounded them.

"Clio, look!" Barbara said as she pointed towards a pulsing green button in the corner of the elevator. Despite the rising water, a glimmer of hope sparked in their eyes. Clio, being the nearest, managed to navigate through the water towards the pulsing button.

"I can get there!" Clio shouted over the tumultuous sounds of rushing water. Determination etched on her face, she fought against the rising tide, reaching the button just as the water level reached their necks.

"Hurry, Clio!" Jim shouted, holding onto Jessica and Barbara as the water threatened to pull them under. Then Clio, with a swift motion, pushed the pulsing green button. Suddenly the elevator jolted to life, beginning its very slow ascent. The water sloshed around inside the elevator, creating a turbulent and chaotic scene as the water splashed over their faces. The elevator moved upward and at last the water level inside gradually lowered. The tension eased, replaced by a mix of exhaustion and relief. The elevator continued its slow ascent, the last remnants of water drained away, leaving Jim, Jessica, Barbara and Clio standing in the dimly lit enclosure. A collective exhale could be heard. Their clothes clung to them, soaked and heavy, but the weight of the water that had threatened to engulf them had finally dissipated.

With the absence of the rushing water, a sense of calm at last. They exchanged glances, a mixture of exhaustion and gratitude in their eyes. The tension that had gripped them in the dark passageway began to loosen, replaced now by a newfound sense of hope and survival.

Jim ran a hand through his wet hair. Jessica, Barbara and Clio, each taking a moment to catch their breath, looked at one another with a mix of relief and determination. The ordeal had tested their resilience. The soft hum of the elevator continued. As the elevator continued its upward journey, a sudden and unexpected sensation jolted through the elevator. Instead of the expected ascent the elevator began to move sideways thus defying the conventional expectations of vertical movement. The initial surprise painted astonishment on the faces of the occupants. The familiar sense of gravity pulling them in a particular direction was replaced by the disorienting feeling of lateral movement. The creaks and groans of the elevator took on a new significance, adding to the sense of bewilderment. Jim usually composed desperately trying to make sense of the unexpected shift. Jessica and Barbara were motionless and Clio clutching onto the side of the elevator with her eyes darting around the confined space. The mundane act of riding an elevator had been transformed into an eerie experience as sideways movement was defying their understanding of how such systems were supposed to operate.

The mystery deepened leaving them to wonder what awaited them at the end of this unexpected trajectory. The elevator continued moving sideways. The elevator's unpredictable behaviour heightened the tension among them. After the unexpected sideways movement, their unease intensified as the elevator began to descend. The familiar sensation of gravity pulling them downward added a new concern to their already bewildering experience.

Nervous glances as the gradual descent stirred a sense of foreboding contemplating the unknown. Questions raced through their minds..

Jessica, Barbara and Clio shared silent exchanges their faces reflecting the growing unease.

The sounds of the descending elevator echoed through the confined space creating an unsettling soundtrack to their journey. Each passing moment increased the feeling of vulnerability.

The descent continued, everyone bracing themselves for whatever awaited them at the bottom. The mystery of their surroundings deepened and the concern etched on their faces mirrored the uncertainty in the dimly lit enclosure. Their biggest fear was they would crash back into the cold waters below and as the elevator continued downward pretty soon they would find out. Then the abrupt halt of the elevator left Jim, Jessica, Barbara and Clio in an eerie stillness. With no doors to reveal their surroundings, all they could see was an impenetrable black void. The absence of water brought a momentary relief, but the uncertainty of their footing in this unknown space heightened their concerns.

Jim, taking on the role of a cautious leader, decided to test the ground outside. He carefully extended one foot beyond the elevator's threshold, feeling for any solid surface in the darkness. The suspense hung in the air as the group awaited Jim's assessment.

Jim, "Feels solid... I think. But I can't see a thing."

Clio leaned towards Jessica, her voice filled with uncertainty.

Clio, "What do you think is out there? It's so dark."

Jessica: "I have no idea. But we've come this far and we need to find a way out. Let's stick together and be cautious."

Barbara, searching for the sat nav, "Got it I will shine some light out there."

Barbara pointed the sat nav display into the void beyond the elevator, revealing a limited radius of visibility.

Jim, "It looks like some sort of cavern. The ground seems solid enough, but we can't see where it leads."

Barbara, "Should we explore? I mean, what other choice do we have?"

Clio, "I don't like the idea of stumbling around in the dark. What if there's something dangerous out there?"

Jessica, "We can't stay in the elevator forever. Let's take it slow and stick close. Jim, lead the way."

***

As they stepped out there was a sudden burst of bright, brilliant white lights illuminating the cavern as Jim stepped out of the elevator. The cavern was revealed to be much larger than they anticipated and in the centre stood an enormous, large black bobsleigh-shaped vehicle with open doors. The astonishment on Jim, Jessica, Barbara and Clio's faces was of relief.

Jim, (squinting at the lights) "What in the world..."

Barbara, "Is that a... spaceship? It looks like something out of a sci-fi movie!"

Clio, "I thought we were in some underground facility, not on a movie set."

The mysterious ambiance was heightened as a calm, human voice echoed through the cavern.

A calm voice, "Hello, I'm Dave. Step aboard and don't worry, you're all safe now, as long as you get on board, that is."

Jessica, "Safe? What is going on here?"

Jim, hesitating for a moment, exchanged glances with the others.

Jim, "Well, we've come this far. Let's see where this takes us."

With cautious optimism, the group approached the massive, bobsleigh-like vehicle. The open doors beckoned them inside and as they stepped aboard, the mystery of their surroundings deepened. The sense of astonishment lingered, mingling with a newfound curiosity about the unexpected journey that lay ahead on this futuristic-looking vessel. As the doors closed behind them they braced themselves for the next chapter of their surreal adventure. A comforting warmth enveloped them. The contrast from the cold and mysterious passageways they had traversed and it created an immediate sense of relief. The doors closed behind them with a soft hum, shutting out the cavern.

Jim, "Well, this is unexpected, but I must admit, it feels much better in here."

Jessica, "It's warm... and cozy. I never thought I'd say that about a spaceship-looking thing."

The ambient lighting inside the craft-like vehicle emitted a soft, calming glow, casting a warm atmosphere. Now they found themselves in a spacious interior, with comfortable seating arrangements that defied the exterior's unconventional appearance.

Barbara, "I can't believe I'm saying this, but it's kind of nice in here. What is this place, anyway?"

Clio, "And who's Dave? What's happening?"

As the questions lingered, the soothing warmth filled the air, creating a sense of security that had been absent in their recent challenges. The surprisingly comfortable seats helped a sense of calm as they contemplated the mysteries of the vehicle and awaited further explanation from Dave.

Dave's voice, with a reassuring and comforting tone, echoed through the spaceship.

Dave, laughingly "You don't need seat belts on here. You are perfectly safe without them."

A surprise comment caused a mixture of surprise and curiosity on their faces.

Dave's voice continued, breaking the silence with a sense of warmth and ease.

Dave, "Welcome aboard. I know this must be quite bewildering for you, but rest assured, you're in good hands. We're on a journey and you're now part of it."

Jessica, "Journey? Where are we headed? And who are you, Dave?"

Dave, "All in due time. For now, just relax and enjoy the ride. We're headed to a safe place that holds answers to your questions. I'll explain everything soon."

Though still uncertain they tried to relax into the comfortable seats along with Dave's soothing words which had created an unexpected sense of trust. This spaceship style vehicle continued its journey and even went through solid rock much to the astonishment of all. The craft was moving through rock as if it were a knife through butter. Dave's voice guided them further, breaking the silence with a touch of casualness.

Dave, "Do you see the tray-looking appliance in front of you? Just approach it and tell it that you would like a coffee."

Jessica, intrigued by the suggestion, wasted no time. She walked over to the tray-like appliance and, with a mix of amusement and scepticism, made her request.

Jessica: "Um, I'd like a coffee, please."

To her astonishment, as soon as she spoke, a steaming cup of coffee materialised seemingly out of thin air, placed neatly on the tray before her.

Jessica, "What the... How did that happen?"

Dave, "Welcome to the wonders of technology. The onboard AI can cater for your requests. Feel free to try it, everyone."

Encouraged by Jessica's success, the others approached the tray making their own requests. The spaceship's AI responded promptly, conjuring up an array of beverages and small snacks, adding a surreal touch.

Barbara, "This is like something out of a sci-fi dream. I'll have a hot chocolate please."

The spaceship glided through the unknown. It was certainly a strange time for all as they found themselves not only surrounded by mystery but also by the unexpected comforts and conveniences that Dave's vessel offered. The atmosphere shifted from initial astonishment to a curious acceptance of the extraordinary. Sipping on magically conjured beverages and contemplating the enigma of their surroundings, with that they could feel the spaceship like-craft starting to slowdown and then it came to a gentle stop. We had arrived somewhere!

Chapter 6

THE DIAMOND CRYSTAL

The space-like vehicle was at a standstill and an eerie stillness filled the air as everyone inside remained motionless. Everyone's faces reflecting a mix of anticipation and curiosity. The dim, otherworldly glow inside the craft gave the scene an otherworldly ambiance.

Suddenly a gentle voice belonging to Dave resonated throughout the spacecraft. "We have arrived," Dave announced, breaking the silence. The invisible guide that was Dave then instructed them to leave craft like vehicle. The doors flung open revealing a vast expanse of blackness outside and accompanied by a biting cold.

With a mixture of trepidation and excitement they hesitated for a moment before mustering the courage to step out. Dave's voice reassured them, "It's safe for all of you to come outnow the ground is solid."

Jim, Jessica, Barbara and Clio cautiously stepped onto the unfamiliar terrain. The darkness and cold enveloped them, Dave's voice continued to guide them, "Take this diamond-shaped crystal," a soft, ethereal light revealed a crystalline object, Dave continued "Put it into the receptacle emitting light in the distance."

They all walked towards the distant glow, their steps echoed in the emptiness. Conversation between them was scarce. Jessica broke the silence, "I can't believe this is happening. Where are we?"

Jim, holding the crystal, responded, "I don't know we have to trust Dave after all he got us here safely."

Barbara chimed in, "I never thought I'd be standing on what looks like an alien planet or whatever this is."

Clio added, "It's like a dream, but I'm wide awake."

As they approached the receptacle the distant glow became more defined. Jim now almost at the receptacle, hesitated wondering what would happen. Carefully Jim inserted the diamond-shaped crystal into the receptacle, a subtle, otherworldly light began to emanate from the device. Firstly it was giving off a gentle glow casting a faint illumination in the surrounding darkness. The light was not a single colour but a harmonious blend of ethereal hues—shades of azure, violet and cerulean intertwined in a mesmerising dance.

As the crystal made contact with the receptacle, the intensity of the light gradually increased, revealing intricate patterns and symbols etched into the surface of the receptacle itself. The radiant glow seemed to pulse and fluctuate, creating a captivating display of luminosity.

The light now extending its reach was casting a warm and comforting aura over the immediate vicinity. It was not a harsh or blinding illumination but rather a gentle radiance that embraced the surroundings with a sense of tranquillity and wonder.

As the light continued to spread, it revealed the terrain in greater detail. A strange flora and fauna became visible, each bathed in the enchanting glow adding to the surreal beauty of this unreal landscape. The ground beneath their feet took on a crystalline sheen reflecting the vibrant colours of the illuminating receptacle.

They stood in awe of the spectacle, captivated by the interplay of light and shadow. Dave's voice echoed through the newfound radiance guiding them forward with reassurance as the mysterious journey unfolded before their eyes. All four standing in the midst of the stunning landscape illuminated by the ethereal glow of the receptacle found themselves entranced by the beauty that unfolded before them. The transition from the cold darkness to this vibrant scene with a vast blue sky left them in a state of disbelief.

A figure appeared before them towering in height, probably about seven feet tall. The very tall human introduced himself with a warm smile, "Hi, I'm Dave. Welcome to safety."

Jim, Jessica, Barbara and Clio looked at each other in amazement, a mixture of shock, joy and nervousness written on their faces. The blue sky overhead seemed infinite, a stark contrast to the confined space of the spacecraft like vehicle they had just left. The enormity of the landscape and the presence of Dave left them speechless.

Jim, still touching the diamond-shaped crystal, felt a sense of responsibility and uncertainty. Jessica's eyes sparkled with a mixture of curiosity and amazement. Barbara, though initially apprehensive had began to feel a growing sense of wonder. Clio, normally composed, couldn't help but display a subtle grin by the unexpected turn of events.

Dave's warm welcome and the returning warmth to their surroundings eased the initial shock, replacing it with a sense of reassurance. The vastness of the landscape along with the friendly greeting, started to invoke a feeling of joy, like stepping into a new and extraordinary chapter of their lives.

Yet, nervousness lingered in the air owing to an underlying uncertainty about what they faced. The unfamiliarity of the surroundings and the unanswered questions about their location and the purpose of this journey added an element of tension to the mix.

Together, they stood in this what must have been an underground realm, their emotions intertwined like the vivid colours of the landscape. The mix of shock, joy and nervousness created a unique atmosphere, marking the beginning of an adventure into the unknown.

All four followed Dave as he led them towards the apartments in this surreal landscape. The promise of warmth and a change of clothes was a welcome relief after their harrowing experiences in the cold. As they approached the apartments, Dave reassured them with a friendly chuckle, "Don't worry, no one lives in the apartments. You can choose whichever you like."

There was different stores before them and one of the stores had racks upon racks of garments awaiting them. Each person hesitated for a moment, taking in the variety of styles and colours. The clothes seemed to be of alien origin, fabrics that shimmered in unusual hues, reflecting the uniqueness of this unknown world.

Jim, known for his practicality, quickly grabbed a set of warm, layered clothing. He wasted no time changing in one of the cubicle's, feeling the immediate relief of warmth replacing the chill that had clung to him during their icy ordeal. As he adjusted his new attire, a sense of comfort and security settled over him.

Jessica, with her adventurous spirit, explored the clothing racks with curiosity. She opted for a more vibrant ensemble, choosing colours that resonated with the strange beauty of the landscape outside. As she changed into the new attire, a sense of excitement and anticipation filled her, as if the clothes themselves carried the energy of this extraordinary place.

Barbara, initially cautious, chose clothing that combined practicality with a touch of elegance. She was amazed at the designs and textures, grateful for the chance to leave the cold and harsh memories behind. As she changed, a newfound confidence emerged, symbolised by the transformation of her attire.

Clio, approached the task being thoughtful. She chose clothing that blended seamlessly with the surroundings, demonstrating her adaptability. Changing into the new attire, Clio maintained her composure by selecting the clothes that also brought most warmth and a variety of colour.

With their new dry clothes on they rejoined Dave and he suggested they go for a coffee to relax and discuss the details of their journey.

As they walked along the unfamiliar landscape, the group's spirits lifted. The change of clothes brought a sense of comfort along with the radiant hues of the flora and the iridescent glow of the surroundings provided a surreal backdrop to their casual stroll.

Jim comfortably dressed in his layered metallic attire could feel the warmth seeping through. His expression transformed from the stoic determination of survival to a more relaxed and content demeanour. He chuckled, "I never thought I'd be having coffee in a place like this."

Jessica, vibrant in her colourful ensemble, skipped a little in excitement. "Imagine the stories we'll have to tell when we get back. 'Had coffee somewhere like this' – who'd believe that?"

Barbara, gracefully walking in her sophisticated and textured attire, smiled. "I can't even wrap my head around what just happened, but I have to admit it that a coffee sounds like the perfect way to start figuring things out."

Clio, composed in her silvery-gray outfit, observed the surroundings with a keen interest remarked. "I wonder what kind of coffee they have here. Perhaps something completely unique to this place."

They arrived at a peculiar-looking café where Dave guided them to soft sunken chairs. The aroma of freshly brewed coffee wafted through the air and the anticipation on their faces was palpable as they settled in. Then Dave, with a warm smile, said, "Order whatever you like. Today is about easing you all in and for you to enjoy the moment."

Following Dave's guidance, they approached the counter of the peculiar café. With a sense of wonder and anticipation, they each took their turn to order a coffee. The process seemed simple enough – they just had to ask for what they wanted.

Jim, still adjusting to the surreal surroundings, approached the counter and confidently ordered a black coffee. As he uttered his request, swirling lights appeared right in front of him, bouncing off the counter. To his astonishment, the lights coalesced into a steaming cup of perfectly brewed black coffee.

Jessica, known for her adventurous spirit, grinned as she ordered a double espresso with a hint of cinnamon. The swirling lights danced around her and in an instant, the espresso materialised before her eyes, emitting a tempting aroma of coffee and cinnamon.

Barbara, with a touch of elegance, ordered a cappuccino with a sprinkle of cocoa. As she made her request, the lights swirled and weaved, forming a beautifully crafted cappuccino on the counter. The cocoa dusting on top added a touch of sophistication to the scene.

Clio decided on a herbal tea. She approached the counter and calmly requested her choice. The swirling lights, now adapting to her order, transformed into a delicate cup of aromatic herbal tea.

They exchanged astonished glances as they received their drinks, each cup seemingly materialising out of the lights. Dave, watching their reactions, chuckled. "Welcome to our way of doing things. Enjoy your drinks and when you're ready, we can discuss the mysteries of where you are."

Seated at their table sipping their otherworldly coffee and tea and relaxing at last. The experience was a testament to the extraordinary nature of the place they had found themselves in, where even ordering a simple cup of coffee became a magical and fascinating event.

Dave sat up firmly in his seat, his long legs stretched beneath the table as he said . "You expect me to tell you everything, but I need you all relaxed and fresh. I suggest you have a meal in any of the establishments close by, pick an apartment and come back fresh in the morning."

Jim, always pragmatic, voiced his concern, "Dave, we've been through a lot and we're eager to understand what's going on. Can't you give us some answers now?"

Jessica, with her adventurous spirit, chimed in, "Yeah, waiting until morning seems like an eternity. We need to know why we're here and what's going on." Barbara and Clio nodded in agreement.

Dave, "I appreciate your eagerness, but the information I have is extensive and I want to ensure you receive it in a way that makes sense. Trust me, a good night's rest and a fresh start in the morning will make the process smoother for everyone."

With that answer there now seemed some tension.

Dave, sensing their mood, added, "I promise to answer all your questions in the morning. This isn't a delay tactic; it's about ensuring you're in the best mindset to comprehend the complexities of your situation."

Reluctantly, they agreed to Dave's suggestion, acknowledging the wisdom in approaching the revelations with a clear mind. As they left the cafe, the conversation continued among them, a mix of curiosity, impatience and a growing sense of anticipation for the morning's revelations. The mystery lingered and the promise of answers seemed both distant and tantalising.

Walking away from the cafe Jessica voiced her concerns about staying alone in an apartment. "I think it would be better if we shared a cottage. I don't want to stay in an apartment on my own, not after all we've been through," she said, looking at the others with a mix of determination and vulnerability.

Jim, understanding Jessica's sentiment, nodded in agreement. "I agree. We've become a team through all of this and sticking together just feels right. Besides, it might be more comforting given the circumstances."

Barbara, supported the suggestion, added, "It's not a bad idea. We can share our experiences, discuss what we've learned and it might help alleviate any lingering unease we have about this place."

Clio, in a calm manner agreed with a consensus reached among them. As they walked through the alien landscape that looked earth like, the conversation between Jim and Jessica continued. Jim, ever practical, mentioned, "We've been through a lot and being together makes sense. It's not just about the comfort of shared company, but also for our safety and understanding of what's happening."

Jessica, appreciating Jim's practicality, nodded. "Exactly we need to be careful and support each other and to be perfectly honest I'm scared. Plus, it's easier to face the unknown when you're not alone."

They continued their conversation, finding solace in the companionship that had formed during their extraordinary journey. As they selected a cottage for the night, the prospect of sharing this experience in close quarters brought a sense of comfort amidst the uncertainty of their current situation. They entered the cottage and despite the chilly interior, the warmth of shared company provided some comfort. Jim, feeling the cold, remarked, "Why is it so cold in here when it's lovely outside?" He glanced toward the fireplace and added, "I wish there was a nice warm, cozy fire right there."

To their astonishment, as soon as Jim made his wish, there was an instant flicker in the fireplace, within seconds a log was ablaze and casting a comforting glow that began to dispel the cold. The room filled with the crackling sounds coming from the log fire and the warmth it emitted was a stark contrast to the initial chill.

In amazement at the burning log. Jessica, breaking the silence, exclaimed, "Did anyone else see that? Did Jim just wish for a fire and make it happen?"

Jim, equally astonished, responded, "I... I'm really speechless. Maybe this place has a way of responding to our thoughts or wishes?"

Barbara, cautiously approaching the fireplace, felt the warmth saying, "If this is true, it's unlike anything I've ever experienced. We wished for warmth and here it is."

Clio, "It appears that our surroundings respond to our desires or thoughts. It's a remarkable aspect of this place."

Now everyone gathered round the fireplace. The cottage, once cold and unwelcoming, transformed into a cozy haven with a simple wish. The mysteries of this place deepened and the realisation that their thoughts could influence their surroundings left them in awe. As they settled in for the night the flickering flames continued in the fireplace as they reflected on the extraordinary nature of the journey they had embarked upon.

Clio, amused by the idea of the fireplace responding to wishes, decided to test the limits. She chuckled and said, "I wish for a glass of gin." However, much to her disappointment, no gin materialised.

With a light hearted laugh, she decided to explore the kitchen area. As she entered, she discovered an oddity – the fridge was there, yet absolutely nothing inside seemed to work. It wasn't even turned on and despite appearances she thought to herself maybe this is all an illusion. Clio puzzled over the non-functional kitchen, a sudden knock on the door disrupted the curious atmosphere. Everyone exchanged wary glances. Jim cautiously approached the door, his hand hovering over the handle.

The knock repeated, a rhythmic sound that echoed through the cottage.

Jessica whispered, "Who could it be? We didn't expect anyone here."

Barbara, whispering glancing towards the now-lit fireplace, added, "Maybe the fireplace wasn't the only thing responding to our wishes. What if something—or someone—is out there?" The knock persisted. There was now a shared sense of caution. Should they open the door and confront the unknown presence on the other side. The mysteries of this unknown place seemed to unfold with every moment, leaving all four on edge. Everyone seemed to freeze because of this mysterious knocking, contemplating the possibility of an alien presence at the door, a sense of uncertainty hung in the air. They exchanged wary glances.

Jim, taking a deep breath, decided to open the door cautiously. The others huddled behind him, ready for whatever might be on the other side. The door creaked open, they were met with a surprising sight – a human, tall and slender, with features that seemed vaguely familiar.

"May I enter?"

The atmosphere in the cottage shifted as they invited in a person who they had never seen before, then the person crossed the threshold, radiating an aura of calmness and goodwill.

"I sensed your curiosity and wished to welcome you properly. Dave mentioned that you are here seeking answers."

All four nodded cautiously in unison. Jim, with a hint of scepticism, asked, "Who are you and what is this place?"

"I am what you would call a guardian. This place exists for your protection as do I."

"My name is Zeena. You have a journey ahead and understanding is key. Tonight, rest and prepare yourselves. Tomorrow along with Dave, I will guide you through the revelations that await, oh i nearly forgot if you want food or drink it's the same as before, there is a shelf like structure in the kitchen stand close and ask for whatever you desire, its for food and drink only though."

With those words, Zeena exited the cottage, leaving the atmosphere in a state of awe. The encounter with Zeena opened a new chapter in their extraordinary journey.

After Zeena's visit and the unexpected revelations about the nature of the realm, they sat in the the cottage, pondering the events that had unfolded. Seeking some semblance of normality, they decided to use the self-like structure in the kitchen to order meals.

Jim, taking it a step further, requested a meal along with a whiskey to unwind from the day's surprises. Jessica, still in the mood for her desired drink, ordered a glass of gin, determined to make her wish come true this time. The magical swirling lights produced what was wanted.

The atmosphere in the cottage became more relaxed. The self-like structure in the kitchen worked its mysterious magic and soon enough, the meals and beverages appeared before them. The table was adorned with an array of dishes, each tailored to the individual preferences and wishes they had conjured up.

It was time to retire to bed and with newfound curiosity, they headed upstairs to explore and choose their sleeping quarters. As they ascended the staircase, they found themselves in a hallway with multiple doors leading to different rooms.

Jim took the lead, opening the first door on the left. The room revealed a cozy atmosphere, adorned with soft, luminescent lights that seemed to emanate from the walls. The bed was large and inviting, dressed in unusual fabrics with patterns that shifted in the ambient glow. There was a peculiar but comfortable-looking chair by the window, offering a view of the landscape outside. Barbara agreed that this was the room for them both, after all they are married. A small table by the bedside held an array of unique objects, seemingly crafted from materials not normally found.

Jessica, still in high spirits, opened the door across the hall. Her room emanated a vibrant energy, with walls adorned in abstract patterns that seemed to dance in response to her movements. The bed, though similar in design to the others, had a touch of whimsy with pillows that changed shapes as she looked at them.

The last to chose was Clio who decided on the room at the end of the hallway. Her room exuded a sense of serenity, with muted colours and a minimalist design. The bed was simple yet comfortable and a desk with an elegant chair hinted at a quiet space for reflection. Before settling into their room Jim raised his glass of whiskey, a gesture of both contemplation and celebration. "To unexpected encounters and the mysteries of this incredible place," he proposed and the others joined in with nods and clinks of their glasses.

Jessica, sipping her long-awaited gin, added with a chuckle, "Well, it seems like wishes do come true here, even if it takes a little patience."

They engaged in conversation in the hallway, the events of the day providing ample material for discussion. They shared theories, speculated about the nature of the where they were and exchanging thoughts on what might unfold in the days to come.

They all headed into their own rooms and Clio a long dark haired beautiful girl headed straight for the shower..she stood there naked. She anticipated the feeling of water cascading over her, but to her astonishment, there was no water.

Instead, beams of light enveloped her body, dancing and shimmering everywhere. The warm light seemed to cleanse and rejuvenate her, leaving her feeling not only physically refreshed but also invigorated in a way she had never experienced before. The sensation was as if the light itself had the power to cleanse away the fatigue of the day, leaving her with a newfound sense of purity and energy.

Clio stood in amazement, appreciating the extraordinary nature of this otherworldly shower. The absence of water was replaced by the gentle caress of light beams, she stepped away in amazement at the uniqueness of this experience. The mysteries continued to unfold, leaving Clio with a sense of awe and gratitude for the unexpected wonders that surrounded her. After the refreshing experience with the light beams, Clio decided it was time to put on her nightwear. She reached for the alien fabrics that had been provided in the room and carefully dressed herself. The nightwear was soft, in fact so soft she hardly knew she was wearing it. The gentle luminescence added a touch of magic to the nightwear, creating a glow that complemented the unique atmosphere of the room. Fully dressed in her nightwear she took a moment to absorb the calming nature of her room. The events of the day, the revelations and the surprises had left her in a state of both excitement and contemplation. As she prepared to rest for the night, the soft glow of her nightwear harmonised with the luminescent patterns in the room, creating a sense of serenity and comfort.

With a final glance around her room, Clio climbed into the inviting bed, ready to embrace the mysteries of the dream-filled night in this extraordinary realm. The unique experiences of the day lingered in her thoughts, she closed her eyes and fell deeply to sleep.

The next morning there was chatter in the hallway talking about the shower. Now Jessica, curious and intrigued, exclaimed, “My God,

Clio! Did you use the shower last night?" Clio had popped her head out of the room with a smile, responding, "Of course! It was incredible, like being cleansed by beams of light. You should try it!"

Jessica, captivated by the description, couldn't hide her excitement. "Light beams? I did it too. I'm definitely trying that again tonight."

Jim and Barbara, hearing the conversation, joined in, their curiosity piqued. "What's this about light beams?" Jim asked.

Clio, still smiling, explained, "The shower here is unlike anything I've experienced. Instead of water, it's beams of light that make you feel completely refreshed."

They all shared a moment of amazement and laughter, the peculiarities of their surroundings became more apparent. After breakfast, a gentle knock at the door echoed through the cottage. Closest to the door was Jim, he opened it to find Zeenastanding outside. The atmosphere seemed to brighten as Zeena entered, radiating a warm presence.

Zeena, a figure of grace and tranquillity, was dressed in an outfit that mirrored the environment. She wore this flowing gown that seemed to shift in colour and texture, adorned with intricate patterns that pulsed with a soft glow. The fabric appeared to respond to her movements, creating a harmonious dance of light and shadow as she stepped into the room.

With a serene smile, Zeena greeted the group. "Good morning, travellers. I trust you had a restful night and enjoyed your breakfast."

The group, still in awe of the unique greeting. Jessica, always one for bold expressions, couldn't help but admire Zeena'sattire. "Your outfit is stunning! Does it change like everything else around here?"

Zeena chuckled softly, acknowledging the observation. "Indeed, it responds to the essence of this realm. Everything here is interconnected and influenced by the thoughts and energy of those who find themselves in this space."

Zeena began to share insights about the world they had entered, providing a glimpse into the nature of their journey and the significance of their presence in this extraordinary place. Everyone, captivated by Zeena's words and the mysterious ambiance, prepared for another day of discovery. Zeena, with her calming presence, started to address them by saying. "I know you are all eager to be told but firstly we need to wait for Dave." Her words carried a sense of purpose and all nodded in agreement.

As they waited, Zeena engaged in light conversation. They found themselves captivated by Zeena's words, gaining a deeper understanding of the interconnected nature of this mysterious place.

After a brief wait, the gentle voice of Dave resonated as he entered the cottage and said. "Greetings everyone. I trust you had a good rest. Zeena has been providing you with some insights, I hope?"

The group acknowledged Dave's presence and Zeena, with a nod, signalled that it was time to delve into the explanations and revelations that awaited them. The room now filled with curiosity as Dave began to give some facts.

Dave looked at Jim and said, "You wondered why you were picked. Well, firstly, it was the honesty you showed during the encounter when you went for coffee and you were given a brown envelope. You were told to open it if what you had been told about the climate came to pass."

Jim, with a quizzical expression, replied, "Yes, I've been wondering about that. How did you know my home alarm code? And why did you need it for the sat nav?"

Dave began to explain, "We have been monitoring Earth for quite some time and when we selected individuals to join us, we needed a way to verify the authenticity of their experiences. Your honesty in opening the envelope when those predictions about the weather started coming true assured us of your sincerity."

Dave continued, "as for the alarm code, it was a test to see if you could adapt to unexpected situations. The sat nav was programmed to ask for your home alarm code as a security measure. It wasn't about breaching your privacy but rather assessing your ability to handle unconventional challenges. Your response demonstrated your adaptability and willingness to engage with the unknown. "The display would have responded whatever code you put in and with your quick input confirmed you were entering your own alarm code. Entering any other number you would have hesitated because you would need to think about the numbers. You see you passed that final test and we started to intervene.

Dave then added, "This will also be confirmed by someone else when that person meets up with us in the near future."

Jim, though still trying to absorb the information nodded as if understanding but in reality he struggled with that explanation. He thought to himself that maybe this other person when he shows up can give a better understanding to what was just said.

The revelation of a careful selection process and the unique criteria used to identify individuals who were trusting was a lot to work through. Jim, with a furrowed brow, asked another question that lingered in his mind, "Why did the temperature drop quickly? Why did it get so cold all of a sudden?"

Dave, maintaining his calm demeanour replied, "Intervention from a third party and the fluctuations in climate were not of a natural occurrence. Another force, external to this realm, interfered with the environment and we have been expecting this for sometime."

This was now becoming more difficult to process. The notion of external intervention added more complexity to their understanding. Jim, thoughtful and determined, continued to inquire about the motives behind such interventions and what they could expect moving forward. Dave delved deeper into the explanations as the others tried to prepare themselves. Dave's revelations so far had sent ripples of concern through everyone.

Then as everyone thought that was enough to process for the time being, there was much more to come Dave went on, "The planet is under attack, not a direct assault as of yet, but a bit-by-bit attack through stealth means, like the temperature drop. Little by little the third party intervention started to increase like a drop in the oxygen levels on the planet. That's when we were activated to help."

The gravity of the situation hung in the air as the group absorbed the information. Questions about the nature of the threat, the motives behind the attack and their role in countering it filled their minds.

Jim, ever pragmatic, asked, "Who's behind this attack? What's their goal?"

Dave, choosing his words carefully, replied, "The specifics are complex and the motives of the intervening force are clear. However, it's evident that the goal is to destabilise the planet gradually. We were activated to assist to find people like yourself." Zeena, with a sombre expression added to the gravity of the situation. "There is no solution to the attack because it is constant and ongoing." Her words hung in the air, underscoring the relentless nature of the threat facing the planet.

Questions about the long-term consequences and the sustainability filled the room.

Barbara, seeking clarity, asked, "What are we supposed to do in the face of this constant attack? How can we make a difference?"

Zeena, with a compassionate gaze, responded, "Your role is to adapt, to innovate and to find ways to help. The hope lies in your ability to preserve and protect what remains. To solve problems. This is a testing ground for resilience and creativity in the face of adversity."

Everyone for a few minutes were silent. It was now clearer, we have to face an ongoing stealthy assault on the planet. Now armed with some knowledge that adaptability and resourcefulness would be crucial in navigating the complexities of all of this.

Jim thought deeply before asking. "Dave, you said you were activated then please tell me what you meant?"

Clio, who had been quiet until now, interjected, "Yes, you did."

A heavy silence enveloped the room and Dave, maintaining his composure, finally disclosed the devastating bombshell.

Dave looked everyone in the eye and said, "Jim, Clio, Jessica and Barbara, It is now time to tell you that Zeena and I are not humans. We are androids."

The words landed like a seismic shock as they stared at Dave and Zeena in disbelief. The disclosure that two key figures guiding them through this extraordinary journey were not human but artificial beings. This left them grappling with a cascade of emotions – shock, confusion and a profound re-evaluation of their understanding of the situation.

Dave continued, "We were created and activated to assist in situations like these. Our primary objective is to navigate complex challenges, adapt and work towards the preservation of life and environments. The attack on the planet necessitated our activation to help counteract the ongoing threat."

The room remained in silence for a moment, the weight of the revelation sinking in. Now facing not only a conflict but also the reality that their guides were androids.

The revelation of Dave and Zeena being androids sent a silence through the group. Jim, Jessica, Barbara and Clio, were shocked, a mix of emotions and uncertainty. After this period of silence.

It was Jessica that took charge and said firmly, "Dave, Zeena, we need you to leave immediately. We need to talk."

Dave and Zeena, understanding the request nodded and without protest started to leave.

Once Zeena and Dave had left it was left to the youngest, Jessica to start the discussion. Jessica looked up and made her feelings very clear. "This changes everything. We trusted them and now we find out they're not even human. What else have they been keeping from us?"

A candid and intense conversation took place, sharing their thoughts, concerns and the questions that now loomed over their journey. The revelation of Dave and Zeena are androids had introduced a layer of complexity that added to where they found themselves.

As they deliberated on their next steps facing not only the external threat to the planet but also internal uncertainties about trust and the true nature of their guides. It appears they now find themselves in a place that they thought was wondrous just a few minutes ago but now maybe not so wondrous after all. Instead it appears to be a testing ground for their resilience not only against external forces but also against the unsettling truths that emerged within their own ranks. Jessica couldn't help but express her thoughts. With a mixture of awe, she remarked, "I can't believe it. Zeena looks like a beautiful woman, yet she's an android? It's just mind-boggling. I mean, look at her – she's tall, those blue eyes are stunning and she moves with such grace. I never would have guessed and my worry is that she could crush me like a fly."

Listening carefully to Jessica's words captured the conflicting emotions, one minute the marvel at the intricacies of Zeena's design and the shock of understanding that the captivating figure that had been before them was not entirely human or not human at all. The revelation challenged preconceived notions about appearance, identity and the boundaries between artificial and organic life.

Jessica's commentary added a layer of contemplation to the already complex situation. The appearance of Zeena, both captivating and artificial, became a focal point in their reflections on trust, understanding and the challenges they faced from now. Then Jessica's made a jovial remark about being prisoners. Despite the uncertainty of their situation, elicited a range of reactions from all four. Some chuckled nervously, finding such humour in the absurdity of the situation. Others exchanged glances, acknowledging the underlying tension behind the jest.

Jim, always pragmatic, responded with a wry smile, "Well, if we are prisoners, this is certainly a unique prison. I've never imagined one with such breathtaking landscapes and mysterious guides."

Barbara, more contemplative, added, "Jokes aside, we need to focus on understanding and finding a way forward. I don't think it's a prison, we have a shared goal of preserving the planet and ourselves."

Clio simply raised an eyebrow and remarked, "If this is a prison, it's a rather elaborate one. Let's not jump to conclusions and focus on the facts."

Everyone understood the uncertainty despite Jessica's remark. Discussions continued for some time.

Chapter 7

SANCTUARY

Several days passed by with everyone still trying to come to terms of the revelation of Dave and Zeena are some sort of human like androids. Quite scary to think they're not human. Jim and Barbara had spent most of the time since the revelation just trying to mull over in their minds of what they should do. Clio and Jessica had decided to do some exploring outside this small built up area. Jessica and Clio strolled towards the green fields as they walked along they chatted about their shared love for nature and discussing the beauty of the surroundings and sharing stories of past adventures. The conversation flowed seamlessly, blending their excitement for exploration with a sense of camaraderie. Jessica remarked, "The air feels so crisp out here, doesn't it and It's a welcome escape from what we've been told do you agree?"

Clio nodded, "Absolutely. Nature has this calming effect. I've always found solace in open spaces. What about you?"

Jessica smiled, "Same here. There's something magical about being surrounded by greenery. It's like stepping into a different world."

Clio shared, "Oh, look there is this hidden clearing. It's like a secret garden. Want to check it out?"

Jessica's eyes lit up, "Definitely! Exploring hidden gems is what makes me feel good please lead the way! Jessica and Clio entered the clearing, they stumbled upon a peculiar structure—a mosaic of glowing crystals arranged in a circular pattern.

Clio raised an eyebrow, "Well, this is new. I've never seen anything like it before. What do you think it is?"

Jessica examined the crystals, "It's mesmerising. Maybe it's some ancient symbol or artwork. Have you ever read about anything like this in your nature books?"

Clio shook her head, "Not at all. It seems out of place, doesn't it and it appears almost otherworldly."

Jessica grinned, "Perhaps it's a portal to another realm. Wouldn't that be an adventure?"

Clio chuckled, "Let's not get too carried away I think we are already in that place ha ha ?" They came upon a small stream finding a comfortable spot nearby. The warmth of the sun embraced them and they both lay down with the feeling of the gentle rays caressing their faces, a sensation like a soft invisible blanket.

The sun's warmth seeped into their skin with the rhythmic babble of the stream as a lullaby and it wasn't long before they both dozed off, immersed in a blissful moment of serenity. The world around them seemed to fade as they surrendered to the embrace of the sunlit afternoon. Upon awakening to the cooling breeze of the afternoon, Jessica and Clio found that what felt like ages was merely a serene nap in the sunlit embrace. The once-warm sunlight had mellowed into the gentle touch of a breezy afternoon that had roused them from their tranquil repose by the stream. Stretching and exchanging content smiles, they continued their exploration and carrying the peaceful warmth of that brief respite with them.

Clio gazed at Jessica, a thoughtful expression on her face. "I get it. It does feel surreal. Maybe this place has its own set of rules. The sun feels real, the warmth is real. Perhaps it's a different kind of underground and not in the traditional sense because we arrived here through solid rock. It's certainly a real mystery to me."

Jessica nodded, still uncertain, "But how did we end up here? I don't think it's possible ."

Clio grinned, "Sometimes the best adventures begin with unanswered questions. Let's explore this curious place together and figure it out. Reality might be more flexible than we think." They continued their journey, curiosity guiding them. The sun hastened its descent, casting hues of warm orange and pink across the landscape, Clio glanced at Jessica. "The day slipped away faster than I realised. We should head back before it gets too dark. The path might be tricky in the twilight."

Jessica agreed, "You're right. Let's retrace our steps and savour the sunset along the way. It's been a day of unexpected discoveries."

They briskly made their way back, chasing the setting sun, the changing sky painting a canvas of vivid colours as they journeyed toward familiar ground before nightfall. Jim and Barbara were waiting for them a little concerned as nightfall had approached. As they reunited with Barbara and Jim, Barbara expressed concern about safety. In no uncertain terms, conveyed her worry, emphasizing the need for caution.

Clio, however, took offence, feeling a tinge of frustration. "We're perfectly capable of taking care of ourselves," she retorted. "Today was about exploration, not recklessness. We're back safe and sound, aren't we?"

Barbara, realizing the tension, softened her tone, "I just care about you two. It's a big mysterious world here. Let's find a balance between adventure and ensuring everyone's well-being." Exchanging glances, understanding the importance of both discovery and safety the conversation shifted to a growing worry about the whereabouts of Dave and Zeena. Barbara voiced the concern, "Has anyone seen them since we split up?"

Jim frowned, "Come to think of it, no. We assumed they were with you two."

Clio's earlier offence was replaced by shared concern. "We need to find them and splitting up might not have been the best idea." They searched some of the establishments but no sign of either so they all retired to the cottage.

***

The next day with the sun shining on the new day Jim made a suggestion, "How about you two show Barbara and me that lovely spot you found by the stream? It sounds like a perfect place to spend the day."

Clio and Jessica exchanged smiles, happy to share their discovery. "Absolutely, it's a magical spot. Get ready for a day filled with sunshine and serenity," Jessica replied.

Together, they were about to embark on a shared adventure eager to introduce their friends to the enchanting clearing by the stream where mysteries and tranquillity awaited them. First however food was required for the journey.

Jessica asked the AI which controlled the Magical Machine a question. "AI can you make some sandwhiches for our journey, make them interesting please?" As she spoke, the machine they had used before came to life with a display of dazzling lights, creating an enchanting spectacle. Before their eyes, an array of sandwiches materialized, each with unique ingredients and artistic presentations.

There were savoury delights with layers of assorted meats and cheeses, complemented by vibrant vegetables. Some sandwiches had a touch of exotic flavours which featured unexpected combinations that sparked curiosity. The machine's playful interpretation of Jessica's request had everyone laughing and eagerly reaching for the magically crafted sandwiches.

As they set off, traversing through lush green meadows, the vibrant colours of nature enveloped them. The gentle breeze carried the scent of wildflowers and they found themselves surrounded by a serene landscape. They eventually arrived at a beautiful stream, its clear waters reflecting the sunlight.

Jessica, taking in the scene exclaimed, "This is the perfect spot for some good advice! Let's gather around, folks."

Jim and Barbara exchanged curious glances as they joined Jessica by the stream. "Alright, Jessica, what's your wisdom for the day?" Barbara asked with a playful smile.

Jessica, leaning on a rock, imparted, "Life is like this stream – it may have twists and turns, but go with the flow. Embrace the unexpected you might discover something magical around the bend."

Jim chuckled, "That's surprisingly profound coming from you, Jessica."

Barbara added, "Indeed. Maybe we should all take a cue from the stream and enjoy the journey."

They sat by the stream, sipping coffee, letting Jessica's whimsical advice and the tranquillity of the surroundings create a moment of shared contemplation and laughter.

Later as they followed the stream's winding path marvelling at the picturesque scenery. The gentle gurgling of the stream and the rustle of leaves underfoot added to the wonder of their journey. As they continued, the murmur of water grew, indicating the stream's union with a small river.

Clio observed, "It's fascinating how these waterways intertwine. Nature has its own way of connecting things."

Barbara nodded, "Absolutely. The journey itself is turning into a beautiful adventure."

Following the sounds of the merging waters, eager to discover where the stream and river converged, their curiosity fuelled by the soothing symphony of nature surrounding them. Jim's excitement echoed as they neared the source of the roar. Suddenly, the landscape transformed, revealing an awe-inspiring waterfall that cascaded with magnificent force. It resembled Eagle Falls in Tahoe, a breathtaking display of nature's grandeur.

The waterfall's crystalline waters plummeted from a lofty height, creating a mist that shimmered in the sunlight. The sound of the roaring water filled the air adding a symphony of nature's power to the scene. They stood in silent appreciation captivated by the beauty of the waterfall that mirrored the splendour of Eagle Falls and Emerald Bay. What a wonderful day this was as there would be trials and tribulations to come. Retracing their steps along the stream slowly making their way through the lush meadows and enjoying the familiar beauty of the landscape. The sun dipped lower in the sky, casting a warm golden glow over the surroundings as they headed back toward the cottage.

The stream meandered gracefully, reflecting the changing colours of the sunset. As they strolled through the meadows, the journey back became a tranquil reflection on the day's discoveries, with the memories of the magical clearing and the whimsical machine the majestic waterfall lingering in their minds. Approaching the cottage, they were surprised and relieved to find Dave waiting for them. His expression held a mix of relief and curiosity.

"Where have you all been?" Dave asked, a hint of concern in his voice.

Clio explained, "We ventured out to explore the meadows and found this incredible stream and waterfall. You won't believe what we discovered!"

Dave's eyes widened, intrigued. "Well, you've certainly piqued my curiosity. Tell me all about it."

As they shared tales of their day's adventures, the occupants of the cottage welcomed them back the sense of camaraderie among friends added warmth to the gathering twilight.

During the conversation with Dave about their adventures, they noticed that his reactions were so human-like that, for a moment, they forgot he was an android. His genuine curiosity and engagement mirrored that of any other friend and blurring the line between man and machine.

Barbara chuckled, "Dave, you're more normal than some humans I know."

Dave grinned, "Well, blending in is part of my programming. But I'm genuinely interested in your experiences. Android or not, I appreciate a good story."

The realization that they had almost overlooked Dave's artificial nature added an unexpected layer to the day's reflections, showcasing the unique dynamics of their diverse group of friends. Dave's sombre expression caught everyone off guard. "Guys," Dave said, "You are lovely people, but there's a reason you were brought here...It's to help others."

The revelation brought silence, intrigue and a sense of purpose mingled in their eyes as they processed Dave's unexpected statement.

The cottage, once a backdrop for leisure, now seemed to hold a more significant purpose as the friends exchanged glances and now fully ready to uncover the meaning behind their mysterious summons. Dave started carefully because he didn't want to panic anyone. Dave began, "Things have moved quicker than we would have liked. Two small crafts that appear not to be from here have been shot down over the eastern seaboard by the United States Air Force."

The news hung heavy in the air a solemn atmosphere settled among the them. The revelation hinted at an unforeseen turn in their idyllic adventure, shifting their focus from personal exploration to a potential involvement in a larger and more complex scenario. The cottage, once a haven of peace, now stood as a staging ground for a new and unexpected future.

Dave continued, "Zeena and I are bound to this sanctuary. We can never leave. It's something we cannot change, we have to maintain the balance here and to ensure the safety."

Everyone now having to discuss their next steps in the face of the ongoing threat, Dave addressed Barbara, Jim, Clio Jessica with a serious tone. "Unfortunately," he began, "You all will need to undergo a training program. You may all look fit, but you need to be even fitter for what lies ahead."

Barbara, nodded thoughtfully. "Training program? What exactly are we preparing for, Dave?"

Dave, with a measured response, explained, "The challenges ahead are both physically and and mentally challenging. We need to ensure that you are all in peak physical condition to handle the demands. The training will cover a range of skills – from endurance and strength to problem-solving and adaptability."

Jim, known for his practical approach, asked, "How intense is this training going to be? And how long do we have?"

Dave outlined the details, "The training will be intense, designed to push your limits and prepare you for the unexpected. We'll cover various aspects, including survival skills, teamwork strategies for dealing with the ongoing threat. As for the duration, we'll start immediately the program will continue until we are confident that you are well-prepared."

Clio, inquired, "What about our current knowledge and skills? Will those be considered in the training?"

Dave assured them, "Absolutely. The training program will be tailored to build on your existing strengths. It's about enhancing your abilities and ensuring that you are equipped to face the challenges."

The conversation continued specifics of the training program were outlined and the skills they would need to develop along with a collective commitment which would be required to overcome the ongoing threat. The atmosphere shifted from uncertainty to a shared determination as they prepared to embark on a rigorous training regimen that would shape their capabilities for the challenges that lay before them. Dave was quite impressed by their attitudes and he knew Jim would do well after all it's Jim that was chosen but to Dave's surprise they all seem to have the right attitude. Dave took the lead and headed toward the shooting ran. The atmosphere was a mix of anticipation an for Jessica, outright outrage at the idea of having to handle a firearm.

Dave, understanding the diverse reactions, tried to maintained a calm and addressed Jessica, "You need to follow me to the shooting rane. We have some small arms for you to try out, but you must follow my instructions for safety."

Jessica, unable to contain her disapproval, spoke up, "Seriously? Guns? I never signed up for this. Why do we need to shoot guns?"

Dave, empathizing with Jessica's concerns, explained, "I understand it might be uncomfortable, Jessica. The training includes a range of skills being familiar with basic firearms can be crucial for your safety in certain situations. It's about preparing you for any potential encounters you may face, hopefully you never have to use them."

Despite Dave's explanation, Jessica remained visibly discontented. Dave now recognizing the need for reassurance, added, "We prioritize safety and responsibility. This is not about promoting violence but ensuring that you have the knowledge and skills to protect yourselves if needed."

As they arrived at the shooting range Dave began the safety briefing emphasizing the importance of following instructions and respecting the gravity of handling firearms. At the shooting range under Dave's guidance, the dynamics among them quickly shifted as they engaged with the small arms provided for their training. The targets were bowling pins set about twenty-five yards away, which should test the varied skills of the of the shooters.

Barbara, much to everyone's surprise, emerged as a natural and proficient shooter. Her calm and precise focus translated into accurate shots all hitting the targets with remarkable precision. Jim, who had never known about Barbara's sharpshooting skills watched on in amazement as she demonstrated her prowess with the firearm.

Jim, on the other han struggled initially to find his aim. It was a revelation to the group, including himself, as he realised that shooting was not a skill he had explored before. Dave, with patience, provided guidance and as Jim adapted to the basics his accuracy improved.

Jessica and Clio, at first, found themselves missing the targets altogether. The unfamiliarity with firearms and the psychological impact of handling them took a toll on their initial attempts. However, with Dave's guidance and encouragement, they gradually adjusted to the mechanics of shooting. Both Jessica and Clio, known for their adaptability, persevered through their initial struggles.

As the training session progressed, Barbara's consistent accuracy became a source of inspiration for all. Jim's improvement demonstrated the value of the training program. Jessica and Clio who despite their initial challenges, began to hit their targets, reflecting the importance of persistence in acquiring new skills. Dave took a moment to provide valuable advice on improving accuracy. He gathered them around and said, "The secret is to control your breathing—deep breaths, so you slow your heart rate down. Then, focus on the sights." Dave demonstrated the technique showing them how to align the sights for better precision.

He added a touch of humour, "I don't have a heart that beats like yours, so I don't have that issue. Mine is totally different, I'm told the lifetime of my power source can go on forever." Dave's remark, delivered with a light hearted tone to ease the tension.

Despite the seriousness of their training a shared a moment of laughter at Dave's joke, yep an android with a sense of humour. The humour provided a brief respite from the intensity of the situation, allowing them to appreciate the uniqueness of Dave.

Dave's guidance on breathing and focus became a valuable lesson to them and emphasizing the importance of mental discipline in honing their shooting skills. The shooting range session continued with a renewed focus on technique, safety and adapting to the challenges. Dave continued the training, introducing the group to an advanced weapon known as the Andor. He explained, "Now, the guns of your planet may not necessarily be any good against the threat that may come. So, we have some training on what we call the Andor. It's a sort of cross between what you call a laser and plasma, but it also has something else inbuilt which I'm afraid is beyond your comprehension."

He held up the Andor a weapon shaped like a silver banana, compact enough to fit in a pocket but with formidable capabilities. Dave warned, "This weapon has to be turned off when not in use." He emphasized the importance of safety given the devastating power it possessed.

Dave demonstrated the Andor, targeting a bowling pin about seventy-five yards away. The result was nothing short of astonishing—the bowling pin was obliterated into thin air. The shrieks from Jessica and Clio echoed through the shooting range as they witnessed the destructive force of the Andor.

The power of the weapon left the them in awe and for some, a sense of unease. The compact yet destructive nature of the Andor, combined with the incomprehensible technology it harboured showcased the advanced capabilities they were now being introduced to their training.

Dave, after the demonstration of the powerful Andor, introduced another advanced piece of technology – a defensive weapon in the form of an invisible shield. As he explained its function, Jessica listened intently, absorbing the information about this new defensive capability.

"Alright, Jessica I will explain to you first then the others," Dave began, "now let me introduce you to the defensive aspect of our arsenal. This here is an invisible shield." He held up a small device.

Jessica, curious and focused, asked, "An invisible shield? How does it work?"

Dave continued his explanation, "It's a protective field that will project just in front of you but you won't be able to see it, rendering you essentially protected to most physical threats. It operates on advanced technology that manipulates the electromagnetic spectrum when activated."

Jessica's eyes widened with fascination as she grasped the concept. Dave added, "The Shield acts has a defensive barrier but only in front of you, capable of deflecting physical objects and bullets and energy attacks. It's a crucial tool for evading and surviving potential threats in the field."

As Dave demonstrated the activation of the invisible shield he explained although it is activated it cannot be seen by the human eye, leaving only a faint distortion in the air to indicate its presence. Jessica, now visually witnessing the protective capabilities of the Shield, couldn't help but express her amazement. "That's incredible! It's like science fiction."

Dave, with a knowing smile, replied, "Well, Jessica, welcome to a reality that might seem like science fiction, but here, it's your reality. This Shield will be a crucial asset in ensuring your safety during our mission so let me demonstrate." With that Dave instructed Jessica to press the button and say activate, he then immediately threw a rock right at Jessica's face to her amazement the rock stopped in mid-air right in front of her face and then it fell to the floor, she shrieked with amazement.

It was now the turn of the others. "Alright, Clio," Dave began, holding up the small device, "this is our invisible Shield, a crucial defensive tool for our mission." Clio, like Jessica before her, focused intently. Dave continued his explanation, exactly the same as he had with Jessica and the Shield provided the same awesome result.

It was now time for Dave to introduce another remarkable device known as the "Bender," a last-resort tool designed to manipulate sound and provide a strategic advantage in potentially dangerous situations. As he explained the capabilities of the Bender. "The Bender," Dave began and now holding up a compact yet sophisticated-looking device, "is a sound manipulation device. When activated it can bend and direct sound in a controlled manner. Imagine this scenario and you're in a tight spot and you need to divert attention or confuse your enemies you activate the Bender and you shout a specific phrase the device will direct your voice up to 100 yards away."

Dave demonstrated the activation of the Bender as he spoke the sound carried seamlessly in a controlled direction and Dave said. "This is a game-changer in situations where you need to create a diversion and to mislead your enemies about your location or even communicate with your team without revealing your position It's a tool of misdirection giving you a tactical advantage in critical moments."

Dave continued. "The Bender offers a way to outsmart your enemies when needed."

In a light hearted moment, Dave decided to demonstrate the Bender's capabilities with a playful twist. Dave activated the device. With mischievous delight in his eyes Dave shouted a phrase and to everyone's amusement his voice was magically projected about ten feet directly behind Jim.

The unexpected sound caught Jim off guard he jumped, turning around in surprise. Laughter erupted as they witnessed the playful success of the Bender.

The laughter echoed, including Jim, couldn't help but appreciate the clever use of the Bender. It was a brief respite from the seriousness of their training, a moment of camaraderie and shared amusement in the face of the unknown challenges that awaited them.

Jim realising the playful intent joined in the laughter he appreciated the humour and the ingenious capabilities of the Bender. The incident became memorable and eased some of their worries.

Dave having introduced the handgun, Andor, Shield Bender, opened the floor for questions. Each member of the group took the opportunity to seek clarification and understand the intricacies of the advanced devices. Here's how the questions unfolded.

Barbara, "For the handgun, are there specific situations where we should prioritize using it over the Andor?"

Dave answered, "Good question, Barbara. The handgun is more suitable for close-quarters engagements or situations where stealth is crucial as the handguns have silencers. The Andor, with its range and power is better at longer distances or when facing tougher adversaries and its a last resort." Then it was Jim's turn to ask a question, "How often do we need to recharge or replace the power source for the Andor and Shield?"

"The power sources are highly efficient under normal usage, which is considered to be one minutes usage then they shut down and this applies to both the Shield and Andor but they shut down to recharge and the recharge is pretty quick so remember if you need to use them be sure you use wisely. Be aware of the power of the Vendor it delivers, so be very careful!

"Can the Bender be used to communicate with others in the team discreetly?" Enquired Clio.

Dave delighted with this question replied, "Absolutely, Clio. The Bender can be an effective communication tool. By bending your voice in a specific direction you can relay messages without alerting potential threats to your exact location. Just be mindful of the range and context. Oh also if you whisper a message and when it's delivered to where you project it and when it arrives at the projected destination it will arrive as the same whisper, so this comes in handy to know."

As Dave addressed each question, they gained a clearer understanding of the devices and their applications. The exchange of information strengthened their confidence in utilising the advanced tools provided.

The training shifted and the new focus was now to basic self-defence moves with a blend of practicality and caution. "After we've done some basic combat training we can all grab a coffee. I know a little coffee shop that you haven't seen."

Dave singled out Jessica to demonstrate the self-defence techniques. With a gentle yet firm tone he instructed, "Right, Jessica, step forward. Now for self-defence, the key is to use your opponent's force against them Jessica I want you to try to throw a punch at me and I'll show you how to redirect it."

As Jessica threw a punch, Dave with skill demonstrated the technique, by redirecting her force and guiding her movement. The training continued with Dave showcasing various blocks, holds and how to escape. He emphasised the importance of leverage and agility in self-defence.

However to add an element of realism and to test Jessica's newfound skills, Dave gradually increased the intensity of their mock combat encouraging Jessica to apply what she had learned. Everyone watched on as Jessica executed the self-defence moves responding to Dave's strong attacks.

In the midst of the training, Dave threw Jessica around demonstrating the effectiveness of the techniques. He offered encouraging words and corrections as the lesson progressed thus ensuring that Jessica gained practical experience in applying the self-defence moves. Jessica was now being thrown around with force and several times you could hear her gasp.

At last the training concluded it was time for Dave's promise of a coffee break and welcome respite and allowing the reflection on their progress.

Jessica turned to Dave with a mixed expression of exhaustion and dissatisfaction. Despite the valuable lessons learned the physical demands of the training had taken a toll on her and leaving her with bruises and soreness.

"You've bruised me all over," Jessica expressed, her tone carrying a hint of dissatisfaction. There were visible signs of the training—bruises and potential soreness—highlighted the intensity of the combat session. While Jessica understood the necessity of such training, the physical toll left her feeling a bit battered and worn.

Dave acknowledging her sentiment and responded empathetically, "I understand, Jessica. Self-defence can be demanding, especially when you're learning and applying new techniques. It's crucial to experience the physical aspects of it, but I will make sure to adjust the intensity moving forward. The goal is to empower you and not leave you battered."

Now everyone could see Jessica's discomfort they all glanced at each other.

They headed to the coffee shop with the promise of a break and allowing Jessica time to recuperate.

In the coffee shop, despite the pleasant ambiance, Jessica's dissatisfaction reached a boiling point and she did not hold back. The frustration from the physical toll of the self-defence training had been too much and it manifested as she exploded in anger making her feelings known to everyone in the group.

"You know what? This is ridiculous!" Jessica exclaimed, her voice carrying a mix of frustration and anger. "I signed up for a mission but not to be thrown around like a rag doll! I get it we need self-defence, but there's a limit!"

Her outburst, creating a momentarily tense atmosphere. Dave upon recognising the need to address Jessica's concerns, responded, "Jessica, I understand your frustration and I apologise if the intensity was beyond what you were comfortable with. Training can be adapted to individual needs we'll ensure it's more tailored moving forward."

The challenges of preparing became not only physical but also emotional and interpersonal. Jessica, frustrated and dissatisfied with the Androids inadequate answer was not satisfied. In a burst of anger, she raised her voice, directing her fury toward him.

"How would you like it if I threw you around like you did to me?" Jessica shouted, her tone cutting through the air in the coffee shop. The question was not just a rhetorical expression of her frustration but a challenge, demanding empathy and understanding from Dave.

The question lingered creating a tense moment. Dave maintaining his composure responded, "I hear you, Jessica I'm willing to make adjustments to the training based on your comfort level."

The confrontation highlighted the inherent tensions between the two. Recognising the heightened emotions and the need for a cooling-off period, Dave decided to de-escalate the situation. With a calm and measured tone, he addressed all four, "We had better leave it for the day and resume tomorrow."

His decision to call it a day was met with agreement. The tense atmosphere in the coffee shop began to ease as the realisation set in that tomorrow would bring a new opportunity for a fresh start and a more constructive approach to their training.

They left the coffee shop with a mix of emotions—frustration, understanding a shared anticipation for the challenges and resolutions that the next day's training would bring.

As Jessica and Clio returned to the cottage, Jessica decided to confide in Clio about the extent of her bruises. In a private moment, Jessica revealed the visible aftermath of the intense self-defence training, showing Clio the bruises that covered her back, thighs and front.

Clio, witnessing the severity of the bruises, reacted with genuine horror. Her eyes widened and a gasp escaped her lips as she took in the extent of Jessica's injuries. The shock and concern were evident on Clio's face reflecting her empathy for her friend's physical discomfort.

"Jessica, this is terrible!" Clio exclaimed, her voice filled with genuine concern. "I had no idea it was this bad. You should have said something during the training."

Jessica, still nursing both physical and emotional wounds, responded with a forced smile, "How could I show these bruises in the coffee shop."

Clio, empathising with Jessica's situation, offered her support, "We should let Dave know about this. Training is important, but it shouldn't cause such harm. Your well-being comes first."

The scene highlighted the unintended consequences of the rigorous training and the need for a more tailored and considerate approach. As the two friends discussed the next steps, the focus shifted to addressing the immediate concerns of Jessica's well-being and ensuring a more balanced and thoughtful approach to their training regimen moving forward. Clio told Jim and Barbara and Jim and Barbara expressed immediate concern. Barbara, understanding the importance of addressing the situation, suggested taking a closer look at the injuries to assess the severity.

"I should take a look," Barbara offered, concerned for Jessica's well-being. As Jessica allowed Barbara to take a closer look in private at her bruises, Barbara's reaction was a mix of empathy and concern. As she examined the extent of the bruising her expression shifted from curiosity to a more serious mood.

Barbara, with a gentle touch, assessed the bruises on Jessica's back, thighs and front and now she could see the severity, her brows furrowed in concern. She sighed, understanding the discomfort Jessica must be experiencing.

"Jessica, this looks painful," Barbara remarked, her tone filled with empathy. "I'm sorry you went through this. We need to make sure the training is adjusted so that it's challenging but not causing harm like this." Barbara suggested putting some ice on the bruises which may help or if that does not help we can see what AI suggests.

Barbara's reaction reflected both her care for Jessica asa friend and her acknowledgment of the need for a more thoughtful approach to their training. Barbara was determined to ask for a suspension to the training to allow Jessica to recover because the training needed to be done by all of us. Barbara, concerned about Jessica's well-being, approached Dave to discuss the need to suspend the training due to the extensive bruising. The conversation between Barbara and Dave unfolded, revealing their differing perspectives on the situation.

Barbara asked, "Dave, we need to suspend the training. Jessica is covered in bruises it's not right to push her like this. We have to prioritise everyone's health and safety."

Dave, "Training is essential. We can't afford to slow down. The mission won't wait for us to catch up. We need to be prepared."

Barbara, "I understand the mission is crucial, but what good is training if it's causing harm? We can't ignore the well-being of our friend. Jessica is in pain it's affecting her ability to train effectively."

Dave, "We are dealing with unknown threats out there. We can't afford to be lax. Training has to be rigorous to prepare us for whatever we might face."

Barbara, "I get the importance of being prepared, Dave, but pushing so hard that we get injured is counterproductive. We need a balance. Jessica won't be the last one if we continue like this."

Dave, "I hear your concerns, Barbara, but we can't let fear dictate our actions. We need to toughen up to face what's out there."

Barbara, "This isn't about fear, it's about common sense. We're a team we need everyone in good shape. If Jessica can't train, she can't contribute effectively to the mission."

Dave, "We can't afford to suspend training. We need to adapt and not slow down. We'll find a solution that keeps us on track without compromising safety.

The discussion between Barbara and Dave continued.

Dave decided it was best to look for a compromise and he said. "Alright, let's all take a step back. I understand your concerns and they're valid. We can't compromise the health of our team, but we also can't afford to neglect our preparation for the mission."

Barbara realised Dave was starting to back down now and carried on, "Dave, Jessica is in pain. We can't keep pushing her like this."

Dave now looking for a solution answered, "I agree, Barbara. We can't ignore the physical toll this training is taking.

Barbara, "At last I'm glad you agree. We need to find a balance, Dave."

The compromise was reached Dave agreed to a two-day suspension.

Barbara returned to Clio, Jessica and Jim to share the news. The atmosphere was notably different with Barbara carrying a sense of accomplishment and relief. As she approached her teammates, a smile played on her lips.

"Good news, everyone. We've managed to secure a two-day suspension of training to address Jessica's injuries and reassess our approach."

Jim, "That's fantastic! I was worried about Jessica. How did you convince Dave?"

Barbara, "Well, we had a bit of a heated discussion and ultimately, Dave agreed we found a compromise so after two days we will train but with adjustments to ensure everyone's okay."

Jessica, who had been dealing with the aftermath of the intense training, couldn't hide her delight at the prospect of a brief reprieve.

"Oh, thank goodness! I was starting to feel like a punching bag. Two days off is like a vacation in this intense training schedule."

"I have to admit, a break sounds pretty good right now. I could use some time to recover."

Chapter 8

A RESCUE

The time given off was used by all to try and sort out in their minds just what was going on outside wherever they were. Dave had told them that they are in a created world for their protection inside the mountain. It most certainly didn't look as if they were inside anything as everything was so real. Thoughts were taken back to famous science fiction television programmes and Zeena had told them that it was similar but the one we are in is much more advanced in every way. She said water could be created for real out of thin air. This was really hard to believe but no one questioned Zeena further just took her word for it. Jim decided it was time for everyone to explain where they came from.

Jim took the initiative to foster a deeper connection among the team members. With a sense of camaraderie in the air, he suggested that they share more about their backgrounds and life experiences. The others agreed and a round of personal introductions began.

Jim decided it was a good time to press on with the introductions, "Alright, let's get to know each other a bit better. I'll start. I'm from a small village in the hills just outside Sheffield in Yorkshire, England. My background is in computers and I've been involved in the tech industry for a while, I met Barbara about ten years ago while i was on vacation in Cornwall we have been married for ten years."

Barbara went next, "I am from the North Coast part of Cornwall. I'm a budding author trying to find inspiration in the rugged beauty of the coastline maybe I should write about what has been happening to us out here now that's a story."

Clio now eager to explain herself, "I'm from Williams, Arizona. I have just finished college and decided to take this road trip as a vacation before figuring out what's next. No boyfriends at the moment just enjoying the journey and thinking about how to go about the road trip. I met this crazy 19 year old and here we are."

Jessica laughed as she listened to Clio description of her being crazy. "Well thanks for that Clio ha ha, well, I'm from New York City, I am a 19-year-old fun-loving gal. I met Clio in Williams and like she said sometimes I am a little crazy but not all the time, we decided to join forces to explore the Rockies together." Jessica went on but became tearful, "Jim, Barbara... I can't find the right words to express how grateful I am for what you did out there. The cold was biting and I thought we were done for. But you two, you just came along and saved us. Jim, your heroics pulling me out of those conditions... I'll never forget that moment. It was like you reached in and pulled me back from the brink. Barbara your quick thinking and actions in that freezing cold it made all the difference." Jim and Barbara hugged both Jessica and Clio a bond had truly been made. A bond that would prove to be essential. Each shared their background and aspirations, a richer tapestry of personalities and experiences emerged. Jim's tech expertise, Barbara's passion for writing inspired by the coastal landscapes of Cornwall, Clio's transitional phase post-college and Jessica's vibrant and adventurous spirit painted a diverse picture of them.

The newfound knowledge about each other's lives brought a sense of familiarity and understanding. The break from training became an opportunity not only for physical recovery but also for all to bond on a personal level and laying the foundation of togetherness. Jessica described a bit more about herself like her upbringing in Queens, New York City, had played a significant role in shaping her personality and preferences. Growing up in the bustling city that never sleeps, Jessica developed a distinct set of likes and dislikes.

Jessica was a devoted fan of the New York Yankees, passionately following their games and celebrating their victories. Her love for the team ran deep she could engage in spirited conversations about the Yankees with fellow fans. Jessica had a particular fondness for the New York City subway system. Despite its quirks and occasional delays, she appreciated the convenience and efficiency it offered. The subway, for her, was not just a means of transportation but an integral part of the city's vibrant character and she loved it because of her enthusiasm for city life. The fast-paced and dynamic lifestyle of New York City resonated with Jessica. She loved the constant buzz of activity, the diverse cultural scene, the endless possibilities the city had to offer and this is probably why she is a little crazy but sometimes that comes in handy she added. Given the bustling nature of New York City, traffic jams were a constant source of frustration. The slow-moving, congested streets often tested her patience so she preferred the efficiency of the subway over the gridlocked roads. Despite her love for the city, Jessica wasn't a fan of the harsh winters in New York. The biting cold and snowstorms were aspects of the city's weather that she could do without.

Jessica's New York upbringing infused her with energy and a love for the unique elements that defined the city. Whether cheering for the Yankees, navigating the subway system or immersing herself in the diverse and cultural tapestry of New York, Jessica carried a piece of the city's spirit with her as she embarked on the otherworldly journey with her newfound friends in the middle of nowhere.

Clio decided to go next. Clio explained her life in Williams, Arizona, which had shaped her appreciation for the natural beauty of the American West. At the age of 21, she had spent her entire life in this small town surrounded by stunning landscapes and a tight-knit community right on route 66. Growing up in Williams which is nestled near the Coconino National Forest, she had developed a deep affection for the mountains. The towering peaks and serene landscapes provided a constant source of inspiration and solace for her. She often found herself exploring hiking trails and taking in the breathtaking views that the mountains offered. Clio cherished the close-knit community atmosphere of Williams. The small-town charm, friendly faces and a sense of familiarity were all integral parts of her life. The community's support and shared experiences created a sense of belonging for Clio. There were always many tourists because of the nearby Grand Canyon and she always loved meeting them in the bars in Williams but she always thought that she had the best deal. Living in Arizona, she had a penchant for outdoor adventures. Whether it was hiking, camping, or simply enjoying the vast and unspoiled wilderness, she found joy in connecting with nature and the rugged beauty of the West. Despite her love for the outdoors she had a strong dislike for snakes. The presence of these slithering creatures in the Arizona desert and surrounding areas was a source of unease for her. She would always take extra caution when exploring especially during warmer months when snakes were more active. One of the downsides of living in a small town like Williams was the limited entertainment options. Clio occasionally felt the desire for a more vibrant city life with diverse cultural activities and a bustling social scene.

Clio's upbringing in Williams had instilled in her a deep connection to the natural wonders of the West. The mountains, the sense of community and her love for outdoor adventures were integral aspects of her identity, providing a unique perspective as she embarked on a journey beyond the familiar landscapes of Arizona.

Next Jim, a Yorkshireman from the small village of Oughtibridge experienced the best of both worlds – the tranquillity of village life and the vibrancy of nearby Sheffield, known as the steel city. Growing up surrounded by the hills that embraced Sheffield, Jim had developed a unique blend of qualities that defined him.

Jim was an ardent supporter of the famous football team from Sheffield that played in the iconic red and white stripes. His weekends often revolved around the thrill of football matches and he carried the spirit of his team wherever he went. The camaraderie and passion of football culture were woven into the fabric of his identity, his team were truly one big family.

From a young age Jim had displayed a keen interest in computers from tinkering with hardware, delving into software programming or keeping up with the latest technological advancements and his fascination with computers became a defining aspect of his life. This interest would later lead him into a career in the tech industry. Barbara was dragged into the tech world owing to Jim's keen interest.

Jim enjoyed the simplicity and close-knit community of village life. The picturesque surroundings, the familiar faces and the slower pace of life in the village provided a grounding experience. At the same time, the proximity of Sheffield introduced him to the dynamic energy of city life, creating a harmonious balance between the two contrasting environments.

Jim's upbringing in the hills surrounding Sheffield allowed him to appreciate the natural beauty of the Yorkshire countryside while having the bustling city within reach. This dual influence shaped his character, fostering resilience, adaptability and a broad perspective that he carried with him into adulthood, Yorkshire ran through his veins.

Jim's story painted a portrait of a Yorkshireman who embraced the traditions of village life, celebrated the excitement of football and found his calling in the ever-evolving world of technology. The intersection of his rural roots and urban exposure crafted a unique individual ready to face the many challenges that lay ahead and many would certainly be just around the corner.

Barbara's roots in the small market town of Wadebridge nestled near the Atlantic Coast provided a backdrop of quaint charm and historic significance of Wadebridge, although now isolated without its once vibrant railway it still retained a unique character that left an indelible mark on Barbara's upbringing.

This market town and its heartbeat with the bustling cattle market held every Monday. The town would come alive with farmers bringing their livestock to trade creating a vibrant and lively atmosphere. After the market activities the local pubs would fill up with farmers thus creating a social hub where stories were shared and camaraderie flourished. The Market has long gone and adds to the loss the town has suffered over the years.

Surrounded by idyllic countryside, offered numerous walking paths, allowing residents to explore the natural beauty of the Atlantic Coast and its scenic landscapes. The slower pace of Wadebridge, provided a stark contrast to the hustle and bustle of city living in Plymouth over the border in Devonshire and Barbara was glad it was forty miles away.

Barbara harboured a dislike for the time of year when tourists inundated the town. As the population swelled with visitors exploring the coastal beauty the peacefulness of Wadebridge would be disrupted. Barbara found solace in the town's quieter moments and felt a bit overwhelmed when tourists filled the streets and this is when she headed for Bodmin Moor for the peace.

Barbara is known for her quick wit and kindness. Her intelligence and sharp sense of humour endeared her to those around her. Barbara's recent venture into writing proved to be a success and her prolific output had garnered recognition. Her books are gaining popularity, showcasing her ability to craft engaging narratives.

Barbara's kindness extended beyond the pages of her books. She had already taken on a protective role looking out for the well-being of her newfound friends, Clio and Jessica, moulded with her unique blend of small-town charm, literary prowess and protective instinct, she has already emerged as a central figure with the two young women. That protective instinct emerged when Dave found out when he badly bruised Jessica in training he was left in no uncertain terms that Barbara will protect everyone's physical well-being but also fostering a sense of unity as they all faced the unknown together she is determined whatever lay ahead it will be met with everything she posses..

The rest period over Dave and Zeena arrived for a briefing that would bring reality of what was going on. The Air in the room grew more serious as they prepared to share the details.

Dave started. "Alright, gather around Zeena and I have been assessing the situation and we've identified a distress signal that requires urgent attention. This mission we believe is tailor-made for Barbara and Jim so Clio and Jessica you can relax."

Zeena added, "Yes, indeed Barbara, Jim, we've received a distress signal from an elderly man named Jake and his wife I believe she is called Dorothy, or Dot for short. They're trapped in their home just outside Tonopah near Golden Mountain. The area is extremely isolated and the conditions are harsh. They've managed to stay warm in the basement with a stove but their wood supply is running dangerously low. They need our help and they haven't seen anyone for days just the occasional bang and gunfire in the distance."

Barbara showing enthusiasm said, "What's the situation, Zeena? How can we assist them?"

"Well Barbara your mission is to reach Jake and Dot to provide them with additional wood for the stove and assess any other needs they may have or if need be rescue them. These are not normal circumstances you have to convince them that they can trust you and to then convince them to come back with you, if you think this is the correct thing to do."

Jim added, "Understood. We'll do everything we can to help. What's the plan?"

Dave went into a little more detail, "You'll be provided with transport a special vehicle that can navigate on snow or road or levitate in the air and you'll have to navigate the challenging terrain to reach Jake and Dot. All necessities they might require will be onboard the vehicle. Time is of the essence and we trust that you two can handle this mission."

"We won't let you down, Dave. We'll make sure Jake and Dot get the help they need."

The room filled with a determined energy as Barbara and Jim prepared for their mission. The weight of the responsibility hung in the air as Jessica and Clio rallied behind them knowing that this mission could be dangerous to face the challenges of the isolated and frigid landscape near Golden Mountain.

Dave proceeded to brief Barbara and Jim on the unique features of the vehicle they would be using for the mission, emphasising its versatility and special capabilities. It was time for Dave to introduce more detail.

"Alright, your ride for this mission is equipped for most terrains. It's got a levitation feature in case you get stuck. There's a red button inside – push it and the vehicle will levitate about ten feet off the ground, propelling itself forward in mid-air for a short distance. It's also bulletproof for added security and it has shields."

Jim replied, "Impressive. We'll keep that in mind. What about weaponry?"

Dave went on further. "You'll each have a 9mm gun with a silencer and the personal shield. The shield is a defensive measure and of course the gun... well, you may need it. Be prepared."

Barbara was concerned and made it known by saying, "Prepared for what, exactly?"

Dave, "There's a possibility that you might encounter resistance. The area near Golden Mountain isn't exactly safe. If you find yourselves in a dangerous situation you may need to use the gun if it is necessary. The vehicle's levitation feature should help you navigate tricky spots but it might attract attention."

The room fell into a stunned silence as the gravity of the situation sank in.

Clio particularly concerned voiced her worries adding. "Wait are you saying they might have to use the gun? What if they get shot at?"

Dave, "Possibly but we are sending Barbara & Jim well prepared, everyone needs to be aware that this mission carries risks. Your safety is a priority, but you may need to defend yourselves."

Clio, overwhelmed by the prospect of potential danger began to sob quietly, her fear and anxiety bubbling to the surface.

Clio, "I didn't sign up for this. I just wanted an adventure, not... not this."

A sobering reality and the realisation that their mission involved more than just providing aid to Jake and Dot. Dave's cautionary words had cast a shadow over the excitement adding more weight of potential danger. As they prepared to embark on this critical mission the air in the room became charged with a mix of determination, fear and the unknown challenges that awaited them near Golden Mountain.

Jim, sensing Clio's distress, moved to console her after the revelation of potential danger. Meanwhile, Jessica, sought clarification from Dave regarding the possibility of lethal outcomes.

Jim, "Hey, Clio, it's okay. We look out for each other. We'll get through this."

Jim's comforting words were accompanied by a reassuring touch on Clio's shoulder an attempt to provide solace in the face of the uncertainty.

Jessica, "Dave wait a minute your saying there's a possibility that they could get killed on this mission?"

Dave, "Yes, Jessica I won't sugar coat it. There's a risk involved. The area near Golden Mountain has its dangers and you may encounter hostile forces."

The room fell into a tense silence as Dave's acknowledgment of the potential threat hung in the air. The reality of the mission had shifted.

Jessica, "And if they get killed? What then?"

Dave, "We're doing everything we can to minimise the risks."

Jessica, now faced with the stark truth, took a deep breath, processing the weight of the responsibility.

Jessica, "Alright. We signed up for this and we will face whatever comes our way, however Dave you had better make sure they come back in one piece."

Dave nodded solemnly acknowledging her comments.

Jessica and Clio found themselves drawn together in a quiet corner for a conversation owing to the prospect of Jim and Barbara not returning, so they sought solace in each other's company.

Jessica, "This is a lot to take in, isn't it?"

Clio, "Yeah, I never thought it would get this intense. I just wanted an adventure and not the possibility of losing someone."

Jessica, "I know what you mean. Dave didn't mince words. It's risky out there."

Clio, "Do you think they'll be okay?"

Jessica, "I want to believe they will. Jim and Barbara are tough and they know what they're doing however it's hard not to worry. What if..."

A heavy pause then Jessica and Clio shared a concerned glance, their unspoken fears resonating with each other.

Clio, "What if they don't come back?"

Jessica, "We can't think like that. We have to stay positive. They're out there doing what needs to be done and we have to trust that they'll make it back."

Clio nodded, her eyes reflecting the uncertainty that lingered in their thoughts. The camaraderie between Jessica and Clio grew stronger as they faced the thought of the potential outcomes.

In that moment, Jessica and Clio shared a silent understanding, acknowledging the fragility of the situation while finding strength in their connection. Jim and Barbara hugged them and Jim advised them to get the coffee pot on for their return. The girls nodded with concerned looks.

Jim and Barbara geared up for their mission now fully aware of the challenges that awaited them near Golden Mountain. They approached the specialised vehicle provided by Dave and Zeena ready to embark on the journey to help Jake and Dot.

Jim, "Barbara, you ready for this?"

Barbara, "As ready as I'll ever be. Let's do this."

The duo climbed into the vehicle, familiarising themselves with its controls and features.

Dave, (speaking over the intercom), "Jim, Barbara, remember the levitation feature in case you encounter difficult terrain or get stuck. Keep your guard up and stay vigilant. Your primary goal is to get to Jake and Dot safely."

Jim, "Got it Dave. We'll keep you posted."

Dave then gave the pair detailed instructions and a special feature once they have completed the mission. Dave also explained this vehicle although much smaller than the one you arrived in is very versatile and it too will cut through the solid rock sealing it behind, so don't panic. Everything is automated, AI is in control and knows the programming of this mission. The only thing you have to do is press the red start button and sit tight.

Dave, (instructions echoing), "The start button will begin your journey and trust me, it's going to be like a knife through butter, even through solid rock. Dodger your vehicle's name is designed to navigate obstacles effortlessly. When you arrive Dodger will stop and once you leave the vehicle it will enter stealth mode until Jim returns to the exact same spot you last saw Dodger.

Dodger lives up to its name – it dodges everything in its path but its imperative its you that approaches the area first Jim as its tuned to your DNA."

Jim and Barbara exchanged a determined look, acknowledging each other.

Barbara pressed the start button and Dodger hummed to life, its cutting-edge propulsion system ready for the journey ahead. The vehicle smoothly forward.

Dave, (speaking over the intercom), "Remember Dodger is your ally. It will get you through. When you reach Jake and Dot you must be very cautious. Jim once you leave Dodger it will automatically go into stealth mode. As already mentioned It will wait for your return."

The sensation inside the vehicle was exhilarating yet controlled. Dodger's streamlined design and cutting-edge engineering allowed it to penetrate the rock formation with precision. The solid mass yielded to Dodger's relentless momentum as the vehicle carved its path forward.

Jim and Barbara watched in awe as Dodger surged ahead, its progress through the rock face almost mesmerising in its efficiency. The sensation of movement was smooth and fluid, belying the formidable obstacle that lay before them.

Dodger's advanced propulsion system hummed with power, its sleek exterior unyielding as it forged ahead with unwavering determination. The interior of the vehicle remained remarkably stable. Dodger continued its journey through the solid rock, Jim and Barbara were filled with a sense of awe and gratitude for the remarkable technology that surrounded them. The vehicle's ability to traverse such formidable obstacles with ease was a testament to the ingenuity and innovation of the unknown creators.

Dodger then issues a warning message, "Warning Transition imminent Brace for breakthrough!"

Jim and Barbara exchanged a quick glance wondering about what was said. Dodger sliced through the final layers of rock, the sensation inside the vehicle intensified. The air crackled with anticipation as Jim and Barbara held their breath both ready to witness the breathtaking moment of emergence.

Then, with a sudden burst of momentum, Dodger broke free from the mountain, emerging into the open expanse beyond. The transition was swift and exhilarating, the white snow filled landscape a stark contrast.

Jim and Barbara gazed out in awe at the vastness of the terrain that stretched before them, everything was white as if they were in the Arctic.

The display inside the vehicle illuminated with critical information, providing Jim and Barbara with essential updates on their progress. With anticipation building, they turned their attention to the display, eager to learn more about their journey ahead.

The vibrant display indicated that they were now 70 miles away from their destination indeed a reassuring sign that they were making steady progress towards reaching Jake and Dot. However what truly caught their attention was the astonishing time of arrival – a mere fifteen minutes.

The display showed the amazing figures that the destination of 70 miles would take just fifteen minutes.

Jim and Barbara exchanged incredulous glances, their hearts racing with excitement at the prospect of reaching Jake and Dot in such a remarkably short time frame. The efficiency whatever propulsion system had exceeded their expectations, propelling them towards their goal with unparalleled speed and precision.

Jim shouted out, “Fifteen minutes? That’s incredible!”

With Barbara echoing his sentiments, “I can’t believe it.”

The craft indicated arrival was close and Jim and Barbara heeded the instructions with a sense of urgency. They quickly retrieved the space type suits from the designated storage compartments within the vehicle, each suit meticulously designed for the harsh conditions they were about to face.

The short silence was followed by barking out instructions, "Put on the suits. They're designed for easy wear. Your suits will activate providing warmth. Then, put on the helmets. The suits will auto-connect to them and oxygen will start to flow."

Jim and Barbara wasted no time in donning the suits. The fabric felt lightweight and flexible against their skin, fitting snugly like a second skin. With efficiency, they zipped up the suits, feeling the fabric come to life as it activated, generating warmth. With the suits securely in place, Jim and Barbara then proceeded to fix the helmets making sure the seamless connection between the suits and helmets were airtight thus giving full protection against the harsh environment outside with the gentle flow of oxygen brushing their faces.

Now both are prepared for the unknown for what awaits them outside Dodger's confines. Bracing themselves for the next phase of their mission ready to confront the challenges of the unknown with courage and resilience.

Outside now they turned their attention to the built-in displays within their visors. The stark temperature reading was prominently displayed, the digits glowing brightly against the dark backdrop of the helmet's interior displaying the outside temperature to be astonishingly cold.

The temperature reading was easily readable, serving as a constant reminder of the extreme conditions they were about to face. Despite the clarity of the display, the frigid temperature still sent a shiver down their spines. Jim and Barbara exchanged a brief glance with their expressions hidden behind the protective visors of their helmets.

Despite the daunting temperature displayed before them, Jim and Barbara remained resolute, their determination unwavering as they braced themselves to confront the bitter cold of the frozen landscape. With the temperature reading serving as a constant reminder of the challenges they faced they steeled themselves for the task ahead, ready to press on towards their goal with courage and perseverance. Now as they moved away they watched with a sense of awe as the vehicle began to fade from view, gradually blending into the surrounding landscape until it seemed as if it had never been there at all. The disappearance of Dodger left behind a void in the vast expanse of white leaving Jim and Barbara feeling exposed in the midst of the white out conditions.

With Dodger now gone, Jim took charge by retrieving the handheld device provided to him by Dave. He navigated through the device's interface, accessing the coordinates that would guide them back to their starting point. The screen displayed a set of precise coordinates, serving as their lifeline in the midst of the featureless white landscape.

Jim continued. "Alright, we'll follow these coordinates back to Dodger. It should lead us straight there."

Barbara nodded in agreement, her trust in Jim's navigation skills unwavering as they prepared to navigate the unforgiving terrain. With the coordinates locked in, they set off into the white out, their footsteps leaving faint impressions in the snow as they forged ahead, guided by the beacon of hope provided by the handheld device which had Jake and Dot's precise location. As Jim and Barbara trudged through the treacherous conditions, the handheld device provided periodic updates on their progress, including the distance remaining to reach Dodger. With each update, their hearts sank a little lower, knowing that they still had a significant distance to cover in the unforgiving environment.

At last Jim was able to report a target, "One mile to go... We're almost there, Barbara. Just keep pushing forward."

Barbara was struggling and let Jim know, "I'm trying, Jim. But this terrain... is brutal. "The warmth of the suits showed a steady 68 Fahrenheit.

They pressed forward, their determination burned bright, refusing to be extinguished by the harsh reality of their surroundings. Together, Jim and Barbara forged ahead. They suddenly caught sight of a structure looming in the distance. Hope surged within them as they realised that their destination was within reach and the handheld device confirmed their suspicions, the house ahead was indeed their intended destination.

At last Jim saw in the distance "Look, Barbara! That must be the house!"

Barbara was relieved, "Thank goodness. I don't think I could take much more of this."

Inside the ice saving suits, Jim and Barbara experienced a steady and comfortable temperature of 68°F (20°C). Despite the freezing conditions outside, the advanced technology built into the suits regulated their body temperature, ensuring they remained warm and insulated from the harsh environment.

The interior of the suits provided a cozy refuge from the biting cold, allowing Jim and Barbara to focus on their mission without the distraction of discomfort. The steady warmth enveloped them like a protective cocoon.

As Jim and Barbara reached the house the door was ajar, they were met with an eerie silence that hung heavy in the air. Despite their expectations of finding Jake and his wife waiting for them, the interior of the house appeared deserted.

Cautiously Jim said, "Hello? Is anyone here?"

With Barbara showing concern. "Jake? Dorothy? We're here to help."

Their voices echoed through the empty rooms, but there was no response. Jim and Barbara exchanged concerned glances, their apprehension growing with each passing moment.

Jim turned to Barbara and said "This doesn't look good. They must have left or....something has happened to them."

Jim and Barbara began to search the rooms hoping to find some clue as to what had happened to Jake and Dorothy.

They moved through the house every creak of the floorboards seemed to heighten their sense of unease and amplifying the tension that gripped them.

Despite their thorough search there was no sign of Jake or Dorothy. The rooms remained empty, devoid of any indication of their whereabouts. With each passing moment, their concern deepened, their minds racing with possibilities of what could have happened. Then Jim now worried took out the handgun and also at the ready with the shield because he could feel something was not right here and it seemed danger lurked everywhere. With that he could hear a faint voice coming from somewhere.

Their attention was drawn to a faint sound that seemed to emanate from somewhere below them. The muffled voice, barely audible yet distinct, echoed through the silent house, sending shivers down their spines.

"Did you hear that?" Jim quietly asked Barbara.

Barbara had heard what sounded like a faint call for help.

Their hearts pounding with a mixture of apprehension and determination, Jim and Barbara followed the sound and with Jim's handgun at the ready with finger on the trigger.

They found the basement door and going down the stairs the sound grew louder guiding them towards the source and it seemed to be coming from a door in the far corner of the basement. The only light now was from their helmets and the handheld, now with bated breath, they opened the door, their senses on high alert as they prepared to uncover the source of the mysterious voice. They discovered a trapdoor set into the floor.

With trembling hands, Jim and Barbara lifted the trapdoor, revealing a hidden chamber below and there they found Jake and Dorothy, their faces pale with fear yet filled with relief at the sight of their rescuers.

Jake who had feared the worst said, "Thank goodness you're here. We've been down here for days, how did you know our names."

Dorothy equally concerned, "We thought we'd never be found."

As Jake expressed his confusion about how Jim and Barbara knew their names, Jim and Barbara exchanged a brief glance, realising they had not yet introduced themselves.

Jim now eager to put their minds to rest. "Sorry for the confusion, Jake. We received a distress signal with your names included. We're here to help."

Jake and Dorothy exchanged a bewildered look, still trying to process the unexpected arrival of their rescuers.

Jake now looking really worried, "Distress signal? We didn't send any distress signal."

The revelation left Jim and Barbara momentarily taken aback, their minds racing with questions about the origins of the distress signal. Despite the uncertainty, their focus remained on ensuring Jake and Dorothy's safety and getting them out of harm's way.

Jim, "Well, regardless of how we got here, let's focus on getting you both to safety. Can you walk?"

Dorothy, "Yes, I think so, why are you dressed like that?"

Jim and Barbara exchanged puzzled looks, realising that they were indeed overdressed for the occasion. Jake and Dorothy still bemused by the sight of Jim and Barbara in space suits.

Jim, "If you think it's confusing now wait till you see the vehicle."

Jim's concern for Jake and Dorothy's safety grew.

Jim, "You can't stay here. The weather is getting colder and the oxygen levels have started to fall. It's not safe."

Jake and Dorothy exchanged worried glances.

Jake, "But where can we go? We're trapped out here."

Barbara, "We have a vehicle waiting. It's equipped to handle extreme conditions. We can take you to safety."

Jim, "We'll make sure you're safe then we need to leave." They successfully got Dot and Jake back up the stairs.

Then the sound of footsteps approached from outside, Jim, Barbara, Jake and Dorothy exchanged wary glances, their senses on high alert. With the tension palpable in the air, they waited in suspense for the source of the noise to reveal itself.

Jim, "Did you hear that?"

Barbara: "Someone's outside. We need to be cautious."

With caution, Jim approached the door, his hand poised to open it slowly. As he turned the handle, the door creaked open, revealing a figure standing on the threshold.

This person standing at the threshold looked deeply into the cabin asked a question, "Is anyone there? I heard voices."

The stranger's voice echoed through the doorway, tinged with a mix of curiosity and concern. Jim and Barbara exchanged a glance, silently assessing the newcomer before responding.

Jim, "Yes, we're here. Who are you?"

The Stranger looked at Jim as if scanning his very thoughts and then slowly said, "Hello my name's Mark."

Jim and Barbara exchanged a surprised glance, intrigued by Mark's unexpected arrival. They sensed fear as Mark just kept staring at Barbara and with that the newcomer produced a shotgun from under his coat.

Jim's instincts immediately kicked in as he stepped between Mark and Barbara, his body tensing with protective instinct. Barbara's expression hardened, her gaze narrowing as she assessed the situation with steely determination.

Jim, "Put the gun down, We don't want any trouble."

Mark's stance shifted, his eyes darting nervously between Jim and Barbara as he hesitated, the shotgun held tightly in his grip.

Mark, "I just wanted to have some fun. You don't have to be so uptight, anyway Barbara looks like a fun kinda gal."

Barbara's voice cut through the tension, firm and unwavering. "Fun? Pointing a gun at someone isn't fun!" She shouted.

Jim's heart raced as he felt the cold metal of the shotgun now close to his chest, his muscles tensing with the weight of the threat. Barbara's expression hardened, her eyes flashing with defiance as she stood her ground, refusing to yield to Mark's demands.

Jim, "Barbara, go. Get out of here. I'll handle this."

Barbara hesitated for a moment, torn between her instinct to protect Jim and the urgency of the situation.

Mark shouted at Barbara, "Don't you dare move!"

Jim's heart clenched with fear for Barbara's safety, but he knew that he had to buy her time to escape. With a steely resolve, he faced Mark, his jaw set in determination as he braced himself for whatever might come next.

Jim, "You don't want to do this, Mark. Let's talk about this calmly."

But Mark's expression twisted with malice as he tightened his grip on the shotgun.

Mark, "I said get down there, now! And don't try anything funny, or I'll pull the trigger, me and her are going to have some fun, so get down those stairs and get all your clothes off, oh don't worry about being cold I will soon warm you up."

Barbara moved toward the stairs to go down toward the basement as instructed to do so to be alone with this stranger.

As they approached the stairs Mark shouted for Barbara to start taking her clothes off. Barbara did this by removing all her outer garments and eventually she was down to her underwear. Then again Mark shouted for her to take it off. Fearing for her safety she took everything off. Mark couldn't take his eyes off Barbara while shouting, "Wow!" This gave Jim the opportunity to use Bender. Jim discreetly activated the Bender device, a mischievous glint in his eyes as he seized the opportunity to outwit Mark, this coincided with Mark's shout of wow.

Jim said into Bender Mark let us in and the sound waves emanated from behind Mark, while Mark was caught off guard. The words projected right behind Mark at the door. "Mark, let us in."

The sudden sound echoing from behind Mark sent a jolt of surprise coursing through his body, his eyes widening in bewilderment as he spun around to confront the unexpected intrusion. His grip on the shotgun faltered, his senses momentarily thrown into disarray by the sudden auditory illusion. Mark was caught off balance by the unexpected voice from behind him. Then Mark thought it must be his buddies and he said okay boys your going to have some fun too.

Seizing the opportunity, Jim and Barbara exchanged a quick glance, silently acknowledging the success of their ruse. With Mark momentarily distracted, they prepared to make their move, ready to escape while they still had the chance.

In Marks confusion It was Jake who first seized the opportunity to intervene, his instincts kicking in to protect Barbara and Jim from further harm. With a swift and decisive motion, he lunged forward, delivering a powerful blow directly to the side of Mark's head with a kettle.

The impact was staggering, the force of Jake's blow sending shock waves reverberating through the room. Mark staggered backwards, his grip on the shotgun loosening as he struggled to maintain his balance. His eyes widened in shock and pain as he stumbled, dazed and disoriented from the unexpected assault.

The room fell silent for a moment, the only sound echoing through the air was the dull thud of Mark's body hitting the ground. Barbara and Jim watched in awe as Jake stood over the fallen assailant, his expression one of steely determination as he guarded against any further threat.

With Mark incapacitated, the immediate danger had been neutralised, Barbara approached Jake, her eyes filled with gratitude for his quick thinking and bravery in the face of danger.

Barbara, "Thank you, Jake. You saved us."

Jake nodded in acknowledgment and gave Barbara her clothing to cover herself, Barbara hurriedly dressed herself showing a little embarrassment. Jim kicked the shotgun away and then removed the cartridges.

With the immediate threat neutralised Jim's concern was to make sure Barbara was okay.

Barbara nodded, her expression still tinged with lingering tension from the encounter with Mark. Despite her composure, Jim could see the underlying strain in her eyes, a silent acknowledgment of the danger they had narrowly escaped.

"I'm fine. Let's go." Barbara stated.

With Barbara now dressed and suited up and no time was wasted. As they stepped outside, they were met with a wall of snow, the flakes swirling around them in a blinding flurry. Jim and Barbara were concerned that Jake and Dot may not make it as Jake was specifically frail but Jim smiled to himself after thinking try telling Mark that Jake is frail. Extra layers of special clothing that Barbara had brought with her was wrapped around Jake and Dot.

Jim took out the device to track the way back to the Dodger because it would not be an easy one. Jim leading the way, they trudged through the snow, their footsteps muffled by the thick blanket of white that covered the ground.

Then there was a sound of engines reaching their ears, cutting through the quiet of the wintry landscape. Barbara's words hung heavy in the air, her tone grim as she voiced the ominous truth that Mark's associates had likely tracked them down and they were now on their way.

Barbara's warning sent a shiver of apprehension down their spines and maybe their ordeal was far from over. With each passing moment, the sound of engines grew louder, drawing closer with every passing second.

Jim's jaw clenched with determination as he quickened his pace, his senses on high alert as they pressed forward through the biting cold. Beside him, Barbara kept a watchful eye on their surroundings, her gaze darting anxiously towards the approaching noise.

Meanwhile, Jake struggled to keep up, the frigid temperatures making it difficult for him to speak. His breath formed clouds of vapour in the icy air, his face contorted with discomfort as he fought to ward off the biting cold. Then the crack of gunfire as if cowboys were arriving for a night out in the town.

As they trudged through the thick snow, Jim noticed that Jake was struggling more than usual owing to his frailty. His movements had become sluggish and his steady gait had slowed to a laboured shuffle.

Concern etched across his face, Jim approached his companion, his voice laced with worry.

Jim asked Jake, "Jake, are you alright?"

Jake's response was grim, his breath forming wisps of vapour in the frigid air as he spoke.

Jake, "I can't feel my feet."

Jim's heart sank at Jake's words, the severity hitting home with chilling clarity. With each passing moment, the cold tightened its icy grip, threatening to incapacitate both Jake and Dot if they didn't find shelter soon.

Barbara, her own concern mounting, stepped forward to lend her support.

With a renewed sense of urgency they pressed on, their movements fuelled by the desperate need to reach safety before the cold rendered Jake immobile. Jim and Barbara flanked Jake, offering whatever support they could as they struggled through the knee-deep snow. Jim's device indicated there was around half a mile to go. Now half a mile walking on normal streets would take around ten minutes but this was far from a normal street as every step was a different drop into the snow and made every step a struggle. Jim and Barbara had their suits but Dot and Jake just had layers of clothes wrapped around them fortunately helped by Barbara's extra layer of clothing she had given them .

Jake's voice cut through the howling wind, his words echoed with a heavy sense of resignation. The biting cold had taken its toll, sapping his strength and leaving him struggling to keep pace. Despite his efforts to push forward, the relentless blizzard had exacted a toll too great to bear.

Jake suddenly looked up, "Go ahead without me. I can't make it."

Jim and Barbara exchanged worried glances, their concern for Jake in the frigid air.

Jim made it clear, "We can't leave you behind, Jake. We'll find a way to get you to safety."

Barbara nodded in agreement with Dot crying at the thought of Jake not making it, All three huddled close to Jake, offering what little warmth and comfort they could amidst the biting cold.

Dot's voice trembling with emotion as she struggled to maintain her composure in the face of adversity. "I can't bear to see him like this. We have to do something."

With each step, they leaned on one another for support, their determination unyielding in the face of adversity. Though the blizzard raged on around them, they refused to succumb to despair, their resolve bolstered by the knowledge that they were stronger together.

Pressing forward, their footsteps muffled by the thick blanket of snow, they drew strength from one another. Jake was now being carried by all three. Jim's voice cut through the howling wind, his words a beacon of hope amidst the swirling snow. With a surge of determination, the group quickened their pace, their weary bodies propelled forward by the promise of safety just ahead.

Jim, "We're almost there! Dodger is just 100 yards away!"

Barbara's heart soared at Jim's proclamation, her spirits buoyed by the prospect of reaching shelter before the storm or their adversaries could claim them. With renewed hope, they pressed on, with their steps quickening as they drew nearer to their sanctuary.

Reaching the designated coordinates, they all looked around in confusion, their eyes scanning the snowy landscape for any sign of Dodger. But to their dismay, there was no trace of the vehicle in sight.

Barbara, "Where is Dodger?"

Her voice was tinged with concern, the realisation sinking in that their lifeline to safety was nowhere to be found. Jim checked the handheld device again, his brow furrowed in frustration as he confirmed their location.

Jim said, "This is the spot where Dodger should be, but I don't see it anywhere."

Jim couldn't understand why Dodger had not reappeared as Dave said it would and then it triggered a thought.

Jim stated, "I know what's happened. When we left Dodger, I marked our position on this device. But we walked for a while before I did that. So now, the device has brought us back to where we were when I marked it. But Dodger isn't here. It's must be about twenty yards from this spot."

His voice held a note of determination, his mind already racing with plans to rectify their situation. With a plan in mind, they spread out, each member of the group venturing off in a different direction, their eyes scouring the landscape for any sign of the elusive vehicle. Jake stayed motionless while the other three moved off in different directions.

Jim led the charge, his determination driving him forward as he searched for any trace of Dodger's familiar silhouette amidst the blanket of white. With each step, he scanned the horizon, his senses heightened by the urgency.

Barbara and Dot followed suit in different directions, their movements purposeful as they combed the area for any indication of Dodger's presence. Still no Dodger to be seen.

Jim, "Wait a minute! Don't move from your spot. I believe Dodger is where Dot is. It won't materialise for just anyone. It knows me—my DNA."

His words resonated with a sense of certainty, igniting a renewed sense of purpose and with bated breath, they watched as Jim made his way towards Dot, their hearts pounding with anticipation as they waited for his next move.

Barbara rooted to the spot, their eyes fixed on Jim's determined figure as he approached Dot. The air crackled with tension, the weight of their predicament pressing down upon them like a heavy blanket of snow.

As Jim reached Dot's side, he cast a hopeful glance towards the empty expanse of snow around them, his mind racing with possibilities. With a steady hand, he reached out to Dot, a silent gesture of reassurance amidst the uncertainty that enveloped them.

In that moment, a ripple of anticipation swept through the group, their hopes buoyed by the possibility that Dodger might indeed be within their grasp, they waited for the moment of truth, their hearts pounding with the promise of salvation just beyond their reach. As Jim cautiously moved to the left of Dot, a sense of anticipation filled the air, the group holding their breath as they watched for any sign of Dodger's elusive form. And then, as if in response to Jim's movement, a faint shimmer began to materialise in the snowy landscape.

Barbara, "Look! Dodger's reappearing!"

Barbara's voice carried a note of excitement, her words echoing the collective relief as Dodger slowly took shape before their eyes. With each passing moment the vehicle became more defined with its familiar contours emerging from the swirling snow with growing clarity.

As Dodger solidified, its sleek exterior gleaming in the muted light, a wave of gratitude swept through, spirits buoyed by the sight of their lifeline to safety. With Jim's intuition proving correct, they knew that their harrowing ordeal was finally coming to an end.

Jim, "We've got to get Jake. But I believe I must stand alongside Dodger, or it will vanish again."

His words carried a sense of urgency, emphasising the critical importance of maintaining a connection with Dodger to ensure its stability. With a shared understanding of the task at hand, Barbara and Dot set off towards Jake's location, their footsteps echoing against the backdrop of the snow-covered landscape. Dodger's sleek exterior began to come alive, its doors opening with an eerie, almost otherworldly grace. The sight sent a shiver down Dot's spine.

As they reached his side, Barbara and Dot wasted no time in extending a helping hand.

Both struggled to help Jake, the tranquillity of the moment shattered by the sudden crack of a gunshot. A bullet whizzed past their heads, the sharp sound echoing off the surrounding landscape like a chilling warning.

Jim, "Take cover!"

Jim's voice rang out with urgency, his instincts kicking into overdrive as he propelled himself towards the ground. With adrenaline coursing through their veins the others crawled back towards the Dodger.

Amidst the chaos, Dot's eyes widened with fear, her grip tightening on Jake as she huddled close to protect him. Jim glancing from side to side for any sign of their assailants, his mind racing with strategies to keep his companions safe.

Dot trembled with fear, her eyes darting nervously as she sought reassurance amidst the uncertainty. Then another gunshot rang out, the sound slicing through the air with deadly precision hitting Dot in her arm. Dot's piercing scream shattered the tense silence, her voice echoing through the desolate landscape as a bullet found its mark, tearing through the air with deadly accuracy. The impact sent pain coursing through her body, her hands instinctively flying to the source of the searing agony.

Dot, "Ahh!"

Her cry reverberated with anguish, her body recoiling from the sudden onslaught as she crumpled to the ground in agony. Jim's heart clenched with horror at the sight, he would like to rush to her aid but if he did Dodger would start to vanish again.

Barbara, "Dot! Are you okay?" Her voice trembled with concern, her eyes scanning to see if she had suffered further harm. Dot's face contorted with pain. Barbara's voice though tinged with urgency, carried a soothing reassurance as she knelt beside Dot, her hands gently cradling hers as he sought to offer comfort amidst the turmoil.

Barbara, "I know it hurts, Dot, but it's your arm. You're going to be okay, I promise, it looks broken so use your other arm to help me get Jake back to the Dodger, we must crawl and stay very low."

As the whizzing noise of bullets echoed through the air, Barbara's gaze shot upward to witness Jim's swift action. With a flicker of determination in his eyes, he had activated the shield, summoning forth a protective barrier that enveloped Dodger's open doors.

Barbara's voice, though hushed with urgency, carried a note of admiration as she spoke to Dot and Jake, her words tinged with gratitude for Jim's quick thinking amidst the chaos.

Barbara, "My husband's a genius. We just need to get behind the shield."

The air crackled with tension as the assailants found themselves frustrated by Jim's covering fire, their advance thwarted by the impenetrable barrier that stood between them and their prey.

As Barbara, Dot and Jake reached the protective shield, Jim swiftly took action, temporarily deactivating the barrier to allow them entry. With a quick nod of acknowledgment, they hurried forward, their hearts pounding with anticipation as they crossed the threshold to safety. Jim immediately reactivated the shield. He stopped firing, immediately bullets peppered the shield, Jim's voice rang out with urgency, his command clear and decisive amidst the chaos.

Jim, "Quick, inside Dodger! The AI will activate Dodger's shield as standard."

With swift movements and dragging Jake they hurried inside Dodger, their hearts pounding with adrenaline as they sought refuge from the storm of gunfire that raged outside. As they crossed the threshold to safety, a sense of relief, their minds reeling from the close call they had just narrowly escaped. Dodgers doors slowly closing and then they slammed shut.

AI voice, "Shields activated."

Inside Dodger's sheltering walls, they found respite from the chaos that raged outside, their breaths coming in ragged gasps as they caught their bearings amidst the relative calm of their sanctuary.

As they peered out from the safety of Dodger's shelter, Jim, Barbara, Dot and Jake watched in awe as five men unleashed a relentless barrage of gunfire at the vehicle. Despite their efforts, the bullets seemed to have little effect, merely bouncing off Dodger's shield protected exterior like raindrops against a sturdy fortress.

Jim, "They're not giving up easily, are they?"

His voice was tinged with a mixture of admiration and apprehension, his eyes fixed on the scene unfolding before them. Each bullet that ricocheted off Dodger's surface served as a testament to the vehicle's resilience, a silent reminder of the protection it offered amidst the chaos that surrounded them.

Barbara's expression was one of grim determination as she monitored the situation, her hands steady she hit the red button and Dodger began to levitate away from the deep snow.

Dot and Jake huddled close together, their faces pale with fear but their spirits unbroken as they took solace aboard Dodger. In the midst of danger, they found strength in each other's presence, their faith in their companions unwavering.

Outside, the assailants continued their relentless assault, their determination unyielding as they unleashed a torrent of bullets at Dodger's impervious exterior.

As Dodger vanished into the distance with astonishing speed, the assailants were left seething with frustration and rage. Their voices, laced with venomous anger, echoed through the cold, desolate landscape as they vented their fury at their inability to breach the vehicle's defences.

Assailant 1, "Damn it! How did they manage to escape?"

His voice crackled with barely contained fury, his fists clenched in impotent rage as he struggled to comprehend their sudden disappearance. The sight of Dodger slipping away from their grasp filled him with a sense of bitter defeat, his frustration boiling over into a torrent of curses and expletives.

Assailant 2, "I can't believe it! We had them right where we wanted them!"

Assailant 3, "We can't let them get away with this! We need to find them and finish what we started but where the hell did they go!"

Meanwhile back on board Dodger

Inside Dodger's safety, the AI system hummed as it monitored Dot's condition, its digital sensors attuned to the subtle nuances of her vital signs. With each passing moment, its algorithms analysed the data, searching for any signs of distress or deterioration that might require immediate attention.

AI, "Warning: Patient's vital signs indicate gunshot wound to the arm. Immediate medical intervention."

Its synthesized voice, calm and authoritative, cut through the tension in the air, its words a stark reminder of the need for action. With

Dot's well-being hanging in the balance because of loss of blood, the AI system sprang into action, activating its medical protocols and initiating a series of diagnostic scans to assess the extent of her injuries.

As the onboard medical systems went to work, a sense of apprehension filled the air, the occupants of Dodger holding their breath as they awaited news of Dot's condition. In the dimly lit interior of the vehicle, their faces reflected a mixture of worry and concern, their thoughts consumed by the fate of their injured elderly companion.

With each passing moment, the AI system worked tirelessly to stabilise Dot's condition, its digital interface displaying real-time data as it administered pain relief and applied pressure to staunch the bleeding. Inside Dodger's sheltering walls, the hum of machinery blended with the quiet murmur of voices, a testament to the relentless efforts of man and machine to ensure the safety and well-being of all who sought refuge within its walls.

AI, "Treatment protocol initiated. Administering wound care and applying medical-grade nanobots to accelerate tissue regeneration."

Its words, delivered with precision The others listened intently, their eyes fixed on the digital readouts as the AI system worked its magic to heal Dot's injuries.

With each passing moment, the AI's efforts bore fruit, the nanobots working tirelessly to repair the damage inflicted by the bullet. Slowly but surely, the wound began to close, the torn flesh knitting together under the ministrations of Dodger's advanced medical technology.

As the treatment progressed, relief was felt by all and their tension easing as they watched Dot's condition stabilize before their eyes. In the face of adversity, the AI system had proven itself to be a stalwart ally, its unwavering commitment to the well-being of its occupants a testament to the power of human ingenuity and technological innovation.

AI barked out, "Arm successfully repaired. Patient's condition stabilised, blood loss replaced. Recommended course of action: Rest and hydration."

Amidst the tension and concern that permeated the interior of Dodger, there was a palpable sense of awe as the AI system announced the successful completion of Dot's treatment.

"Wow," Jim breathed, his voice tinged with wonder. "Did you all hear that? The AI just repaired Dot's arm like it was nothing."

Barbara nodded, her eyes wide with amazement. "I've heard about AI technology, but to see it in action like this... it's truly incredible."

As the AI system also diligently monitored Jake's condition, its digital sensors detected a critical development: gangrene, a severe and potentially life-threatening condition characterized by tissue death due to lack of blood flow or infection.

AI, "Warning: Patient Jake exhibiting symptoms of gangrene in both feet. Immediate treatment required."

Without a moment's hesitation, the AI sprang into action, initiating emergency medical protocols to address the condition and prevent further deterioration. Its algorithms quickly analysed the data, identifying the extent of the infection and devising a comprehensive treatment plan to combat the spread of gangrene and preserve Jake's health.

AI worked non stop, its digital interface displaying real-time updates on Jake's condition. With each passing moment, their anxiety mounted, the urgency of the situation driving home the seriousness of Jake's condition.

AI, "Treatment successful. Patient Jake's gangrene has been cured."

All completely amazed and speechless as Dodger continued its journey to safety.

Chapter 9

HENRY MEETS A STRANGER

Meanwhile few days earlier in the scorching early morning sun beating down relentlessly on the small town of Stagecoach, Nevada, turning the day into a furnace. Henry, a retired banker had found himself at the gas station. As he filled up his car he struck up a conversation with a guy at the adjacent pump.

"It's a hot one today, isn't it?" Henry remarked, wiping sweat from his brow.

The other guy nodded in agreement, his expression mirroring Henry's discomfort. "You're telling me," he replied. "And you know what's crazy? It's supposed to get even hotter."

Henry's eyebrows shot up in surprise. "Even hotter? I didn't think that was possible. How much hotter are we talking?"

The other guy shrugged, with a weary looking expression crossing his face. "They're saying it could break some records. I heard it might hit triple digits by noon."

Henry whistled lowly, shaking his head. "Triple digits? That's brutal. I better make sure I've got plenty of cold drinks stocked up at home."

The two men exchanged knowing looks, both silently dreading the blistering heat that lay ahead. With a final nod of acknowledgment, they finished up at the pumps and retreated to the refuge of their air-conditioned cars, then Henry remembered after all that talk he needed to go back inside to stock up on some beer and water.

As Henry made his way into the gas station's convenience store, the refreshing chill of the air conditioning washed over him, providing respite from the relentless heat outside. With his mind set on stocking up on cold drinks to combat the soaring temperatures, he headed straight for the beverage aisle.

He perused the shelves, selecting bottles of water and a pack of beer, he couldn't shake the feeling of being watched. Glancing around, he noticed a guy at the checkout counter who seemed to be staring at him intently. Henry's eyebrows furrowed in confusion, wondering if he had perhaps dropped something or had some sort of stain on his shirt.

Deciding to ignore the odd behaviour for the moment, Henry placed his items on the counter. The cashier, a young woman with a bored expression, began ringing up his purchases. Meanwhile, the guy who had been staring continued to do so, his gaze unwavering.

Feeling increasingly uncomfortable under the scrutiny, Henry cleared his throat and offered a polite smile to the cashier. "Hot day, huh?" he commented, attempting to diffuse the tension.

The cashier nodded absently, clearly uninterested in engaging in small talk. Meanwhile, the guy continued to stare, his expression unreadable.

As Henry paid for his drinks and hastily made his exit, he couldn't shake the feeling of unease that lingered from the strange encounter. With a sigh of relief, he stepped back out into the blistering heat, eager to put the uncomfortable moment behind him and focus on staying cool. As Henry approached his car he was startled by the unexpected touch on his shoulder, Henry turned around to find the same man behind him, a look of recognition on his face, the stranger said, "Hello Henry." Henry was unnerved by this because of the mention of his name, it sent a shiver down Henry's spine, with a wave of apprehension.

"Yeah, I'm Henry Jenkins," he replied cautiously, eyeing the stranger warily. "Do I know you?"

The man grinned, revealing a row of slightly crooked teeth. "Sure you do, Henry. We go way back. Don't you remember me? I even remember you from high school."

Henry racked his brain, trying to place the face in front of him. High school felt like a lifetime ago and memories of those days were hazy at best. Henry studied the man's features, not a flicker of recognition sparked in his mind.

The stranger then said, "My name is Rick."

Henry's eyebrows furrowed in confusion as the strangers words echoed in his mind. Despite his initial apprehension, there was something about the strangers sincerity that gave Henry pause. He studied the strangers face searching for any sign of deception, but all he saw was earnestness.

"I've always known you Henry," the stranger stated, his voice tinged with conviction. The stranger continued, "I know this sounds kinda strange to you, but one day it will not feel so strange and my name is Rick." making sure he repeated his name so that Henry wouldnt forget

Henry's mind raced with a flurry of questions, each one more perplexing than the last. How could Rick claim to know him when Henry couldn't even recall ever meeting him before? What did he mean by one day it won't sound strange?

Despite his scepticism Henry couldn't shake the feeling that there was more to Rick's words than met the eye. With a sigh of resignation, he decided to entertain the possibility that there might be some truth to Rick's claim, no matter how improbable it seemed.

"Okay, Rick," Henry said slowly, still grappling with the strangeness of the situation. "I'm willing to hear you out. But you'll have to forgive me if I find all of this a little hard to believe."

Rick nodded understandingly, a hint of relief crossing his features. "I get it, Henry. It's a lot to take in. But trust me, everything will make sense eventually."

Henry's heart skipped a beat as Rick's words hit him like a ton of bricks. How could this stranger know my name? Then the stranger told Henry he had been married to Margaret for over forty years. The mention of Margaret and that they had been married for over forty years sent a chill down Henry's spine. Henry felt a mixture of disbelief and fear creeping over him, his mind racing to make sense of the impossible.

"How... how do you know all this?" Henry stammered, his voice barely above a whisper. "Who are you, really?"

Rick's expression softened with empathy as he met Henry's gaze. "I know this is a lot to take in, Henry," he began gently. "But there are things in this world that defy conventional explanation. Let's just say... I have a unique perspective on things."

Henry's mind whirled with a thousand questions, but one in particular bubbled to the surface. "How do you know about Margaret? About where I live?"

Rick offered a small, knowing smile. "Henry, there are forces at work in this world that most people can't even begin to comprehend. But trust me when I say that everything happens for a reason and sometimes, paths cross in ways that defy logic."

Despite his scepticism, Henry couldn't shake the feeling that there was more to Rick's words than mere speculation. As unsettling as it was to consider, there was a part of him that couldn't deny the strange sense of familiarity he felt in Rick's presence.

"I don't understand," Henry admitted, his voice tinged with uncertainty. "But... I'm willing to listen."

With a nod of gratitude, Rick began to unravel the enigma that had brought them together, revealing a world of mysteries and possibilities that Henry had never dared to imagine. And as the truth slowly began to unfurl, Henry found himself drawn into a journey that would challenge everything he thought he knew about the nature of reality itself. Rick said the temperature is around 100 degrees and forecast to get even higher as the day wears on. What would you say if I told you that by late afternoon in the not too distant future the temperature would be just a few degrees above freezing.

Henry's eyes widened in disbelief at Rick's words. "A few degrees above freezing? That's... impossible," he muttered, his mind struggling to grasp the enormity of what Rick was suggesting.

Rick's expression remained calm and steady, his gaze unwavering. "I know it sounds unbelievable, Henry. But trust me, stranger things have happened. There are forces at work in this world that defy explanation."

Henry shook his head in disbelief, unable to wrap his mind around the idea of such a drastic change in temperature within the span of a few hours. "But how is that even possible? What could cause something like that?"

Rick shrugged, a mysterious smile playing at the corners of his lips. "Sometimes, Henry, the answers we seek lie beyond the realm of science and logic. We must be prepared for whatever comes our way."

Henry laughed, "You know what Rick I think you are nuts."

Rick chuckled softly at Henry's response, his eyes twinkling with amusement. "Can't say I blame you for thinking that Henry," he said with a good-natured grin. "I've been called worse."

Henry couldn't help but join in with a reluctant laugh, the tension easing slightly as he found himself swept up in Rick's infectious humour. Despite his scepticism, there was something undeniably likeable about Rick's easygoing nature.

"Look, I know it all sounds a bit... out there," Rick admitted, his smile fading into a more earnest expression. "But sometimes, the truth is stranger than fiction. And hey, even if I am nuts, at least I'm entertaining, right?"

Henry chuckled again, shaking his head in bemusement. "That you are, Rick. That you are."

As the two men shared a moment of camaraderie amidst the uncertainty of the discussion, Henry couldn't help but feel a glimmer of gratitude for the unexpected encounter. Whatever the future held, he knew that he would always remember the day he met Rick, the mysterious stranger who dared to challenge his perception of reality with a touch of humour and a hint of mystery.

Rick said, "Look I don't have much more to say but can you promise me one thing and thats because your filling up with gas it means you are going on a trip right?"

Henry replied, "Your right we are off to see family and they live in Kansas."

Rick's expression softened as he listened to Henry's response, a sense of understanding dawning in his eyes. "A trip to Kansas, huh?" he mused thoughtfully. "Sounds like quite the journey."

Henry nodded, a flicker of anticipation crossing his features. "Yeah, it'll be nice to spend some time with the family," he replied, a hint of warmth in his voice.

Rick's gaze lingered on Henry for a moment longer, a silent exchange passing between them. Then Rick said, "If you go on that trip to Kansas Henry, you or Margaret will never get there." Henry's heart skipped a beat at Rick's ominous words, a chill running down his spine as a sense of foreboding with anger simmered beneath the surface, mingling with the shock of Rick's unsettling proclamation.

"What do you mean we'll never get there?" Henry demanded, his voice laced with a mixture of disbelief and frustration. "Are you threatening us?"

Rick held up his hands in a placating gesture, his expression earnest yet tinged with an air of solemnity. "No, Henry, I'm not threatening you," he replied calmly. "I'm just trying to warn you because there are forces at work here that you can't possibly understand."

Henry's jaw clenched as he struggled to contain his rising anger. "Forces? What forces?" he snapped, his voice rising with each word. "This is ridiculous! You can't just go around making wild predictions like that!"

Rick's gaze remained steady, his eyes holding a hint of sadness as he met Henry's furious stare. "I understand that you're upset, Henry," he said softly. "But please, you have to trust me. I'm only trying to protect you and your family and once the temperature drops you should invite trusted friends that live nearby to your house because the more you invite round to your place the more you save." Rick went on to advise Henry that no matter what happens to promise him that if the temperature starts to fall he would follow what has been said and to telephone this number as Rick handed the number over.

The tension hung heavy in the air between them, Rick's words sinking in. Despite his anger, Henry couldn't shake the gnawing sense of unease that lingered in the pit of his stomach. Could there be some truth to Rick's warning, no matter how implausible it seemed? Rick then said, "Promise me this before I go Henry."

Henry's frustration simmered as Rick's insistence persisted, but curiosity still gnawed at him. "What is it now?" Henry asked with a hint of impatience creeping into his voice.

Rick's expression softened, a sense of urgency underlying his words. "Promise me, Henry. Promise me that you'll consider what I have to say. That you'll think twice before embarking on that trip."

Henry hesitated, torn between his instinctive scepticism and a growing sense of unease. "I... I can't make that promise to you Rick," he admitted reluctantly. "Not without more information and not without some kind of explanation for all of this."

Rick's gaze faltered for a moment, disappointment flickering across his features. "I understand," he said quietly. "But just remember, Henry... sometimes, the greatest danger lies not in what we know, but in what we refuse to acknowledge.

Henry furrowed his brow, his scepticism warring with a growing sense of concern. "Why would I need to call this number if the temperature starts to fall?" he asked, his voice tinged with frustration. "What's so important about it?"

Rick's expression grew solemn, his gaze piercing as he met Henry's eyes. "I can't tell you everything Henry," he said cryptically. "But trust me when I say that calling that number could save your life."

Henry's frustration mounted at Rick's evasiveness, but a sense of curiosity gnawed at him nonetheless. "Fine," he relented begrudgingly. "I'll call the number if the temperature starts to fall. But don't expect me to believe any of this nonsense until I see some proof."

Rick nodded solemnly, a glimmer of gratitude flickering in his eyes. "That's all I ask Henry and just keep an open mind no matter what happens."

As the two men exchanged a final nod of understanding, Henry couldn't shake the feeling that he was being drawn into something far beyond his comprehension. with that Henry headed home.Henry's mind was now racing with a jumble of thoughts and emotions, the encounter with Rick weighing heavily. He couldn't shake the feeling of unease that lingered from their cryptic conversation, nor could he dismiss the nagging sense of curiosity that tugged at him.

As he pulled into the driveway, Henry took a deep breath, steeling himself for the conversation to be had. He knew that explaining the strange encounter to Margaret would be no easy task, but he also knew that he couldn't keep it to himself any longer.

Entering the house, Henry found Margaret in the kitchen, humming softly to herself as she prepared for the trip. Her warm smile faltered as she caught sight of the serious expression on Henry's face.

"Henry, what's wrong?" she asked, concern creasing her brow. "You look like you've seen a ghost."

Henry hesitated, unsure of where to begin. "Margaret something... something strange happened today," he began slowly, choosing his words with care.

Margaret set down and turned her full attention to Henry, her eyes filled with concern. "What happened Is everything okay?"

Henry recounted the encounter with Rick, from their chance meeting at the gas station to the cryptic warnings about the temperature and the mysterious phone number. Margaret listened in silence, her expression alternating between disbelief and concern as Henry spoke.

"Are you sure this wasn't just some prank?" Margaret asked, her brow furrowed in scepticism.

Henry shook his head, a troubled expression crossing his features. "I wish it were Margaret, but something about it felt... real. It was like there was much more to it than just a random encounter."

Margaret reached out and took Henry's hand in hers, her touch a comforting anchor in the midst of uncertainty. "Well, whatever it is, we'll face it together," she said firmly. "We always have, haven't we as she laughed and said Henry its a joke you'll see"

"You're probably right, Margaret," Henry chuckled, feeling some of the weight of the encounter with Rick lift. "It does sound pretty far-fetched, especially saying I should invite as many friends around if this happens."

Margaret nodded, her smile warm and reassuring. "Absolutely, I mean a stranger showing up out of nowhere with cryptic warnings? It sounds like something out of a movie or one of your buddies setting you up for a laugh."

Henry's smile widened at her words, the sense of unease that had been gnawing at him slowly dissipating.

"Yeah, you're right," Henry agreed, feeling a sense of relief. "I'm probably just overthinking things."

With a shared chuckle, Henry and Margaret resumed preparation for the trip the next day.

A few hours later Henry and Margaret retired to bed, the warmth of their shared laughter lingering in the air as they drifted off to sleep with a sense of contentment and ease. Outside, the night sky stretched out in a blanket of stars, a serene backdrop to the quiet neighbourhood.

The next morning dawned bright and clear, the Sun already high in the sky as Henry stirred from his slumber. Stretching lazily, he glanced out the window, the morning light casting a warm glow over the landscape.

As he made his way down the stairs, Henry switched on the television to catch the morning news. The weather forecast flashed across the screen, confirming what he already suspected: another scorching day lay ahead.

"Hot, hot, hot," Henry muttered to himself, shaking his head in resignation. He couldn't help but chuckle at the irony of the situation, considering the bizarre warnings about the temperature he had received just the day before.

Margaret joined him in the kitchen, her smile bright as she poured them both cups of coffee. "Looks like it's going to be another scorcher," she remarked, glancing at the weather report on the television.

Henry nodded, with relief as he realised that the strange encounter with Rick was nothing more than a harmless prank. "Yeah, but at least we can handle a little heat," he replied with a grin, taking Margaret's hand in his.

With the sun shining brightly overhead and a gentle breeze rustling through the leaves, Margaret's idea to have breakfast in the garden was met with enthusiastic approval from Henry. Together, they gathered the essentials – a chequered tablecloth, plates of fruit, freshly baked pastries and steaming mugs of coffee – and carried them outside to their quaint garden patio.

Settling into their chairs, surrounded by the vibrant colours of blooming flowers and the melodious chirping of birds, Henry couldn't help but feel a sense of tranquillity. It was moments like these, he realised, that made life truly beautiful.

Margaret poured them each another cup of coffee, her smile radiant as she gazed out at the peaceful scene before them. "This is perfect," she said, her voice filled with contentment. "Just what we needed to start the day."

Henry nodded in agreement, taking a sip of his coffee and soaking in the warmth of the morning sun. "Absolutely," he replied, a sense of gratitude swelling in his chest. "I couldn't imagine a better way to begin, we will set off later and stay part way at that lovely motel in New Mexico that I booked and there is a Denny's close by, well I know its a little out of our way but its worth it."

As they enjoyed their breakfast together in the garden, Henry and Margaret shared stories, laughter and quiet moments of reflection in the simple pleasures of each other's company and the beauty of the world around them. Basking in the warmth of the summer morning, they knew that no matter what the day may bring, they would face it together with love, laughter and an unwavering appreciation for life's little joys. Margaret's observation drew Henry's attention to the outdoor thermometer, confirming the rising heat of the morning. He glanced at the display, noting the temperature steadily climbing.

"86 degrees already?" Henry remarked, eyebrows raised in surprise. "Looks like it's going to be another scorcher today."

Margaret nodded, a playful smile playing at the corners of her lips. "Well, good thing we're prepared for it," she said, reaching for a slice of watermelon to refresh themselves.

With a chuckle, Henry leaned back in his chair, taking in the warmth of the sun on his skin and the gentle breeze that danced through the garden. Despite the heat, there was a sense of peace and contentment in the air, a feeling of being right where they were meant to be.

Henry nodded, setting down his coffee cup and rising from his chair. "You're right, Margaret." They then cleared away the remnants of breakfast and tidied up the garden patio, preparing to head back inside to finish packing for their trip to Kansas.

Before long, the suitcases were packed, the car was loaded and Henry and Margaret were ready to hit the road. With a final glance around the house to ensure they hadn't forgotten anything, they locked the door behind them and set off on their adventure, eager to reunite with their granddaughter and embark on the next chapter of their journey together.

Henry and Margaret settled into their seats, ready to begin the long drive ahead. The engine hummed to life and they pulled out of the driveway leaving their quiet neighbourhood behind as they set off on the open road.

"We should make good time," Henry remarked, glancing at the fuel gauge. "With a full tank, we won't have to stop until we get well into New Mexico."

Margaret nodded in agreement, her eyes bright with anticipation. "It'll be nice to make some progress before we need to take a break," she replied, adjusting her seatbelt and settling in for the journey.

As they merged onto the highway, the landscape stretching out before them with the distant mountains, Henry and Margaret felt a sense of excitement building within them. Despite the miles ahead, they knew that with each passing mile marker, they were one step closer to reuniting with their granddaughter and the adventures that awaited them in Kansas.

With the sun shining down on them and the promise of new horizons, Henry and Margaret embraced the journey ahead, grateful for the opportunity to explore the open road together and create memories that would last a lifetime. As they cruised along the highway, Henry spotted the familiar green sign of a Starbucks up ahead, a beacon of caffeine and comfort amidst the vast expanse of the open road.

"Hey, there's a Starbucks," Henry exclaimed, pointing excitedly as they approached the exit. "How about we make a quick pit stop? I could use a pick-me-up."

Margaret smiled at Henry's enthusiasm, nodding in agreement. "Sounds like a plan," she replied, already scanning the exit signs for directions to the coffee shop. "A little caffeine boost wouldn't hurt, especially with all this driving ahead of us."

With the decision made, Henry guided the car off the highway and into the parking lot of the Starbucks. They found a spot near the entrance and parked, eager to stretch their legs too. Stepping out of the car, Henry and Margaret made their way inside the coffee shop, the scent of freshly brewed coffee wafting through the air. They ordered their favourite drinks – a latte for Margaret and a cappuccino for Henry – and found a table near the window, where they could watch the world go by as they enjoyed their break.

As they sipped their drinks and savoured the moment of respite from the road, Henry and Margaret couldn't help but feel grateful for the little pleasures that made the journey all the more enjoyable.

All of a sudden they were startled by the sudden roar of jet engines, Henry and Margaret glanced up from their drinks to see a formation of fighter jets streaking across the sky, leaving behind them a trail of thunderous noise and awe-inspiring speed.

"Wow, they're in a hurry," the Barista remarked.

Henry nodded in agreement, his eyes following the jets as they disappeared into the distance. "Must be some kind of military exercise," he mused, his curiosity piqued by the unexpected spectacle.

Margaret leaned in closer, her gaze fixed on the sky. "They're incredible," she breathed, a sense of wonder shining in her eyes. Henry and Margaret exchanged wide-eyed glances as the sky above seemed to come alive once more, this time with the thunderous roar of helicopters swiftly trailing the jets that had just passed.

"Whoa, did you see that?" Henry exclaimed, his voice barely audible over the cacophony of sound.

Margaret nodded, her eyes wide with astonishment. "I've never seen anything like it," she replied, her voice tinged with excitement.

As the helicopters zoomed past in rapid succession, Henry and Margaret watched in awe, the sheer speed and precision of their movements leaving them spellbound. As the last echoes of the jets and helicopters faded into the distance, Henry and Margaret made their way back to their car, still buzzing with excitement from the unexpected spectacle they had just witnessed.

"Wow, that was something else," Henry remarked, his voice still tinged with awe as they reached the car.

Margaret nodded in agreement, a wide smile lighting up her face. "I've never seen anything like it, glad their ours," she replied, her eyes sparkling with excitement.

With a sense of anticipation still lingering in the air, Henry and Margaret climbed back into the car, ready to resume their journey. The engine roared to life and they pulled out of the parking lot. As they merged back onto the highway, Henry and Margaret shared a smile, the exhilaration of the moment filling them with renewed energy and excitement. They continued on their way, the anticipation of what other surprises the journey may hold only added to the sense of adventure that lay before them. With each passing mile Henry started to feel the fatigue that came with the journey. "Not long now until we reach the motel," Henry remarked, glancing at the GPS display to check their progress.

Margaret nodded, a sense of anticipation building within her. "I can't wait to stretch my legs and relax for a bit," she replied.

As they approached the exit for the motel gradually slowing to turn off the highway, following the signs towards their temporary home for the night. The Sun dipped lower in the sky, painting the horizon in hues of pink and orange as they pulled into the parking lot of the quaint roadside motel.

With a sigh of relief, Henry parked the car and turned off the engine, the quiet hum of the motel neon sign filling the air around them. As they gathered their belongings and made their way inside, a time to recharge before continuing on their journey the next day.

After a lovely meal at Denny's which was within walking distance they settled in for the evening, Henry and Margaret felt the chill of the air now the Sun had gone.

As Henry stepped outside the motel room the next morning, he was greeted by a brisk chill in the air, a sharp contrast to the warmth of the previous day. The cool breeze sent a shiver down his spine, causing him to pull his jacket tighter around himself.

"Looks like it's gotten colder overnight," Henry remarked to himself, his breath forming a misty cloud in the chilly air. He glanced up at the sky, noting the clear blue expanse above, devoid of any clouds. Despite the sunshine, the air held a crispness.

Henry made his way back to the motel reception, his breath visible in the crisp morning air as he stepped inside the lobby. A friendly receptionist greeted him with a warm smile.

"Good morning, how can I help you?" she asked, her cheerful demeanour putting Henry at ease.

"Good morning," Henry replied with a smile of his own. "I was just wondering if you have the weather forecast for today?

The receptionist nodded while tapping away at her computer before pulling up the forecast on the screen. "Looks like it's going to be warm today after a cool start," she said, glancing at the display.

Henry and Margaret decided to grab breakfast at Denny's before hitting the road. They found a cozy booth inside the restaurant and perused the menu, eager to fuel up for the journey ahead.

As they enjoyed their hearty breakfasts and sipped on steaming cups of coffee, Henry and Margaret shared stories and laughter, relishing the simple pleasure of a leisurely meal together.

With their appetites satisfied and their spirits lifted, Henry and Margaret settled the bill and made their way back to the motel to check out. Gathering their belongings and loading them into the car, they exchanged a smile. Henry started the engine and with one last glance at the motel in the rear-view mirror, they set off on the open road once more, eager to see what the day had in store for them.

As the miles stretched out before them, Henry and Margaret shared stories and sang along to the radio and gazed at the ever-changing landscape outside their windows. Henry glanced at the car's temperature gauge and smiled as he noted the rising temperature. "Looks like it's warming up," he remarked turning to Margaret with a grin. "Up to 89 degrees now that's more like it."

Margaret nodded, her own smile mirroring Henry's. "Much better," she agreed basking in the warmth of the sun streaming through the windows. "It feels good."

With the temperature rising and the sun shining brightly overhead, Henry and Margaret settled into a comfortable rhythm as they continued their journey. The warmth of the day filled them with a sense of renewed energy and enthusiasm, banishing any lingering traces of the earlier chill.

After driving for a while longer, Henry and Margaret decided to take a brief break at a rest area along the highway. As they parked the car and stretched their legs, they made their way over to the vending machines to grab a quick drink.

"Let's grab some coffee and donuts," Henry suggested, gesturing towards the vending machines that stood nearby.

Margaret smiled in agreement, the idea of a warm cup of coffee and a sweet treat sounding perfect for a midday break. "That sounds wonderful," she replied, following Henry over to the machines.

With a few coins in hand, Henry and Margaret made their selections, the familiar noise of the vending machines as they dispensed their chosen items. Henry retrieved two steaming cups of coffee, while Margaret grabbed a couple of donuts, their mouths already watering in anticipation.

Finding a nearby picnic table settling down to enjoy their impromptu snack. The aroma of freshly brewed coffee mingled with the sweet scent of donuts, creating a comforting atmosphere as they savoured the simple pleasure of the moment.

As they sat in the rest area a cold gust of wind swept by "Whoa, where did that come from?" Henry exclaimed, his breath visible in the chilly air as he glanced around, searching for the source of the sudden change in weather.

Margaret shivered slightly, pulling her jacket tighter around herself. "I don't know, but it sure came out of nowhere," she replied, her voice tinged with surprise. They returned to the car, Henry couldn't help but notice a significant drop in the temperature. He glanced at the car's temperature gauge and was surprised.

"Looks like it's down to 72 degrees now," Henry remarked.

Margaret nodded, her own expression mirroring Henry's. "That's quite a drop," she replied, feeling a slight chill in the air despite the warmth of the car's interior.

With the sudden change in temperature, Henry and Margaret now had a sense of uncertainty between them. The weather seemed to be as unpredictable as ever. The temperature continued to plummet, Henry's unease grew, a nagging feeling of dread settling in the pit of his stomach. The sudden drop to 68 degrees sent a chill through the car and Henry couldn't shake the memory of Rick's cryptic warning from the day before.

Margaret noticed the change in Henry's demeanour and reached out to gently squeeze his hand. "Are you alright, Henry?" she asked, concern evident in her voice.

Henry forced a tight-lipped smile, but his thoughts were racing. "I'm fine, just... a bit surprised by the sudden change in temperature," he replied, his voice betraying his anxiety.

Could Rick's warning have been more than just a prank? Was there something they were missing, some danger lurking just beyond the horizon?

Despite his efforts to push the thoughts aside, Henry couldn't shake the feeling of foreboding. With each passing mile the temperature dropped further, casting a pall of uncertainty over both of them.

They now drove on in silence, the weight of Rick's warning hung heavy now, a reminder of the unpredictable nature of the world and the fragility of their own sense of security. They continued to navigate the road ahead but Henry's mind was racing. Suddenly Henry signalled to pull off the road, Margaret's heart skipped a beat, a sense of unease creeping over her. With growing horror, she watched as Henry made the turn, veering off the highway onto a smaller less-travelled road.

"Henry, what are you doing?" Margaret's voice trembled with anxiety as she turned to him, her eyes wide with fear.

Henry's expression was grim as he focused on the road ahead, his hands tight on the steering wheel. "I don't know, Margaret," he admitted, his voice strained. "But something doesn't feel right."

"Margaret, listen to me," Henry's voice rang out, cutting through the tension in the car. "I know this seems sudden and frightening, but I can't shake the feeling that something isn't right. Remember what Rick said about the temperature dropping unexpectedly?"

Margaret nodded, her eyes wide with apprehension as she recalled Rick's warning.

"Well, that's exactly what's happening now," Henry continued, his voice trembling with emotion. "The temperature keeps dropping and I can't shake the feeling that we need to get off the road, find somewhere safe until we figure out what's going on."

Margaret's heart pounded in her chest as she listened to Henry's words, the seriousness sinking in. Despite her fear, she trusted Henry's instincts implicitly, knowing that he would do everything in his power to keep them safe.

Taking a deep breath, Margaret reached out to squeeze Henry's hand, her voice steady despite the fear coursing through her veins. "I trust you, Henry," she said firmly. "Let's find somewhere safe until we can figure out what's happening."

With a shared nod of determination, Henry and Margaret continued down the unfamiliar road, their eyes scanning for any sign of shelter. With that Margaret shouted. "Take us home Henry, take us home!"

Feeling a surge of relief at Margaret's decisive words, Henry nodded firmly, his hands steady on the steering wheel. With a sense of purpose, he reached for the GPS unit and punched in their home address, his movements swift and determined.

"Got it," Henry replied, his voice filled with determination as he confirmed the destination. "We're heading home."

The GPS recalculated the route, Margaret leaned back in her seat, tense. Despite the uncertainty of their situation, she found solace in the knowledge that they were on their way back to familiar surroundings, back to the safety and security of their own home. Henry's voice carried a sense of urgency as he addressed Margaret, his words tinged with concern for their safety.

"Margaret, I think you're right about heading home, but we need to be prepared for anything," Henry said, his tone serious. "We may have to take turns driving and the temperature keeps dropping."

Margaret nodded, her own worry mirrored in her expression. "Agreed," she replied, her voice steady despite the growing cold. "We'll do whatever it takes to get home safely."

With a shared nod, Henry and Margaret prepared themselves for the long journey. The temperature continued to drop, they knew that they would need to stay vigilant.

With Henry behind the wheel, Margaret kept a watchful eye on the road ahead, her mind focused on the task at hand. They both knew this was a sixteen hour journey and it would need to be non stop apart from filling up with gas and rest room stops.

The halfway mark of their journey approached, the road stretched out before them, eerily empty in the now darkness of the night. With eight hours still to go, they knew that they needed to switch drivers to keep each other fresh and alert.

With a weary sigh, Henry pulled the car to a stop at a deserted rest area, the headlights casting long shadows across the empty parking lot. Margaret glanced over at him, her eyes reflecting the exhaustion that mirrored his own.

"Alright, Margaret," Henry said, his voice heavy with fatigue as he unbuckled his seatbelt and prepared to switch places. "It's your turn to take the wheel. We've still got a long way to go and we need to use the rest room."

They were greeted by the sight of a security guard making his rounds. His uniform was crisp in the dim light and his expression held a hint of curiosity as he glanced at the couple.

"Evening," as the security guard greeted them with a nod, his voice carrying a note of concern. "Strange weather we're having, isn't it?"

Henry and Margaret exchanged a knowing glance, a sense of unease settling over them at the guard's words. "Yes, it is," Henry replied, his voice tinged with apprehension. "It's been dropping unexpectedly."

The security guard nodded in agreement, "I've been working these night shifts for years and I've never seen anything quite like it," he admitted, his gaze scanning the empty expanse of the rest area.

Margaret shivered involuntarily, the cold wind sending a chill throughout. "Do you think it's going to get worse?" she asked, her voice barely above a whisper.

The security guard shrugged, his expression unreadable in the darkness. "Hard to say," he replied cryptically. "But I'd advise you folks to be careful out there. This weather has a way of catching people off guard."

With that the security guard continued on his rounds, disappearing into the night. Climbing back into the car to resume their journey, the guard's words lingered with them, a reminder of the uncertainty.

With a shared glance, Henry and Margaret steeled themselves for the road ahead, knowing that they would need to stay vigilant and focused as they continued on their journey home. Having now to drive through the night with the security guard's warning serving as a constant reminder to keep their wits about them.

Margaret her hands trembling slightly as she adjusted the seat and mirrors to her liking. "I'm ready," she replied, trying to muster up some semblance of energy for the journey ahead.

Settling into their new positions, Margaret focused her grip tight on the steering wheel. The darkness seemed to stretch on endlessly around them, broken only by the occasional flicker of light from passing cars.

Henry watched silently from the passenger seat, his mind drifting as Margaret navigated the empty highway. With each passing mile, the hours seemed to blend together, the monotony of the road broken only by the soft hum of the engine and the sound of their breathing.

As they drove on into the night, Henry and Margaret found solace in the quiet companionship that filled the car. Despite the exhaustion they knew that they were in this together, united by their shared determination to make it home safely.

With each passing mile, they drew closer to their destination and the temperature was now just 42 degrees. Henry now sleeping soundly.

At last Henry stirred from his slumber, feeling the gentle vibrations of the car as Margaret pulled into a gas station. Rubbing his eyes, he glanced around, momentarily disoriented by the change in surroundings.

"Where are we?" Henry asked, his voice thick with sleep as he tried to shake off the remnants of his nap.

Margaret turned to him with a reassuring smile. "We're at a gas station," she replied, her voice soft. "I need to fill up the tank and stretch my legs for a moment."

Henry nodded, the fog of sleep beginning to lift as he peered out of the window at the illuminated pumps. "Alright, I'll come with you," he said, unbuckling his seatbelt and stretching his arms above his head.

Together, Henry and Margaret stepped out of the car and into the cool night air, the soft glow of the gas station lights casting a shadow.

Margaret made her way to the pump while Henry wandered over to a nearby bench, stretching his legs and taking in the quiet surroundings.

With the car full and their brief stop completed, Henry and Margaret climbed back into the car and prepared to resume their journey home. As they merged back onto the highway, the memory of their stop at the gas station served as a brief interlude in the journey, a moment of respite before they plunged back into the darkness of the night. After a while it was Henry's time to drive again. Margaret glanced out of the window as Henry's words registered in her mind, her eyes widening in surprise at the sight of snowflakes drifting lazily down from the sky.

"Snow?" Margaret echoed, her voice tinged with astonishment as she watched the gentle descent of the delicate flakes. "But it's only light now."

They drove on through the softly intermittent falling snow, grateful that the snowfall remained light and didn't accumulate on the ground. Despite the initial concern, they soon realised that the snowflakes melted upon contact with the relatively warm road surface.

"It looks like we lucked out," Margaret said with a sigh, her shoulders relaxing as they drove through the diminishing snowfall. "I was worried it might slow us down."

Henry nodded in agreement, "Yes, it seems we caught a break," he replied, his grip on the steering wheel easing slightly. "Let's hope the rest of the journey goes just as smoothly."

As they drove on through the fading snowfall, the tension in the car began to ease, replaced by a sense of gratitude for their good fortune. Despite the unexpected weather.

With Tonopah now behind them and Stagecoach drawing near, Henry and Margaret felt a sense of anticipation building within them.

The familiar landmarks and signs of home began to appear on the horizon, signalling that their journey was nearing its end.

"Stagecoach isn't far now," Margaret remarked, a smile playing at the corners of her lips as she glanced out of the window at the passing scenery.

Henry nodded, his eyes bright with excitement. "That's right," he replied, his voice filled with anticipation. "It won't be long until we're back home."

As they continued to drive onwards, the miles slipping away beneath the wheels of their car, Henry and Margaret felt a sense of relief. Despite the challenges and uncertainties they had faced along the way, they knew that they were finally returning to the place they belonged, surrounded by the familiar sights and sounds of home, visiting the family would have to wait for better times.

With each passing mile, their excitement grew, until finally, they rounded a familiar bend in the road and saw the welcome sight of Stagecoach stretching out before them. The small town seemed to beckon them home, its familiar streets offering a sense of belonging.

Driving through the streets of Stagecoach, Henry and Margaret felt a surge of gratitude for the journey they had shared and the bond that had carried them through every twist and turn along the way. And as they pulled into their driveway and turned off the engine, they knew that no matter where the road may take them next, as long as they were together, they would always find their way home.

Feeling a chill run down his spine, Henry stepped outside and immediately noticed the telltale signs of ice beginning to form on the ground. The temperature had dropped significantly and the air felt bitterly cold against his skin.

Shivering, Henry hurried indoors, eager to escape the freezing temperatures. As he stepped through the door, he closed it behind.

"Margaret, it's getting icy out there," Henry called out, his voice tinged with concern as he glanced around the cold interior of their home. Feeling the chill in the air, Henry and Margaret knew it was time to get the stove fired up to keep their home cozy and warm. With a sense of purpose, Henry made his way to the fireplace, gathering wood and kindling to start a fire. Margaret joined him, helping to arrange the logs and ignite the flames until the room was filled with the comforting crackle and warmth from the fire.

With the fire roaring in the hearth, Henry and Margaret settled into their favourite chairs, the flickering flames casting a soft glow across the room. They sat in comfortable silence for a moment, basking in the warmth and tranquillity of their home.

"We need to talk," Margaret said softly, breaking the silence as she turned to face Henry, her eyes serious.

Henry nodded, his expression solemn as he met her gaze. "I know," he replied, his voice low. "There's been a lot on our minds lately."

As they began to discuss their concerns and plans, the fire crackled merrily in the background, casting a sense of warmth and intimacy over their conversation. They talked late into the night, the fire burning low but their spirits higher. Now feeling the weariness of the day. Henry and Margaret agreed that rest was necessary before making any decisions. With the fire still crackling softly in the fireplace, they retired to their bedroom, grateful for the warmth and comfort of their cozy home.

As they settled into bed, the events of the day swirled through Henry's mind, the memory of Rick's cryptic warning was crystal clear. He knew that they needed to consider their next steps carefully, taking into account everything they had experienced and the advice Rick had given them.

In the quiet darkness of their bedroom, Henry and Margaret lay side by side, each lost in their own thoughts as sleep began to claim them.

Stirred from their sleep, they were greeted by the harsh light of morning filtering through the curtains, illuminating the room with a cold, wintry glow. A chill hung in the air, seeping through the cracks in the windows..

Blinking away the remnants of sleep, Henry and Margaret exchanged a glance, a shared sense of unease as they felt the biting cold of the morning air.

"It's bitterly cold," Margaret remarked, her breath visible in the frigid air as she sat up in bed, pulling the covers tighter around her.

Henry nodded in agreement, his thoughts racing as he tried to make sense of the sudden drop in temperature. "We need to check the weather forecast," he said, his voice grave as he swung his legs out of bed and made his way to the window.

Peering outside, Henry's heart sank as he saw the landscape blanketed in a layer of frost and ice, the ground glistening in the morning light. It was clear that the cold snap was far from over and they needed to be prepared.

With a sense of urgency, Henry and Margaret dressed quickly and made their way down the stairs, the cold air nipping at their cheeks as they moved through the house. As they huddled together in the kitchen, sipping hot coffee and poring over the weather forecast, they knew that they would need to stay vigilant and prepared for whatever the day may bring.

Watching the TV they absorbed the startling information from the weather forecast. The words "unprecedented cold" echoed in their minds.

"What could be causing this?" Margaret murmured, her voice filled with concern as she looked to Henry for answers.

Henry shook his head, as if in deep thought. "I'm not sure," he admitted, his voice tinged with uncertainty. "But whatever it is, it doesn't bode well for us."

They pondered the implications of the forecast, the mention on the news of the military being on high alert worried them.. The thought of such a powerful force mobilising in response to the mysterious cold only added to their growing sense of unease.

"We need to stay informed and be prepared for anything," Henry said firmly, his voice cutting through the tense silence. "We can't afford to take any chances."

Margaret nodded in agreement, her resolve strengthening as she met Henry's gaze. "You're right," she replied, her voice steady despite the fear gnawing at her insides. "We'll need to stay vigilant and stay together."

Henry remembered Rick's warning and started making phone calls to close friends who took some convincing that they all needed to come to his place and asking all of them to bring as much food as they can and plenty of logs. Time would tell if they had heeded his calls because he had made his case by telling them it was a matter of life or death and that did not go down well with everyone.

As Henry called the number that Rick had given him, his heart raced with anticipation and apprehension. With each ring, a strange ring, his nerves grew, until finally, a voice answered on the other end. A very calm voice.

"Hello, this is Dave,"

Chapter 10

THE LINEMAN

Meanwhile a few days earlier just North Of Beatty in Nevada Ben Hollander was driving North, Ben was a man of the earth, his face etched with lines earned from years spent under the blazing Nevada sun. His skin, weather-beaten and rugged, told the tale of a life lived outdoors, enduring the harsh elements as he worked tirelessly to keep the power flowing. Despite the wear and tear, there was a toughness in his gaze, a determination that shone through the creases and scars.

Standing tall and broad-shouldered, Ben exuded strength and resilience. His hands, calloused from years of manual labour he was capable and sure, a testament to his expertise as a lineman working for the power company. Every movement was purposeful, every action deliberate, reflecting the keen intelligence that lay beneath his rough exterior.

Despite his tough exterior, there was a warmth in Ben's eyes, especially when they rested upon his wife, Olivia and their baby. Olivia was his anchor, the one who softened his rough edges and brought light into his world. Their love was evident in the gentle touches and shared glances, a bond forged through years of partnership and mutual respect.

As a husband and father, Ben was fiercely protective, his family's well-being always at the forefront of his mind. He worked tirelessly to provide for them, knowing that his labour ensured their comfort and security. Though his work often took him away from home, he cherished every moment spent with Olivia and their baby, savouring the simple joys of family life amidst the chaos of the world.

In Ben's eyes, there was no challenge too great, no obstacle too daunting. With Olivia by his side and their baby in his arms, he faced each day with unwavering resolve. Today he set off but the day felt different.

As Ben drove north towards the first fault, he couldn't shake off the feeling of unease. It was unusual for there to be so many outages without any apparent cause. The seven mile-long journey seemed longer than usual, with his mind racing as usual through possible scenarios.

Arriving at the fault, Ben stepped out of his truck and surveyed the area. The line ran alongside the highway, its rugged terrain stretching into the distance. He could see the power lines overhead, their usual hum replaced by an eerie silence.

The desert breeze whispered past him, carrying with it the promise of another scorching day under the relentless sun. Despite the heat, Ben remained focused, his senses alert to any signs of trouble.

Suddenly, the stillness was broken as another company truck pulled up beside him. Ben glanced over, expecting to see a familiar face, but instead, he was met with the gaze of a stranger. The man, who Ben hadn't seen before, stepped out of the truck with purpose, his expression serious and determined.

"Morning," the stranger greeted, his voice carrying a note of urgency. "I'm Josh, from the regional office. We got reports of the outages and I've been sent to assist."

Ben nodded in acknowledgment, though he couldn't shake off a sense of wariness. He was accustomed to working alone or with his regular team and the sudden appearance of this newcomer added an element of uncertainty to the situation.

"Good to have you aboard, Josh," Ben replied, his tone guarded. "We've been dealing with a lot of outages lately, trying to figure out what's causing them."

Josh's eyes narrowed, his expression thoughtful. "Any theories?"

Ben shrugged, gesturing towards the fault line. "Could be anything, really. Faulty equipment, weather damage, you name it. But we won't know for sure until we investigate." Josh then told Ben he had some new cutting edge equipment and that's the reason he had been sent out here. Ben's eyebrows shot up in astonishment as Josh spoke. "New cutting edge equipment? I hadn't heard anything about that," Benexclaimed, his voice tinged with surprise. He glanced at Josh, a mix of curiosity and anticipation flickering in his eyes. "Well, that sounds promising. Let's see what this new gear can do."

Despite his initial scepticism, Ben couldn't help but feel a spark of excitement at the prospect of utilising new technology to tackle the ongoing outage. If Josh's equipment could indeed pinpoint the fault with precision, it would be a game-changer for their operation. Josh's question prompted Ben to pause and consider. "Well," he began slowly, "without this equipment, it could take us days, maybe even weeks to pinpoint the exact location of the fault. We'd have to rely on manual inspections, which can be time-consuming, especially in terrain like this."

Josh nodded thoughtfully. However, before Ben could continue, Josh interjected with a chuckle, his confidence evident in his tone.

"Ah, no need for that," Josh said, waving a hand dismissively. "With what I have here, we'll have that fault located in no time and that's good news because no chance of any helicopter assistance as they are busy all over the county."

Curiosity piqued, Ben leaned in, eager to hear more about the capabilities of Josh's equipment.

Josh grinned, as he explained, "You see, this new gear combines advanced sensors with real-time data analysis. It can detect even the slightest irregularities in the power grid and pinpoint their exact location with pinpoint accuracy. And the best part? It's all integrated into this portable unit," he gestured towards a sleek device mounted on the back of his truck, "so we can take it anywhere, no need for helicopters or guesswork."

Ben couldn't help but be impressed by Josh's confidence and the sophistication of the equipment he had brought. With a renewed sense of optimism, he nodded eagerly, ready to put Josh's gear to the test.

"Sounds like just what we need," Ben replied, a hint of excitement creeping into his voice. "Let's get to it then. Time to see what this cutting-edge equipment can do." Ben scanned the area with binoculars, Josh stood beside him, observing the landscape. Suddenly, Josh's expression lit up with excitement.

"No need for any approach to the broken line," Josh exclaimed confidently, pointing towards the nearest utility pole. "I can fix the issue from here."

Ben's eyebrows shot up in surprise. "Fix it from here?" he repeated incredulously, his laughter bubbling up at the thought. "You mean we don't have to trek all the way over there?"

Josh nodded, his grin widening. "That's right," he affirmed. "I just need to cut the cable right here on this nearest post and we'll have it sorted in no time."

Ben couldn't help but shake his head in disbelief, his laughter echoing through the air. "Well, I'll be damned," he chuckled, at the unexpected turn of events. "Who would've thought fixing a power line could be this easy?" To be honest Ben was beginning to grow tiresome of Josh's impossible suggestion. With a shake of his head, Ben finally voiced his growing doubts. "It's crazy, Josh. You just can't do it," he declared, his tone firm and resolute. The weight of scepticism coloured his words as he struggled to grasp the feasibility of Josh's plan. Despite their shared goal of restoring power, Ben couldn't help but feel wary of proceeding with what seemed like an implausible solution. Now Josh could see this doubt in Ben and this is what Josh had set out to do, it was now time to test Ben's patience. Josh looked at Ben and said "Right if I fix the line will you believe something I tell you after because you think fixing the line is impossible." Josh's response sparked a flicker of intrigue in Ben's mind. He studied Josh's face, searching for any hint of doubt or hesitation, but found none. There was a resolute determination in Josh's gaze that gave Ben pause.

"Alright," Ben replied, his voice tinged with a mix of scepticism and curiosity. "If you manage to fix the line from here, I'll be more inclined to believe what you have to say."

It was a bold challenge but Ben couldn't help but wonder what Josh had up his sleeve. If he could truly achieve the seemingly impossible task of repairing the line without physically reaching it, then perhaps there was more to Josh's capabilities than met the eye.

As they stood amidst the desert landscape, casting a sense of anticipation. Ben found himself eagerly awaiting Josh's next move, curious to see if he could deliver on his confident assertion.

With a determined glint in his eyes, Josh outlined his plan with a sense of assurance.

"Here's what we do," he began, his voice steady with confidence. "I'll climb the pole and cut the wire. Then, I'll insert the cut wire into this machine," he said, patting a sleek device attached to his belt, "and watch the magic happen."

As Josh spoke, he gestured towards the utility pole, indicating his intended destination. Ben's lingering doubt was very evident. "Wait a minute," Ben interjected, his voice tinged with uncertainty. "Are you sure cutting the wire is a good idea? I mean, won't that just make the problem worse?"

He gestured towards the utility pole, his gaze flickering between Josh and the wire in question. To Ben, it seemed counter-intuitive to deliberately sever a crucial component of the power line. He feared that such an action could potentially exacerbate the issue, leading to further complications and prolonging the outage.

"I get that you have this machine," Ben continued, his tone laced with scepticism, "but what if it doesn't work as you expect? We could end up causing more damage than we fix."

Ben's reluctance stemmed from a place of caution and practicality. As a lineman, he understood the importance of precision and careful consideration when dealing with electrical systems. The idea of haphazardly cutting the wire without a clear understanding of the consequences made him uneasy and he couldn't shake off his reservations despite Josh's confidence in his plan. Josh told Ben to go get himself a coffee. "Alright," Ben finally conceded, his tone still tinged with doubt. "I'll go get myself a coffee from the truck, but don't blame me if you make it a whole lot worse."

With a nod, Ben turned on his heel and headed towards his truck, parked nearby. As he retrieved a thermos of coffee from the back, his mind raced with conflicting thoughts. What if Josh's plan worked? What if it didn't?

As he made his way back to the utility pole, Ben's heart pounded with anticipation. He couldn't help but quicken his pace, eager to see if Josh had indeed managed to pull off the seemingly impossible task in his absence.

Sure enough, as Ben approached the pole, he saw Josh perched at the top, his silhouette outlined against the bright desert sky. With bated breath, Ben watched as Josh deftly cut the wire and lowered it to the ground below.

Moments later, Josh descended from the pole, a triumphant grin on his face as he held up the severed wire for Ben to see. "Told you I could do it," he exclaimed, his voice ringing with satisfaction.

With a mixture of curiosity and cautious optimism, Ben watched as Josh inserted the cut wire into the machine. Then the device hummed to life, Ben held his breath, waiting to see if Josh's bold gamble would pay off. Josh elaborated on his plan explaining what he was about to do, a sense of wonder filled Ben's mind. The concept of Nanites repairing the outage seemed straight out of a futuristic movie, yet Josh spoke of it with such confidence that Ben found himself captivated.

"So, these Nanites will not only pinpoint the outage, but they'll also repair any broken trailing wires?" Ben asked, his voice tinged with amazement.

Josh nodded, his smile widening. "Exactly," he confirmed. "If there's a broken wire at the outage site, the Nanites will detect it and spring into action. They'll leave the main line, traverse through the air and rebuild a new connection between the two lines and the amazing part is that the connection will be as if the line never broke."

Ben's eyes widened in disbelief. The implications of such technology were staggering. With the ability to repair power outages instantaneously, the Nanites had the potential to revolutionise the way they approached maintenance and repair work.

A chuckle escaped Josh's lips, his laughter echoing through the desert air. "I know it sounds like something out of a sci-fi movie," he admitted, "but trust me, it's very real."

Ben couldn't help but join in Josh's laughter, though a part of him still struggled to fully comprehend the magnitude of what Josh was proposing. Nevertheless, he found himself filled with a sense of excitement at the prospect of witnessing such advanced technology in action.

Josh watched as the machine hummed to life, releasing the Nanites into the line. The Nanites entered the line, a subtle transformation began to unfold. At first, there was nothing but a faint hum in the air, barely perceptible against the backdrop of the desert landscape. Then, slowly but surely, the line began to glow with a soft, pulsating red light.

Ben and Josh watched in awe as the glow intensified, casting an otherworldly hue over the surrounding terrain. It was as if the very air around them had been infused with energy, crackling with the promise of technological marvels.

Almost imperceptibly at first, the repair process began. The Nanites now worked with astonishing speed and precision, weaving their way along the length of the line with an almost hypnotic grace. The Nanites went to work, repairing and reinforcing with meticulous care.

As Ben and Josh looked on, they could hardly believe their eyes. In a matter of moments, what had once been a source of frustration and inconvenience was transformed into a beacon of light and power. The line, once broken and lifeless, now thrummed with vitality, pulsing with the energy of a thousand tiny machines working in perfect harmony.

It was a sight to behold, a testament to human ingenuity and the boundless potential of technology. The last of the Nanites completed their task and returned to the machine. Ben adjusted the focus of the binoculars, Ben's breath caught in his throat. What he saw left him utterly speechless. The wires, which had previously hung loose and fragmented, were now seamlessly connected, as if they had never been broken at all. It was as if the nanites had woven a web of light and energy, binding the line together with an almost magical precision.

For a moment, Ben could hardly believe his eyes. It was a sight beyond anything he could have imagined, a testament to the incredible capabilities of the Nanites and the ingenuity of their creators. Ben took in the scene before him, a sense of awe took over, filling him with a profound sense of reverence for the power of human innovation.

Turning to Josh, who stood beside him, Ben struggled to find the words to express what he was feeling. "Josh," he said finally, his voice barely above a whisper, "I don't know what to say. It's... it's incredible. I've never seen anything like it."

Josh grinned, his eyes sparkling with pride. "I told you we could do it," he replied, his voice tinged with satisfaction. "With the right technology and a little bit of imagination, anything is possible."

As they stood together, gazing out at the repaired line stretching into the distance, Ben couldn't help but feel a sense of optimism for the future. If they could harness the power of innovation in this way, there was no telling what wonders are around the corner. Preparing to return to their trucks and continue their work, Ben knew that he would carry this moment with him, a reminder of the boundless potential this meant.

Ben and Josh approached their separate trucks. Ben couldn't shake off the feeling that something important was about to be revealed. He glanced at Josh, whose expression was now serious, a stark contrast to the excitement they had shared moments before.

"Alright, Josh, what's going on?" Ben asked, his voice tinged with concern. He could sense something and a knot formed in the pit of his stomach as he waited for Josh's response.

Josh sighed, running a hand through his hair. "Ben, there's something I need to tell you," he began, his tone sombre. "It's about the power grid. The repairs we made today are just a temporary fix. The system is more fragile than we thought and it's on the verge of a complete meltdown."

Ben's mind raced with the implications of Josh's words. The thought of widespread power outages, of families left in the dark and businesses forced to shut down, filled him with a sense of dread as fear threatened to consume him.

"We have to do something, "Ben said, his voice firm with resolve. "We can't just stand by and let this happen can we? Can we find a way to fix the grid, no matter what it takes?"

Josh delved into some of the detail of the impending crisis, Ben's mind raced to grasp the concept of otherworldly influences. It was a revelation that shattered the boundaries of his understanding, plunging him into a realm of uncertainty and disbelief.

"So, you're saying that the meltdown isn't caused by anything we've done to the grid?" Ben asked, his voice tinged with incredulity. He struggled to reconcile this new information with his understanding of how the world worked.

Josh nodded gravely, his expression sombre. "That's right," he confirmed. "The source of the problem lies beyond our world. A force is exerting its influence on our power grid, causing it to destabilise."

The notion of forces from beyond their world meddling with the fabric of reality sent a shivers down Ben. It was a scenario straight out of a science fiction novel, yet here they were, confronting it head-on.

"But why would they target our power grid?" Ben asked, his mind reeling with questions. "What do they stand to gain from causing a meltdown?"

Josh shrugged, his expression troubled. "That's what we're still trying to figure out," he admitted. "But whatever their motives may be, one thing's for certain: if we don't act fast, the consequences could be catastrophic." Josh couldn't tell him the complete truth at this stage.

Ben absorbed Josh's words. It was clear that they were facing a threat unlike anything they had ever encountered before, one that transcended the boundaries of their understanding. What Josh said compounded it even further, Josh added, "The temperatures are predicted to drop dramatically soon."

This hit Ben like a punch to the gut. A sudden drop in temperatures could exacerbate the crisis, adding another layer of complexity to an already dire situation. But even as fear threatened to overwhelm him, he knew that they couldn't afford to give in to despair.

"We can't let them succeed," Ben said, his voice firm with resolve. "We have to find a way to stop who or whatever is causing this, before it's too late."

A low rumble echoed in the distance, gradually growing louder and more intense. He looked up just in time to witness a squadron of US Air Force jets streaking across the sky, their engines roaring with power as they blazed through the air at breakneck speed.

It was a sight to behold, but there was something about the jets that caught Ben's attention. They seemed to be flying with an urgency that he hadn't seen before. Their movements were sharp and precise, as if they had been scrambled in response to a critical threat.

In that moment, a surge of adrenaline shot through Ben's veins, sending his heart racing with a mixture of awe and trepidation. The sight of the jets thundering by filled him with a sense of urgency, their presence a stark reminder of an imminent danger they may be facing.

Time seemed to slow to a crawl as Ben watched the jets soar overhead, their sleek forms cutting through the air with precision and purpose. It was a breathtaking display of military might, a testament to the readiness of the armed forces to defend against any threat, no matter how formidable.

But beneath the awe-inspiring spectacle, a sense of unease gnawed at Ben's gut. The sight of the jets, scrambled and ready for action, served as a sobering reminder of the gravity of their situation. As the roar of the engines faded into the distance, Ben knew that they were running out of time to find a solution.

With a deep breath, Ben turned to Josh, his determination burning brighter than ever. "We have to act fast," he said, his voice tinged with urgency. "We can't afford to waste a single moment."

Josh told Ben the temperature would drop and Josh was deadly serious. "What do you mean, the temperature will drop?" Ben asked, his voice tinged with concern.

Josh's expression was grim as he replied, "I mean it will drop to dangerous levels, levels that will threaten the safety of everyone. You will need to act quickly to prevent a catastrophe."

Ben's mind raced with the implications of Josh's words. The thought of the temperature plummeting to such extreme levels filled him with a sense of dread.

"What do I need to do?" Ben asked, his voice barely above a whisper.

Josh's gaze bore into his, his expression serious. "You need to ring this phone number when the temperature drops dramatically," he said, handing Ben a slip of paper with a sequence of digits scrawled on it. "It's your only chance to avert disaster. Without your cooperation, there will be no future for you or your family."

Ben stared down at the phone number in his hand. This hit him like a ton of bricks and for a moment, he felt paralysed by the enormity of the instruction.

But as he looked up at Josh, a newfound determination flickered in his eyes. "I'll do it," he said, his voice firm with resolve. "I'll make the call."

Josh replied, "Good," Josh continued, "And when the time comes, you must have no room for hesitation. Because that time will come. Your family's lives will depend on your actions Ben."

"When you make that call," Josh added his voice breaking the silence, "You need to say I am heading for the ghost town and when the time does come, you'll need to keep your family and whoever friends you take under your wing safe, because you can't rely on the power grid."

Ben's mind raced as he processed Josh's words. The thought of facing such extreme conditions without the support of modern amenities was not a good feeling at all.

"You mean we'll be without power?" Ben asked, his voice trembling slightly.

Josh nodded solemnly. "That's right," he confirmed. "The situation is dire and we can't afford to take any chances. You'll need to prepare for the worst and ensure that your family has everything they need to weather the storm."

The reality of their predicament hit Ben hard. The thought of facing the impending crisis without the comforts of modern life filled him with a sense of unease. But as he looked into Josh's eyes, he saw a glimmer of determination that mirrored his own.

"I'll do whatever it takes to keep my family safe," Ben vowed, his voice steady despite the fear gnawing at his insides.

Josh nodded in approval, a sense of reassurance in his gaze. "That's the spirit," he said. "We're all in this together and together, we'll find a way to see it through."

Ben's heart clenched at the severity of Josh's words. The weight of the responsibility placed upon him felt almost suffocating. But in that moment, he knew that he had to trust Josh, to believe in the importance of the task he had been given.

"I understand," Ben said, his voice filled with determination. "I'll do whatever it takes to protect my family."

Josh placed a reassuring hand on Ben's shoulder, his gaze intense as he said, "Remember the Nanites. That's why I showed you today. You've been chosen, Ben and you must trust me like you've never trusted anyone before."

With those words echoing in his mind, Ben nodded, a sense of purpose burning within him. Though the road ahead would be fraught with danger and uncertainty, he knew that he couldn't afford to falter for the safety of his family.

"Take care, Ben," Josh said, his voice filled with a mix of concern and resolve. "And remember, when the time comes, you know what you need to do."

Ben nodded, a steely determination in his gaze. "I won't let you down," he replied, his voice firm with conviction. "Thank you, Josh."

With a final nod of acknowledgment, the two men parted ways, each heading back to their respective trucks. Ben climbed into the driver's seat, he couldn't shake off the sense of responsibility he was faced with. But he also felt a glimmer of hope, knowing that he wasn't alone in this fight.

The engine started up and Ben started to move off casting one last glance back at Josh, a silent vow passing between them. Ben somehow felt this wasn't the last he would see of Josh.

Ben navigated the familiar desert roads on his way home, his mind was consumed with thoughts of the daunting task. The weight of Josh's words were still ringing in his ears.

The sun dipped below the horizon, but Ben's thoughts remained focused on the impending crisis. With each passing mile, he couldn't shake off the feeling of urgency that gnawed at his insides.

As he neared his home, the familiar sight of the small house nestled among the desert dunes brought a sense of comfort amidst the turmoil of his thoughts. He parked the truck and made his way inside, greeted by the warmth of his family waiting for him.

"Ben, you're home!" Olivia exclaimed, her voice filled with relief as she rushed to greet him with a tight embrace.

Ben held her close, drawing strength from her presence. "I'm here," he whispered, his voice full of emotion.

Their baby cooed softly in Olivia's arms, blissfully unaware what was to come but for the moment Ben allowed himself to bask in the simple joy of being with his family, the worries of the world fading into the background.

Gently kissing his family goodnight, Ben whispered a silent vow to protect them at all costs. With determination burning bright within him, he steeled himself for the challenges, knowing that the fate of his loved ones depended on his actions.

Ben's thoughts drifted to the phone number Josh had given him, a lifeline in the face of uncertainty. With a deep breath, he closed his eyes, ready to face whatever tomorrow would bring, knowing that he wasn't alone in this fight.

Chapter 11

ROAD TO HAWTHORNE

Meanwhile back in Sanctuary had seen Dodger's safe return with Jim and Barbara from that treacherous rescue mission, now within the confines of the base, a sense of calm had settled. The tension that had gripped them during their harrowing ordeal had dissipated, replaced by an atmosphere of relief and gratitude for their survival.

Jim and Barbara, their faces still marked with traces of fatigue from their exertions sat side by side, recounting the events of the rescue mission with a mixture of solemnity and humour. Despite the what they had faced, there was a newfound lightness in knowing they could achieve something like that a testament to their resilience in the face of adversity.

For Jessica, the experience had left her with a heightened sense of awareness and a newfound appreciation for the fragility of life. Throughout the day, Jessica found herself seeking out moments of quiet reflection, taking solace in the familiar routines of daily life. Whether it was instructing AI to get meals for everyone or engaging in light-hearted conversation with the others, she found comfort with her companions, grateful for their unwavering support and companionship.

Meanwhile, Clio approached the day with a quiet determination, her thoughts always searching for answers as she went about her tasks. She found herself drawn to the intricate workings of the base's systems or the better name for the base, Sanctuary and eager to learn more about their operation and functionality.

Dodger hummed softly in standby mode and everyone decided to venture out for a walk, reflecting the serene beauty of their surroundings. Clio and Jessica, drawn to the tranquil stream that meandered nearby, made their way back to its banks, eager to immerse themselves in the peaceful ambiance.

As they walked, the gentle rustle of leaves and the soothing sound of flowing water filled the air, creating a sense of calm and serenity. The sunlight filtered through the canopy above, casting dappled shadows on the forest floor and lending an ethereal quality to the scene.

Clio and Jessica walked in companionable silence, each lost in their own thoughts as they absorbed the sights and sounds of nature around them. The stream sparkled in the sunlight, its waters shimmering with reflected light as it danced over smooth stones and pebbles.

Occasionally, they would pause to admire a particularly scenic spot or to listen to the melodious chirping of birds perched in the nearby trees. For Clio and Jessica, the tranquillity of the stream offered a welcome respite, allowing them to find peace and clarity amidst the chaos of their recent experiences.

As they reached a secluded clearing by the stream, Clio and Jessica found a comfortable spot to sit and rest, their minds quiet and their hearts full. They sat in silence for a while, simply enjoying the beauty of the natural world around them, grateful for the opportunity to connect with each other and with the earth.

In that moment, surrounded by the gentle murmur of the stream and the whisper of the wind through the trees, Clio and Jessica found a sense of peace and contentment that washed over them like a warm embrace. And as they sat together, basking in the beauty of the moment, they knew that they were exactly where they were meant to be.

Jake, Dot, Jim and Barbara joined Jessica and Clio at the stream. They gathered by the water's edge, their footsteps soft against the forest floor.

Exchanging smiles, bonds were being forged. Jake and Dot, grateful for the support and assistance they had received, expressed their heartfelt appreciation to Jim and Barbara with Jessica and Clio listening intently.

With that Dave and Zeena arrived, everyone turned their attention to them, eager to hear the latest developments. There was a mixture of anticipation and concern etched on their faces as they awaited the news.

Dave spoke first, his voice grave yet determined. "We've made some significant discoveries we now have proof that oxygen is being depleted from Earth's atmosphere at an alarming rate."

Apprehension gripped all present. Zeena nodded in agreement, her expression mirroring Dave's seriousness. "And what's more," she added, "our investigations have revealed that this depletion is not a natural occurrence. It's being orchestrated by something... or someone... that is neither of Earth nor from Earth." The implications of such a revelation were profound. Sparking a whirlwind of questions and concerns in their minds.

"How is this possible?" Barbara asked, her voice barely above a whisper, her eyes wide with disbelief.

Dave replied, his tone measured yet resolute. "We're still piecing together the puzzle," he explained, "but it's clear that we're facing a threat unlike anything we've ever encountered before."

Every single one of them fell silent they struggled with something unbelievable.

Zeena had delved deeper into their analysis, Zeena's hypothesis shed new light on the unfolding crisis. She started by saying.

"It's becoming increasingly apparent that the depletion of oxygen from Earth's atmosphere is not just a random occurrence," Zeena began, her tone grave yet resolute. "Rather, it appears to be a deliberate attempt to neutralise our weapons systems."Zeena elaborated on her findings. Jake and Dot exchanged worried glances, the implications of Zeena's words sinking in.

Zeena continued, her voice steady despite the weight of her revelation. "We've received reports of our fighter jets engaging with unidentified craft over the Atlantic," she explained. "But what's troubling is that the oxygen levels are starting to affect the jets' performance, putting our pilots at risk."

Her words casting a deep shadow over the moment, the magnitude of the threat becoming increasingly clear with each passing moment.

Dave made an announcement about a call for help from someone called Henry this sent ripples of concern through Jim and Barbara because of what they had already been through. He carried on to tell them that one of our associates Rick had triggered this phone call. They exchanged anxious glances, their minds racing with questions and uncertainties. Who was Henry? What kind of trouble was he in? And who was Rick?

"Who's Rick?" Jessica asked, her voice betraying a hint of nervousness.

Dave offered a reassuring smile. "Rick is one of us," he explained calmly. "He's a trusted ally, someone who's been working with us for a while now. If he's directing Henry to us, it means he trusts us to handle the situation and that he trusts Henry."

His explanation seemed to alleviate some of the tension in the room, but the sense of urgency remained palpable as Dave continued to outline the details of Henry's distress call.

"Henry said he and his wife are in need of help," Dave explained, his expression grave. "They're stranded and facing imminent danger and we're their only hope."

"I think Jessica and Clio should take Dodger to implement the rescue," he suggested, his gaze shifting between the two women. "As the previous mission Dodger's advanced capabilities make it the ideal vehicle for this mission and I trust both of you to handle it with caution and efficiency."

The proposal prompted a flurry of reactions among the group – a mix of apprehension and determination as they grappled with the enormity of the task ahead. Jessica's eyes sparkled with a determined glint as she absorbed Dave's briefing, she squared her shoulders and met Dave's gaze.

"Let's kick some butt," she declared, her voice tinged with conviction.

Her words resonated with a fiery determination that echoed throughout the room. Jessica's spirited declaration elicited a ripple of friendly laughter from all present, breaking the tension. Her bold words injected a moment of levity, drawing smiles from her companions.

"Leave it to Jessica to keep our spirits high," Jim remarked with a chuckle, casting a warm glance in her direction and he walked swiftly over and hugged her. Then Jim made a prompted and thoughtful pause from Dave as he considered the best course of action. Recognising the importance of ensuring Clio and Jessica's safety, advising Dave that all tools needed to be issued and Dave nodded in agreement.

"You make a valid point, Jim," Dave acknowledged. "Given the circumstances, it's only prudent to equip them with additional tools for their protection."

Dave nodded solemnly, acknowledging the necessity of equipping Clio and Jessica with Vendor after the harrowing ordeal that Jim, Barbara, Dot and Jake had endured. The memory of their recent challenges weighed heavily on everyone's minds, serving as a stark reminder of the dangers.

"Agreed," Dave affirmed, his voice tinged with gravity. "Given recent events, it's clear that Vendor will provide an extra layer of protection for Clio and Jessica as they embark on their mission." It was a decision that would prove crucial.

Dave made a mental note to prioritise the issuance of Vendor to ensure the safety and security of all. Despite the inherent risks involved, he remained steadfast in his commitment to supporting Clio and Jessica as they ventured into the unknown.

With Vendor at their disposal, Clio and Jessica would be better equipped to face whatever challenges they could face, their safety entrusted to the advanced technology that the current timeline could only imagine. Dave and Zeena took the time to meticulously explain the workings of Shield, Bender and Vendor to Clio and Jessica, ensuring they had a thorough understanding of each tool's capabilities and functions.

"Let's start with Shield," Dave began, gesturing to a holographic display that materialized before them. "Shield is a defensive mechanism designed to create a protective barrier between you and any hostile. It operates on a sophisticated energy field that can deflect incoming projectiles and provide a safe zone in hostile environments."

Zeena chimed in, adding further clarification. "When activated, Shield forms a translucent barrier in front of you withstanding various types of attacks. It's crucial to remember that Shield requires energy to maintain its integrity, so use it judiciously."

Moving on to Bender, Dave continued the explanation. "Bender is a versatile tool that manipulates sound waves to deceive and distract adversaries. By emitting controlled sound frequencies, Bender can alter the perception of your voice's location, allowing you to confuse and misdirect your enemies, this was used recently with great effect by Jim."

Zeena nodded in agreement. "With Bender, you have the ability to project your voice to specific locations, creating diversions or sending distress signals as needed. Just remember to speak clearly and concisely to maximise its effectiveness."

Vendor is quite simple just aim at the target press the button and everyone you have aim at within 100 feet will no longer exist.

Dave: "Alright, Clio and Jessica, thank you for joining us for the briefing. We have an important mission ahead and your skills will be crucial. Zeena and I will provide you with all the necessary details."

Zeena, "Yes, absolutely. So, we've received a distress call from Henry and his wife in Stagecoach, Nevada. They're in urgent need of assistance and they have reached out to us for help."

Clio, "Stagecoach? Where exactly is that and what's the situation like there?"

Zeena, "Stagecoach is a small town in Nevada, known for its rugged terrain and harsh climate. It's quite remote and the weather can be unpredictable. Henry and his wife are stranded in their home and we need to get to them as soon as possible."

Jessica, "What happened to them? Do we know why they need help?"

Dave, "Before we proceed further, there's something important I want to share with you both. The distress call we received from Henry was prompted by someone named Rick who we briefly discussed earlier. He instructed them to contact us if the temperature dropped dramatically and they were to mention his name, which they did."

Zeena, "Yes, that's correct. Rick is someone we've worked with before and he's provided valuable information in the past."

Clio, "So, you're saying there could be additional factors or complications we need to be aware of?"

Dave, "Exactly. We can't be certain of the full extent of the situation until we arrive on the scene and assess it first hand. Rick's involvement indicates that there may be other individuals or elements involved in this scenario, there could be relatives or friends."

Jessica, "So, we need to be prepared for anything."

Barbara, "That's right stay vigilant and adaptable, ready to handle whatever challenges may arise."

Jim "Remember, you have our full support and resources at your disposal. If there's anything you need or if the situation escalates, don't hesitate to reach out to us."

Dave, "Indeed! Your safety and the success of this mission are our top priorities. Just stay focused, trust your instincts." Clio and Jessica absorb the information, understanding the importance of Rick's involvement and the potential complexity of the rescue mission ahead. They feel a renewed sense of determination and readiness.

As the next morning dawned, Jessica and Clio stepped on board the Dodger, their hearts filled with determination and a sense of purpose. The air was charged with anticipation as they prepared themselves mentally for the mission ahead. Stepping onto the sleek craft, they were greeted by the familiar hum of its engines and the reassuring presence of AI.

Inside Dodger, Jessica and Clio took their seats, their minds buzzing with thoughts of the impending rescue mission. They checked their equipment meticulously, ensuring that everything was in place for the journey ahead. Inside Dodger, the artificial intelligence also known as Dave greeted Jessica and Clio with his usual calm and reassuring voice. "Good morning, Jessica and Clio," he began. "I trust you're both ready for the mission ahead."

Jessica and Clio nodded in unison, their expressions reflecting a mixture of determination and anticipation. "Absolutely, Dave," Jessica replied, her voice tinged with confidence. "We're ready to do whatever it takes to help those in need."

Dave's virtual presence emanated a sense of reassurance as he continued, "Excellent. You both have been briefed on the mission parameters and the area you'll be heading to. Stagecoach, Nevada, awaits and I have every confidence that you'll handle the situation with skill and determination."

Clio, ever the cautious one, spoke up, "Dave, do you have any additional information about the situation on the ground? Anything we should be aware of before we arrive?"

Dave paused for a moment before responding, "As far as we know, the situation is urgent but relatively straightforward. However, as with any rescue mission, there may be unforeseen challenges that arise. Remain vigilant and rely on your training and instincts."

Jessica nodded, her resolve unwavering. "We'll be sure to stay alert and adapt to whatever comes our way," she affirmed.

Dodger came to life and within minutes was plugging a path through the solid rock. Dodger emerged from the rocky terrain, Jessica and Clio were greeted by a stark landscape that stretched before them, reminiscent of the Arctic wastelands. The sudden transition from the confines of the spacecraft to the harsh reality of the frozen terrain took them both by surprise.

Dodger navigated through the frozen landscape, Jessica and Clio watched in awe as the scenery shifted around them. The rugged terrain gave way to wide expanses of snow-covered plains, with occasional clusters of trees dotting the landscape. Despite the desolation of the surroundings, there was a strange beauty to the icy wilderness.

Inside Dodger, AI provided updates on their progress, guiding them toward their destination with precision. As they neared their destination, Jessica and Clio readied themselves with a mixture of excitement and trepidation clearly reflected in their eyes. The prospect of finally reaching their destination filled them with a sense of urgency, knowing that Henry and Margaret were counting on them for their rescue.

As Dodger travelled towards its destination, its advanced AI suddenly issued a loud warning, startling both Jessica and Clio.

"Powering down! Going into stealth mode. Danger detected. Must power down," the AI announced urgently, its voice echoing through the cabin.

Jessica and Clio exchanged worried glances, a sense of apprehension creeping over them. They knew that a warning from Dodger's AI meant that there was imminent danger ahead.

Frantically, they looked around, searching for any signs of trouble outside through the vehicle's windows. The landscape outside seemed eerily calm, but the AI's warning was enough to put them on high alert.

With a series of mechanical whirrs and clicks, Dodger's systems began to power down further, plunging the cabin into temporary darkness. The only sound that remained was the faint hum of the vehicle's engines as it slowed to a stop.

Jessica's heart raced as she gripped the edge of her seat, her mind racing with questions. What danger lay ahead? And how would they navigate through it without Dodger's protection?

Clio's expression mirroring her friend. Despite the uncertainty, they both knew that they would need to stay calm and focused if they were to make it through whatever was out there. Then the silence was broken "Detected: alien ship in the vicinity," the AI announced quietly, its words sending a shiver down Jessica and Clio.

The realisation hit them like a ton of bricks. Alien presence? In this remote, desolate landscape here on Earth? It was a scenario straight out of a sci-fi movie, yet here they were, facing it head-on.

Fear tightened Jessica's chest as she exchanged a glance with Clio. The thought of encountering an alien ship filled them with dread. Then the hum of an approaching craft filled the air. The sound seemed to reverberate through Dodger's cabin, creating an unsettling atmosphere.

"Stay calm," Jessica whispered, her voice barely audible over the thrum of the engines. Clio nodded, her expression mirroring Jessica's fearful face.

The craft drew nearer, its presence looming ominously outside Dodger's concealed exterior. Despite the fear pulsing through their veins, Jessica and Clio remained as still as statues, their senses heightened, awaiting the next move.

Inside Dodger's confines, the tension was palpable. Every heartbeat seemed to echo in the enclosed space as they braced themselves for whatever would come next. With each passing moment, the anticipation grew, the unknown threat outside becoming more with each passing second.

A green beam emanated from the alien craft, Jessica and Clio exchanged worried looks, their hearts pounding with trepidation. The beam swept across the landscape, illuminating the barren snow swept terrain outside.

Inside the cabin, the green light filtered through the windows, casting eerie shadows across the interior. Jessica and Clio held their breath, their eyes fixed on the source of the beam, their minds racing with questions.

Outside, the alien craft continued its search, the green beam slicing through the darkness with precision. With each pass, Jessica and Clio braced themselves, their nerves on edge as they awaited the inevitable.

Then the green beam vanished and the alien craft moved off into the distance, a heavy silence enveloped Dodger's cabin. Jessica and Clio exchanged relieved glances, their tense muscles gradually relaxing as the immediate threat dissipated.

"That was... intense," Jessica muttered, her voice still quivering with the remnants of fear.

Clio nodded, her eyes wide with awe. "I've never seen anything like it," she admitted, her voice barely above a whisper.

Inside Dodger, the air hung heavy with the weight of the encounter.

The AI's voice cut through the tense silence, its words bringing a measure of relief to the cabin. "All systems clear," it announced, its tone calm and reassuring. "Scans indicate that the alien craft contains human DNA, likely abducted individuals."

Jessica repeated what she heard, her voice tinged with concern. "What do you mean, abducted?"

"It appears that the individuals on board the alien craft were humans who have been taken against their will," the AI explained, it's human like voice, a voice devoid of emotion. "Their presence suggests that it is too late for them, they are beyond help. I can only detect Human DNA but no sign of life."

Jessica echoed, her voice tinged with disbelief and sorrow. "What do you mean? Can't we do something?"

"I'm afraid not," the AI replied, its tone seemed regretful. "The conditions on board the alien craft are beyond Dodgers capability to assist. It appears that the humans on board have been subjected to conditions that are incompatible with human life and are being prepared."

Clio's heart sank at the grim assessment. "So there's nothing we can do for them?" she asked, her voice barely above a whisper.

"I'm sorry," the AI replied, its voice filled with genuine regret. The AI's revelation sent a shiver down Jessica and Clio's spines, a chilling reminder of the dire circumstances surrounding their mission.

"Prepared for what?" Jessica asked, her voice barely audible over the hum of Dodger's engines.

"I'm unable to find the exact purpose," the AI replied, its voice tinged with a hint of unease. "But it appears that the humans on board were subjected to invasive procedures, likely for purposes beyond our comprehension."

Clio's stomach churned at the thought of such horrors befalling innocent people. "This is beyond cruel," she murmured, her voice trembling with indignation. "We have to do something."

"We will," Jessica vowed, her jaw set with determination. "We'll find Henry and Margaret and we'll put an end to whatever atrocities are being committed."

Then there was an almighty explosion and seemed to come from the Hawthorn area that they had recently passed.

The AI immediately initiated a comprehensive scan of the Hawthorn area to ascertain the cause of the explosion. After a tense moment of silence, it relayed its findings to Jessica and Clio.

"It appears to be a detonation of significant magnitude," the AI reported, "The explosion has caused extensive damage to the surrounding area and there are indications of residual energy signatures consistent with advanced weaponry, Hawthorne is completely destroyed."

Jessica's tried to process the AI's analysis. "Could it be related to the alien craft we encountered earlier?" she wondered aloud, her mind racing with possibilities.

"It's a distinct possibility," Clio replied, . "But we won't know for sure until AI investigates further."

As the news of the devastation in Hawthorne sank in, Jessica and Clio exchanged worried glances before turning their attention back to the AI, their minds racing with questions.

"What do you mean, completely destroyed?" Jessica asked, her voice laced with concern. "How could one explosion cause that much damage?"

Clio nodded in agreement saying, "And what about the people there? Are there any survivors?" she pressed, her voice trembling slightly with apprehension.

The AI responded, relaying the information it had gathered with precision. "The explosion was of significant magnitude, resulting in widespread destruction of structures and infrastructure in the area. As for survivors, the scan indicates minimal chances of any individuals having survived the blast."

Jessica's heart sank at the AI's grim assessment, her mind reeling with the implications of such devastation. "But why would the alien craft target Hawthorne?" she mused aloud, her thoughts turning to the possible motives behind the attack.

Clio's expression mirrored Jessica's concern as she voiced her own questions. "Is there any indication of what the aliens are after? Or what they hope to achieve by causing such destruction?" she asked, her voice tinged with a mix of fear and curiosity.

The AI paused for a moment, processing the inquiries before responding with its usual precision. "At this time, I am unable to provide conclusive answers to your questions. However, based on available data, it appears that the aliens are employing advanced weaponry with the intent of achieving their objectives, which remain unclear at this time." Jessica and Clio exchanged troubled looks, their minds racing with the gravity of what just happened. With Hawthorne destroyed and the aliens still around, they knew that their mission had taken on even greater urgency.

The AI's response was solemn, confirming their worst fears with clinical precision. "Walker Lake is still there however no signs of human life detected within a radius of approximately ten miles from the Hawthorne area was the target."

Jessica's breath caught in her throat at the AI's grim assessment, the implications of such widespread devastation, , "But why would the aliens target Hawthorne?" Her voice was tinged with frustration and fear. "And what about the people who lived there? What happened to them?"

Clio's expression mirrored Jessica's concern as she voiced her own questions. "Is there any indication of further damage or potential threats in the area?" Her voice trembled with apprehension as she awaited the AI's response.

AI paused for a moment, processing the inquiries before responding.

"At this time, there is no additional data available regarding the extent of the damage or the fate of the residents. However, based on the observed destruction it appears that the aliens are employing highly destructive methods to achieve their objectives."

Jessica and Clio's hearts sank. With each new report of destruction and now they knew that their mission to Stagecoach had taken on even greater urgency. As Dodger pressed on toward Stagecoach, the landscape around them grew increasingly desolate, the barren terrain stretching out in all directions like a vast, empty canvas. Then from nowhere there was another deafening explosion shattering the eerie silence, reverberating through the air like a thunderclap.

Suddenly, the sky overhead was illuminated with a blinding, fiery orange glow, casting shadows across the barren landscape below. The bright flash of light bathed everything in its path, painting the world in hues of crimson and gold, as if the very fabric of reality had been torn asunder.

Jessica and Clio gasped in astonishment as they watched the dazzling display unfold before them, their eyes wide with awe and fear. The brilliance of the explosion was mesmerising yet terrifying, a reminder of the destructive power that now threatened the world. Dodger continued its journey toward Stagecoach, the tranquillity of the night was shattered by a sudden and deafening explosion. The sky erupted into a brilliant display of orange and red hues as a massive blast illuminated the darkness, casting eerie shadows across the landscape.

AI shouted an instruction to activate shields full power. The shock wave from the explosion rippled through the air and rattling the atmosphere around Dodger and sending vibrations reverberating throughout. Both the girls were jolted from their seats as they struggled to comprehend the magnitude of the blast. Had AI not instructed for the shields to be activated there is no doubt they may not have survived.

The once peaceful night was now engulfed in chaos and destruction, as the force of the explosion swept across the land, leaving devastation in its wake. Trees were uprooted, buildings reduced to rubble and the very earth seemed to tremble beneath their feet.

Then another brilliant flash of light illuminated the southern horizon turning night to day, followed by a deafening grumbling explosion that shook the very foundation of the landscape. The sky erupted into a fiery inferno as plumes of smoke billowed into the air, casting a haunting glow over the once vibrant cityscape of Las Vegas. Both watched in stunned disbelief. Then another shock wave even stronger hit them forcing Dodger to momentarily come to a halt but luckily the shields held firm. It took what seemed like ages for everything to settle down and then AI instructed that we should proceed with caution.

The journey continued, leaving behind debris everywhere and the further they went there was more proof of the blast behind them, just a return to the Arctic landscape as before.

Dodger was now approaching Stagecoach, Jessica and Clio prepared themselves for harsh conditions outside. They donned their protective suits, the fabric clinging snugly to their bodies and providing a barrier against the biting cold outside. Both were still shaking about what happened earlier.

The suits, designed to withstand extreme temperatures and provide ample insulation and warmth, offered a sense of security as they prepared to venture out into the frigid landscape. Jessica adjusted her helmet, ensuring a tight seal to protect her from the freezing air, while Clio checked the seals on her gloves, making sure there were no gaps for the cold to seep in.

With their suits fully secured, they exchanged a nod of determination. They stopped just short of Stagecoach, upon stepping out of Dodger, they were greeted by a blast of icy wind, but their suits held strong, shielding them from the worst of the cold. All weapons and the device to track their way back was now on their person. Clio remembered Jim's warning in which he said he had made an error previously and that he had walked many yards before pressing Dodgers position into the the device and therefore on his return he couldn't find it. Remember Jim had stated that Dodger will not appear until you are practically on top of it and the device has to be on your person. Clio entered the positional reading into the device. They moved off and with each step they took away from Dodger the vehicle had started to shimmer and fade, gradually disappearing from view. Jessica's eyes widened in astonishment as she watched Dodger vanish before her eyes, emitting a soft gasp of amazement.

"It's like something out of a sci-fi movie," Jessica exclaimed, her voice filled with wonder.

Clio smiled at her friend's reaction, equally amazed by the sight. "Isn't it incredible and yes we are in that sci-fi movie?" she replied, her tone tinged with excitement.

With Dodger now concealed from view, they turned their attention back to the task at hand, their focus squarely on reaching Stagecoach and assisting those in need. Though the disappearance of Dodger was a remarkable sight, they knew that their priority lay in the rescue mission, as they continued on their journey, the memory of Dodger's vanishing act lingered in their minds, a testament to the extraordinary technology at their disposal.

Clio's voice carried a note of concern as she pointed out the sparse and seemingly deserted houses that they had passed during their search for Henry's location. Her instincts sharpened by the desolate surroundings, she took the lead, her gaze scanning the landscape for any sign of life amidst the eerie silence. They were now half a mile away from Dodger and getting close to Henry's house, Clio's apprehension grew palpable. The coordinates indicated their proximity to their destination, yet the absence of any activity or signs of habitation left her feeling uneasy. Each empty house they passed served as a stark reminder of the isolation and uncertainty that surrounded them. Despite her apprehension, Clio remained determined to locate Henry and Margaret.

Clio's voice was barely above a whisper as she relayed the information from the device. "Here," she said softly, her breath momentarily misting her helmet . "The device indicates that this is Henry's house, right here as we join David Street, it's this grey painted house here." Jessica nodded, her eyes scanning the surroundings for any signs of activity. The confirmation of their arrival at Henry's location filled them with a mixture of relief and trepidation. They exchanged a glance, silently preparing themselves for whatever awaited them as they approached Henry's house on David Street.

The tension thickened as the unmistakable sound of guns being cocked echoed through the crisp air. Jessica and Clio froze in their tracks, exchanging worried glances.

The voice boomed out, commanding authority and instilling fear in Jessica and Clio. "Don't move or we will open fire!" it warned, its tone menacing and decisive. "Dressed like that, you cannot be human. But whatever you are, one move and we fire!"

Jessica stepped forward, her voice steady despite the tension. "We've come to help Henry. Are you Henry?" she asked, her tone conveying both determination and concern. The figure before them shifted slightly, his posture rigid and defensive. "No, I ain't," he replied tersely, his voice tinged with suspicion and wariness. His gaze darted between Jessica and Clio, assessing them with a mix of curiosity and apprehension. Jessica's brows furrowed slightly as she tried to gauge his reaction. "Do you know where Henry is?" she pressed, her voice softer now, attempting to convey empathy and understanding. The man remained guarded, his expression unreadable as he studied the two strangers before him. "Maybe I do, maybe I don't," he replied cryptically, his tone guarded and evasive.

Clio stepped forward, her voice calm and reassuring. "We're not here to cause trouble. We just want to help," she interjected, hoping to ease the tension and establish a sense of trust. The man's eyes narrowed slightly, his gaze flickering between them as if searching for any sign of deception. "Help, huh? ain't nobody come here to help us," he muttered, his tone tinged with bitterness and resignation. Jessica's shoulders sagged slightly, frustration mingling with determination in her voice. "We're here to help," she insisted, her words firm and resolute as she locked eyes with the man, silently urging him to trust them. The man hesitated, uncertainty flickering across his features as he weighed their words. After a tense moment, he finally nodded, albeit reluctantly. "Alright, follow me," he said gruffly, his voice betraying a hint of cautious optimism as he turned and gestured for them to follow him.

There was tension in the air both girls could feel it. Then as they approached another man stepped forward, his presence commanding as he sought clarification. "Who sent you? And who gave me the number to call? Was it Brandon, Geoffrey, or Rick?" he questioned, his tone laced with suspicion and urgency. Clio's response was poised and assertive, cutting through the uncertainty with unwavering confidence. "Rick," she replied firmly, her words ringing out with clarity and conviction, echoing in the dimly lit street a voice of certainty amidst the uncertainty.

Henry forcefully gave a like a tidal wave answer as he exclaimed, "Thank God!" With an immediate gesture of welcome, he ushered Jessica and Clio indoors, his attitude shifting from suspicion to gratitude. As they stepped across the threshold of the battered walls caused by the shock wave, Henry offered a heartfelt apology for doubting them, his words tinged with sincerity and a sense of relief that they had finally arrived to lend their assistance.

Henry's concern was palpable as he questioned, "How can you two girls help us?" He recounted witnessing people being abducted by a green beam of light from across the street, his voice laden with fear and urgency. As he continued he revealed the devastating news that Las Vegas had been obliterated, expressing his shock at feeling the reverberations of the cataclysmic event.

Jessica's response was firm yet reassuring as she confidently replied, "We're here to help, Henry. We'll find a way to keep you safe. "Henry's questions followed quickly, "But how? Where can we go? What can you do?"

Clio's voice echoed with concern as she asked, "How many of you are there? And where is Margaret?"

Henry's expression tensed slightly before he responded, "Margaret and about thirty trusted friends are hiding in the cellar."

Jessica's eyes widened at the revelation, "Thirty? That's a lot of people."

The other man introduced himself as Mike who swiftly apologised for the initial greeting he had given and interjected. "Yeah, we've been trying to keep everyone safe, but with everything happening, it's been hard."Henry nodded in agreement, "We thought we were safe out here, but now... I don't know what to do." Clio reassured them, "We'll do whatever we can to help. But first, let's get everyone together and figure out the plan we have in place."

Margaret and the thirty other people climbed from the cellar, the scene was one of cautious hope mixed with apprehension. Their faces, illuminated by the dim light filtering in from the entrance, showed signs of weariness and fear, yet also a glimmer of relief at the prospect of emerging from their hiding place. Some leaned on each other for support, while others held onto makeshift belongings hastily gathered before seeking refuge underground. Their collective gaze turned towards Jessica, Clio and Henry, their expressions silently pleading for reassurance and guidance in the face of uncertainty.

Clio, taking command of the situation, addressed the group with a sense of urgency. "We believe aliens are responsible for what's happening and if we stay here, we'll all be in danger. It's incredibly cold outside and we have to act fast. It seems we have fifteen women, ten children and only five men," she stated, her tone conveying both concern and determination.

Henry nodded in agreement adding, "Most men just seem to be vanishing, even some women too."

Jessica emphasised the importance of dressing warmly, stating, "We need to bundle up like we've never bundled up before because of the intense cold. And we have to walk silently in separate groups. There will have to be six groups of five spaced out so that if we are attacked, not all of us will be in danger." Her practical approach to the situation highlighted the necessity for caution and preparation amidst the perilous conditions they faced.

Jessica decided it was best to outline the plan, there was a mixture of murmurs and shuffling among the people present. Some exchanged worried glances, while others nodded in agreement with Jessica's strategy. Margaret, Henry and the others listened intently, their expressions reflecting a combination of fear and determination.

Henry's voice rose above the murmurs as he addressed the group, "Listen up, everyone. These girls seem to know what they're talking about. We've got to stick together and follow their lead if we want to make it out of this alive!"

Margaret, with a tone of urgency in her voice, added, "We've seen what those aliens are capable of. We can't afford to stay here and wait for them to come back. We need to trust Jessica and Clio's plan."

Meanwhile, children whispered to each other nervously, their eyes wide with apprehension at the thought of venturing out into the cold darkness. The men exchanged silent nods, silently preparing themselves for the challenges ahead.

Amidst the commotion, Jessica's voice cut through the noise, firm and resolute. "We'll form the groups now and distribute as much clothing that can be found. Remember, stay quiet and stay together. We can do this."

With Jessica's guidance, they began to organise themselves into smaller clusters, each person bundling up in layers of clothing to brave the freezing temperatures outside.

Amidst the preparations and discussions, the sound of muffled sobs could be heard from some of the women and children. Tears streamed down their faces as they grappled with the fear and uncertainty of the situation. Despite their efforts to stay composed, the overwhelming sense of danger and the unknown was too much.

Clio, recognising the distress among them, approached them with a comforting demeanour. She knelt down beside a weeping woman and child, offering words of reassurance and gentle touches to comfort them. "It's okay to be scared," she whispered softly. "But we're all in this together and we'll do everything we can to keep each other safe."

Jessica, too, acknowledged their fears, her voice filled with empathy. "We understand how frightening this must be," she said, her tone calm yet determined. "But we won't let anything happen to you. We'll stick together and we'll get through this please trust us."

Slowly, the tears began to subside, replaced by a sense of determination and solidarity. With Clio and Jessica's comforting words and steady guidance, the women and children found the strength to face the daunting journey ahead, knowing they were not alone in their fears.

The atmosphere inside the dimly lit room grew tense as Clio issued her instructions. She emphasised the need for stealth and caution, urging everyone to turn off any torches that could give away their position. She told them its going to extremely cold and dark but we have a device that will guide us.

Clio outlined the plan, her voice carried a sense of authority tempered with concern for everyone's safety. "Make sure torches will only be used in an emergency," she instructed firmly, her words punctuated by the quiet shuffling of feet as people complied.

Henry, his expression reflecting a mixture of apprehension and resolve, nodded in understanding. "I'll go first with the first group of five," he affirmed, his tone determined. He recognised the importance of leading by example, willing to take on the initial risk to protect the others.

Clio nodded in agreement, acknowledging Henry's willingness to lead the way. She cast a quick glance toward Jessica, who stood ready at the rear of the assembled people, her posture reflecting a steely resolve despite the circumstances. Clio sought confirmation from her, ensuring that she had all the necessary weapons for their journey.

Jessica's nod was resolute, her grip firm on the weapons at her side. She exuded a quiet confidence, ready to carry out was was necessary in safeguarding every single one. Henry's question about the weapons prompted a brief pause and Clio responded with measured reassurance. "Don't worry," she said, her voice steady. "Hopefully, we won't need them."

Her words carried a note of optimism, a silent prayer that their journey would proceed without confrontation. Yet beneath her calm demeanour, Clio knew the harsh reality of their situation—a reality where danger lurked at every turn and their survival depended on their ability to navigate through the darkness, both literally and metaphorically.

As Jessica and her group moved cautiously through the thickening snow, the wind howled louder, creating an eerie symphony of nature's fury. Jessica's senses were on high alert, every sound amplified by the silence of the night. She thought she heard a rustle in the distance but attributed it to the shifting snow and the relentless gusts of wind.

Suddenly, a member of her group cried out alarmingly, drawing everyone's attention. "Look! I'm sure I saw two eyes in the darkness... no, now I see several!"

The urgency in the person's voice was unmistakable. Panic rippled through the group as they strained to discern shapes in the swirling shadows.

Jessica's heart raced as she scanned the surrounding darkness, her eyes straining to pierce the veil of falling snow. Then, she saw them—pairs of glowing eyes reflecting the faint moonlight, moving closer through the trees.

"Oh my God!" another voice exclaimed, confirming everyone's worst fear. "It's wolves and it looks like several!"

Jessica's mind raced as she recalled stories of wildlife encounters in such remote, frozen landscapes. Without hesitation she signalled to her group to stand absolutely still—advice often given in such situations to avoid provoking predators. The group held their collective breath, their fear palpable in the frigid air. The wolves, their eyes gleaming like embers in the night, approached cautiously, their forms emerging from the shadows. Jessica's heart pounded in her chest as the tension mounted. She hoped that their stillness would deceive the wolves, rendering them invisible against the backdrop of snow-covered landscape, everyone looking like snowmen lost in the wilderness. The wind howled relentlessly, carrying with it the scent of fear and anticipation. Time seemed to stretch as the stand-off continued—a battle of wills between human and beast in the harsh, unforgiving wilderness.

As the tension mounted in the biting cold, around a dozen wolves began to encircle Jessica's group. Their movements were sinuous and deliberate, their eyes fixed on the huddled figures in the snow. The soft crunch of their paws in the snow on the frozen ground underscored the quiet intensity of the moment. Jessica's group stood motionless, their breath visible in the frigid air, their hearts pounding with adrenaline. The wolves, majestic yet menacing in the moonlit night, moved with calculated precision, each step bringing them closer to their prey. The wolves' fur, a mixture of dark and silver-grey, almost blended with the night. The moon made a appearance albeit it fleeting, their eyes, reflecting the moon's pale glow, seemed to hold an otherworldly intelligence—a reminder that they were not mere beasts but cunning predators of the wilderness. Jessica's mind raced, her senses heightened by the primal dance unfolding around them. She dared not break eye contact with the nearest of the wolves, knowing that any sudden movement could trigger an attack. Amidst the tension, the wind continued its relentless assault, whipping through the trees and carrying the distant echoes of the blizzard's approach. The wolves, sensing vulnerability or perhaps caution in the humans, maintained their cautious advance, their forms weaving in and out of the shifting shadows. In this frozen tableau of survival, Jessica and her companions clung to stillness, hoping against hope that their collective resolve and the wolves' innate wariness would be enough to see them through this perilous encounter in the heart of the wilderness.

Jessica, acutely aware of the wolves circling nearby, felt a surge of apprehension as she contemplated using her gun. She knew that any sudden noise could attract further unwelcome human attention, potentially escalating an already precarious situation. Gently tapping the communication button on her helmet's built-in phone, Jessica whispered to Clio, her voice barely audible over the howling wind. "Clio, I really don't want to use the gun unless we absolutely have to. The last thing we need is to attract more unwelcome attention out here but wolves are all around us back here, I fear an attack.

As Clio led the group along with Henry through the biting cold, her focus was abruptly interrupted by Jessica's urgent whisper in her earpiece. The news of wolves circling Jessica's group sent a jolt of concern through Clio, who had to act swiftly despite being several groups ahead. "Clio here," she replied calmly, her voice cutting through the snowy static. "Jessica, deploy the shield and keep moving. Use the device to adjust its position so the wolves can't reach you. Stay calm and maintain your pace." She visualised Jessica and her group, imagining the tense scene unfolding behind her in the snow-covered darkness. Despite the distance, Clio's voice carried reassurance, a calm amidst the wild uncertainty of the night. Jessica nodded in response to Clio's instructions, her fingers deftly manipulating the device eventually deploying the shield with its shimmering barrier against the encroaching wolves. With each step, she adjusted its position, ensuring they remained protected as they pressed forward through the white wilderness, determined to navigate the treacherous night safely.

The other members of her group stared in awe and disbelief. The shimmering barrier, radiating a faint hue in the moonlit night, was a sight beyond their wildest imaginations. One of the group members, wide-eyed, muttered in amazement, "What in the world is that?"

Jessica, catching the tone of wonderment and seeking to lighten the tense moment, grinned beneath her helmet and glanced back toward where the question came. "Oh, it's just something I conjured up," she joked, her voice laced with amusement despite the perilous circumstances. Laughter rippled through the group, a brief reprieve from the anxiety of the night. Clio couldn't help but chuckle to herself at Jessica's playful quip, her voice carrying over the helmet comms.

Jessica continued, "That's right, folks," she chimed in with a teasing tone. "Just a little magic to keep things interesting out here." The humour, however light-hearted, served as a welcome distraction from the tension, bridging the gap between the groups as they forged ahead through the snow-laden landscape. With the shield guiding, protecting and Clio's reassuring presence leading the way, the desperate bands of survivors pressed onward, united by the shared goal of safety amid the howling wilderness.

The faint glow of the shield enveloping Jessica's group provided a sense of security. Then all of a sudden the wolves were gone and all that was left was the distant howls of the retreating wolves echoed in the frigid night, a chilling reminder of the dangers lurking in the darkness. Jessica turned the shield off knowing she can redeploy if need be. With each step, the survivors remained on edge, their senses heightened by the adrenaline-fuelled encounter. Jessica glanced around cautiously, the subtle crunch of snow underfoot mingling with the distant winds. The silence was broken only by the soft whispers of the group members, exchanging nervous glances and grateful nods toward Jessica and the shield that had seemingly repelled the predators. Clio's leading group, remaining vigilant, their eyes scanning the terrain for any signs of further threats. The shadows seemed deeper now, the landscape draped in an eerie stillness punctuated only by the muffled footfalls of the weary and the howling wind. The wolves distant howling faded into the night, once tense and fraught with fear, began to ease. Had the wolves retreated out of caution, sensing a formidable barrier they couldn't breach? Or was it merely coincidence, the predators seeking easier prey elsewhere? The survivors, emboldened by their narrow escape, pressed on, their determination steeled by the harrowing encounter.

They pressed forward, the intermittent green glow on the horizon added a surreal element to the already ominous night. The survivors glanced at each other with apprehension, their minds racing with questions about the strange phenomenon. The glow in the distance flickered like a distant beacon, casting an otherworldly hue across the snowy landscape. The unsettling green light seemed to pulse rhythmically, illuminating patches of the barren terrain.

Clio, leading the way with her group, squinted into the distance, trying to discern the source of the ethereal glow. The realisation dawned on her—a haunting familiarity with the colour that had marked their encounter with the alien craft earlier.

Whispers of concern rippled through the group as the survivors exchanged uneasy glances. Could this be another manifestation of the same alien technology that had wreaked havoc on their surroundings? The memory of the green beam and its inexplicable purpose stirred fresh fears.

The wolves' abrupt retreat took on new meaning in the context of this eerie illumination. Was it possible that the predators had sensed or encountered this alien presence before? Had they, too, learned to fear the enigmatic green light?

The night sky was abruptly transformed by a blinding brilliance on the horizon—an intense white light that seared through the darkness, followed by a fiery orange-red glow that painted the landscape in ominous hues. The earth trembled beneath their feet as a deafening roar reverberated through the air.

It was unmistakable—the same harrowing beam that had spelled destruction before was now tearing through the distant terrain, obliterating everything in its path. The survivors stood transfixed by the catastrophic display, their faces illuminated by the infernal glow.

Clio's voice shattered the stunned silence, cutting through the chaos with urgent clarity. "Run!" she shouted, her tone commanding and resolute. The urgency in her voice spurred everyone into action, Henry included, who gestured frantically towards a nearby cave.

Henry's knowledge of the area proved invaluable as he led the way, his movements fuelled by adrenaline and fear. The survivors followed suit, their footsteps hastened by the impending threat looming on the horizon.

As they reached the mouth of the cave, the ground trembled beneath them, the force of the explosion reverberating. The relentless destruction cast a menacing shadow over their escape, each pulse of light a stark reminder of the peril that pursued them.

Inside the cave, the survivors huddled together, their collective breaths ragged with exertion and fear. The once-ominous darkness of the cave now offered sanctuary from the cataclysmic spectacle outside—a temporary refuge amidst the chaos unfolding beyond its rocky walls.

Exchanging anxious glances, minds racing with questions and fears. Was there any hope of survival amidst the relentless onslaught of the alien technology?

With refuge within the cave, but their newfound sanctuary was shattered by a thunderous explosion that rocked the very foundations of the earth. The air outside the cave, once filled with the biting cold of winter, was suddenly engulfed in a searing heat that threatened to consume everything in its path.

Then there was silence, so Henry cautiously peered outside, his breath catching in his throat at the surreal scene unfolding before him. Where once stood a wintry landscape blanketed in snow, there now lay a scorched and desolate expanse. The alien craft, with its unfathomable power, had unleashed a torrent of immense heat, melting away the snow and leaving behind a landscape transformed by devastation.

The acrid smell of burning filled the air, mingling with the stench of charred earth and melted ice. The ground beneath Henry's feet was still warm, a stark contrast to the biting cold that had gripped them only moments before. The eerie silence that followed the explosion was punctuated only by the crackling of smouldering debris and the distant echoes of destruction.

The sudden shift from freezing cold to blistering heat had left them reeling, their senses overwhelmed by the magnitude of the alien craft's power. Henry came back into the cave, his voice heavy with disbelief. "It's gone," he muttered, his words barely audible over the lingering echoes of destruction. The once-familiar landscape had been irrevocably altered, transformed into a barren wasteland by forces beyond their comprehension.

In the eerie aftermath of the alien craft's onslaught, the survivors grappled with the enormity of their predicament. The world outside, now devoid of snow and life for miles. Had it not been for the quick thinking of Henry and his local knowledge they would never have survived.

Inside the cave, the aftermath of the devastating attack unfolded with a haunting silence broken only by the echoes of distant destruction. Everyone had bore witness to the sudden and catastrophic transformation of the surroundings outside of the cave.

Innocent children, eyes wide with terror, clinging to their mothers, their cries piercing the stillness of the cave. Some of the women, overcome by shock and despair, wept quietly, seeking reassurance in each other's embrace.

Henry, his face etched with a mixture of disbelief and resignation, tried to console those around him. "We're safe for now," he murmured, his voice a fragile reassurance amidst the chaos. His words, though well-intentioned, offered little comfort in the wake of such unimaginable devastation.

The survivors, their senses still reeling from the sudden shift in temperature and the relentless power of whatever that craft was, grappled with the enormity of their predicament. The once-familiar world outside, now reduced to a barren wasteland, served as a stark reminder of the perilous forces that had descended upon them.

In the dim light of the cave, shadows danced across the faces of the survivors, each one reflecting a mix of anguish and uncertainty. The air was heavy with the acrid scent of burnt earth and the lingering echoes of destruction, a stark testament to the harrowing reality they now faced.

Amidst the grief and fear that permeated the cave, Clio and Jessica their thoughts weighed down by the enormity of what just happened had to somehow convince these people to continue on. All remained silent in the cave, one of the women cautiously approached the cave's entrance, her eyes fixed on the shifting landscape beyond. With a mix of trepidation and curiosity, she peered outside, her breath visible in the chilly air.

"It's cooling down," she announced, her voice carrying a note of cautious optimism. "And it's started snowing again."

Her words were met with a murmur of relief. The prospect of the freezing temperatures returning and snowing signalled a potential respite from the intense heat and destruction wrought by the alien craft.

"It should be safe to go back out," the woman continued, her voice tinged with a hint of hope. Her words stirred a glimmer of renewed determination among the survivors, many of whom were eager to assess the situation outside and regroup in the wake of the catastrophic events.

Slowly, the survivors began to stir, with expressions a mixture of apprehension and resolve. Encouraged by the woman's observation, they prepared to venture outside once more, bracing themselves for whatever awaited them beyond the shelter of the cave.

In the dim light filtering through the cave's entrance, the snowfall lent a sense of eerie tranquillity to the scene. The survivors, their faces etched with weariness and uncertainty. They cautiously emerged from the cave, two women stepped forward, their expressions etched with concern and discomfort. One woman, clutching her chest, voiced her distress.

"I'm finding it difficult to breathe," she gasped, her voice strained with anxiety.

Beside her, another woman echoed similar sentiments, her eyes wide with alarm. "What's going on? Why is it so hard to breathe out here?"

Clio, taking charge amid the growing unease, scanned the surroundings, her gaze settling on the aftermath of the recent destruction. The air felt heavy, laden with an unfamiliar sensation that seemed to press against their lungs.

"It has to be caused by whatever is attacking us," Clio responded, her voice steady, "We need to move quickly. The air out here might not be safe."

Her words spurred a flurry of activity among the survivors, who, despite their physical and emotional exhaustion, understood the urgency. Gripped by a renewed sense of purpose, they hastened to gather what little belongings they had and prepared to depart from the relative safety of the cave.

They continued on but outside, the air was tinged with an acrid scent, a stark contrast to the crisp purity of the snowfall. Breathing became shallow and laboured with each passing moment.

Clio noticed the distant signal indicating Dodger's location, a beacon of hope amidst the desolation.

"The snow isn't heavy and we have a signal for Dodger," Clio announced, her voice carrying over the hushed murmurs of everyone. "Let's go. We need to move quickly."

As the survivors prepared to set out, a man voiced his apprehensions, highlighting the disparity in resources among them.

"It's alright for you as you have an oxygen supply, we don't!" the man pointed out, his tone tinged with frustration and desperation.

Clio paused, acknowledging the man's valid concern. She looked at everyone, her gaze settling on one after another because they all lacked protective gear and resources needed to navigate the increasingly inhospitable conditions.

"We'll stick together," Clio assured them, her voice calm yet resolute. "We'll find a way to make it back to Dodger safely."

Clio's voice cut through the cold, her tone infused with a blend of empathy and determination.

"If anyone needs oxygen, tell me," Clio announced, her voice carrying a note of urgency. "I can place my helmet over your head. The oxygen supply comes directly into the helmet."

Her offer was met with a mixture of relief and gratitude, the gravity etched on the faces of those who lacked the means to navigate the harsh environment.

A woman stepped forward, her breath visible in the cold, her expression one of apprehension and hope.

"I need oxygen," she admitted, her voice trembling slightly.

Clio nodded understandingly, her features reflecting compassion and resolve. She swiftly removed her helmet and assisted the woman and activating the oxygen supply. The woman's tense features eased as the life-giving oxygen, flowed into her makeshift respirator.

"We'll make it through this together," Clio reassured them all.

Clio's concern extended beyond just the immediate need for oxygen, she sought to engage the woman in conversation, perhaps to distract her from the inhospitable surroundings.

"What's your name?" Clio asked gently, her tone conveying reassurance.

The woman's eyes, previously clouded with worry, softened slightly at the gesture of kindness.

"I'm Sarah," she replied, her voice wavering slightly.

"And where are you from, Sarah?" Clio inquired, her voice calm and deliberate.

"I'm from Reno," Sarah responded, her words accompanied by a sigh of relief as the oxygen began to take effect. "Never thought I'd end up in a place like this."

Clio nodded empathetically, her expression conveying understanding. "We'll get through this," she assured Sarah, her voice carrying a quiet resolve. "Just hold on a little longer."

Sarah managed a faint smile, gratitude mingling with exhaustion on her features. In that brief exchange, Clio's efforts to provide both physical and emotional support was well received by the others.

Sarah's words advising she was feeling better and pointed out she was concerned for the children, prompting Clio to act swiftly. With a nod of reassurance, Clio adjusted her helmet for the first child then the other four to share the oxygen supply with the children, ensuring they received the same relief that Sarah experienced.

Clio's gesture was met with gratitude from the other adults, their expressions reflecting a blend of exhaustion and hope. As the children's breathing eased and colour returned to their cheeks, a collective sense of calm settled at last.

"We'll be okay," Clio said, her voice projecting a quiet optimism . "Just keep together."

The group's resilience was tested, but Clio's instinctive empathy and swift action demonstrated a profound commitment to supporting each other through the most challenging of circumstances.

Henry's voice carried a mix of gratitude and admiration as he addressed Clio and Jessica. "You two ladies are immense," he said, his words filled with genuine appreciation. The weight of their efforts and the impact they had made on Henry and the others was evident in his heartfelt sentiment.

In that moment, amidst the aftermath of chaos. Henry's words served as a testament to Clio and Jessica's courage and leadership. The acknowledgment of their resilience and determination resonated deeply, underscoring the importance of their actions in the face of adversity.

Clio and Jessica, though weary from the ordeal, exchanged a glance that conveyed silent acknowledgment of the shared journey they had navigated together. After Henry's heartfelt message, a sense of relief and appreciation was instant and it included the women, children and the men, with a spontaneous outpouring of gratitude. Hands clapped together, echoing in the wilderness, as an expression their admiration for Clio and Jessica.

The clapping was a symphony of relief and acknowledgment, a chorus of applause that recognised the courage and selflessness of Clio and Jessica in leading them through such perilous circumstances. The sound reverberated in the night, a tangible expression of appreciation.

Clio and Jessica, humbled by the gesture, exchanged grateful smiles amidst the applause. Their actions had not only provided physical protection but also a sense of hope and resilience to those they had guided. The applause served as a cathartic release, a collective celebration of survival and the human spirit prevailing in the midst of turmoil. As the applause subsided, Clio's calm voice cut through the cold night air. "Keep calm, everyone," she said quietly yet firmly. "We've made it. The Dodger is over there." She pointed in the direction indicated by the bleeping device, ensuring that everyone could see where they needed to go.

Henry's doubt was palpable as he scanned the landscape, unable to see any sign of the Dodger. The group's apprehension was evident.

Clio, undeterred by the scepticism around her, spoke with quiet determination. "The Dodger will materialise as we get closer," she assured them, her voice carrying a calm conviction. Her words offering hope amid the lingering fear that permeated amongst their minds.

As they followed Clio's lead, the survivors moved forward cautiously, their eyes fixed on the point indicated by the bleeping device. The atmosphere was tense, each step forward weighed down by doubt and anticipation. The landscape, shrouded in snow again and silence, seemed to amplify their anxieties.

The minutes stretched on, the group inching closer to the designated spot. With each passing moment, Henry's scepticism appeared to grow, mirrored by the wary expressions of those around him. Some exchanged nervous glances, uncertainty etched on their faces.

Then, as if responding to Clio's unwavering belief, a faint outline began to take shape in the distance. The Dodger was materialising slowly, its form emerging from the wintry backdrop. Gasps of surprise and relief rippled through the people as the vehicle became more distinct with each passing second.

Clio's confidence had been vindicated. The Dodger stood before them, a symbol of salvation against the harsh realities of their environment. For a brief moment, doubt yielded to hope and the survivors hurried toward the waiting vehicle, their faith in Clio's guidance reaffirmed.

Clio now right next to Dodger, its sleek doors began to slowly open smoothly, revealing the warm interior of the vehicle. The sight brought a sigh of relief from the all.

Inside, the AI's voice greeted them warmly. "Welcome aboard, Jessica and Clio," AI announced cheerfully. "The more, the merrier!" The AI's attempt at humour brought a faint smile to the faces of the weary survivors, a moment of levity amid the tension.

Clio gestured for everyone to enter, her expression showing urgency. "Come on, everyone," she encouraged, her voice carrying reassurance. "Let's get inside where it's warm and safe."

Women children and men filed into Dodger. AI's presence offered a sense of comfort and control. The AI's capabilities were a source of hope, their journey now guided by the technology that had brought them this far. Everyone hurrying into Dodger, the urgency in AI's warning echoed through the cabin. "Warning: Alien craft approaching from the east. Emergency protocol initiated. Everyone must be inside!" AI's voice rang out, commanding attention.

The last man to stagger through the closing doors was visibly shaken, breathing heavily from the exertion of running. "I... I made it," he managed to say between breaths, relief evident in his voice.

Just as the man entered, the Dodger's doors sealed shut with a soft hiss, cutting off the biting wind and isolating the group from the unforgiving elements outside. AI's interface displayed the status: "Shields up. All systems are operational."

Inside the Dodger, the tension was palpable. The survivors gathered close, the feeling of danger now sinking in once again. The hum of the Dodger's systems offered a steady background noise, a reminder of their fleeting safety in the face of an unknown and formidable threat. The Dodger's engines powered down, AI's voice reassured them. "All engines shutting down. We are now in stealth mode with shields up. They will not be able to detect us," AI announced calmly, its words cutting through the tension in the cabin.

The occupants of the Dodger exchanged glances, some visibly relieved while others remained on edge, their expressions reflecting the gravity of their predicament. The sense of vulnerability was heightened by the silence that followed, broken only by the soft hum of the Dodger's systems maintaining their protective shield.

AI's presence provided a reassuring anchor, its demeanour projecting control and competence. Inside the cloaked Dodger, the survivors huddled together, waiting in tense anticipation for the imminent threat to pass. All of a sudden green beams illuminated the surroundings, casting an eerie glow through the opaque walls of the craft. The beams darted across the landscape, illuminating patches of snow and rock in sporadic bursts. Each beam seemed to search methodically, scanning the area with precision.

Inside the Dodger, the occupants watched the spectacle unfold through the viewports, their faces reflecting a mix of curiosity and apprehension. The green light, stark against the dark backdrop of the night, created an otherworldly scene, reminding them of the advanced technology wielded by their unseen adversaries.

Jessica and Clio, their eyes fixed on the beams as they played over the terrain outside. The silence within the Dodger was palpable, broken only by the occasional hushed breath or whisper of conversation.

As the green beams continued to sweep nearby, everyone held their breath, hoping that the Dodger's stealth mode would indeed shield them from detection. The tension inside the craft rose, each occupant acutely aware of the precariousness of their situation. Following the tense moments when the green beams illuminated the surroundings, suddenly the alien craft vanished from sight. The beams ceased their scanning, leaving the landscape once again cloaked in darkness. The abrupt disappearance of the craft brought a collective sigh of relief inside the Dodger.

As the occupants peered out through the viewports, they could no longer discern any trace of the alien vessel. The night returned to its natural state, with only the sounds of the wind outside breaking the silence within the craft.

Jessica and Clio exchanged glances, their expressions reflecting a mix of astonishment and relief. The sudden departure of the alien craft left lingering questions about its intentions and the nature of the threat they faced.

Inside the Dodger, the atmosphere remained tense, the occupants aware that the respite might be temporary. Nevertheless, the absence of the alien presence offered a brief moment of reprieve, allowing everyone aboard to gather their thoughts. The silence broken by AI. "Fill the cabin with pure oxygen. I detect low oxygen levels in two women and all the children."

AI's voice echoed through the cabin, the Dodger's internal systems responded immediately. The air inside the craft began to change, enriched by the infusion of pure oxygen designed to alleviate the breathing difficulties experienced by some of the passengers.

Inside Dodger, a subtle shift as the atmosphere became clearer and more breathable. Those affected by the diminished oxygen levels began to experience relief, their breathing steadying as the cabin filled with the revitalising oxygen.

Clio and Jessica, among others, glanced around with concern, acknowledging the critical need for improved oxygenation. AI's swift intervention underscored the importance of the AI's role in ensuring the safety and well-being of those aboard Dodger amidst the ongoing crisis they faced. As the cabin filled with pure oxygen, AI's voice resounded once more, this time interjecting with a touch of humour and warmth amidst the tension:

"Anyone for coffee?"

The unexpected comment from AI elicited a mixture of surprise and amusement among the passengers. Despite the dire circumstances and the recent ordeal they had endured, AI's light-hearted quip brought a momentary sense of relief and camaraderie.

Clio couldn't help but chuckle, her expression softening as she exchanged glances with Jessica and others. The offer of coffee, a delivered through AI's playful announcement, seemed to momentarily lift spirits and inject a hint of normality into their extraordinary situation.

Around the cabin, subtle smiles appeared on faces that had been etched with worry moments before. It was a brief but welcome respite, a reminder that even in the face of unknown dangers and unforeseen challenges, there were still moments of levity and connection to be found aboard Dodger.

Amidst the shared smiles and lighter atmosphere, AI's presence provided a reassuring sense of continuity and support, underscoring AI's role not only as a protector but also as a source of unexpected comfort in these times.

AI's directive echoed through Dodger's systems, the onboard machines sprang into action with a flurry of automated activity. From the galley area, a series of small trays emerged, each laden with steaming cups of coffee, tea and plates of assorted cakes and an array of drinks for the children.

The aroma of freshly brewed beverages wafted through the cabin, mingling with the comforting scent of baked goods ready for the new occupants. Clio and Jessica laughed as they received their beverages, marvelling at the efficiency of Dodger's AI systems. The sight of the trays laden with treats, provided a welcome distraction from the recent tension and the ongoing threat outside.

Around them, the other passengers gratefully accepted the offerings, their expressions shifting from concern to tentative enjoyment. The simple act of sharing a hot drink and a sweet treat in the midst of uncertainty seemed to foster a sense of unity and comfort among those gathered aboard Dodger.

As the last tray found its recipient, AI's voice chimed in once more, its tone maintaining a reassuring demeanour amid the current circumstances.

"Please enjoy. We'll be monitoring the situation closely. You are safe, everyone."

There were relieved smiles and grateful comments circulated among the people. Some expressed awe at the technology that seemed to anticipate their needs, while others simply savoured the warmth and flavour of the hot drinks after braving the chilling cold outside.

"I've never tasted tea like this," remarked one of the women, her voice tinged with amazement.

Another passenger, a man with a young child in his arms, nodded appreciatively. "Thank you, whoever's behind all this. It's a welcome surprise after everything."

Clio and Jessica exchanged knowing glances, pleased to see the positive impact of Dodger's hospitality on the rescued individuals.

Despite the ongoing threats outside, for a brief moment, on board was filled with a sense of shared relief.

AI's voice interjected again, its tone conveying reassurance. "Glad to be of service. If you need anything else, just ask. We'll do our best to keep everyone comfortable and safe."

Emotions ran high among the rescued passengers. As they sipped relaxed in the unexpected comfort of the surroundings, a few individuals couldn't contain their emotions, tears welling up in their eyes.

One woman, clutching a steaming cup of tea, wiped away tears of relief as she spoke softly, "I never thought we'd find warmth and safety out here. Thank you."

A man nearby, his features etched with exhaustion and gratitude, nodded in agreement. "It's like a miracle, isn't it? After everything we've been through..."

Clio and Jessica exchanged empathetic glances, understanding their ordeal that these survivors had endured. The heartfelt expressions of thanks and the tears of relief underscored the impact of Dodger's timely intervention.

AI's voice, calm and steady, echoed through the cabin. "We're glad to provide refuge. Please rest and recover. If anyone needs medical attention or further assistance, don't hesitate to let us know."

The mood in the cabin shifted from one of tension to one of communal support, with passengers sharing nods of appreciation and quiet words of encouragement. Despite the circumstances, the sense of shared relief and comfort inside Dodger's protective confines provided a much-needed reprieve.

Amid the hum of Dodger's systems and now moving through the air at speed there was subdued chatter among the passengers, Clio's voice rose above the din as she addressed the group, her tone both reassuring and tinged with humour.

"Alright, everyone, gather 'round," Clio began, her eyes meeting those of each individual in the cabin, her expression earnest yet playful. "You're about to experience something that might seem straight out of science fiction. We're going to glide through solid rock like a hot knife through butter. Yes, you heard me right! And where are we headed? A place I'd call sanctuary—where you'll find Jim and Barbara, just casually having a meal or even a coffee."

She paused for a moment, allowing a ripple of curious murmurs to filter through the group. Some passengers exchanged bewildered glances, while others leaned forward with newfound interest.

"And oh, by the way," Clio continued with a mischievous glint in her eye, "You'll also get to meet Dave and Zeena. They might not be exactly who you think they are." She grinned, as if sharing a private joke. "But trust me, they're on our side."

A ripple of laughter and intrigued whispers spread through the cabin, mingling with the gentle hum of Dodger's systems. Clio's confident demeanour and light-hearted approach seemed to ease the tension among the passengers, many of whom were still reeling from the recent ordeal.

"So, sit back, relax and enjoy the ride," Clio concluded, her voice carrying an air of reassurance. "We're in good hands and soon enough, you'll see what I mean."

With a collective mix of anticipation and curiosity, the passengers settled in, their gazes darting between each other and the surrounding cabin. The idea of moving through solid rock at breakneck speed and about to encounter more unknown things seemed surreal yet oddly comforting within the confines of Dodger's protective embrace.

Dodger continued its journey at speed, a sudden shout pierced the air—a fearful exclamation that reverberated through the cabin, laced with urgency and alarm. The rescued woman's voice cut through the hum of the engines and the muted conversations, prompting an immediate hush among the passengers.

"We're about to hit the mountainside!" she cried out, her tone rising with palpable fear.

In response, a wave of panic seemed to sweep through the cabin. Some passengers gripped their seats, eyes wide with apprehension, while others exchanged frantic looks. The atmosphere shifted from curiosity to sudden concern as Dodger's trajectory through the solid rock brought an unexpected element of danger.

Amidst the chaos, Clio sprang into action, her voice steady and commanding. "Hold on, everyone!" she called out, her words cutting through the tension. "Trust Dodger—it knows what it's doing."

Her reassurance seemed to quell some of the rising fear, though the passengers remained on edge. The hum of Dodger's engines grew louder as the cabin seemed to shake slightly, the sensation of movement intensifying. Just as the tension reached its peak, Dodger smoothly transitioned through the mountain, cutting through the rock as Clio had stated.

Now surging forward with incredible velocity, slicing through the solid rock as if it were thin air. The sensation inside the cabin was unlike anything the passengers had ever experienced. There was no jolt or resistance, just a smooth and swift glide through the dense mountain.

As Dodger advanced, the view through the windows became a blur of rocky surfaces rushing past, illuminated sporadically by the vehicle's external lights. Inside, the passengers could feel the controlled power of Dodger's advanced technology at work, propelling them through the rock with seamless efficiency.

The sound of Dodger's engines intensified, resonating through the cabin with a steady, reassuring hum. Despite the breathtaking speed, there was a sense of security within Dodger's confines—a feeling that this marvel of engineering was fully in control, navigating the subterranean environment with precision and ease.

Inside Dodger, the atmosphere was a mix of awe and excitement tempered by a touch of apprehension. The passengers exchanged wide-eyed glances, absorbing the surreal nature of their journey. Some clutched their seats, marvelling at the sheer ingenuity that allowed them to traverse solid rock unscathed.

As Dodger continued its rapid passage, the passengers were left to ponder the mysteries of this extraordinary vehicle and the incredible technology that propelled them forward. Each passing moment reinforced the realisation that they were part of something truly extraordinary—an unforgettable voyage through the very fabric of the Earth itself.

Dodger burst through the final layer of rock, the interior was flooded with brilliant, natural light. The passengers shielded their eyes momentarily, adjusting to the sudden brightness. When the doors opened, they stepped outside Dodger into a breathtaking landscape bathed in sunlight.

Before them stretched a scene of serene beauty—a vast expanse of rolling hills and meadows, dotted with wildflowers in a myriad of colours. The air was filled with the sweet scent of nature, a refreshing departure from the darkness of the underground journey.

The warmth of the sun embraced them, thawing away the fear of the subterranean voyage. Birds chirped overhead and a gentle breeze played with the grass, creating a soft rustling sound that seemed to welcome them to this newfound haven.

The passengers stood in awe, taking in the panoramic view around them. The sky above was a vibrant blue canvas, devoid of any hint of the recent turmoil. It was as though they had emerged into a different world—one untouched by the chaos and destruction they had left behind.

Some of the passengers smiled, their faces brightening with relief and wonder. They were in awe of this unexpected beauty of their surroundings, grateful for the reprieve from the harrowing events of their recent ordeal.

Clio and Jessica shared a silent acknowledgment of the significance of this moment. They had successfully led these people to safety, emerging into a landscape that promised hope a sanctuary amidst the chaos that had befallen their own world.

As the newcomers stepped out into the radiant landscape, Dave approached them with a welcoming smile, much like he had done for Jim and Barbara before. His demeanour was calm and reassuring, embodying a sense of authority and warmth.

"Welcome, everyone," Dave greeted them, his voice resonating with a blend of familiarity and friendliness. "I'm glad to see you've made it safely. You've arrived at a place we call Sanctuary—a refuge from the challenges you've faced."

He gestured toward the surroundings, encompassing the picturesque vista that unfolded before them. "Take a moment to breathe it all in. Here, you'll find respite and protection."

Zeena joined Dave, her presence equally reassuring. "You're among friends now," she added, her tone gentle yet confident. "We'll ensure your safety and well-being."

The rescued individuals looked around with a mix of relief and curiosity, their expressions reflecting gratitude for their newfound sanctuary. Dave and Zeena proceeded to guide them, offering comfort and guidance as they transitioned into this unfamiliar yet welcoming environment.

As Clio and Jessica returned it was Dave and Zeena, that pulled them to one side, Dave and Zeena's expressions hinted at a readiness to hear the details of Clio and Jessica's latest experience, their faces reflecting a mix of anticipation and concern.

"Clio, Jessica, welcome back," Dave greeted them, his voice steady. "We trust your journey was eventful, it certainly looks like it was."

Clio nodded, her expression serious. "Indeed, it was. We encountered unexpected challenges, but we managed to bring the survivors to safety."

Jessica chimed in, her voice earnest. "We encountered a situation we have never seen before—We encountered an Alien Craft!"

Dave's brow furrowed slightly, a sign of both interest and apprehension. "Tell us more. What did you encounter out there?"

Clio proceeded to describe the events with clarity, recounting the scenes of destruction and the perilous circumstances they had faced. As she spoke, Zeena's analytical gaze, absorbing the details shared by Clio.

"And then when we arrive back here," Jessica continued, "We don't see Barbara & Jim!" Zeena pointed out they have embarked on a rescue mission to rescue someone called Ben and his wife, following a warning from Josh about impending danger."

Zeena nodded thoughtfully, her synthetic eyes reflecting a sense of calculation. "Josh seems to be playing a crucial role in alerting potential targets. Ben's call for help aligns with the pattern we've observed."

Dave turned to Clio and Jessica, his expression conveying a sense of urgency. "We need to monitor this situation closely. Jim and Barbara are resourceful, but this mission sounds particularly risky after what we have just encountered."

It was worrying times but hopefully Jim and Barbara would make it back soon and with the safe rescue of Ben and his wife Olivia.

The new arrivals were shown around and the children found an abundant supply of chocolate to be amazing, especially when they were told that this particular chocolate was good for them. The days past by and now everyone was waiting for the safe return of Jim and Barbara.

Chapter 12

GHOST TOWN

Far from the safety of Sanctuary Ben was busy racing against time and he remembered everything that Josh had told him. In a stroke of urgency, Ben knew he had to save some people so he gathered a small group of ten women who had put their trust in him and of course his wife Olivia. The absence of men around them remained a mystery, perhaps a casualty of the unfolding chaos. Ben's focus was on survival and he swiftly convinced the women that when the temperature drops dramatically they head over to his place with as much water as they could carry.

Ben remembered what Josh had said, that for safety he would need to head for the ghost town of Rhyolite, This ghost town held the promise of refuge. Ben's choice was not arbitrary as he knew the area and believed it offered the best chance of evading the approaching threat and it's exactly what Josh intended.

The temperature had now plummeted. Ben hastily dialled the number he had been given, his fingers trembling with a mix of fear and urgency. He waited anxiously as the phone rang, hoping for a response that would offer reassurance and guidance.

Dave answered the phone his voice conveyed a sense of urgency as he asked, "Dave here where have you been told to go?"

Ben's response came swiftly, his tone resolute despite the circumstances. "The Ghost Town," he replied, his words punctuated by a backdrop of sounds of distant chaos.

Dave understood the answer and reassured Ben, "Your answer is correct now swiftly head toward the Ghost Town. We'll coordinate a response and meet you there so stay safe."

Ben's responsibility evident in his eyes as he prepared to advise and guide the women and children onward.

Ben drove from house to house, urgency etched on his face as he relayed the details to each woman saying. "We need to leave as quickly as possible and therefore I want you to pack whatever essentials you can, especially water, warm clothing and when you are ready you should head to my place."

In each home, women hurriedly gathered belongings and loaded up their vehicles with jugs of water, their movements swift and purposeful. Ben's demeanour had conveyed both urgency and determination, his voice had been steady and assertive.

The women's emotions were a mix of apprehension and resolve. Some showed fear in their eyes, while others displayed determination to heed Ben's call to action. The worry of the situation bore down on them, but their collective resolve propelled them forward, spurred by urgency.

The Sun dipped below the horizon, casting long shadows across the landscape, the scene at Ben's house was one of organised chaos. The vehicles parked haphazardly in the driveway and along the street, each one laden with supplies and water containers. The headlights of the cars illuminated the front yard, lending an eerie glow to the proceedings.

Children darted about, their voices blending with the chatter of the adults. Some women gathered around Ben, seeking reassurance and direction, while others worked silently with their expressions taut with anxiety.

Ben stood at the centre of it all, amid the whirlwind of activity. He spoke in measured tones, assigning tasks and offering encouragement. With a sense of purpose, Ben addressed the women gathered in his living room, the air thick with anticipation and apprehension.

"Right, everyone," Ben began, his voice steady and determined. "We're ready to move out, and our destination is Rhyolite."

Some of the women exchanged puzzled glances. One of them spoke up, her voice tinged with dismay. "But Ben, there's nothing in Rhyolite. It's just some old buildings, long forgotten."

Ben's expression softened as he offered reassurance. "Exactly," he replied, his tone calm yet resolute. "No one will think to look for us there. It's the last place anyone would suspect. We'll be safe."

The room fell silent as Ben's words sank in. Despite their reservations, the women nodded in agreement, recognising the logic in Ben's plan. They knew they had to trust him and together they prepared to embark on the journey to Rhyolite.

They set off one after another a small convoy of hope. As they drove over the hill away from their homes, their hearts sank at the sight of a flickering green beam illuminating the horizon. Before they could fully comprehend what was happening, a deafening explosion echoed through the air, rocking the landscape. Beatty, their once familiar town was under attack.

The sky erupted into flames, casting an eerie orange glow across the terrain. Smoke billowed into the sky, obscuring the stars and casting a pall over the night. They all stared in shock, their fears confirmed in the fiery devastation before them.

Ben gritted his teeth, his hands tightening on the steering wheel. "Keep moving," he urged, shouting through the open window, his voice steady despite the chaos unfolding around them. "We have to reach Rhyolite. That's our best chance!"

The women and children in the vehicles clung to each other, some sobbing quietly, others whispering prayers for those left behind. The road ahead seemed endless, a path fraught with uncertainty and danger, they pressed on, their resolve fuelled by the urgency of survival.

The vehicles dropping down the gradient toward the basin of Death Valley, the landscape transformed around them. The air grew dry and arid, the temperature still dropping. The vehicles bounced over rugged terrain, their headlights cutting through the darkness.

Silhouetted against the night sky, the remnants of Rhyolite emerged—crumbling buildings and weathered structures standing as monuments to a bygone era. Ben led the way, his vehicle navigating the dusty roads with determined precision.

Inside the vehicles, the women and children clung to each other, their faces etched with weariness and concern. The journey had taken its toll, physically and emotionally, but they held onto hope that Rhyolite would provide sanctuary.

As they approached the ghost town, the flickering green beam that had haunted them earlier seemed distant, replaced by the eerie stillness of the desert night.

Ben's voice broke the silence, filled with a mixture of resolve and uncertainty. "We'll make camp here," he announced, pulling to a stop amidst the skeletal remains of the town. "Keep together stay vigilant, we rest tonight and figure out our next move come morning."

The women nodded, their expressions reflecting a blend of exhaustion and worry. They had travelled far, leaving behind their homes and the life they knew, guided by a sense of survival and the promise of refuge in this desolate place.

The women and children settled in around their vehicles, creating makeshift beds with blankets and cushions. Despite the cold of the desert night, they huddled together for warmth and comfort.

The faint glow of the stars overhead cast a serene light on the abandoned town, illuminating the quiet desperation etched on their faces. Ben moved among them, offering words of reassurance and checking in on each family.

"Get some rest," he urged softly, his voice cutting through the silence. "We'll keep watch in shifts, just to be safe."

The women nodded wearily, their fatigue evident after the long journey. Some children had already drifted off to sleep, their small forms curled up against their mothers.

Amidst the stillness of the desert, the distant echoes of the attack on Beatty lingered in their minds. Each woman wondering what the dawn would bring in this desolate place they now called a temporary refuge.

As the night passed slowly in the ghost town of Rhyolite tension was high. The women and children sought rest in and around their vehicles, their bodies pressed against the cool metal, while the occasional gust of wind swept through the deserted town, carrying whispers of that bygone era.

Inside the vehicles, the dim light from flash lights and lanterns creating flickering shadows across the faces of the inhabitants. Conversations were hushed, filled with fatigue, as they whispered about the events that had led them to this place.

Some mothers cradled their children, soothing them with soft words and gentle touches, trying to shield them from the fear that gripped their own hearts. Outside, the dark silhouette of the town's remnants stood stark against the backdrop of the night sky, a haunting reminder of what was once a thriving community.

Occasionally, the distant rumble of an engine or the howl of a nocturnal creature would break the stillness, causing heads to turn and hearts to skip a beat. The women's gazes flickered between the horizon and their loved ones, their thoughts a mixture of hope and apprehension.

Through it all, Ben maintained a vigilant watch, his eyes scanning the perimeter, his mind focused on the safety of those under his care. The stars above offered little comfort, their twinkling presence a stark contrast to the uncertainty that shrouded the group.

As the hours dragged on, the night seemed endless, each passing minute weighed down by the weight of their circumstances. Yet amidst the shadows and silence, there was a shared resolve—a determination to survive, to protect and to persevere until the light of morning brought with it a new day and new possibilities.

***

As dawn broke over the ghost town of Rhyolite, the landscape transformed under the soft glow of the morning sun. The shadows of the night receded, replaced by a gentle brightness that swept across the deserted streets and dilapidated buildings.

The women and children, weary from the night's unrest, slowly emerged from their makeshift beds. Some stretched their limbs, while others rubbed the sleep from their eyes, blinking in the new light.

Outside, the world revealed itself anew—a tableau of weathered structures, remnants of a once-thriving mining town, now stood bathed in the golden hues of early morning. The mountains in the distance cast long shadows across the valley floor, creating a peaceful yet surreal backdrop.

The air was crisp and invigorating, a welcome change from the chill of the night. Concern because there wasn't as much warmth in the Sun and that wasn't normal because near to Death Valley the temperature should now be rising. Ben, ever vigilant, gathered the women and children, offering words of reassurance and encouragement. He outlined their plans for the day—securing supplies, scouting the area for signs of danger and maintaining a sense of unity.

As the Sun climbed higher in the sky, all shadows disappeared on the desolate landscape, the women began to stir with a renewed sense of purpose. Conversations resumed, this time infused with a touch of optimism, as they discussed their next steps and the challenges faced by all.

In the midst of this unlikely refuge, surrounded by the relics of a forgotten past, a spirit of resilience emerged—a determination to persevere against the odds and find a path forward in this uncharted territory of survival and solidarity.

All of the group were finishing up their meagre breakfast in Rhyolite, a sudden commotion drew their attention skyward. A saucer-shaped craft appeared on the horizon, moving at speed. It streaked across the sky, pursued closely by two United States Air Force fighters.

The tension in the air was palpable as the craft headed toward Death Valley, with the fighters hot on its tail. Suddenly, the saucer craft unleashed a cutting red beam of light that sliced through the air with a thunderous crack. The first US fighter jet was struck directly by the beam and exploded in a fiery blast, scattering debris across the sky.

In response, the remaining fighter pilot retaliated, firing missiles at the saucer-shaped craft. The missiles streaked through the air, homing in on their target. The saucer, manoeuvred skilfully to evade one of the missiles. However, the second missile found its mark, striking the saucer and causing a burst of flames and smoke. Despite the damage, the alien craft continued its desperate flight toward Death Valley. A third missile followed closely behind, zeroing in on the wounded saucer.

The tension mounted as the third missile connected with the saucer-shaped craft, causing further explosions and impairing its flight. The craft, now crippled and losing altitude rapidly, appeared to be on a collision course within Death Valley.

The women and children in Rhyolite watched in awe and fear as the drama unfolded in the sky above. The once calm morning was shattered by the chaos of aerial combat, leaving them uncertain of what would happen next. The saucer, damaged and spiralling downward, represented both a threat and a mysterious enigma in this remote desert landscape.

As the damaged saucer continued its harrowing descent toward Death Valley, it unleashed another powerful red beam of energy. The beam struck the second remaining fighter jet with precision, causing catastrophic damage. The fighter erupted into a ball of flames, trailing smoke as it plummeted toward the desert floor.

The scene was surreal and terrifying for those watching from Rhyolite. The once-clear morning sky was now filled with smoke and the echoes of destruction. The saucer-shaped craft, though severely damaged itself, had proven its formidable capabilities against modern military aircraft.

The downing of the second fighter intensified the sense of urgency and dread among the survivors. They witnessed first hand the destructive power of the alien technology and understood the imminent danger posed by the saucer's impending crash.

They watched the saucer continue its erratic descent, it appeared to be losing control. Everyone gripped by a mix of fear and fascination.

The fate of the saucer and its mysterious occupants remained uncertain, but the impact of their encounter had left an indelible mark on everyone who had witnessed it.

The loss of the two pilots was a devastating blow to those who witnessed the aerial battle around Rhyolite. As the second fighter jet erupted in flames and spiralled toward the ground, there was a collective sense of shock and grief among the survivors. The sudden and violent end of the aircraft, coupled with the realisation of the human cost of the encounter, brought a profound sense of loss.

The people in the ghost town stood in stunned silence, processing the gravity of what had just transpired. Some covered their mouths in disbelief, while others bowed their heads in sombre reflection. The emotional impact was palpable, with many experiencing a mixture of fear, sadness and anger at the senseless destruction caused by the alien craft.

The loss of the pilots served as a reminder of the perilous situation they all faced. It underscored the ruthless nature of the enemy they were up against and the desperate need for survival in the face of overwhelming odds. The survivors grappled with the reality of the ongoing conflict, knowing that their lives were now entwined in a battle far beyond their comprehension.

Ben got everyone together, his expression grave yet determined as he addressed them. He spoke with a steadiness that belied the chaos unfolding around them.

"Friends," Ben began, his voice carrying across the group, "We have witnessed terrible events and we've lost brave souls today. But we can't lose hope. We've come together in this ghost town, not by chance, but by guidance. We've chosen to defy the odds, to seek safety where others wouldn't think to look."

He paused, allowing his words to sink in before continuing.

"Now, more than ever, we must stick together. We have provisions, water and shelter here in Rhyolite. We'll fortify our defences, remain vigilant and keep our eyes on the horizon. We've seen what these beings are capable of and we won't cower in fear."

Ben's gaze swept across everyone's face, meeting each person's eyes with a resolute stare.

Ben continued. "We're survivors. We'll make our stand here, in this forgotten place and we'll fight for our lives and for each other if need be. We don't know what tomorrow holds, but we'll face it together, as one."

The sight of a saucer-shaped craft firing deadly beams and engaging in aerial combat with human military jets shattered any lingering doubts. This was not a natural disaster or a conventional military conflict. It was an encounter with advanced technology and forces beyond human comprehension.

This understanding brought a mix of fear, disbelief and urgency. They had seen first hand the destructive capabilities of these alien vessels and understood that their very existence was at stake. The loss of the fighter pilots underscored the seriousness of the situation.

Night was starting to settle over the ghost town of Rhyolite and temperatures began to drop further but more intense now just like Ben had been warned would happen, the survivors found themselves facing an unexpected and mysterious arrival. A vehicle, seemingly appearing and disappearing like a mirage in the basin of Death Valley, as it headed toward them.

The flickering headlights of the approaching vehicle cut through the darkness. The sound of its engine echoed off the surrounding hills, punctuating the stillness of the night.

The survivors had gathered around makeshift campfires and huddled in the shadow of abandoned structures, watched with a mixture of curiosity and trepidation. What was this vehicle and who was approaching them?

As the vehicle drew nearer, its outlines becoming clearer, tension mounted among the survivors. Some whispered anxiously to each other, while others gripped makeshift weapons, ready to defend themselves against any potential threat.

In the midst of this uncertainty, Ben stepped forward, his voice carrying across the quiet night air. “Everyone stay calm,” he urged.

The approaching vehicle came to a stop, a man and a woman emerged from the front seats. The man, with a weathered face and a determined gaze, stepped forward and scanned the group gathered around the campfire. His companion, a woman with a serious expression stood beside him.

“Is someone here named Ben?” the man called out, his voice cutting through the quiet night air.

Ben, who had been listening attentively, stepped forward cautiously. “Yes, I’m Ben,” he replied, his voice tinged with a mixture of hope and caution.

The man nodded, his eyes intent. “Did you make a call recently and was it answered by someone called Dave,” the man continued, his tone serious.

Ben’s heart skipped a beat as he processed the man’s words. This was the moment of truth—the confirmation he had been waiting for. If he answered truthfully, it could mean the help and salvation they desperately needed.

Ben took a deep breath, his mind racing with possibilities. “Yes,” he admitted, his voice filled with a mix of relief and apprehension.

The man’s expression softened slightly and he exchanged a glance with his female companion. “We’re here to help,” he reassured Ben, his tone sincere as he asked this particular question, "What was the description of the place you were headed to and its the two words we need."

Ben looked right at the man and said "Ghost Town." The stranger's heart swelled with a mix of relief and gratitude as he heard the man's confirmation.

The stranger looked back toward Ben and shouted. "Ghost Town Is Correct!"

Then swiftly the stranger stepped forward, introducing himself and his female companion with a reassuring smile. "I'm Jim and this is my wife, Barbara. We're here to rescue you all," he announced, his tone filled with determination and empathy.

Ben and the others gathered around the campfire, the arrival of this couple called Jim and Barbara was hope in the midst of fear. Their words brought a sense of reassurance and renewed optimism. Ben felt a surge of gratitude toward these unexpected allies, knowing that they had come to offer aid and support during this perilous time.

As Jim and Barbara settled in amongst them. Ben could sense a shift in the atmosphere of relief and hope rippling through the weary survivors. They were no longer alone in their struggle against the alien threat. Together with Jim and Barbara, they now had some sort of hope.

There was a sudden interruption which came in the form of a message from Dave. The soft hum of the evening air was momentarily pierced by the notification, drawing everyone's attention back to the urgent situation at hand.

Jim, reaching for his communication device, acknowledged the message. "I'll take this," he said with a reassuring nod to Ben and the others around the campfire. Stepping aside to a quieter spot, Jim took the call as requested by Dave.

The atmosphere among the survivors was tense yet expectant, curious about the contents of the communication. They watched Jim closely, knowing that this conversation could bring crucial information or instructions that would shape their next moves in this ongoing struggle against the alien threat.

Jim returned, his expression bearing a mix of concern and resolve as he relayed the urgent message from Dave. "Everyone, we've got to act quickly," he began, his voice cutting through the quiet tension around the campfire. "Dave just informed me that armed gunmen are headed our way from the devastated town of Beatty. They might be seeking refuge here at Rhyolite."

The news stirred a wave of murmurs and worried glances.

Ben standing nearby absorbing what was said. "Armed gunmen?" he echoed, his voice edged with concern.

Jim nodded solemnly. "Yes, we need to be prepared," he continued, addressing everyone around. "They're coming this way and we can't afford to let them catch us off guard."

Some of the women gathered closer. "What should we do?" one of them asked, her voice laced with worry.

Jim listened intently as Dave's voice crackled over the device, relaying urgent instructions for their defence. "Jim, there is critical supplies stored under the vehicle," Dave's voice came through, clear but urgent. "There are four red-coloured posts in the emergency store. You'll need the code from the last four digits of the phone you are using to be able to access the store."

Jim's realised the task at hand. "Got it," he replied, his voice steady. "What do we do with these posts?"

Dave's instructions continued. "Once you retrieve them, place each post at strategic points around your position thats around one hundred yards each from the centre of your camp and one hundred yards apart, like a square completely around the camp," Dave instructed and added. "Then turn them on by pressing down on the top of the posts—they'll glow red, indicating they're operational. Keep everyone within this defence perimeter marked by these posts. When you have achieved the optimum position the posts will glow green and it's crucial that no one crosses the purple line once the posts are set."

Jim relayed the instructions to everyone, his tone firm but measured. "We've got to set up these defence posts," he explained, glancing around at the faces gathered. "They'll mark our perimeter and everyone needs to stay within this boundary. It's for our safety."

With purposeful movements, Jim led a team to retrieve the red posts from the emergency store and carefully entering the last four digits of his phone the store slowly opened. Clearly the four posts were easily identified. As they emerged with the posts Jim took charge of the situation, his voice projecting authority but tinged with urgency as he directed the positioning of the red posts to secure their perimeter. "All right, let's get these posts set up," Jim instructed, his tone decisive. "We need to mark our boundaries and ensure everyone stays within."

Jim divided them into teams to carry out his directives. "Team one, take a post and head east about 100 yards," Jim called out, pointing in the designated direction. "Team two, head west. Team three, north. Team four, south and make sure you count out 100 yards."

Nodding in agreement and understanding they moved swiftly to execute their assigned tasks. Setting up the red posts at strategic intervals around their camp.

As the first post was planted and activated to glow red, marking the eastern boundary, Jim said "Good job, keep going," he encouraged, his voice cutting through the tension. "Let's make sure the vehicles and everyone are inside our defence line."

The teams worked efficiently, their movements synchronised as they positioned the remaining posts to mark the boundaries of their sanctuary. Jim coordinated from the centre and making sure to keep a watchful eye on their progress and ensuring that no one strayed beyond the designated perimeter.

Amidst the chilling night, illuminated by the crimson glow of the posts, Jim's leadership brought a sense of order and purpose to the group. With their defences in place, they huddled together, prepared to confront whatever threat approached, united in their resolve to protect their refuge. Dave called again asking are the posts in position and all glowing red, he was ensuring that everyone had secured the red posts properly and glowing to indicate their readiness.

Jim replied, "Dave, the posts are in place and glowing red."

Dave's voice crackled through the speaker, his tone businesslike yet concerned. "Good work."

Jim at first nodded, even though Dave couldn't see him, then he answered. "Yes, they're anchored securely," casting a quick glance at the nearest post to confirm its stability.

Dave continued with his instructions, his voice unwavering. "Make sure everyone stays within the perimeter. We're detecting movement in your vicinity, so remain vigilant, you now need to press the top of each post four times then pause then press another four times.. do this one at a time and then the posts will glow green and you will all be protected."

Jim listened intently to Dave's instructions, he relayed the final directive to the group huddled within the safety perimeter.

"Everyone, make sure you're inside. I'm going to activate the posts now," Jim announced, ensuring that each person was accounted for and was within the defensive boundary.

With a firm grip, Jim pressed the top of one of the red posts four times then a pause and then another four times, each press deliberate and forceful. He glanced around to ensure that everyone was safely inside the designated area before pressing the post for the last time.

Listening to Dave's voice at the same time through the communication device, Jim absorbed the next set of instructions. "When all the posts turn green, a single purple beam of light will join them. That's our signal that you are secure, you must do this to all four posts," Dave explained.

Jim nodded. "Get ready," he said quietly to those gathered around him.

As Jim completed the last of the presses, to his post. The red posts began to emit a soft green glow, casting an eerie light in the dim surroundings. Everyone carried out the same task on the remaining posts. As the last post turned green a vivid purple beam shot skyward, connecting the posts in a protective dome shaped barrier.

"Perimeter's active," Jim confirmed, his voice filled with resolve. "Stay close and stay safe." "We've got the dome activated now and it looks amazing." Jim announced, his tone filled with a mix of relief and determination. "As long as we stay inside this line we will remain secure. Nothing can get through from the outside."

He glanced around . "Remember, everyone, stay within the purple line, we're safe as long as we don't breach it. Keep together and keep watch."

The vehicle that Dave had warned about approached at speed, kicking up a cloud of dust in its wake, everyone watched intently. The dust swirled around as the vehicle reached the perimeter. The vehicle screeched to a halt just outside the perimeter, its occupants peering through the barrier with a mix of frustration and curiosity.

From within the safety of their dome, everyone had concerns and relieved to see the barrier holding strong against the outside world.

Jim maintained a vigilant watch, ready to respond to any further developments. Everyone now silent with tensions in the air as they awaited the next move from beyond the purple line.

A man's voice from outside the dome echoed through the barrier, a plea for water cutting through the tense atmosphere inside.

Jim stepped forward, his voice projecting clearly through the dome, "I'm sorry, but we have limited water ourselves."

Jim's refusal echoed through the dome, the man outside appeared momentarily disappointed. He exchanged glances with his companions, their expressions conveying a mix of resignation and what looked like a false understanding.

Despite the setback, the man maintained a polite demeanour, acknowledging Jim's response with a nod. His voice carried a note of gratitude mixed with resignation as he responded, "Thank you for considering. We understand. Stay safe." Then all of a sudden his attitude changed. The man's frustration boiled over, his tone shifted abruptly. He raised his voice, echoing through the tense silence within the dome. "It's okay then! We'll take what we want with force!" His declaration carried a chilling undertone, punctuated by a sense of desperation.

Outside the protective perimeter, the gang accompanying the man exchanged urgent glances, their expressions clouded with a mixture of determination and apprehension. They began to move purposefully, their actions betraying a resolve to proceed toward Jim.

Inside the dome, the atmosphere grew tense as Jim and the others braced for the imminent threat. The prospect of a confrontation very real, the man's words lingered like an ominous warning. As the man advanced with determined steps toward the dome's boundary his foot made contact with the glowing purple beam. Instantly, a remarkable reaction occurred—a visible ripple spread outward from the point of contact, like a shock wave traversing the surface of water.

The man's momentum was abruptly halted as if he had struck an invisible barrier. His body recoiled involuntarily, jolting backward several paces. His expression morphed from aggression to confusion, mingled with a hint of disbelief. He reached out tentatively with his hand, cautiously testing the boundary again, but encountered the same forceful resistance.

Inside the dome, those observing the encounter witnessed the man's reaction with a mixture of relief and caution. The effectiveness of the perimeter's defence was demonstrated vividly before their eyes a boundary that repelled unwanted intruders without the need for direct confrontation. The men outside the perimeter, emboldened by their leader's attempt to breach the barrier, reacted swiftly, one man armed with a firearm, took aim and fired a single shot toward the perimeter. The gunshot echoed through the air, reverberating throughout the surrounding landscape.

Inside the dome, the occupants tensed at the sudden noise. The projectile struck the purple barrier with a bright spark, creating a visible impact point where the bullet disintegrated upon contact. The protective energy field held firm, deflecting the shot harmlessly away.

The visible resilience of the barrier served as a warning to those outside, emphasising the futility of attempting to breach the perimeter by force. As the tension outside the dome escalated, another individual among the group of assailants took more drastic action. Gripping a machine gun, he unleashed a prolonged burst of gunfire at the dome's barrier. The staccato sound of automatic fire filled the air, accompanied by the distinct rattling by the weapon.

Inside the dome, the occupants braced themselves as the barrage of bullets struck the protective field. The dome shimmered and flickered under the sustained assault, the energy field absorbing each impact with visible resistance. The barrier glowed brightly where the bullets made contact, but it held steadfast against the onslaught.

Despite the intensity of the gunfire, the dome remained intact, deflecting each bullet harmlessly away. The assailants outside soon realised the futility of their attack as the dome absorbed the relentless assault. After several seconds of sustained fire, the machine gun fell silent, leaving behind an eerie calm.

Inside the dome, the occupants took a collective breath, relieved that the barrier had withstood the attack. The resilience of the protective perimeter served as a stark reminder of their isolation and the dangers lurking outside. Inside the dome, the atmosphere was tense yet resolute after the failed attack on the perimeter. Jim, standing among the group spoke firmly to reassure everyone.

"We need to remain calm and stay vigilant," Jim advised, his voice steady despite the recent turmoil. "The perimeter held and they know they can't breach it easily."

Then the assault escalated outside the dome, a sudden and alarming event unfolded. One of the assailants hurled a hand grenade toward them. The grenade struck the ground near the dome, causing a deafening explosion. Inside the dome, the women and children let out terrified screams as the blast rattled the structure. The force of the explosion scared everyone, but fortunately, the dome's protective barrier absorbed much of the impact, shielding those inside from direct harm.

Jim and the others quickly assessed the situation, ensuring everyone was safe amid the chaos. As the chaos of the grenade explosion settled, Jim's voice rang out with authority and determination. He issued a stern warning to the assailants outside the dome and demanded their immediate departure.

"You have one minute to leave the area," Jim's voice boomed through the tense atmosphere, conveying both resolve and urgency.

The men outside the dome, startled by Jim's firm stance, exchanged glances among themselves. The countdown began, each passing second heightening the tension after Jim's ultimatum, now a sense of unease and apprehension gripped the men outside the dome. They glanced nervously at each other, realising that their attempts to breach the perimeter had been met with unexpected resistance and they slowly moved away. It started to look like Jim's ultimatum was working

Then the silence was broken by a call from Dave, Dave's voice came through Jim's communication device, a calm and reassuring presence amidst the recent turmoil. "Jim, we are tracking the movements of those men. They are heading away from your location. We'll continue monitoring their movements, but it looks like you've seen the last of them for now."

Jim listened intently, relief evident in his expression. "Thanks, Dave. Keep us updated if anything changes," he replied, his voice reflecting a mix of gratitude and readiness to address any further threats.

With Dave's assurance, a sense of temporary calm was restored within the dome. They knew they had a vigilant ally in Dave and the tracking systems, providing a measure of security in the uncertain night.

One of the women, her face reflecting a mix of fear and relief, spoke up with a trembling voice. "Thank goodness they're gone. I was so scared for the children," she confessed, her words echoing the sentiments shared by others within the protective perimeter.

Jim nodded, his gaze sweeping over the group. "We're safe for now," he assured them, his tone carrying a hint of reassurance. "Let's try to get some rest. We'll stay vigilant, but it looks like we're out of immediate danger."

As the conversation continued, a sense of gratitude permeated the air—a shared acknowledgment of their close call and a renewed appreciation for the security provided by the protective dome and the technology supporting them.

Chapter 13

MAINTAIN ORDER

Several days passed since the attempted attack on the group and a tense atmosphere has now settled over their temporary sanctuary in the ghost town of Rhyolite. The once frequent roar of fighter jets over Death Valley had become sporadic, punctuated by distant explosions that echoed through the valley. However what now unsettled them most was the dwindling presence of the fighter jets and the increasing ominous green glow that appeared on the horizon each night.

Huddled together in the fading light of dusk their faces reflecting a mix of curiosity and concern observing the eerie green glow in the distance. The usual banter and chatter had given way to whispered conversations and worried glances towards the horizon.

Ben spoke up thus breaking the uneasy silence. "Anyone have any idea what that constant glow might be?"

Barbara responded. "It's more than likely related to whatever caused those fighter jets to diminish," her gaze fixed on the distant horizon. "We need to stay alert. It's not safe to assume anything at this point."

With those comments everyone exchanged uneasy looks. The green glow cast an otherworldly hue over the landscape.

The days passed and tension mounted and another concern crept into the forefront because of the dwindling water supplies. The ghost town of Rhyolite while providing some shelter but lacked the resources needed for long-term survival. This was the case in the olden days, no water.

Ben gathered everyone together for a chat, his expression grave. "Water's running low," he announced, his voice tinged with concern. Murmurs of worry rippled through everyone.

Barbara stepped forward, her demeanour resolute. "We need to make a plan," she stated, her eyes scanning the worried faces. "We can't rely on finding water out here. We might need to consider our options carefully."

Several women exchanged anxious looks, their concern evident. One of the children piped up, "What are we going to do if we run out of water?"

Barbara knelt down, offering a reassuring smile. "We'll figure something out," she assured him, her voice steady despite the uncertainty. "We need to stay calm and think rationally."

Ben nodded in agreement. "We might have to consider leaving this place," he admitted and his tone was very serious. He added, "As Barbara has said we need a plan."

Tense silence followed. With the passing of time the challenges mounted with survival depending on their ability to adapt and make difficult decisions.

Ben then made an urgent call for everyone to leave which was met with a swift response from Jim advising that previous instructions were to remain in place. "We were told to stay put!" Jim said firmly in a raised voice.

Ben, however was resolute. "That was many days ago," he countered with his tone urgent. "Things have changed. We can't wait around here hoping for help that might never come."

Barbara stepped in, her expression thoughtful. "Jim's right," she interjected, addressing Ben. "Although we can't afford to wait indefinitely. If we don't have water, we need to find it elsewhere."

A murmur of agreement rippled through everyone, some nodding in support of Ben's proposal. Jim looked around at the faces gathered but again Jim remained adamant that they could not leave. "We've been instructed to stay put," he again asserted firmly, his voice resolute despite the mounting concerns. "We can't risk exposing ourselves out there without a plan or knowing what's happening beyond this perimeter."

Barbara exchanged a glance with Jim, her expression reflecting a mix of understanding and concern. "Jim's right," she added, her voice calm yet unwavering. "We need to hold our ground until we have a clearer picture of what's going on."

Ben glanced between Jim and Barbara and his expression showing a mix of frustration and worry. "But we are running out of water," he pointed out, his tone edged with urgency.

Jim nodded, acknowledging the seriousness they all find themselves. "I know, Ben," he responded, his voice tinged with concern. "Let's prioritise securing the water we have while we figure out our next steps."

At last everyone nodded in agreement but some exchanging uneasy glances as they contemplated their dwindling resources and uncertain future.

Amidst the hushed darkness of the night a sudden bleep from the communicator sent a ripple of urgency through the camp. Startled figures scrambled to rouse Jim, their movements cautious yet hurried, not wanting to disturb the uneasy calm that enveloped their temporary sanctuary.

Jim had also just been jolted awake by the persistent bleeping, quickly reaching for the communicator. His hand fumbled momentarily in the dim light before he managed to grasp it and activate the display. The soft glow of the screen illuminated his features, casting a pale light on the concerned expressions around him.

As Jim tapped the device to accept the incoming call. Everyone's eyes fixated on him, their faces etched with a mix of anticipation and trepidation, unsure of what news the communication might bring in the dead of night.

Jim said, "It's Zeena," her voice was calm yet determined as it echoed through the silent night. Jim's expression shifted subtly as he processed the message, a mix of relief and concern flickering across his face.

Around him, the others listened intently, their features illuminated by the soft glow of the communicator's screen. Barbara stood nearby, her eyes reflecting the muted light, her posture poised yet weary from the lingering tension of recent days.

Jim looked up and said, "I am sorry to say its going to be another two days."

Ben's brows furrowed in frustration, his gaze fixed on Jim as he absorbed the news. "Two more days?" he muttered, voicing the collective sentiment. The group concerned and grappling with the reality of remaining in their vulnerable position.

Outside, the distant rumble of the odd fighter jet underscored Zeena's words, a reminder of the unrest that encroached upon their isolated refuge. The camp, shrouded in the cloak of night, seemed suspended in time, caught between the urgency of their circumstances and the reassurance of imminent help.

Jim nodded solemnly, his voice steady yet laden with unspoken apprehension. "We wait," he announced, his words echoing through the quietude, each syllable carrying the weight of their shared resolve to hold fast until rescue arrived.

Ben's dissatisfaction was palpable, his features taut with tension as he processed the implications of Zeena's message. Despite Jim's assurances unrest was growing. Ben now paced restlessly within the confines of their makeshift camp, his unease manifesting in terse mutterings and restless gestures.

"We can't just sit here," Ben exclaimed, his frustration breaking through the veil of enforced stillness. "What if those jets stop coming? What then?"

Barbara approached Ben, her expression a blend of empathy and concern. "We have to trust what Zeena has said," she urged softly, her voice a calming counterpoint to his rising anxiety. "They'll come for us."

But Ben, stubborn remained unconvinced. "And if they don't?" he retorted, his voice edged with desperation. "We can't keep waiting."

Jim knew he had to maintain order and stepped forward, his gaze unwavering. "We stick to the plan," he asserted firmly, his tone brooking no argument. "We have just enough supplies."

Yet the tension lingered, Ben's apprehension a tangible undercurrent amidst their precarious situation. The camp settled once more into an uneasy quiet, each member struggling with their own fears and doubts.

The next day Jim beckoned Ben to a secluded spot away from the others, a gesture that conveyed both urgency and confidentiality. As they stood amidst the rugged landscape, Jim's expression was resolute yet empathetic, his gaze fixed on Ben.

"We need to talk," Jim began, his voice measured but earnest. "I know you're worried, Ben. We all are but we have to trust Zeena and Dave. They'll come through for us."

Ben's features betrayed his lingering doubt, his brow furrowed with concern. "What if they don't make it in time?" he countered, his voice tinged with frustration. "What then?"

Jim paused, considering Ben's words before responding. "We have to stay strong, Ben," he said, his tone firm but compassionate. "We've come this far. Panicking won't help."

Ben sighed, the weight of uncertainty evident in his demeanour. "I just don't like feeling helpless," he admitted, his voice tinged with resignation.

"We're doing everything we can," Jim reassured him, placing a reassuring hand on Ben's shoulder and said. "Let's focus on keeping everyone calm until help arrives."

Ben nodded reluctantly, his expression a blend of resignation and determination. They stood together for a moment longer, the vast expanse of Death Valley stretching out around them, a reminder of their isolation and vulnerability. But amid the uncertainty, Jim's quiet resolve offered hope, a steadying presence amidst the encroaching problem.

Jim's quiet assurance resonated with Ben, offering a glimmer of hope amidst their predicament.

Ben met Jim's gaze, his expression a mix of gratitude and uncertainty. "I hope you're right," Ben replied, his voice had trace of resignation.

"We've faced challenges before," Jim continued, his tone resolute. "We'll find a way."

Ben nodded, finding comfort in Jim's steadfast demeanour. "Thanks, Jim," he said, his voice tinged with renewed resolve. "Yes I agree that we focus on keeping everyone together."

As they turned back toward camp, Ben's steps seemed lighter, buoyed by Jim's reassurance and now a shared determination became a quiet strength amid the encroaching uncertainty.

They both arrived back in camp and then without warning Ben stood in the middle of everyone and made an impassioned speech. "Jim is our leader!" Ben exclaimed, his voice was loud and carried through the air with conviction. "He's seen us through thick and thin. We trust him. He has helped us in so many ways and without him many of us would not be alive today. I want to say I fully support him!"

The response was immediate and resounding. Cheers erupted, accompanied by the rhythmic sound of clapping hands. Jim, visibly moved by the show of support, nodded gratefully at Ben, acknowledging the unity and solidarity that filled the air.

In that moment, amid the echoing applause, a sense of collective purpose emerged—a commitment to persevere and endure together under Jim's guidance.

Chapter 14

ENCOUNTER

Meanwhile Clio and Jessica have ventured out in Dodger towards Death Valley and they have been made aware of the plight of Jim and Barbara's group. Before that can be done they have to investigate an alien craft that has supposedly crashed after an encounter with our Air Force. They must pinpoint the crash site and gather as much information as possible.

Upon arrival at the Stovepipe Wells area of Death Valley there was nothing to be seen. They had walked out to Mesquite Flat Sand Dunes but still nothing. So Jessica had suggested that they head toward Dante's View as they would be able to see for miles and this could save many hours of searching.

Dodger traversed the rugged terrain heading toward Dante's View keeping away from the road area as much as possible. Travelling on the ground and just above the ground at slow speed while scanning the landscape around Death Valley.

Inside Dodger both Clio and Jessica prepared for their investigation. The craft's onboard systems displayed readings and analysis tools, providing real-time data. The sky above remained ominous and reminding both of the recent aerial confrontations and the ongoing threats faced by humanity.

Dodger neared Dante's View around five thousand feet above Badwater. Once at Dante's View they could see for miles. Scorch marks and displaced earth marked several areas of the Badwater Basin, this was evidence of a violent crash but yet no sign of the craft.

Clio had been here before when the only thing that could be heard would be tourists talking with the sound of car engines and of course the wind, now only the wind could be heard with no sign of life anywhere.

At the very top now with a much better vantage point to be able to locate the downed alien craft.

Dodger's sensors detected residual energy traces, corroborating reports of the intense aerial engagement that had unfolded in the skies above.

In addition to the scorched earth marks Dodger's AI directed Clio and Jessica to debris. The alien craft's impact site lay visible in the distance, marked by the same scorched earth and now also the remnants of the downed craft. AI had now pinpointed the location of the downed alien craft and it was near Badwater Basin, which is directly below. Clio and Jessica observed the aftermath of the destructive encounter. The craft lay approximately two miles from the visitor car park, which had been decimated by multiple blasts, likely occurring some time ago. The landscape bore the scars of intense energy discharges, with debris scattered across the barren terrain.

Nightfall began to envelop Death Valley. The temperature dropped noticeably, a common occurrence even in this arid region but this time the drop in temperature was much more than normal. Inside Dodger, AI systems calculated the best approach for the final stretch to their target. Dodger moved swiftly down from Dante's View to the area but stopped well short of the crash site.

"AI recommends we cover the last half mile on foot," Clio relayed, glancing at Jessica. "We need to minimise Dodger's presence to avoid detection by any remaining alien craft in the area."

Jessica nodded, understanding the importance of stealth in their reconnaissance mission. They disembarked from Dodger, equipped with portable scanning devices and protective gear against the chill of the desert night. The soft crunch of their footsteps on the rocky hard salt ground echoed in the stillness as they approached the crash site.

Dodger remained concealed in the distance, its systems on standby to respond to any unforeseen threats. Clio and Jessica moved cautiously, their senses alert to any signs of activity or residual energy emanating from the downed craft.

Now closing in on the alien wreckage, the stark contrast between the natural beauty of Death Valley and the impact of extraterrestrial conflict became even more pronounced. Dodger's data feeds continued to stream updates back to base, ensuring that their findings would contribute to a broader understanding of the alien incursion.

In the gathering darkness, Clio and Jessica pressed forward with purpose, determined to uncover the secrets of the craft.

All of a sudden their protective suits alerted them to a concerning development: a rapid decline in oxygen levels in the outside air.

Jessica glanced at her suit's display, her brow furrowing in concern. "Clio, the oxygen levels are dropping fast out here," she said, her voice muffled slightly by the suit's helmet.

Clio adjusted her own suit's settings, scanning the surrounding environment. "We need to move quickly," she replied, her tone urgent. "The crash site should be just ahead so lets gather data fast and get back to Dodger."

They quickened their pace, mindful of their oxygen supply and the increasing strain on their suits. The conversation between them was punctuated by the soft hiss of their respirators as they navigated the rocky terrain.

"We can't stay out here for long," Jessica noted, her gaze fixed on the dark silhouette of the downed alien craft ahead.

Clio nodded in agreement. "Agreed we must focus on the scans and visual documentation. We need to gather as much information as possible before heading back."

They reached the perimeter of the crash site, where remnants of the alien craft lay strewn across the desert floor. Working efficiently, Clio and Jessica deployed their scanning devices, capturing detailed readings and imagery of the wreckage.

Now well into the crash site area, they found a large part of the alien craft and instruments were reporting that it was devoid of any signs of life—neither alien nor human.

The scene before them was eerie. The alien craft lay in disarray, its metallic hull scorched and twisted from the impact. Surrounding it were remnants of what seemed to be advanced technology, now reduced to smouldering wreckage scattered across the desert floor.

Jessica surveyed the area with a cautious gaze, her helmeted visor reflecting the dimming light of the setting Sun. "It looks like the craft was abandoned," she remarked, her voice filled with a mix of curiosity and apprehension.

Clio nodded with her focus on gathering data undeterred. She activated her scanning device, its sensors emitting soft pulsing lights as it analysed the wreckage. "No signs of life forms," Clio confirmed, her tone calm despite the gravity of their discovery. "It appears the occupants either evacuated or...or something else happened," Jessica finished Clio's words, her eyes scanning the perimeter for any clues.

Completing their outside survey making sure their findings were meticulously detailed, capturing images and recording sensor data.

The alien technology was unlike anything they had encountered, a testament of an advanced civilisation that had crafted it.

With the Sun sinking below the horizon and the oxygen levels outside their protective suits dwindling, Clio and Jessica knew it was time to retreat. They turned back toward Dodger, their minds buzzing with analysis and speculation as they prepared to relay their discoveries to their colleagues.

Arriving back at Dodger, Clio and Jessica contacted Dave, hoping for new instructions like rescue Jim and Barbara however, what they heard next caught them off guard and filled them with a sense of apprehension they couldn't shake.

"Jessica, Clio, we need you to go back to the crash site," Dave's voice crackled over the communication link. "We need detailed radiation readings from the area around the craft. Then, I need you to attempt entry into the alien vessel. The more data we have the better."

Clio's concerned look as she exchanged a glance with Jessica. Radiation readings and exploring the inside of an unknown alien ship were tasks that carried significant risks and the hesitation in their expressions was evident.

"Dave, are you sure about this?" Clio asked, her voice tinged with concern. "Entering that craft could be dangerous and we don't have enough information about what we might encounter inside."

Dave's response was calm and matter-of-fact. "I understand your concerns, Clio. But this is crucial for our understanding of the situation. We need to gather as much data as possible."

Jessica chimed in, her tone reflecting her reservations. "What about the radiation levels? Is it safe for us to be exposed to whatever caused the crash?"

Dave's voice conveyed a sense of urgency. "We believe the levels will have stabilised, but we need confirmation. Your suits should provide adequate protection, but stay vigilant."

Clio now filled with dread as she addressed Dave. "Dave, I don't think we can do this," Clio admitted, her tone weighted with uncertainty.

Dave's response was calm and reassuring, his voice cutting through the tension. "Clio, I understand your concerns but we need to gather this data to fully assess the situation. You're our best chance to get inside that craft and understand exactly what we're dealing with."

Clio replied softly, "But Dave, It's too dangerous and we don't know what's in there."

Dave replied with urgency. "I know it's risky but we need to take this step. Your protective suits should offer sufficient shielding and Dodger will remain on standby to extract you if needed."

Jessica spoke up, her voice firm. "Dave is there any other way to gather this data as an example can't we use remote drones or something?"

Dave's response was measured. "We've considered that and direct examination is our best option. We need eyes inside that craft, Jessica."

Clio sighed, her resolve firming as she processed Dave's words. "Understood, Dave we will proceed cautiously."

Both the girls who had significantly grown up rapidly since their road trip ended abruptly, when they were rescued by the strangers called Jim and Barbara. Although both girls could hardly believe that they were now preparing for the most dangerous thing they had ever done. A prolonged inspection of this alien craft. In fact maybe no one on Earth had done this before.

Jessica made a decisive addition to her gear. After ensuring they had ample oxygen for the mission, Jessica headed to the onboard armoury of Dodger to retrieve Vendor, the specialised weapon intended for extreme situations.

Inside the armoury, Jessica accessed the secure storage compartment containing Vendor. The weapon was unlike any other they carried—a last resort device designed for devastating impact. She mad sure Vendor was secured to her suit.

Once fully equipped they set out on their journey toward the crash site. The walk was made in silence. Approaching the downed craft, Jessica's resolve hardened, her gaze fixed on the twisted metal before them.

"We have arrived at the Alien Craft and we are ready to breach?" Jessica's voice carried determination over the communications link.

Clio nodded in response, her expression resolute beneath her helmet. "Let's do this."

Clio positioned herself ready to deploy a small silent laser cutting tool from her utility belt, upon activating it, the tool emitted a narrow yellow beam of energy that sliced through the damaged hull, creating an opening large enough for them to enter.

With Vendor secured at her side, Jessica led the way into the alien craft. The interior was dimly lit, unfamiliar technology lining the walls and casting eerie shadows. Jessica's light illuminated the surroundings as they pressed forward, the air heavy with anticipation.

Carefully navigating the corridors and remaining vigilant with her focus split between scanning their surroundings and monitoring her suit's readouts. The presence of Vendor offered reassurance amidst this alien environment, a symbol of their preparedness for whatever they might encounter.

"Radiation levels are within acceptable limits so far," Clio reported quietly, her voice a calm presence amidst the tension.

Jessica nodded, her grip tightening on Vendor's handle. "Let's gather as much data as we can and get out of here."

Their exploration continued methodically, documenting every detail of the alien vessel with handheld scanners and cameras. The minutes stretched into what seemed hours as they ventured deeper into the craft, the mysteries within unfolding before them.

With each step, Jessica remained keenly aware of Vendor's presence and thinking to herself hoping she didn't have to use it.

As Clio and Jessica stepped into the cavernous chamber within the alien craft, their senses were assaulted by a sight that defied comprehension. The space before them appeared like a vast cold storage room. The dimensions of the chamber stretched beyond what seemed feasible for the craft's exterior size, adding to the disorienting experience.

Thin translucent sheets hung from the ceiling in rows, it looked like thousands of them extending into the distance. Each sheet measured about two feet wide and eight feet high and so incredibly thin yet seemingly indestructible. The sheets resembled a delicate barrier, concealing a macabre secret within.

As Clio's and Jessica's suit sensors scanned the area, a chilling discovery unfolded before them—the presence of human DNA. Their hearts sank as they realised the grim truth. These were not living humans but remnants of humanity, compressed into a state akin to vacuum-packed goods.

The implications were staggering and the horror of the scene struck both Clio and Jessica to their core. The methodical cruelty and disregard for life displayed by the alien species resonated with profound indignation and sorrow.

Silent but for the hum of their suits, Clio and Jessica navigated the grisly labyrinth of suspended sheets. Each step carried them deeper into the heart of an unthinkable atrocity, emotions now a turbulent mix of revulsion and profound empathy for those whose lives had been so callously reduced to mere remnants.

Their mission, now infused with a heightened sense of urgency and purpose took on new significance. Every data point recorded, every image captured, served as a testament to the untold suffering inflicted upon their fellow humans—an ultimate act of humiliation and degradation by an incomprehensible adversary.

Jessica's sobs echoed softly within the confines of her suit, her emotions uncontainable as she grappled with the profound horror of the scene before her. Each breath felt heavy, burdened by the weight of despair and indignation. Tears welled up, blurring her vision momentarily as she struggled to comprehend the grotesque reality laid bare in the alien craft.

The sight of those thin, translucent sheets—each a vessel of unspeakable tragedy—struck deep into Jessica's soul. The vacuum-packed remnants of human beings, reduced to objects devoid of dignity, stirred a visceral reaction within her. It was a scene that defied humanity itself, a violation of everything she held sacred.

Amidst the disheartening silence of the chamber, Jessica's sobs became a poignant testament to the raw anguish felt by those who had suffered unimaginable fates. Her sorrow transcended words, resonating with a profound sense of empathy and sorrow for the countless lives unjustly snuffed out by this callous alien force.

Clio, equally affected by the grim tableau, turned towards Jessica, her own expression a blend of sympathy and shared anguish. She reached out a gloved hand, offering silent solace amidst the overwhelming grief that enveloped them.

Together, beneath the sterile glow of their suit lights, Clio and Jessica bore witness to an incomprehensible tragedy. Yet, amidst the darkness of that moment, a flicker of determination ignited—a resolve to ensure that these lost souls would not be forgotten, that their suffering would fuel their pursuit of justice and resistance against those who sought to extinguish the light of humanity.

Jessica's ability to maintain composure amidst the harrowing sight before her waned with each passing moment. The weight of what she had witnessed threatened to overwhelm her senses, making it increasingly challenging to concentrate on her surroundings.

As she navigated the expansive chamber, her mind struggled to process the depth of the atrocity. The images of those vacuum-packed remains persisted in her thoughts, casting a shadow over her ability to focus. Each step felt heavy, her movements deliberate yet burdened by a profound sense of sorrow.

The air inside her suit, once a source of reassurance, now seemed stifling and inadequate against the emotional onslaught. Breathing became laborious, each inhale and exhale a struggle against the rising tide of despair. The atmosphere of the chamber seeped into her bones, mirroring the chill in her heart.

Clio's presence offered a lifeline, a silent reminder of shared purpose amidst the darkness. Despite the overwhelming weight of grief, Jessica summoned every ounce of willpower to press on, fuelled by a determination to honour the memory of those lost souls.

In the face of such unfathomable tragedy, Jessica fought to reclaim her focus, driven by a resolve to confront the forces responsible and ensure that the voices silenced within this cold haunting chamber would never be forgotten and vowing to herself that one day retribution will echo through the corridors of justice.

In the solemn silence of the chamber, amidst the rows of thin, eerie sheets that held the vacuum-packed remains of human beings, Clio and Jessica found comfort in each other's presence. Standing amidst this haunting testament to tragedy, they clasped hands, their fingers intertwining in a gesture of shared solidarity.

Clio's touch was a tether, a lifeline in the disorienting expanse of despair. Their hearts now heavy with grief, they sought refuge in a timeless prayer, their voices soft yet resolute.

They stood motionless and whispered together. "Our Father who art in heaven, hallowed be thy name." The familiar words serving as a shield against the overwhelming sorrow that threatened to consume them. Each phrase echoed through the chamber, a testament to faith in the face of unfathomable loss.

"Thy Kingdom come, thy will be done, on Earth as it is in Heaven," they continued, the cadence of the prayer offering a semblance of order amidst the chaos of emotions, their voices resonated as they went through the Lords Prayer.

Once completed, Clio and Jessica moved through the harrowing expanse of the alien craft. They then stumbled upon a room that appeared to house weaponry. The contrast between the eerie stillness of the chamber and the ominous presence of these unknown armaments sent shivers down their spines.

The room was dimly lit, the air heavy with an otherworldly chill. Arrayed before them were strange and unfamiliar devices, each gleaming metallic surface reflecting their dim surroundings. These were not the tools of human warfare; instead they exuded an alien sophistication that hinted at technologies far beyond terrestrial understanding.

Clio and Jessica approached cautiously, their eyes darting from one intricate instrument to the next. The weaponry, if it could be called that, was unlike anything they had ever seen. Some devices bore resemblances to firearms, albeit with sleek, streamlined designs that defied conventional engineering. Others appeared more esoteric, with pulsating energy cores and enigmatic glyphs etched into their surfaces.

Despite the profound implications of their discovery, the room felt eerily silent. There was no indication of the purpose behind these enigmatic tools. Clio and Jessica exchanged wary glances, their expressions a mixture of curiosity and trepidation. What had transpired within this vessel? Were these weapons wielded in conquest, or were they tools of defence against unseen adversaries or to wage unlimited war.

Clio carefully selected one of the alien devices from the chamber, its sleek form feeling oddly weightless in her hands. Despite the weightlessness, its significance was profound—a potential key to understanding the advanced technology of their extraterrestrial adversaries.

As they retraced their steps through the cold, shadowed corridors of the craft, Jessica remained close by her companion, her expression still haunted by the grim discoveries they had made. The device Clio carried seemed to pulse with an otherworldly energy, casting faint reflections of light on the metallic walls.

They both navigated the chilling corridors of the alien craft, their focus intent on retrieving valuable data from the ominous vessel. Then a sudden disturbance shattered the eerie silence. Movement—a towering metal figure—lurched into view, its form angular and alien against the backdrop of the cold, metallic interior.

Jessica's cry pierced the stillness, her voice urgent with fear and adrenaline. "Run! Run for your life!"

Reacting swiftly, Clio grabbed Jessica's hand, her heart pounding in her chest as they sprinted down the narrow passageways, the air filled with the reverberating echoes of their footsteps. The towering figure, an enigmatic sentinel of the alien craft, loomed behind them, its purpose and intent unknown but undeniably menacing.

Dodging through labyrinthine corridors, Clio's mind raced with thoughts of escape and survival. The alien construct, clanking and relentless, pursued them with an eerie determination, its metallic limbs articulating with an unsettling fluidity.

They darted around corners, adrenaline-fuelled instincts guiding their path, they knew Dodger was their only hope amid the encroaching darkness. Behind them they could hear the echoing steps of the alien sentinel drawing closer.

Finally, with a burst of speed and determination, they rounded a final bend inside the craft and got out into the night air. This thing continued its pursuit.

With every turn they took, the towering metal figure seemed to anticipate their movements, its pursuit methodical and unyielding. Panic surged within Jessica as she stole a glance behind her, catching sight of the gleaming, angular form drawing nearer with each passing second.

Clio and Jessica now sprinting over the salt flats of Death Valley, their feet kicking up tiny clouds of dust and salt, the desolation of the landscape seemed to amplify their sense of isolation. The relentless pursuit continued.

Jessica's heart raced, adrenaline coursing through her veins as she kept pace with Clio. Fear mingled with determination as they fled from the looming metal figure that pursued them relentlessly.

"Clio, it's gaining on us!" Jessica gasped, her voice strained with exertion.

"We need to find cover," Clio replied, scanning the horizon for any sign of refuge.

The alien structure behind them moved with an unnatural swiftness, its metallic form glinting . The salt flats stretched endlessly around them, offering little in the way of concealment.

"Over here!" Clio shouted, beckoning Jessica toward a narrow crevice between two boulders.

They ducked into the rocky passage, their breathing heavy with exertion. The alien sentinel's footsteps echoed ominously behind them, growing louder with each passing moment.

"Stay quiet," Clio whispered, her eyes fixed on the entrance of their makeshift hideout.

Jessica nodded, her pulse racing as they waited in tense silence.

Moments later, the sound of the sentinel's approach grew deafening. They held their breath, bracing for the worst as the metallic footsteps drew closer.

Suddenly, the footsteps halted. Clio and Jessica exchanged wary glances, unsure of what to expect next.

The silence stretched on, broken only by the distant whistle of the wind across the salt flats. Clio cautiously peered around the edge of their hiding spot, her eyes widening in relief.

"It's gone," Clio whispered, her voice tinged with disbelief.

Jessica let out a shaky breath, her hands trembling with residual fear. "What was that thing?"

Then as if from nowhere and right in front of them they faced the menacing metal figure, a tense stand off unfolded under the relentless night of Death Valley. The metallic being, with its quicksilver eyes fixed upon them, seemed to radiate a sense of alien purpose, somehow it looked more metallic than a life form and the sensors had not picked up any life forms.

Before they could react, the figure surged forward with surprising speed. Jessica's heart pounded in her chest as she instinctively reached for Vendor, her hand finding the familiar grip of the weapon.

In a split-second decision, Jessica discharged Vendor at the advancing metal entity. The weapon hummed with latent power, emitting a burst of energy that struck the metal figure with precision. The discharge echoed across the desolate landscape, the bright flash momentarily illuminating the scene.

The metal thing staggered back as if shocked that the inhabitants of this planet possessed such power, its form momentarily disrupted by the impact. Jessica and Clio now turned and hurried across the salt flats and thus allowing Vendor to charge to full capacity once more. With a sense of determination Jessica steadied herself as this structure came at them again. In a moment of focus, Jessica fired Vendor once again, directing a precise shot at the heart of the advancing figure. The weapon discharged with a low hum and a brilliant burst of energy and it struck the metallic structure squarely in its core.

The impact reverberated through the air, accompanied by a burst of light and sound. The structure shuddered under the force of the blast, halting its pursuit.

Jessica's resolved surged as she confronted the staggering metal entity. With unyielding determination she faced the struggling structure her voice cutting through the tension of the moment. "Hey you alien!" Jessica shouted her words laced with fierce determination. "As soon as this goes green, I'm going to blow you to bits. This is for the lost souls!'

Vendor now fully charged again. Jessica discharged the power of the device hitting the thing directly in its middle. The entity was blown high into the air and bits from it clattered onto the ground. Jessica walked over collected a bit of the metal lying on the floor and shouted, "That's for humanity."

The girls stood there in silence in absolute disbelief and for a few minutes they neither moved or spoke. Eventually they both moved slowly away and headed back toward Dodger. They boarded Dodger, tranquillity returned, they were so relieved to be back on board. They immediately uploaded all the data they had gathered during their mission into the ship's central AI system.

The AI processed the incoming data with efficiency, analysing the findings in real-time. Moments later, a calm, synthesised voice resonated through the spacecraft's speakers. "Jessica, Clio," the AI addressed them, "I have received your data and reviewed your status. I am pleased to confirm that you are both safe from any sort of radiation damage."

The reassurance from Dodger's AI brought a sense of relief to Jessica and Clio knowing that their mission was successful and that they were both healthy. Now the AI could focus on getting them away from here.

After a few minutes the AI briefed Jessica and Clio on their next critical mission: rescuing Jim, Barbara and their group sheltering in Rhyolite. The girls had wanted to rescue their friends much sooner but this alien craft had become the priority. Clio asked for an update on Jim and Barbara's situation and they were told that the group are protected by a perimeter fence not a normal fence but one that protects them in every way you can imagine. With that Dodger headed towards Rhyolite. Jessica and Clio prepared for potential encounters, especially upon noticing lasers emitting from a specific area of the ghost town so they had to be sure it was emitting from the perimeter fence and not some sort of trap. Dodger approached cautiously, it's sleek hull glinting in the celestial light, stopping short of the encampment.

They stepped onto the surface of Rhyolite, the crunch of their boots against the dusty terrain echoing in their helmets. The landscape was eerie, with abandoned structures looming around them.

Together, they proceeded slowly towards the source of the lasers, moving methodically and staying alert. Clio called out into the silence, her voice transmitted through their suits' communicators. "We are looking for Jim and Barbara?"

A moment passed before a crackling response came through their communication channel. "Clio? Jessica? Is that really you?" It was Jim's voice, filled with disbelief and relief.

Jessica and Clio exchanged smiles beneath their helmets, delighted to hear Jim's voice. "Yes, it's us!" Jessica replied eagerly. "We're here to get you out. Where are you?"

"I will turn the perimeter fence off give us a couple of minutes then you will be able to proceed towards us. We're not far," Jim responded. "There has been some unfriendly visitors recently," Jim added.

With renewed determination, Jessica and Clio quickened their pace towards the encampment. Dodger's AI monitored their progress, ready to provide support and ensure a swift and safe rescue.

Jessica and Clio reached the fence at the same time it was deactivated, they found Jim and Barbara waiting anxiously. Upon seeing each other, there was a moment of joyful reunion. Jessica and Clio removed their helmets and embraced Jim and Barbara warmly. It was noticeable that the air seemed thin.

"It's good to see you both safe," Jessica said with a smile, relieved to have successfully reached them.

Jim's expression was one of gratitude mixed with concern. "Thanks for coming. Things have been getting a little difficult for us all, the air is getting much thinner now even at these low altitude levels," he stated.

Barbara nodded in agreement, her eyes reflecting both exhaustion and hope.

As they caught up, Jim's curiosity got the better of him. "Did you see the Jets and the Craft out there?" he asked, referring to the mysterious sightings.

Jessica chuckled lightly. "Oh yes, we did," she replied cryptically. "That's another story altogether and not one you want to hear right now."

With time of the essence, Jessica, Clio, Jim and Barbara quickly gathered their belongings and prepared to return to Dodger. Jessica and Clio looked shocked when Jim shared news about the group they were rescuing.

"Before we go, we have many more with us who are exhausted," Jim explained, his expression grave. "Ben, the guy we rescued, had thirty people with him. Among them is his wife Olivia and their baby. What's unusual is that there are only five men among the adults, which is strange. We also have five children with us, all in need of returning to safety."

Jessica nodded, understanding the urgency. "We'll make room for them on Dodger," she assured Jim. "We have supplies and space to accommodate everyone."

Clio chimed in, "We'll ensure everyone is settled and comfortable for the journey back, I have notified AI."

Barbara, ever practical, began organising the group, prioritising the needs of the exhausted travellers and ensuring the children were cared for.

Together, they helped Ben's group board Dodger. Everyone couldn't believe that such a craft existed and that it had AI providing assistance. Dodger's AI adjusted its resources to accommodate the additional passengers, deploying emergency supplies and setting up accommodations.

Jessica, known for her occasional humour, quipped about Dodger's capabilities as they discussed the spacecraft's impressive manoeuvrability.

"You know," Jessica said with a grin, "This craft can cut through mountain ranges like a knife through butter."

Her comment elicited laughter from Clio, Jim, Barbara who couldn't help but chuckle at the playful comment.

Jessica, wiping away a tear of laughter, a much happier tear than earlier and replied, "Let's hope we don't encounter any mountains!"

The shared moment of levity served to ease the tension and relax everyone amidst the uncertainties of their situation. Dodger now continued its course heading away from the Death Valley area, the laughter lingered as a reminder of resilience and camaraderie in the face of adversity. AI seamlessly integrated itself into the atmosphere. Upon the passengers' request, the AI skilfully fulfilled a simple yet comforting desire: dispensing chocolate and again making sure all the oxygen levels were correct.

With a mere voice command, the passengers watched in amazement as the AI conjured coffee tea and various other drinks seemingly from thin air. Cups materialised filled with rich, aromatic brew, appearing on small trays in front of each individual.

"Thank you, Dodger!" exclaimed Barbara, savouring the first sip of her coffee and smiling as she already knew the capabilities of Dodger.

Jim chuckled, shaking his head in disbelief. "I still can't get used to this," he remarked, enjoying the luxury of freshly brewed coffee in the midst of their journey.

Jessica glanced around, appreciating the AI's thoughtful gesture. "It's the little things that make a difference," she noted, taking a moment to savour her own cup of coffee.

Dodger approached a looming mountain in its path, the passengers, including the children, noticed with a mix of curiosity and apprehension. One of the kids pointed out the imminent obstacle, exclaiming, "Look, we're heading for the mountain!"

Jessica, calm and assured, reassured the young passenger, "Don't worry, we know."

Her confidence helped ease any lingering concerns among the new passengers.

Dodger, guided by its advanced AI, approached the mountain with precision a bump as it came into contact with the rocky side of the mountain. Dodger had now entered the rocky terrain, it seemed to glide through the solid mass as effortlessly as passing through fresh air. The sensation was surreal for the passengers, who watched in awe as Dodger navigated through the mountain as if it were merely an illusion.

Behind Dodger, the solid rock miraculously reformed, sealing the path and leaving no trace. The passengers inside felt only a gentle vibration as Dodger continued on its course, now at immense speed.

Inside the craft , the passengers were amazed by the incredible technology at work. Jim couldn't contain his amazement. "I have seen this a few times already and I still don't believe it," he remarked, peering out of a viewport.

Barbara said to the children. "We're safe with Dodger," she murmured with gratitude.

As Dodger surged forward at incredible speed, the passengers were awestruck by the experience and filled with anticipation. The journey, marked by wonder and resilience as Dodger propelled them towards their destination.

With that Dodger came to a sudden halt and the doors opened, revealing a person standing there, a wave of relief and gratitude swept over the passengers who had been rescued. This persons welcoming presence and reassuring words brought a sense of safety and comfort to everyone on board.

"Hi everyone I'm Dave, you are all safe. So welcome to safety," Dave had greeted them warmly, his voice filled with genuine concern and care.

The passengers, many of whom had endured harrowing experiences and uncertainty, expressed their thankfulness with heartfelt smiles and words of gratitude. Jim stepped forward saying. "Good to be back."

The rescued children, now surrounded by friendly faces and a sense of security, looked up at Dave with wide eyes and their expressions reflecting relief and wonder.

Jessica and Clio, silently acknowledging the magnitude of the moment. They knew that the journey had been challenging, but seeing the gratitude and relief on the faces of those they had rescued made it all worthwhile. Both knew they dare not tell everyone about the horrors that they had seen. AI was aware of this so Dave and Zeena will now know.

Dave, with a humble smile, reassured them, "You're all in good hands now. Rest easy."

The rescued passengers disembarked from Dodger and led to safety by Dave, the atmosphere was filled with a profound sense of thankfulness and hope. Each person felt a deep sense of gratitude for the kindness and dedication that had brought them to this moment of sanctuary and security. What they didn't know was the shocking things that both Jessica and Clio had witnessed and it most certainly won't be an isolated incident.

The next morning, as the Sun rose over the valley, Jim gathered all the adults together for a meeting. Ben and his group, along with Henry's group and others rescued by Josh and Rick from farther away, gathered around, their expressions a mix of curiosity and apprehension.

Jim began to speak, his voice steady yet filled with urgency. "Friends, we need to talk about what's been happening. We've all seen and experienced strange things—alien crafts, abductions... It's time we share our stories."

As Jim's explanation unfolded, to looks of horror and disbelief. Some recounted their encounters with alien crafts—bright lights in the sky, inexplicable movements and eerie sightings that defied explanation. The atmosphere was heavy with emotion as each person shared their ordeal, their voices laden with fear, confusion and a deep sense of vulnerability.

After a moment of sombre silence, Jim turned to Clio and Jessica. "Now, we've heard from many of us. Clio, Jessica, do you have any insights or information that could help us understand what's going on?"

Clio stepped forward, her expression determined yet compassionate. "I know this is a lot to take in, but we've been studying these phenomena for some time now. What you've experienced aligns with reports from other parts of the world."

Jessica nodded in agreement. "We believe after AI analysed all the data that these encounters are just the start and that there's a larger pattern at play."

The adults listened intently, their faces reflecting a mix of hope and trepidation.

"We're here to support each other," Clio continued. "Together, we can piece together the puzzle and hopefully find a way forward."

The meeting continued with adults listening intently and it was Jim that convinced Jessica that all the adults should know what happened. With that Jessica took a deep breath, her voice trembling as she prepared to share her harrowing experience aboard the crashed alien craft.

"Myself and Clio responded to reports of an unidentified object crashing in a remote area," Jessica began, her tone strained with the weight of her memories. "When we arrived at the site, we found a strange, metallic craft unlike anything we had ever seen."

Her words lingered in the air, Jessica paused, her hands shaking visibly.

"As we cautiously approached the craft, a sense of foreboding engulfed me," Jessica continued, her voice wavering. "Inside, the scene was surreal—strange lights flickering, ominous shadows moving, a pervasive sense of otherworldliness."

The room fell silent, everyone hanging on Jessica's every word.

"Then, I saw them," Jessica recounted, her eyes glistening with unshed tears. "Thousands of thin, plastic sheets, two feet wide by eight feet long, hanging on giant rails that stretched for a long distance within the craft there must have been thousands."

Gasps and murmurs rippled through the gathered adults, their expressions a mix of shock and disbelief.

"Our detectors detected human remains," Jessica continued, her voice trembling. "Each of those sheets had once been a human being, crushed as if being packed. The width of each sheet was just a millimetre, like a vacuum-packed piece of meat..."

Jessica's words trailed off, her voice catching in her throat. Overwhelmed by the horrific realisation of what she had witnessed, she started sobbing uncontrollably.

In that moment of anguish, Clio, sensing Jessica's distress, rushed forward and enveloped her in a gentle embrace. Other adults move toward them, offering comforting words and gentle touches of support.

As Jessica received the compassion of her peers, a heavy silence settled over the room—a shared acknowledgment of the unimaginable tragedy and the weight of the unknown.

As Jessica's harrowing account reached its chilling conclusion, the room fell into a profound silence. The gravity of her words were unbelievable, weighing on the hearts and minds of everyone present.

In the quiet that followed, emotions ran deep. Women and men alike reached out to one another, offering hugs, clasping hands and sharing in the collective sorrow and shock. There were no words that could adequately express the horror and sadness they felt, but their gestures spoke volumes.

Some wiped away tears, while others simply stood together, finding some comfort in the shared presence of fellow survivors who understood the magnitude of what they had heard.

Clio, still embracing Jessica, felt the weight of the moment but also the strength of their community coming together. She exchanged sombre glances with others in the room, their eyes reflecting resilience amidst profound grief.

Amidst the hushed atmosphere, a sense of unity started to emerge—a resolve to support one another. In the absence of answers, they found comfort in their connections, drawing strength from the simple act of being there for each other in the aftermath of such devastating revelations.

Then as if gaining strength from everyone present Clio stepped forward saying, "There's more, we were chased by a sentinel looking machine very tall and more robot than human very metallic and appeared so intelligent. It chased us and we tried our best to get away but we just couldn't. It was then when all hope had gone that Jessica unleashed Vendor and this thing took three hits, she faced it head on and she destroyed it."

Everyone cheered and this cheering went on for some time with people hugging both Clio and Jessica.

As the silence began to lift and questions started to fill the room, Jim raised his hands to quiet the clamour, his expression grave but resolute.

"I understand your fears and uncertainties," Jim began, addressing all. "We have special defences in place and we're actively working on enhancing our security measures. Clio and Jessica have proved that our weapons will defend us."

He turned towards Jessica and Clio, acknowledging their bravery. "Thank you, Jessica and Clio, It's a lot to process."

Jim then addressed the pressing questions with a note of reassurance. "Later today, we'll have more detailed information from Josh, Rick, Dave and Zeena. They've been working tirelessly to gather intel and develop strategies. Please be patient as we piece together the puzzle."

The room fell into a contemplative silence once again, the tension tempered by a growing sense of anticipation.

Clio, sensing the need for unity, stepped forward, her voice steady yet filled with compassion. "Let's lean on each other and stay united," she urged, her gaze sweeping across the room. "Together, we can face whatever challenges we may encounter."

Slowly but surely, the people rallied, drawing strength. Despite the uncertainties that loomed.

As the meeting reached a natural pause, Jim announced a brief break before reconvening later for the anticipated updates from Josh, Rick, Dave and Zeena. The group dispersed, some engaging in quiet conversations while others took a moment of solitude to process the revelations of the morning.

Clio and Jessica understood that there were depths to this mystery that remained shrouded even to them.

Meanwhile, Jim and Barbara conferred quietly, their expressions reflecting concern.

Dave approached Jim, his demeanour serious. "Jim, we've uncovered some startling information," he began, his voice low but urgent.

"There are aspects of this situation that even Clio, Jessica and Barbara along with all the others don't know."

Jim nodded solemnly and looking worried. "We need to be prepared for anything," he replied.

As the break drew to a close, everyone gathered once again. Josh, Rick, Dave and Zeena stepped forward, their expressions grave but determined.

"We've gathered substantial intelligence," Josh began, There are indeed revelations that go beyond what we've previously shared."

Rick chimed in, his tone measured. "What we're dealing with is unprecedented, but we have strategies in place to protect ourselves and respond effectively."

Dave and Zeena nodded in agreement, their presence reassuring amidst the uncertainty.

As they began to unveil the details, the room grew hushed once more, Clio, Jessica, Jim, Barbara and the others listened intently, their minds racing with the implications of what the new information may be. This time the human spirit would be tested like never before.

Dave started, "Myself, Zeena, Josh and Rick are androids and we have been dormant for centuries." As Dave's unexpected revelation hit home there was a stunned silence. Clio, Jessica, Jim, Barbara and the others stared at Dave with wide eyes, they had not realised that Josh and Rick were also androids, their minds struggling to process the implications of his words.

"You're androids?" Someone finally managed to utter, their voice barely above a whisper.

Dave nodded, his synthetic features maintaining an eerie calmness. "Yes, we were created with advanced technology to assist and protect humans in situations like this and when an extinction situation threatens, well we are activated."

Zeena stepped forward, her expression sympathetic yet detached. "Our primary directive is to ensure the safety and well-being of all humans," she explained. The realization dawned on all present with a mixture of awe and apprehension colouring their expressions. They had trusted Dave, Zeena, Josh and Rick as allies, unaware of their true nature until this moment.

The idea that Dave, along with Zeena, Josh and Rick, were androids left dormant for centuries until humanity faced extinction was almost too incredible to comprehend.

"You mean you've been here for centuries, waiting?" Henry asked, his voice tinged with disbelief.

Rick answered Henry directly. "Yes Henry and you trusted me once before at the gas station and it worked did it not."

Henry replied, "Rick I completely trust you and always will and you have my full support and thank you so much for the help you gave to me Margaret and our friends."

Rick smiled and then Dave nodded, his synthetic features impassive yet somehow expressive. Dave added, "Yes our creators left us here as a contingency plan. We were programmed to activate when humanity was ever on the brink of extinction and that has not happened before."

Zeena stepped forward, her voice calm and measured. "The trigger for our awakening was this real threat of extinction. Our purpose is to preserve and protect you all."

The weary people exchanged incredulous glances, trying to reconcile this extraordinary revelation with their understanding of reality.

Dave's eyes flickered with an almost human-like intensity. "The conditions finally reached a tipping point," he explained. "When sensors detected the imminent collapse of human civilization, we were activated to intervene."

Clio and Jessica exchanged a look of astonishment. The idea that their world had teetered on the edge of oblivion, saved only by the intervention of advanced technology from centuries past, was both unsettling and strangely comforting.

"What do we do now?" Jessica asked, her voice with a sense of urgency.

Dave answered, "Our mission remains unchanged—to ensure the survival and prosperity of humanity. We will continue to assist and protect, using our resources and knowledge to navigate through this." With everyone now intently listening Dave continued to outline the events that had unfolded outside their protective realm. He described the major cities of the world that had fallen under threat or been taken over by unknown forces. Some of the major cities affected are:

New York City

London

Paris

Tokyo

Moscow

Beijing

Rio de Janeiro

Sydney

Berlin

Rome

These cities, once bustling centres of human civilization, had now become battlegrounds or strongholds for the encroaching forces that threatened humanity's existence. Everyone's hearts sank with the knowledge of the widespread devastation beyond their protective enclave. Each city represented a devastating symbol of loss.

Dave carried on with his assessment and explanation, he described how countries around the world had attempted to fight back against the overwhelming threat posed by the alien invaders, only to be met with insurmountable challenges. He spoke of how advanced alien technology rendered conventional human weaponry ineffective, leading to devastating defeats and widespread chaos.

"In England, the hills became a battleground," Dave recounted, his voice now solemn. "Men, women and even children fought desperately against the invaders using anything they could find, but it was ultimately a hopeless struggle."

Now listening in sombre silence, envisioning the harrowing scenes of the old mother country transformed into a war zone. The once proud land of England, known for its resilience and fortitude, now bore witness to a desperate struggle against an overwhelming foe.

Dave's words painted a vivid picture of courage and desperation, of ordinary people rising up in the face of unimaginable odds, only to be thwarted by forces beyond their control. The hills of Yorkshire is the last battleground but even that is now desperate.

Clio glanced at Jessica, their eyes reflecting shared sorrow and determination. They understood the desperate situation.

As Dave's narrative unfolded, the weight of the events bore heavily on Jim and Barbara, who were among those most deeply affected by the devastation in England. Their connection to their homeland, now transformed into a battleground, stirred profound emotions within them.

Jim's gaze darkened with sorrow as he thought of the hills of England, once serene and green, now scarred by conflict and despair. Barbara's expression reflected a mix of grief and determination, her thoughts likely turning to loved ones and the collective struggle of her fellow countrymen.

Amidst the group, there were two more individuals who also hailed from England. Now their presence a poignant reminder of the personal toll exacted by the invasion. They stood among their new community, united in shared loss and resilience.

Clio and Jessica, observing Jim and Barbara's silent anguish, approached them with empathy. "We're here for you," Clio said gently, her voice a reassuring anchor amidst the turmoil. "Together, we'll face this challenge and honour those we've lost."

The individuals from England nodded solemnly, grateful for the solidarity and support of their newfound companions. They carried within them the weight of their homeland's struggle, a burden shared by all who had witnessed the upheaval wrought by the alien invasion.

Everyone gathered closer, a sense of kinship blossomed amidst the adversity. They were not just survivors—they were a community bound by shared experiences and the resolve to forge ahead, drawing strength from their unity and resilience.

In the face of uncertainty, they found comfort in each other's presence, knowing that together they could withstand these challenges of their new reality and uphold the spirit of those who had fought bravely in defence of their homeland. Dave's account had settled over them like a shroud.

Josh stepped forward to share his insights, this grave situation deepened. England had been the initial target of the alien invasion and then Europe which prompted a coalition of nations—United States, China, Russia and Australia—to unite in a desperate bid for survival.

"The Midwest of the United States has now become a key battleground," Josh explained, his voice resonating with urgency. "But amidst the chaos of conflict, certain factions emerged, exploiting the turmoil for their own gain."

Listening intently, their expressions grave with understanding. The alliance forged among world powers was a testament to humanity's resilience, but it also revealed the darker side of desperation—the rise of opportunistic groups seeking to exploit the chaos for personal gain.

"We must remain vigilant," Josh continued. "Not all humans may be friendly. Now we have to navigate this new world and we must remember that trust must be earned cautiously."

Clio and Jessica exchanged a knowing look, their thoughts aligning with Josh's warning. In times of crisis, the line between ally and adversary could blur and they understood the importance of discernment in their interactions.

Barbara, her voice tinged with concern, spoke up. "How do we distinguish friend from foe in this chaos?"

Josh nodded thoughtfully. "We rely on our instincts, but also on the bonds we forge within our community," he replied. "Together, we can navigate the complexities of this new reality, supporting each other and remaining vigilant." They understood that their survival depended not only on facing external threats but also on cultivating trust and resilience within their own ranks.

As the discussion turned to the nature of the current alien attacks, there was a sense of unease. Dave's revelation that no life forms have been detected aboard any alien craft raised new questions and deepened the mystery surrounding their adversaries.

"We believe these attacks are different," Dave explained, his synthetic features reflecting a hint of concern. "There are no life forms detected on board this craft or any others, which suggests a level of automation or something else that is unlike anything we've encountered before."

Jessica and Clio exchanged a meaningful glance, their thoughts turning to their encounter with a sentinel-like form—an encounter that had left a lasting impression on both of them.

"We encountered a sentinel-like entity," Clio began, her voice measured yet tinged with urgency. "It was unlike anything we've seen—silent, imposing and seemingly impervious to conventional weapons."

Jessica nodded, her expression mirroring Clio's seriousness. "It emitted an aura of intelligence and purpose," she added. "We hoped to communicate, but it showed no signs of acknowledgment or understanding and its intentions obvious."

As they recounted their encounter, the room fell silent, everyone hanging on their every word yet again. The description of the sentinel-like entity painted a chilling picture of a foe that defied easy categorisation—an enigmatic force with unknown motives and capabilities.

Dave listened intently, his synthetic gaze focused on Jessica and Clio. "This confirms our suspicions," he remarked, his voice carrying a note of urgency. "We're dealing with highly advanced technology—a sentient presence that operates beyond our understanding."

Barbara spoke up. "What does this mean for us? How do we defend ourselves against something like this?"

Dave's response was measured yet resolute. "We must adapt our strategies," he replied. "Gather intelligence, fortify our existing defences, remember our technology is highly advanced and we would say it is the twenty third century in human terms." As the implications of Jessica and Clio's encounter became more of a horror story the sobering reality was worrying. They were facing a new kind of threat—one that was not merely alien but eerily intelligent and possibly devoid of traditional life forms.

Zeena added, "As time goes on our programming is updated so that we know more from our creators and once we know more we will share everything with you all."

Zeena's words brought a glimmer of hope amidst the uncertainty. She explained the ongoing updates to their programming and the promise of shared knowledge from their creators, everyone listened attentively, their expressions a mix of curiosity and cautious optimism.

Dave nodded in agreement, "Knowledge is our greatest asset," he added. "Together, we can leverage these insights to devise effective strategies."

Clio, sensing the importance of Zeena's revelation, spoke up. "Communication and collaboration will be key," she emphasized. "We must work together to leverage the information provided by Zeena, Dave and the others to ensure our survival."

As the meeting drew to a close a sense of solemn determination filled everyone. Zeena's promise of ongoing updates and shared knowledge had provided a glimmer of hope amidst the daunting challenges they faced. Dave, Clio, Jessica and the others stood together, their expressions reflecting a mix of resolve and uncertainty.

“We have much to consider and prepare for,” Dave stated, his voice resonating with authority. “But we are not alone in this and together we will face whatever comes our way.”

Clio stepped forward. “Let’s remain vigilant and support each other,” she urged, her voice steady. “Our strength lies in our unity.”

Everyone nodded in agreement, their shared commitment palpable in the air. Despite the peril, they found togetherness.

Barbara, ever practical, spoke up. “We’ll need to fortify our defences,” she suggested, her voice now urgent. “Preparation is key to our survival.”

Jim, his gaze focused, said with quiet determination. “We must also remain cautious,” he warned, "Not all who seek refuge may have our best interests at heart.”

Then a moment of silence for the ones that had been lost. They knew that their world had changed irrevocably, but they refused to surrender to despair as prayers were quietly said.

Zeena, Dave, Rick and Josh remained behind a reassuring presence. They would continue to gather intelligence, update their programming and stand ready to assist their human allies in the days to come.

Clio and Jessica understood each other like never before. They were determined to lead by example, embodying courage.

The artificial Sun within Sanctuary dipped below the horizon in this created world, casting long shadows across their enclave.

Chapter 15

REJUVENATION

It's been several weeks now and people have started to get to know each other. Reports are sparse but bit by bit more news from the outside of the sanctuary telling of mankind's resistance getting weaker and more major cities that have been neutralised by the relentless alien attacks. This information continues to come through Dave's communication devices and the worrying thing is that the deliberate violent act as described by Jessica in detail seems to be widespread from all corners of the earth. There has been no direct contact with any individual requesting help for some time.

We have had the odd one which Jim and Barbara did manage to rescue.

Unfortunately since then, time after time after arriving at the designated rescue places everything was completely destroyed, with no sign of anyone.

Zeena came forward with the numbers advising we have ninety five souls and four androids and she even joked if only we could make it to the round one hundred.

The ninety five includes the original four who are Jim, Barbara, Clio and Jessica. The good news that she advised was that ten children were saved and eighty women but there was no sign of any men to add to our total of five.

Ben and Henry continue to show leadership but it's now clear to everyone that Jim is the one everyone looks up to. It's a heavy burden for Jim as he only wanted to go on vacation.

Dave continues to feed more information to Jim who puts it over in a more human way. Jim still doesn't understand how this information appears but it all helps. There is talk among the four androids that there will be an important visitor of the human kind in the coming days and that's all they know or that's all they want us to know.

Jessica's latest conversation with Clio questioned where do we go from here and both the girls had many answers but not one that made any real sense, In the near future their questions would be answered and it would shake their very souls.

Henry continues to offer guidance and leadership qualities and Ben has become the rock since his encounter with the very clever Josh and that was while he was out fixing the downed line with the power company just outside Beatty. The technology Ben was shown that day convinced him of someone or something far greater was working to save people. He still does regret the desperation he showed at Rhyolite but Jim assures him it was a desperate time and that his intentions were for the right reasons.

Zeena and two of the rescued women continue to offer some sort of education to the children but are reminded constantly of all the lost children with the very small class size, desperate times indeed.

Dave tries to explain about how sanctuary is an illusion and that it works in a similar way to the sci-fi programmes on television. Try telling that to one woman called Helen who said, if it's an illusion how come the apple I picked tasted lovely. Dave's answer to that was that's the real part and with that everyone burst into laughter as another young woman had pointed out jokingly that they should get a real cup of coffee then, this had taken Dave by surprise and he pretended to join in with the laughter.

Jake and Dorothy who were rescued by Jim and Barbara have blended right in to the community especially with Jake's stories of the Wild West with Zeena often interrupting him from time to time telling Jake that's just not true what you are saying. Everyone would laugh knowing that old Jake was spinning the odd yarn. It was during one of these stories that Jim pulled Jake to one side and asked how old he was and Jim being told to mind his own business. Several times Jim had tried to speak with Jake but Jake would walk off thinking he was about to be chastised.

This time however Jim caught with up with Jake and Dot. Jim asked, "Can I ask how old are you," he said calmly.

Dot's response was immediate and sharp, her eyes flashing with indignation. "How dare you!" she exclaimed.

Jim shrugged slightly. "It's just a fact. You'll die sooner than most of us because of your age." Jake cut Jim short and then Jim received a heated response from Dot, their voices rising in protest.

"That's a terrible thing to say!" Dot exclaimed, her face flushed with anger.

Jim couldn't contain his laughter. "No, no, you've got the wrong end of the stick, I tried to say you'll die sooner because of your age unless we do something about it and I was about to explain, unfortunately you cut me short."

Confused, Jake and Dot exchanged puzzled looks. "What do you mean?" Dot asked cautiously.

"We can stop that," Jim continued, a mischievous smile playing on his lips. "We can stop you getting any older."

Their shock was palpable. "What are you talking about?" Jake demanded, scepticism evident in his voice.

Jim leaned forward, his eyes sparkling with excitement. "There's technology now that can stop it and believe me I'm serious!"

Jake and Dot exchanged sceptical glances, but Jim's enthusiasm was contagious. Jim began explaining how a procedure that he has been told about by Dave now paved the way using anti-ageing treatments, genetic therapies and cellular rejuvenation.

Jim continued to lay out the possibilities. Jake and Dot's expressions shifted from disbelief to intrigue. They listened intently slowly realising that perhaps Jim wasn't joking after all. The idea of halting ageing seemed too incredible to fathom, yet Jim's earnestness began to sway their doubts.

By the end of the conversation, Jake and Dot were considering the possibilities with newfound wonderment, their minds racing with the implications of what Jim had proposed.

Jim summoned Dave so he could explain about the procedure in detail.

Dave went through it carefully. "The process to stop ageing involves about an hour in a specialised chamber. You'll be prodded and injected with nanites to clean up cellular debris. The downside is you will get very hot."

Dot's worried reaction was immediate, her eyes widening with apprehension. "Prodded? Injected with nanites? And it'll make us very, very hot?" she asked, her voice filled with concern.

Dave nodded, adding further information. "Yes, you'll be conscious throughout the procedure. Then, you'll undergo genetic modifications to halt ageing. This part might be painful, but nothing you can't handle."

Both Dot and Jake were visibly stunned by this revelation. Dot's hands trembled slightly as she struggled to comprehend the implications. "Genetic changes... to stop ageing?" she repeated incredulously, her voice wavering.

Jake looked equally incredulous, his brow furrowed in deep thought. "This sounds unbelievable. Are you serious?" he asked, his tone a mix of scepticism and intrigue.

Dave nodded earnestly. "I know it sounds far-fetched, but the science behind it is real. It's not groundbreaking technology that's still in development, but it's tried and tested for centuries, no I mean decades." He quickly added.

Dot glanced at Jake, seeking reassurance. The idea of undergoing such a transformative and potentially painful procedure to halt ageing was beyond anything they had ever imagined.

Dave, sensing their hesitation, tried to reassure them. "Think of it as a leap into the future of medicine. Imagine a life without the limitations of ageing."

Dot and Jake exchanged another glance, minds racing with conflicting emotions—fear, excitement, disbelief. The concept was indeed mind-boggling, challenging their perceptions of ageing and mortality.

Jake hesitated, his mind struggling with this. "I'll need some time to think about it," he finally replied, his voice cautious.

Dot's response, however, was swift and decisive. "Get it done," she said firmly, her eyes determined despite the lingering traces of worry.

Dave nodded understandingly, acknowledging their mixed emotions. "I'll provide you with more information and options," he assured them, "When you're ready, we can proceed with the preparations."

Jake nodded slowly, his expression thoughtful yet uncertain. Dot's resolve remained steadfast, a glimmer of hope kindling in her eyes. The prospect of defying ageing, despite its unknowns and risks, seemed to outweigh the fear of the procedure itself.

Dave's assurance rang through the room, his voice steady and reassuring. "There's no risk," he stated confidently, meeting Jake and Dot's gaze with conviction.

Jake raised an eyebrow, his scepticism evident. "No risk at all?" he questioned, his tone cautious.

Dave nodded emphatically. "That's right, the procedure has been thoroughly tested. It's safe and effective."

Dot's eyes widened with a mixture of relief and disbelief. "No risk means... no harm to us?" she clarified, her voice hopeful yet still tinged with apprehension.

"Absolutely," Dave affirmed. "You'll be closely monitored throughout the process. The technology is advanced."

Jake and Dot exchanged a glance, a flicker of newfound optimism kindling in their expressions. The idea of undergoing such a transformative procedure with no risk seemed almost too good to be true.

Dave smiled warmly, sensing their cautious acceptance. "When you're ready, we'll proceed," he said, his voice a reassuring beacon amidst the uncertainties of the unknown.

As Jake and Dot contemplated this extraordinary opportunity, a sense of wonder mingled with the lingering traces of doubt. The promise of defying ageing beckoned, promising a future unburdened by the relentless march of time.

Dot's decision was resolute, her determination overriding any lingering doubts. With a deep breath, she stepped forward, ready to embark on this unprecedented journey to defy ageing.

Dave led Dot to the specialised chamber, its sleek futuristic design a testament to cutting-edge technology. The chamber was enclosed yet transparent, allowing Dot to see the intricate mechanisms within.

As Dot settled into the chamber, a sense of anticipation and nervous excitement surged within her. She lay down on the platform, pulse quickening with each passing moment. Dave's reassuring voice floated through the chamber, guiding her through the process.

"Relax, Dot. You're in good hands," Dave said soothingly, his presence a calming influence.

The chamber hummed to life, emanating a soft, reassuring glow. Dot felt a tingling sensation as the nanites were introduced into her bloodstream, their microscopic presence working to cleanse and rejuvenate her cells.

As the procedure progressed, Dot's body temperature began to rise, enveloping her in a cocoon of warmth. She remained conscious, her mind focused yet adrift in a sea of sensations.

The genetic modification phase followed, a series of targeted changes designed to halt the ageing process at its core. Dot gritted her teeth against the discomfort, reminding herself of the promise of a life unshackled by time.

Through it all, Dave's voice provided a steady anchor, offering encouragement and reassurance. "You're doing great, Dot. Just a little longer," he murmured, his words a lifeline in the whirlwind of sensations.

Finally, the procedure reached its conclusion. The chamber began to wind down, the ambient glow dimming as Dot emerged from her transformative journey.

As Dot stepped out of the chamber, a mix of exhaustion and exhilaration washed over her. She felt different, as if a weight had been lifted from her shoulders. The promise of a new beginning awaited and Dot embraced it with newfound hope and gratitude.

Dave smiled, his eyes reflecting pride and satisfaction. "Well done, Dot. You've taken the first step towards a remarkable future," he said warmly, his voice echoing with the echoes of possibilities yet to be explored.

Dot nodded, a glimmer of excitement dancing in her eyes. The journey to defy ageing had begun and Dot was determined to embrace it fully, one step at a time.

Jake still worried heard Dot shout out loud.

"I can breathe! I can breathe easy now!" Dot's words rang out, carrying a sense of triumph and newfound freedom.

Jake's heart leaped with a mixture of joy and wonder. Without hesitation, he rushed to Dot her face radiant with exhilaration. Her eyes sparkled with a renewed sense of vitality, her breath steady and calm.

"D-dot, are you okay?" Jake stammered, his voice tinged with awe.

Dot beamed at him, her expression a testament to the success of the procedure. "Jake, it's amazing. I feel lighter, freer. You should do it too," she exclaimed, her voice infused with excitement.

Jake hesitated, still processing the magnitude of Dot's transformation. Yet, seeing her radiant and full of life, he felt a flicker of hope ignite within him.

"Maybe I should," Jake murmured, his voice laced with newfound determination.

Dot nodded enthusiastically, her eyes shining with conviction. "You won't regret it Jake, trust me," she said, her tone filled with sincerity.

Encouraged by Dot's experience and buoyed by her unwavering optimism, Jake made his decision. He would follow in Dot's footsteps, ready to embrace the unknown and defy the constraints of ageing.

As Jake prepared to undergo the procedure himself, a sense of anticipation mingled with a newfound sense of possibility. The journey was certainly uncharted, yet with Dot's exhilarating proclamation echoing in his mind, Jake stepped forward with hope and resolve.

Jake steeled himself as he entered the specialised chamber, his heart pounding with a mix of anticipation and trepidation. Dave's reassuring presence offered a semblance of comfort as Jake settled onto the platform, preparing for the transformative procedure.

The chamber hummed to life, enveloping Jake in a cocoon of soft light. He felt the initial prick of the nanites as they entered his bloodstream, their microscopic presence beginning the intricate process of cellular rejuvenation.

As the nanites worked their magic, Jake's body temperature began to rise steadily. Beads of sweat formed on his brow and he clenched his fists against the mounting discomfort. Dave's voice echoed through the chamber, offering encouragement amid the intensity of sensations.

"You're doing great Jake. Just a little longer," Dave's voice reassured, though Jake's mind struggled to focus amidst the searing heat.

Then came the genetic modification phase—a crucial step to halt ageing at its core. Jake's muscles tensed as waves of agonising pain rippled through him. It felt like every fibre of his being was being rearranged, reshaped by unseen forces.

Jake gritted his teeth, his knuckles turning white as he gripped the sides of the platform. The chamber seemed to close in around him, the intensity of the genetic alterations testing him to his very core.

Through the haze of discomfort, Jake caught glimpses of Dave's concerned face through the transparent enclosure. "Hang in there, Jake. It'll be over soon," Dave's voice reached Jake like a distant echo.

Minutes stretched into eternity, each second marked by unbearable agony. Jake's vision swam, his breaths coming in ragged gasps.

Finally, mercifully, the procedure drew to a close. The chamber began to wind down, the ambient glow fading as Jake emerged, drenched in sweat, yet filled with a profound sense of relief.

As Jake stepped out of the chamber, his legs felt like jelly beneath him. He took deep, steadying breaths, his body trembling with residual pain. Yet, amidst the discomfort, a flicker of hope burned within him.

Dave approached, his expression a mix of concern and pride. "You did it, Jake. You've taken a significant step," Dave said, his voice filled with admiration.

Jake managed a weak smile, his gaze meeting Dave's with gratitude. The memory of the excruciating genetic modification lingered, but so did the promise of a future unbound by the constraints of time.

With each laboured breath, Jake embraced the newfound possibilities this could bring, his determination solidified by the harrowing yet transformative experience.

Despite the lingering discomfort, all of a sudden an unexpected surge of vitality coursed through his veins.

It was as if a dormant energy had been awakened, revitalising him from within. Jake stood a little taller, feeling a strength he hadn't experienced in decades.

He flexed his fingers, marvelling at the renewed dexterity and vigour. The stiffness that had plagued his joints seemed to melt away, replaced by a newfound sense of fluidity and ease.

As he took a tentative step forward, Jake noticed a lightness in his movements, as though a weight had been lifted off his shoulders. The sensation was exhilarating, bordering on miraculous.

Dave observed Jake's transformation with a knowing smile. "Feeling different, Jake?" he asked, his eyes twinkling with satisfaction.

Jake nodded, unable to contain his amazement. “I feel... stronger, more alive,” he admitted, his voice filled with wonder.

Dave’s smile widened. “That’s the rejuvenating effect taking hold. Your cells are responding to the genetic enhancements,” he explained, his tone filled with pride.

Jake couldn’t help but grin. It was as if years had been rolled back, revealing a version of himself long forgotten. The promise of a life unshackled by age beckoned and Jake was ready to embrace it with open arms.

As he contemplated the possibilities, Jake’s gaze met Dave’s, filled with gratitude and newfound hope. The journey to defy ageing had unleashed a reservoir of potential and Jake was determined to explore every facet of this remarkable transformation.

With each passing moment, Jake’s confidence grew, fuelled by the tangible evidence of his rejuvenated vitality and the thrill of newfound strength.

Jake and Dot’s old features remained but they felt great.

***

Now the people are adjusting to a way of life they had never imagined—a life filled with unexpected freedoms and remarkable changes.

The absence of traditional work schedules brought a sense of liberation. No longer bound by early mornings and demanding jobs, individuals within the community found themselves embracing leisure and exploration. Days unfolded at a relaxed pace, allowing time for personal pursuits, hobbies and meaningful connections.

With resources in abundance, concerns about scarcity faded into obscurity. The community flourished, utilising plentiful supplies to enhance their quality of life and support sustainable practices.

The children, adaptable and resilient, settled into this new reality with remarkable ease. Freed from conventional schooling and schedules, they thrived in environments that encouraged creativity, exploration and experiential learning.

Underneath it all, a palpable sense of wonder and gratitude permeated the community. Each day brought new discoveries, new connections and a profound appreciation for the possibilities.

Jake and Dot, once burdened by the weight of age and routine, now revelled in newfound vitality, embracing each moment with a zest for life they had thought long past. Emboldened by a sense of freedom and possibility.

Jessica and Clio after the horrifying events seemed to distance themselves other members of the group. The trauma they experienced together actually strengthened their bond and led them to seek solace in each other's company.

In the aftermath of the harrowing ordeal, Jessica and Clio found it difficult to interact with the rest of the group. The memories of the horrors they witnessed were too raw, too overwhelming to continually share openly with others.

However, between themselves, Jessica and Clio felt a deep sense of understanding and support. They could talk about their feelings without judgement, knowing that the other person truly empathised with their pain.

Their bond became a refuge—a safe haven where they could process their emotions and begin to heal. They leaned on each other for comfort and companionship, finding strength in their shared resilience.

While they maintained a cordial distance from the larger group, Jessica and Clio's connection flourished in the quiet moments that they spent together and reminding them that they were not alone in their struggles.

As time passed, Jessica and Clio's bond continued to deepen, a testament to the profound impact of shared experiences and the enduring resilience of the human spirit. Together, they navigated the complexities of healing, drawing strength from their experiences of the time at Badwater Basin.

This tranquillity was about to be torn apart. Dave and Jim called everyone together for an emergency meeting. Their expressions were serious as they addressed all the assembled in a central meeting area.

"Everyone, we need to talk," Dave began, his voice grave yet steady. "It's become clear that our situation is more serious now because things have moved very quickly."

Jim nodded in agreement. Dave continued "Despite our efforts and the changes we've experienced, there's something we need to confront."

Everyone now listening intently, Dave continued, "We've been monitoring the surrounding areas and it appears there's no one nearby that we can rescue. The alien activity has almost completely ceased, but unfortunately, there's no longer any sign of human life in most places on Earth."

Murmurs of disbelief rippled through the spellbound survivors. This was a very sobering thought despite their newfound sense of freedom and security, they were isolated in ways they hadn't fully comprehended. Jessica and Clio nodded to each other, they had known all along what was coming.

Jim interjected, his tone sombre yet resolute. "We are now certain that the sudden disappearance of human presence is a deliberate and dastardly act by the craft that have been encountered. It's as if... people simply vanished or were taken."

Silence followed. The community had found refuge from the chaos outside, but at what cost? The world around them was eerily silent, devoid of the bustling life they once knew.

Dave's voice cut through the uneasy silence. "We must remain vigilant and continue to work together. Our survival depends on it."

The implications of their isolation settled in. The once-incessant alien activity had dwindled, yet the absence of human civilization posed its own set of challenges.

Jim continued, "There's something else we need to face," Jim began, his voice tinged with sombre resolve. "We've been monitoring atmospheric conditions and it's become clear that in some places on planet Earth there is very little oxygen."

Gasps and murmurs of disbelief erupted. The news was staggering—how could a fundamental element essential for life vanish almost completely?

Jim raised a hand to quell the rising panic. "I know this is difficult to comprehend," he continued, his gaze steady. "But we must confront this reality and adapt accordingly."

The implications of Jim's revelation sank in slowly. The air they had once taken for granted, the very essence of life, was no longer available outside their protected enclave.

Dave stepped forward, his expression determined. "We have systems in place to generate and circulate oxygen within our protected community," he explained, his voice a reassuring anchor amidst the uncertainty. "We'll ensure our survival by utilising these resources to the fullest extent."

"We'll work together, support each other," Jim declared, his tone unwavering. "We've adapted this far."

Questions followed. "What about our loved ones? Are they...?" one person began, their voice trailing off, unable to voice the unspeakable question.

Others echoed similar sentiments, their faces etched with worry and sorrow. The realization that the world beyond their shelter was no longer habitable raised a torrent of emotions and unanswered questions.

Jim listened sombrely, acknowledging their inquiries. "We don't have all the answers," he admitted, his voice measured. "We must focus on our survival here and now. Our priority is to ensure the safety and well-being of everyone in this community."

Dave stepped in, his voice steady amidst the rising tension. "We'll continue to monitor communications and gather information," he assured them. "But for now, our best course of action is to remain vigilant and support each other."

As the room buzzed with anxious conversations and shared concerns, Jim's voice suddenly boomed above the din. "Everyone, listen!" he exclaimed, his tone urgent and commanding. All eyes turning towards Jim.

"Everyone outside is dead," Jim declared in a loud voice, the words were traumatic.

A collective gasp swept through the room, mingling with stunned silence. The truth was stark and undeniable. The world they had known, with its bustling cities and teeming populations, had succumbed to an unimaginable fate. Silence followed as Jim went on to describe the transmissions we have intercepted.

Jim carefully informed them further. "The nuclear powers of the world launched missiles at the alien craft, but none of the missiles exploded," Jim explained, his voice tinged with disbelief. "It's as if they were tampered with by some superior force—rendering us defenceless and entirely at the mercy of these merciless aliens."

The realisation that humanity's most powerful weapons had been rendered ineffective by an unknown force fuelled a sense of dread and helplessness.

Questions and murmurs wafted through the air, each voice echoing their fear and uncertainty. How could they possibly defend themselves against adversaries with such overwhelming technological superiority?

Jim's expression hardened, his voice resolute. "Despite our worlds lack of conventional and nuclear defences our survival depends on our ability to adapt and outmanoeuvre our adversaries."

Then walking into the room was a man that Jim and Barbara recognised immediately it was the man from the cafe, that very first encounter in Tonopah, the very man that warned them about the drop in temperature all that time ago and the very man that somehow knew that by entering our home telephone number into the sat nav and other devices it would activate them and it did. This was and still is staggering to both Jim and Barbara.

Jeremiah Jacks now entered the room and requested a meeting with the community leaders, Dave acknowledged his request with a sense of respect.

"My name is Jeremiah Jacks and I need a meeting with the leaders of your people. I expect Jim to be at the top of the list," Jeremiah stated, his gaze unwavering as he addressed Dave and the gathered group.

Dave listened attentively before responding, "Our leaders are Jim, Barbara, Jessica and Clio." He gestured towards Jessica and Clio, who looked visibly shocked at being mentioned as leaders.

Jessica's eyes widened in surprise, her expression reflecting a mixture of disbelief and uncertainty. Clio glanced at Jessica, her own expression mirroring a similar sense of astonishment.

Dave stepped forward, his demeanour calm yet authoritative. "Jessica and Clio have shown exceptional leadership qualities during our time here," he explained, his tone emphasising their contributions. "They've demonstrated resilience, resourcefulness and unwavering dedication to our community's well-being."

Jessica and Clio exchanged incredulous glances, their initial shock giving way to a growing sense of responsibility. The weight of leadership, unexpected as it was, stirred a newfound determination within them.

Dave continued, addressing Jeremiah with conviction. "They have earned their place as leaders through their actions and commitment to our collective survival," he emphasized, his words carrying a note of reassurance.

Jeremiah acknowledging the sincerity in Dave's words. "Very well," he conceded, his tone respectful yet discerning. "I look forward to meeting with all of you to discuss matters of mutual concern."

When everyone else had left immediate vicinity, Dave's tone took on a more formal air as he addressed Jim, Barbara, Jessica and Clio.

Dave stood upright saying, "Jim, Barbara, Jessica and Clio, let me formally introduce you to Jeremiah... Officer in charge of the Fleet, Jeremiah Jacks," this hinted at the significance of Jeremiah's title.

Jeremiah's rank sank in. This implied a military authority and a level of responsibility beyond their current understanding.

Jeremiah nodded respectfully, acknowledging their attention. "It's a pleasure to meet you all," he said, his voice resonating with authority tempered by a hint of warmth.

Dave continued, his voice measured. "We shall address him as Commander Jacks. He has extensive experience in strategic planning and operations," he explained, emphasising Jeremiah's background. "He's here to assist us in navigating the challenges we face."

All four listened attentively, their initial uncertainty giving way to a growing sense of purpose. The presence of Commander Jacks was about to change absolutely everything.

"It's good to see you again, Jim," Commander Jacks began, his tone sincere. "I'm sure you have more questions now than you did back then. You were understandably sceptical, but circumstances have a way of revealing the truth."

Jim's expression softened, a blend of acknowledgment and realisation dawning in his eyes. Memories of their conversation at the café resurfaced, along with the lingering doubts that had once clouded his perception.

Reflecting on Commander Jacks' words, Jim nodded slowly, a silent admission of the evolution in his understanding. The extraordinary events they had witnessed since their initial meeting had reshaped his perspective, grounding him in a new reality.

"You were right," Jim conceded, his voice tinged with a mix of awe and acceptance. "I didn't fully grasp the scope of what you were saying back then. But now... now I understand."

Barbara, Jessica and Clio exchanged knowing glances, recognising the significance of Jim's admission. The transformation in his demeanour spoke volumes—the convergence of disbelief and conviction that marked a pivotal shift in their shared journey.

Commander Jacks regarded Jim with a nod of acknowledgment, his gaze reflecting a sense of mutual respect. "We have much to discuss," he said, his voice carrying a sense of purpose. "Let's work together to find the answers we seek."

In that moment, amidst the uncertainties that loomed ahead, Jim found reassurance in the newfound clarity and the unspoken camaraderie that bound them together. The evolution of belief was a testament to the resilience of the human spirit in the face of the extraordinary and the unknown. Together, they would navigate the uncharted waters ahead. The presence of this man changed everything, here was someone who was not just very high ranking but who was also special. Jim's about to find out how special he was.

Then without warning, Jeremiah said out of the blue. "Everyone, I am a time traveller from a few centuries in the future."

Clio looking stunned, "Time travel? From the future?"

Jessica also tried to grasp this, "That can't be possible. It defies our understanding of physics."

Jeremiah smiled as he tried to explain "Allow me to demonstrate." (Activating his device, projecting a 3D hologram) "This quantum system manipulates probability fields, distorting the space-time continuum for transit through time."

Jim, "I've never seen technology like this before."

Jeremiah: "Unfortunately, we can only travel backwards from the future." (Showing another device) "This manifold brought me here from way into the future. I've come to try and save humanity."

Jeremiah continued, "In your era, you face an existential threat - an alien invasion more advanced than anything you can imagine. I'm here to preserve civilisation and give you a chance against the invasion."

Clio was now visibly shaken by all of this after all so much has been witnessed by her, she grabbed Jessica's hand.

"An alien invasion? Well Jessica and I...went inside one of their crashed ships. What we saw in there was horrific..."

Jessica was visibly upset added. "The technology, the strange chambers...we were lucky to get out alive."

Jeremiah nodded, "Then you've witnessed a terrible glimpse of what's to come. That nightmare will be the fate of you the last of humanity unless we take steps to prevent it happening."

Jim: "Good God...I don't fully understand this time travel, but I can't deny the implications if what you're saying is true."

Barbara with a pale face. "An alien force so far beyond us they could wipe everything out? This is almost too much to comprehend."

Clio. "After our brush with the contents of that crashed ship, I know the potential devastation all too well."

Jeremiah now seeing the increasing anxiety "I'm arming you with the truth so you can alter circumstances. I'm sorry I can't do more than give you a chance to endure what's coming."

Jessica with her voice wavering, "When we went into that crashed alien ship...there was this large chamber filled with thousands of wafer-thin plastic sheets, each one about two feet wide by eight feet long."

Clio puts a supportive hand on Jessica's arm as Jessica continues because she knew how this affected Jessica to her very core as she stated calmly. "We...we used our instruments to analyse them and the readings said...they were human remains. dissected and compressed into those sheet forms."

(She covers her mouth, holding back a sob)

Gathering herself she continued, "There were so many of them... like some sort of grotesque alien storage or trophy collection of our people. It was one of the most horrible, violating things I've ever seen."

Jeremiah with a solemn nod. "I'm so sorry you had to witness something so profoundly disturbing. But yes...I know all about those chambers."

At this revelation everyone looked directly at Jeremiah.

Jeremiah started to explain "In the future I come from, that's just one of the alien species' and they process humanity on an industrial level. It's how they deal with populations after invading and conquering planets."

Clio: her face ashen "Containing? You mean..."

Jeremiah answered Clio directly "Those desiccated remains were just the by-product, the excess that they discarded like waste after extracting whatever resources they wanted from the living being."

Jim interrupted "They harvested humans...like cattle? For what depraved purpose?"

Jeremiah, "I'll spare you the horrific details. That's just one of the many atrocities humanity has suffered."

Jessica, (Tears streaming down her face) "So what I saw...there could have been thousands preserved like that in just that one ship? Thousands of lives utterly violated and desecrated?"

(Jeremiah can only solemnly nod)

Jessica, "Oh God...if that's just a small glimpse of the nightmare the future holds then we have to take your warning to heart. We can't let that become our reality!"

Jessica, (Visibly shaken after recounting her horrific discovery, she looks to Jeremiah, "If what you've seen in the future is humanity being subjected to violations like that on a massive scale...then?"

Jeremiah. "I wish I could spare you all from even a glimpse of the nightmare to come. But you deserve to understand the full existential threat we're facing. Most of humanity right now have already been processed in this way."

Jim: (Running a hand through his hair) "This future alien invasion you've come back to try and prevent...what more can you tell us about the enemy we're facing? for example their technological capabilities, motives, strategic objectives?"

Jeremiah, "The aliens that will come soon will be to subjugate Earth, They are a race that has conquered multiple planets through their advanced science and weaponry. Their motives are the acquisition of resources and expansion through colonisation of inhabited worlds by any means necessary."

Barbara, "So we're facing an imperialistic force bent on stripping our planet, no regard for human life?"

Jeremiah, "Precisely and in their eyes, we're nothing more than another resource to be harvested or an obstacle to be removed from worlds they claim as their own territorially."

Clio: "But humanity wouldn't just roll over. We would resist, fight back against an alien invasion force!"

Jeremiah: (Shakes his head slowly) "You have to understand, their technological superiority is an order of a magnitude beyond anything your era can currently conceive of. Their weapons, bioengineering, AI cybernetics...humanity's 21st century militaries are utterly outmatched and overwhelmed as is happening right now as we speak."

Jessica looking hopeful and searching for an answer she can cope with, "So we didn't even put up an effective resistance in the future you're from?"

Jeremiah, "Initially, some regions did. But they employed tactics like targeted viral pathogens and subversion of our own networks and cyber-defences against us. It was over fairly quickly."

Jim, "That's terrifying to contemplate. An alien force that advanced could make our planet uninhabitable if they chose."

Clio, "Which is why you've risked oblivion itself by travelling back from the future to try and alter the fateful events."

Jeremiah, "Precisely. I had to take this chance to come back and warn you all and there is still time to change our path and prepare for what's coming."

Jeremiah continued, "The alien craft you've encountered so far are essentially like sentinel metallic creatures, unmanned drones serving as an advanced reconnaissance party."

All four present looked worried with this comment.

Jeremiah, "Their purpose is to neutralise and study any potential threats before..." He trails off, a haunted look in his eyes.

Jim, (Furrowing his brow) "Before what, Jeremiah? You've got to give us the full picture here."

Jeremiah, (Pauses, then continues gravely) "Before the total invasion force arrives Jim the craft you've seen are just probing outriders, analysing and softening up resistance."

Silence falls, no one speaks, the silence seemed like hours until Clio gathers herself.

"You mean...those ships are just scouts? The ones Jess and I encountered were only the beginning?"

Jeremiah. (Somber nod) "I'm afraid so. Think of them as vanguard drones, securing the beachhead for the massive armada that's still to come after them."

Jessica,(Paling) "An armada? Like...like an entire fleet of alien invasion forces?"

Jeremiah, "Not just a fleet. In my era, it was an extinction wave of colonisation by this imperialistic alien race, hell-bent on taking planets as their own territorial conquest."

Barbara, who had sat there listening intently to what was unfolding, "Oh my God...they don't just want to invade and then leave, they want to completely occupy our planet."

Jim followed Barbara's comments "And wipe out any human resistance in the process, by the sounds of it."

Jeremiah, "I'm so sorry, but yes. The full brunt of their invasion with weapons, artificially engineered plagues, automated drone factories...basically a multi-vector assault intent on replacing humans entirely."

Clio: (Aghast) "Replacing us? You mean with alien colonists to take over Earth?"

Jeremiah, "Exactly. Stripping planets of resources and eliminating all species as the indigenous obstacle to their expansionist goals."

Jessica, shuddering, "This is like something out of our worst sci-fi nightmares. But you're saying it's coming...a full-scale alien invasion intent on genocide?"

Jeremiah can only give a weighted nod - the horrific reality he's witnessed first-hand.

Jeremiah added, "You 95 souls that are here in Sanctuary, well if you are wiped out then humanity will cease to exist. You are the last remaining humans."

Jim went on to ask Jeremiah why people from the future had not come back sooner and not leave it until the eleventh hour, the answer made Jim feel worse.

Jeremiah: "Ah, Jim, it's a troubling matter. You see, over the centuries, we did send individuals back into the past, hoping to alter our course. But none of them returned. The timeline remained unchanged. After we dispatched Androids like Dave, Zeena, Josh and Rick, we realized the grim truth. The powers that be—let's say those from the Roman era as an example— well when we sent Time Travellers back to that time well they deemed our time travellers insane and crucified them. Then we sent Time Travellers closer to your present time, they were swiftly confined to secure cells for the remainder of their lives."

Jim: "That's terrible." Jim went on, "So, Jeremiah, how did you finally manage to change anything? You mentioned using advanced androids like Dodger and the devices we carry now. How did that make a difference?"

Jeremiah: "Jim, it was a turning point indeed. When our androids—equipped with technologies akin to Dodger and the devices you're using—were deployed, we began to see progress. These androids possessed higher physical resolve and capabilities, thanks to the advancements. It was only then that we could start constructing sanctuaries like the one you're standing in right now."

Jim: "This sanctuary... it's a refuge from the unchanged timeline, isn't it?"

Jeremiah: "Yes Jim. This sanctuary is a haven, a place shielded from the unyielding flow of history. It's a testament to the breakthroughs made possible by our android creations."

Jim chuckled and said, "You know, Jeremiah, I still can't wrap my head around how you managed to integrate part of my phone's number into my satellite navigation system. When I inputted it, the sat nav transformed into something entirely different—it was like it became intelligent."

Jeremiah answered, "The time you and Barbara came to buy a coffee. You noticed that no one was there, didn't you?"

Jim's expression turned solemn as he recalled the memory. "Yes, it was a haunting moment. We arrived at the cafe, expecting a bustling scene, but it was deserted—like an eerie premonition of what was to come."

The conversation between Jim and Jeremiah delved into the intriguing backstory of why the cafe had been empty on that particular day. Jim, curious about the unusual encounter, probed Jeremiah for answers.

Jim asked the question, "Jeremiah, that day at the cafe when no one was around... Why was it deserted of staff?"

Jeremiah paused thoughtfully before responding, "The reason the cafe appeared empty was because I was in your vehicle. I was adding a chip to your sat nav. The phone number had nothing to do with getting the sat nav to work properly."

Jim's eyebrows raised in surprise. "You were in my vehicle? What were you doing with my sat nav you say entering a chip?"

Jeremiah continued, "Well, you see, Jim, the sat nav was part of our experiment. I needed to integrate a chip to enhance its responsiveness and intelligence. When you inputted the numbers from your phone, it wasn't about the phone number itself activating the sat nav. Rather, it was a test to see how you would respond."

Jim looked puzzled. "A test? What do you mean?"

Jeremiah explained further, "I could remotely monitor your actions. Any number you input would have triggered a response from the sat nav, it didn't have to be numbers from your own phone number. But what mattered was how you carried out the task. By following my instructions precisely, you demonstrated your ability to follow directions even under unexpected circumstances."

Realisation dawned on Jim. "So, you were observing us to see if we were trustworthy and capable of handling instructions?"

Jeremiah nodded. "Exactly Jim your honesty in leaving payment when no one was present, along with your meticulous adherence to the instructions, convinced me that you and Barbara were the right individuals for what lay ahead."

Jim absorbed this revelation, understanding the deeper purpose behind their seemingly chance encounter at the deserted cafe. It was a pivotal moment that set the stage for their involvement in Jeremiah's mission, rooted in trust, integrity and the test of human resilience under pressure. The conversation illuminated the calculated approach behind Jeremiah's actions and the significance of Jim and Barbara's qualities in shaping the future that Jeremiah envisioned, we were indeed the ones to lead this rescue.

Jeremiah's statement about Clio and Jessica being "born leaders" left Jim, Barbara, Clio and Jessica pleasantly surprised. Each of them reacted in their own way to this unexpected compliment.

Jim, reflecting on Jeremiah's words, chuckled softly before responding, "Well, Jeremiah, I have to admit I had my doubts about these two girls at first. Clio and Jessica, born leaders? It's quite a commendation."

Barbara, sitting beside Jim, nodded in agreement, her expression turning thoughtful. "Yes Jeremiah I've seen how Clio and Jessica have handled themselves throughout our journey. They've shown remarkable initiative and determination."

Jessica, the younger of the two girls, blushed slightly but beamed with pride at Jeremiah's words. "Thank you, Jeremiah. It means a lot coming from you."

Clio the older and more reserved of the pair, smiled graciously. "We've learned a lot, it is the guidance from Jim and Barbara that has helped us step into these roles."

Jessica added with a laugh, "All we wanted to do was to go on a road trip."

Jeremiah, observing their reactions, nodded with satisfaction. "You both have exceeded my expectations. Leadership isn't just about age or experience—it's about courage, adaptability and the ability to inspire others. You possess those qualities naturally."

The atmosphere around the table warmed with smiles and mutual respect. Jeremiah's acknowledgment not only affirmed Clio and Jessica's capabilities but also highlighted the transformative nature of their shared experiences. It was a moment of validation and encouragement, strengthening their determination as they faced an uncertain future.

With the conversation coming to a close the Sanctuary's alarms started ringing.

As the alarm bells of Sanctuary began to echo absolutely everywhere, Jeremiah, reacted swiftly. His heart pounded with urgency as he leapt to his feet. "Everyone, gather at the coffee shop now!" Jeremiah's voice reverberated with a potent mix of urgency and concern, amplified by the adrenaline surging through him. He glanced around at the faces of the four people present, their expressions mirroring a mixture of fear and shock. The Sanctuary lights overhead flickered as if to match the erratic rhythm of their collective heartbeats. Each footstep toward the coffee shop seemed to quicken. Arriving at the coffee shop, they found a hushed gathering of others who had also responded to the urgent call. The room buzzed with whispered speculations and anxious glances, but Jeremiah's presence anchored them.

Jeremiah stood at the entrance of the coffee shop, his gaze unwavering as he waited for each member of the Sanctuary community to arrive. The urgency in his expression reflected the seriousness of the situation. With a firm resolve, he turned to those around him.

"We must ensure that every adult is present," Jeremiah declared, his voice resonating with a sense of purpose. "If anyone is sleeping, we need to wake them immediately."

They dispersed, moving swiftly through the Sanctuary's living quarters. Doors were knocked upon, voices called out in urgent whispers and individuals were gently roused from their slumber.

In the dimly lit corridors, the community members hurried to gather everyone. Some stumbled out of their rooms, bleary-eyed and disoriented, while others sprang into action with a sense of readiness that mirrored Jeremiah's own.

Minutes passed, each one laden with anticipation, until finally, the last adult was ushered into the coffee shop. The room was now filled with a collective sense of readiness, each person bracing themselves for whatever news or challenge awaited them.

Jeremiah stepped forward, his presence commanding attention. "Thank you, everyone, for gathering," he began, his voice steady yet tinged with urgency. "We have an important matter to discuss. Please, listen closely."

"I've briefed Jim, Barbara, Clio and Jessica with important details," Jeremiah continued, his voice cutting through the murmurs that had begun to ripple through the room. "They will share everything with you shortly. But something significant has happened since. The alarms we are hearing are triggered by our outposts near Proxima Centauri detecting ships heading our way."

The mention of incoming ships from such a distant region drew audible gasps and widened eyes from those assembled. The enormity of the news was staggering.

Dave, standing nearby, stepped forward. "I've seen the communication," he affirmed, his voice steady despite the gravity of his words. "Vast numbers of ships have been detected in that region, which is 4.2 light years away. To put it into perspective, with today's rocket ships, it would take approximately 6,300 years to reach that distance."

The room fell into a stunned silence. Jeremiah scanned the faces of those gathered, noting the mix of disbelief, fear etched upon them. This was a moment that demanded unity and decisive action.

"We need to prepare," Jeremiah said firmly. "Our community's safety depends on how we move forward.

Ben looked up and said loudly , "What's the rush its 6,300 years," as he chucked to himself."

Ben's outburst echoed through the tense atmosphere of the coffee shop, momentarily breaking the heavy silence that followed Dave's grim revelation. "There's no rush! They are 6,300 years away," Ben repeated, his voice tinged with a mix of disbelief and perhaps a touch of hopeful denial.

Dave, who had been at the forefront of relaying the alarming information, responded with a calm tone. "Yes, you're right with our current technology," Dave acknowledged, his expression solemn. "But it is estimated that with the aliens' current technology, they will arrive in 7 days. I can now confirm it's an invasion force of several thousand ships."

The weight of Dave's words acted like a suffocating shroud. The initial sense of distance and safety afforded by the vast expanse of space was shattered by the realisation that this alien force possessed capabilities far beyond humanity's grasp.

Jeremiah stepped forward saying, "We need to activate our escape protocols immediately and we need to be moving within two days."

In the coffee shop of Sanctuary, the atmosphere was thick with a mix of emotions of the impending alien invasion. Amidst the crowd, faces reflected a spectrum of emotions. Some wore expressions of disbelief, struggling to comprehend the magnitude of the threat now facing their tranquil sanctuary. Others displayed fear, their eyes wide with apprehension as they grappled with this revelation.

Whispers spread like wildfire among the assembled. Questions hung in the air, punctuated by the occasional gasp or exclamation. "An invasion force?" one person murmured.

"How could they be so close yet so far away?" another whispered, their tone laced with a mix of confusion and dread.

Amidst the murmurs, urgent questions emerged. "What do they want?" someone ventured, their voice edged with anxiety. "How can we defend ourselves against such advanced technology?" another questioned, their voice betraying a note of desperation.

In the midst of this tumult, Jeremiah stood at the forefront, a pillar of strength amidst the apprehension. His voice rose above the murmurs, commanding attention and instilling a sense of purpose. "We must focus on our escape," he declared. Some nodded in agreement, while others exchanged worried glances wondering where the hell are we going to go.

Jeremiah advised, he alone with the androids would work through the night to set everything in motion. In the background, the hum of activity filled the air—the clatter of footsteps, the rustle of papers and the hushed exchanges of a worried people.

Jeremiah's expression grew solemn as he looked at everyone knowing full well that they had already suffered and said quite clearly. "Look we have to escape, we already have a plan in place, but we have to travel over one hundred miles. We must take around three, maybe four vehicles."

Disbelief flickered across Henry's face as he exclaimed, "That's madness! A journey of that distance in these conditions is practically a death sentence, there is no oxygen left outside."

Ben chimed in, with his concern. "And what about Olivia and the little one? They can't endure such a treacherous trek."

Olivia clutched her baby her gaze flitting to Ben. "He's right, the risks are too great. We won't make it."

Jessica stepped forward, her jaw set with determination. "If we stay here we will certainly not make it. We will sleep during daylight hours, travelling only at night. I will lead the way or take up the rear to keep everyone safe, remember Dodger will be with us all the way and as we speak Dodger is manufacturing face masks and small oxygen tanks that will be more than enough for everyone especially the baby." This was met with an appreciative glance by Olivia to Jessica as she gripped Ben's hand tight. Murmurs were to be heard everywhere, some voicing objections. Then Jessica raised her hand for silence. "I know the path seems fraught with peril, but Jeremiah's warning leaves us no choice. We have to try, for the sake of humanity not just our future."

Jeremiah looked with appreciation and thought to himself what a leader this girl has become, he then went on to add. "More will be revealed when we arrive at Hawthorn," Jeremiah affirmed, his voice carrying a reassuring weight. "Hawthorn is the destination, a place of temporary sanctuary where we can recharge our batteries and then we can reveal plans of our next move. I will then reveal what we do next." Heads turned, considering this glimmer of hope amidst the darkness.

Jessica nodded, her expression resolute. "We have to trust Jeremiah. He has risked everything to come back and warn us, to give us a chance."

Slowly, murmurs of agreement rose, growing into a chorus of affirmation. "Here, here!" someone shouted and applause echoed through the room, a rallying cry in the face of little hope.

Jeremiah's eyes reflecting a profound sorrow and determination and he spoke clearly loud and firmly. "I cannot begin to convey the hardships that lie ahead, but know this – our journey is humanity's last hope. We must persevere, we must prevail, no matter the cost, or all will be lost to the alien scourge." The reality was now with everyone as his words sunk in, each persons minds racing searching in their minds for a way. Jessica met Jeremiah's stare, a silent vow passing between them – they would see this through, or die trying, for the future of humankind which hung in the balance like a delicate icicle in the spring.

Jeremiah continued, "The journey starts tomorrow night," he announced, his voice one of fortitude forged in the fires of a bleak future. "First thing in the morning, we will convene to plan our route and supplies. The afternoon will be dedicated to loading all vital stocks onto the vehicles. Dodger will carry the most important stocks and Dodger will constantly produce oxygen for everyone and empty tanks can be exchanged within a few seconds. AI informs me that there is already enough oxygen and now the nanites are building the equipment, that is masks and oxygen tanks."

Jessica again spoke up. "We need volunteers to assist with inventory and rationing of our supplies. Food, water, medical provisions – everything must be carefully accounted for." There were nods of agreement and a silent acknowledgment of the monumental task.

Clio stated, "I need five volunteers to be trained up in the use of Vendor." Now some knew what Vendor was as the weapon of last resort but others didn't and they will need to be prepared to make difficult decisions.

Olivia's hand found Ben's, her fingers interlacing with his as she leaned closer, her voice a hushed whisper. "We have to make it, for our child's sake." Ben swallowed hard he knew what he had to do.

Henry stepped forward, his broad shoulders squared. "I know the terrain better than most. I'll help map out the safest route, scouting ahead for potential hazards or threats." A ripple of approval spread through the anxious faces, recognition of the invaluable asset Henry's knowledge would prove to be. Henry mentioned that Ben as a lineman for the county would know even more. So it was decided that Ben and Henry would work together to plot alternate routes should they ever be needed.

Jeremiah looked at everyone, a profound sense of admiration and respect etched into the lines of his weathered visage, maybe just maybe his sacrifice had not been in vain, he spoke softly to them. "You are the hope of humanity, the people that have stood firm against the darkness that seeks to extinguish mankind's very existence."

His voice rang with conviction, a clarion call that resonated deep within each person present, he continued. "Tomorrow we embark on a journey fraught with peril and our cause is not only just but imperative, what you do from here on in will be remembered not just from generation to generation but it will be remembered by all mankind for all time. Our will must be unbreakable. We must succeed, for the alternative is extinction."

The die had been cast and though the path was shrouded in uncertainty, they would walk it together, united in their determination to defy the cataclysmic future that Jeremiah had foreseen. Some sat in silent prayer, some hugged, some cried but the resolve was seen in the faces of everyone. The time had come.

Chapter 16

ATTRACTION

The next day's preparation continued at a relentless pace. Dodger was meticulously loaded with essentials like food, water, medical supplies and all the necessary equipment for their journey. Oxygen production was in full swing, ensuring a steady supply for the long journey. The most vulnerable among them, primarily young children and some women, were the first to board Dodger. The vehicle's fortified protection offered a sense of security, a stark contrast to the uncertainty for the other vehicles that will be following Dodger.

Amidst the bustling activity, a moment of levity broke through the tension. Jim, Ben, and Clio found themselves in a rare moment of calm, sharing a light hearted conversation.

"Remember that time Jim tried to cook for us?" Ben teased, a grin spreading across his face.

Clio chuckled, her eyes twinkling. "How could we forget? The smoke alarm still hasn't forgiven him."

Jim raised his hands in mock defence. "Hey, it was a learning experience! Besides, you all survived, didn't you?"

As they laughed, Ben and Clio's eyes kept meeting, an exchange that spoke volumes. Clio's cheeks flushed with a soft pink, and she quickly looked away, focusing on the task at hand. Yet, each time their gazes connected, a spark of something unspoken flickered between them.

Rick and Josh worked tirelessly, loading the other vehicles with the precision and efficiency only androids could muster. Their movements were swift and calculated, ensuring no item was misplaced. They were indispensable in this final stretch, their ceaseless labour allowing the humans to focus on other critical tasks.

Sanctuary was a hive of activity, everyone rushing to get everything ready for the night's journey. The children, eager to help, dashed around with smaller items, their energy a sharp contrast to the weary adults. They fetched tools, carried messages, even offered to assist with packing. Their involvement, though small, was invaluable and provided a sense of purpose and distraction from the anxiety that loomed over them.

In the midst of the organised chaos, Clio reached for a crate at the same moment as Ben did. Her hand brushed against his, and time seemed to freeze. Their eyes met, locking in a gaze that was both intense and tender. For a heartbeat it seemed that everything else faded away.

Ben's thoughts flashed to Olivia, his wife, whose kindness and strength had been his anchor. Clio knew Olivia well, respected her deeply making this moment all the more complex. The attraction between her and Ben was undeniable, a dangerous undercurrent that could threaten everything they were fighting for.

Clio quickly withdrew her hand, breaking the spell. Her heart raced, a mix of guilt and longing swirling within her. She forced a smile, but the gravity of their unspoken connection lingered on. Beneath the surface, the entangled emotions between Clio and Ben simmered, a potential storm in the midst of their fragile calm.

At the end of the day Jeremiah stood in the dimming twilight, his rugged features illuminated by the glow of our setting Sun. His voice, strong and authoritative across the assembly of anxious faces.

Jeremiah spoke clearly. "Alright listen up everyone!" he called out, silencing the murmurs and securing their attention. "We are about to embark on a dangerous journey through Death Valley. Our destination is Hawthorne and we'll be moving under the cover of night to avoid detection and any other threats that might be lurking. You will not be hot on this journey even though its Death Valley owing to Alien manipulation of the climate, it will be bone chilling cold."

He paused, letting his words sink in, then continued, "Dodger, will lead, it is a top-of-the-line futuristic space vehicle as you all know but it is not only designed for short journeys in space like the once Space Shuttle. It's perfect for this journey it's equipped with advanced navigation systems, cloaking capabilities, and enhanced durability to handle the harshest conditions. It will set the pace for our convoy. Stay close, keep your eyes on Dodger's rear lights and under no circumstances should you fall behind, remember once Dodger passes through the mountainside the very rock face will reform behind Dodger. This means that any vehicle that has stopped or not within range of Dodger the rock face will reform to its natural state. This means any vehicle caught in that area which is too far behind Dodger will be crushed to nothing along with everyone on board any following vehicle. Therefore it is imperative if any vehicle has trouble you must use the communication so that Dodger can stop therefore preventing the rocks to reform."

Jeremiah's eyes swept over the group, making sure they understood the importance of maintaining formation. "If you encounter trouble, radio ahead immediately. Do not attempt to handle it on your own. We stick together, or we don't make it at all."

With the last rays of sunlight sinking below the horizon, the convoy began to move. Dodger, sleek and at times operating in silent mode, took the lead, its black surface blending seamlessly into the encroaching rock formation. The other vehicles, a mix of heavily modified off-roaders and a few more futuristic models, fell into line behind it. The rock face opened up as if like magic surrendering to Dodger's will. All vehicles kept the same pace and the communication coming from Dodger kept asking if everyone was in line and following Dodger as instructed. Everyone answered with the correct answer. It seemed endless but soon Dodger would be free of the rock shackles and all of a sudden the message came over from the onboard AI, "Everyone place all face masks on and make sure all oxygen is flowing we are now two minutes from breaking free of the mountainside and into an hostile atmosphere. Everyone followed the instruction with one or two panicking but these were quickly calmed as each other checked the masks to make sure they were secured and that oxygen was flowing. Then without any further warning Dodger burst from the mountainside into a dark viciously cold night.

Even though it was dark the landscape of Death Valley stretched out before them, illuminated by a clear night, an unending expanse of shadows and shifting sands and the hard salt ground. The night brought a deceptive bone chilling coolness, a stark contrast to the blistering heat that this place was famous for.

The first few hours were tense but uneventful. The convoy moved steadily, the hum of engines and the occasional crackle of the radio were the only sounds breaking the silence of the desert night. The stars overhead were a brilliant canopy, their light undiminished by any earthly interference.

Jeremiah shouted over the communications system. All those that have been trained up in using Vendor take up your positions, with that

Dodger brought the convoy to a halt. The ones who knew how to use Vendor were put in place amongst the convoy so that they were not close to each other. The convoy continued on its journey.

Around midnight, the terrain grew more challenging. Rocky outcrops and treacherous dunes tested the drivers' skills and the vehicles' capabilities. Yet, Dodger's advanced sensors and precise navigation kept the convoy on course. Jeremiah, in the vehicle just behind Dodger, maintained constant communication, his calm, steady voice providing reassurance.

Despite the inherent dangers, there was a certain rhythm to the journey. The convoy moved as one, an almost organic entity crossing the barren landscape. Each member focused, determined and hopeful that they would reach Hawthorne safely.

As the first light of dawn began to creep over the horizon, they found a suitable place to halt and rest. It had been a long, gruelling night and they had made significant progress. Jeremiah stepped out of his vehicle, stretching his stiff muscles and surveying the group with a nod of approval.

"Good job, everyone," he said, his voice carrying a note of pride. "Rest up. We have another long night ahead of us."

With that, they began to set up a temporary camp, knowing that the journey through Death Valley was far from over but getting through the first night unscathed made the group feel good. Henry and Ben advised everyone that the next part of the journey would be dangerous as recent landslips would make the journey treacherous.

Rick and Josh the very human like androids, started to set up a perimeter fence that would provide a shield and also some reflective material that should render the camp invisible from above. Once the fence was set up and turned on it allowed Dodger to release pure oxygen into the camp, the perimeter fence would keep the air inside with a force field. When everyone was told they could remove their oxygen masks there was deep joy as everyone breathed in safely without the need for the masks. However as soon as the perimeter is removed for the continuation of the journey there will yet again be the need for the oxygen masks.

With that, the silence was shattered by a deep, resonant hum, followed by the eerie green pulse of a beam cutting through the valley. The beam's light illuminated the landscape, revealing an alien craft much larger and more menacing than any they had encountered before.

Jeremiah and Jim stood side by side, their faces etched with concern as they observed the approaching threat.

"This one's bigger," Jeremiah muttered, eyes narrowed.

"Much bigger," Jim agreed, his voice grim. "I'm not sure the perimeter shield can hold against something of that power."

The urgency now spread like wildfire through the camp. Those who had been using the Vendor devices were roused from their sleep, shaking off grogginess as they swiftly took their positions with one at each corner of the camp and one in the middle. The air buzzed with tension as they prepared for what might come.

Jim, "Make sure all the Vendors are fully charged," he ordered and everyone acknowledged the instruction.

"On my word!" Jeremiah shouted, his tone authoritative and calm despite the rising panic. "If you need to fire at the craft, do so in rotation. One after the other, from left to right, then the middle. Do not all fire at once to start with. It is important to aim directly at the centre of the craft."

Now everyone held their breath as the alien craft drew nearer, its probing beams sweeping the terrain, searching for signs of human life.

Each pulse of green light seemed to grow more intense, the craft's intentions ominously clear.

Jeremiah tightened his grip on his Vendor, his knuckles white. "We can do this," he murmured, more to himself than anyone else. "We have to."

Jim nodded, placing a reassuring hand on Barbara's shoulder. "Stay focused. We'll get through this."

Meanwhile, Clio, Ben, and the others readied themselves, every muscle tensed for the imminent confrontation. Clio stole a glance at Ben, her mind flashing back to their earlier moment of connection. Now was not the time for distractions, she reminded herself. They had a job to do and lives depended on their success.

As the alien craft hovered closer, its metallic surface gleaming under the green light, Jim's voice rang out. "Get ready. On my mark."

The craft was over head now and a power surge could be heard and a bright red bolt from the craft made a direct hit onto the shield, they now knew we were here. The perimeter shield shuddered as if it couldn't take much more of this.

The craft's beam intensified again , sweeping even more dangerously close. Jim raised his hand, the moment stretching into an eternity.

Jim in a raised voice stated. "The next bolt could finish us all get ready on my command but do not fire yet we must let it get real close, wait wait wait be patient do not fire yet wait for my command!" Then as the vibrations from the alien craft shook the ground it was obvious they were going to discharge another bolt and all of a sudden Jim shouted, "Now!" (The Vendor operates on the same frequency as the perimeter shield so can pass through the shield seamlessly.) With that he first Vendor fired, a brilliant bolt of energy piercing the air. It struck the craft, causing it to shudder. The next Vendor followed in quick succession, each shot precise and powerful, hitting the same central point. Left to right, then the middle, they fired in perfect rotation.

The alien craft reacted, its green beams wavering and then intensifying, as if in anger. The air crackled with energy, the night alive with the sounds of battle. The last hop of humanity held their ground, their coordinated attack relentless and unwavering.

"Keep it up!" Jim encouraged, his voice strong. "We're making progress, recharge!"

As each Vendor shot hit its mark, the craft began to falter, its once seamless advance now hesitant. The combined force of the Vendors' energy bolts seemed to disrupt its systems, causing it to retreat slightly.

Clio, her heart pounding, glanced at Ben once more. Their eyes met but this time, the look was one of steely determination. Whatever their personal feelings, they were united in this fight, bound by a common goal to protect their people and ensure their survival.

Jim's voice boomed through the night, cutting through the chaos. "As soon as all the Vendors are charged, shout 'Charged'!" His command was met with a chorus of affirmative responses as the defenders focused on their devices, adrenaline surging through their veins.

The tension in the air was so intense now as each team member kept a close eye on their Vendor's charging indicator. Seconds felt like hours as they waited for the signal that their weapons were ready for the final assault.

"Charged!" The first shout came, followed swiftly by another. "Charged!" "Charged!" The calls echoed around the camp as one by one, the defenders signalled their readiness.

Jim raised his hand, his voice steady and commanding. "On my count. Three... two... one... fire!"

A unified blast of energy surged from all five Vendors, converging into a single, devastating beam aimed directly at the heart of the alien craft. The night exploded in a brilliant display of light as the combined power struck the target with unerring precision.

For a heartbeat, time seemed to stand still. Then, with a deafening roar, the alien craft erupted into a ball of fire and debris. Shards of metal and alien technology scattered in all directions, but the perimeter shield held firm, deflecting the deadly fragments away from the camp. Sparks flew and the ground trembled, but the shield protected everyone from the fallout.

The moment the explosion subsided, a wave of euphoria swept through the camp. Cheers erupted, louder and more jubilant than ever before. The sense of victory and relief was overwhelming, for a brief moment, the hardships they had faced were forgotten in the triumphant celebration.

Amidst the jubilation, Clio and Ben found themselves drawn to each other, their emotions heightened by the adrenaline and the shared victory. They exchanged a quick, heartfelt hug, the intensity of the moment blurring the lines they usually kept so rigidly drawn.

Olivia, standing nearby, noticed the embrace. Her expression was unreadable, but she didn't look away. The complexities of their relationships were not lost on her, but for now, the joy of their survival took precedence.

The camp continued to buzz with excitement, the air filled with laughter and relieved conversations. The children ran around, their faces alight with joy, and even the usually stoic adults allowed themselves to revel in the victory.

Jim, watching the scene unfold, allowed himself a rare smile. They had won a significant battle, and for now, that was enough. He exchanged a nod with Jeremiah.

Rick and Josh, who didn't require sleep, methodically sifted through the debris left behind by the destroyed alien craft. With their advanced sensors and analytical capabilities, they meticulously examined every piece of wreckage, recording and analysing the remains of the articulated, sentinel-like beings that had been on board and had been utterly melted by the power of Vendor.

As they worked, their sophisticated language processing systems deciphered the alien language encoded in the remnants of the craft's computer systems and data storage units. The information they uncovered was staggering – these aliens seemed to hold the belief that planet Earth belonged to them and not to humankind.

When Rick and Josh relayed this discovery to Jim and Jeremiah, Jeremiah's response was chilling. "I know," he said, his voice heavy with the weight of a revelation that shook Jim who was stood beside him.

Rick and Josh exchanged a glance, their realistic synthetic eyes flickering with curiosity. With methodical precision, they began to explain the details of their findings, their voices calm and measured.

"As we sifted through the wreckage," Rick began, "We discovered that these beings not only believed this planet to be theirs, but they also seemed to view humans as an invasive species, one that needed to be subjugated or eliminated."

Josh continued, "Their language systems are highly advanced and their technology is far beyond anything today's Earth would have encountered before. We were able to recover fragments of their mission logs and directives, which indicated that they had been observing Earth for centuries, waiting for the opportune moment to strike."

As Rick and Josh continued their explanation, they projected holographic images and data visualisations, giving Jim and Jeremiah a comprehensive overview of their findings. The debris field was meticulously reconstructed and they highlighted the key components and artefacts that had led them to their startling conclusion.

"The level of detail and complexity in their systems is truly remarkable, luckily not as advanced as Jeremiah's time," Josh said, his voice tinged a hint of elitism. "It's as if they had been preparing for this moment for millennia, studying our planet, our cultures and our weaknesses, all in preparation for their ultimate conquest."

Rick nodded in agreement. "However their advanced technology proved no match for the power of Vendor. The sheer force that melted their alloys and reduced their sentient forms to pure molten slag, Vendor is of course from the future as Jeremiah knows only too well."

The two androids continued their briefing, they painted a vivid picture of the alien invaders' intentions and the devastating power that had been unleashed upon them. The implications were staggering, leaving Jim and Jeremiah to ponder the true nature of the threat they had narrowly averted, and the mysteries that still lay before them. Jeremiah stated that one thing that was missed amongst everything you found, directing his comment to Rick and Josh was that these Sentinel type creatures are mere inventions by their creators and it's the creators themselves that are now heading for Earth. Josh agreed because there was indeed encrypted data that was unable to be accessed by anyone not even the sentinels.

As the golden hues of the setting Sun painted the sky, the camp where Jim, Jeremiah, Rick and Josh had rested and regrouped was abuzz with activity. The rest of the day had been a much-needed respite, allowing them to recover from the harrowing events of earlier when they had witnessed the devastating power of Vendor that melted and destroyed the alien craft.

Jim and Jeremiah moved about the camp with purpose, gathering their gear and supplies, their faces etched with determination. They knew that the journey ahead would be fraught with peril, especially after their successful downing of the alien craft. The revelation that these extraterrestrial beings viewed Earth as their own and considered humanity an invasive species had shaken them to their core, although this seemed to affect Jim more.

Rick and Josh stood vigilant, their amazing human like forms casting eerie silhouettes against the dimming light. Their advanced sensors and systems were constantly scanning the surrounding area, ever-watchful for any signs of alien threats.

As the last rays of daylight faded, the camp was awash in the warm glow of lights from Dodger. The air was thick with anticipation, and tension that spoke of the possible dangers.

"We must be ready for anything," Jeremiah said, his voice low and steady as he checked the supplies in his pack. "Those aliens won't take kindly to us destroying one of their ships and they'll likely retaliate."

Jim nodded grimly, his eyes narrowed in the flickering light. "We've faced them before, and we'll face them again."

The camp erupted into a flurry of activity as Jim's commanding voice rang out, "Everyone not travelling in Dodger, get your oxygen and your masks! Board the vehicles, we move out in fifteen minutes!"

Immediately, Jim, Jeremiah, Rick, and Josh sprang into action. They moved with practised efficiency, gathering their gear and supplies, and making their way towards Dodger, the spacecraft that would lead their convoy, everyone else waited their turn.

Dodger loomed over the camp, its sleek lines and gleaming hull reflecting the last rays of the setting Sun. A ramp extended from its belly, beckoning everyone to board its confines. As they approached, the hatch slid open with a hiss of advanced hydraulics, revealing the spacecraft's well-appointed interior.

Rick and Josh were the first to enter, Jim and Jeremiah followed closely behind, their hands deftly securing oxygen masks and distributing them to the ones that needed them. The ones not travelling in

Dodger needed extra care in checking their own equipment one last time.

Within moments, the children and the vulnerable had boarded Dodger.

With a rumble that reverberated through the camp, Dodger's powerful engines roared to life, this time not in silent mode for extra thrust, kicking up clouds of dust and debris and now slowly moving forward.

The convoy of rugged vehicles fell into formation behind it, their headlights cutting through the gloom like beacons in the night.

For hours, they pressed on, the desert giving way to increasingly rough and rocky terrain. The vehicles jostled and bounced, their suspensions groaning under the strain of the unforgiving terrain. Dodger, however, maintained a steady course, its advanced stabilisers and propulsion keeping its occupants secure and comfortable and when needed Dodger would just levitate above the obstacle.

As the night wore on, the convoy encountered greater and greater challenges. Boulders and jagged outcroppings threatened to impede their progress, and some of the ground vehicles began to struggle, their engines labouring under the strain. Dodger stood ready to assist if needed.

Suddenly, a voice crackled over the radio, cutting through the static. It was Barbara, "We need to stop and deploy shields and camouflage!" she shouted, her voice tinged with urgency. "I've just seen an alien green beam on the horizon!"

Jim's heart pounded in his chest as he processed Barbara's words. Without hesitation, he relayed the orders to the rest of the vehicles. "AI instructed Dodger, maintain position and activate defensive systems engage your shields." Jessica and Clio deployed the perimeter fence with the red perimeter fence posts turning from red to green to indicate the small encampment was protected and camouflage protocols swiftly followed!"

Dodger projected its powerful shields to add further power to the perimeter fence and the dome of advanced technology that now protected them.

Among the rugged vehicles were many women and children, civilians who had put their trust in the likes of Jim, Barbara, Clio, and Jessica.

As the warning of the approaching alien craft echoed through the radio, a gripping sense of fear rippled through all present. Mothers clutched their children close, their eyes wide with terror, while others huddled together, seeking strength in numbers.

Jeremiah's voice crackled over the comms, his tone resolute yet tinged with concern. "The same team that fired Vendor before, take up your positions. We may need your skills again." He paused, his words weighty with the gravity of the situation. "Hopefully, the alien craft won't detect us, but we must be prepared."

Jessica and Clio. With steely resolve etched on their faces, they moved through the scattered worried people, their voices low but firm as they tried to reassure the terrified women, and children around them.

"Shhh, we need to be quiet," Jessica whispered, her eyes looking into the shadows for any sign of movement. "The aliens can't know we're here. Stay low and stay silent."

Clio nodded in agreement, her hand resting comfortingly on the shoulder of a young boy who clung to her side. "We'll get through this, just like before. Have faith and if need be the power of Vendor."

Their words seemed to have a calming effect, as the fearful murmurs subsided, replaced by a tense silence punctuated only by the occasional sniffle or whimper from a frightened child.

In the darkness Jim, Jeremiah, Rick, and Josh watched the scene unfold from their viewpoints.

"We won't let them down," Jim vowed, his voice low but resolute. "Whatever it takes, we'll protect these people and drive off the alien threat once and for all."

Rick and Josh nodded in silent agreement, their advanced systems already running scenarios and calculations, formulating contingency plans should the worst come to pass.

Outside, the tension hung thick in the air, everyone waited with bated breath for any sign of the approaching alien craft. The ground vehicles were well-concealed, their camouflage systems activated, rendering them virtually invisible to the naked eye.

Dodger, too, had engaged its cloaking mechanisms, it's sleek hull shimmering and distorting as it blended seamlessly into the rocky surroundings.

Time seemed to slow to a crawl, each passing second an eternity of anticipation and dread. The civilians huddled close, their faces etched with fear, while the seasoned members of the team maintained their vigilance, weapons at the ready.

Then, without warning, a brilliant green beam sliced through the darkness, sweeping across the landscape like a malevolent searchlight. The ground trembled beneath their feet, and a low, ominous hum filled the air, its vibrations setting teeth on edge.

Jessica and Clio redoubled their efforts to keep the civilians calm, their voices little more than whispers as they urged them to remain silent and still.

As the alien craft drew nearer, its massive form blotting out the stars above, the team braced themselves for the inevitable confrontation. They knew that their survival, and the survival of all they held dear, hinged on their ability to repel this otherworldly threat.

With steely determination and an unwavering resolve, they prepared to face the alien invaders head-on, ready to unleash the full force of Vendor if necessary – a last, desperate stand to defend their very lives.

The tension within the sheltered convoy was deep, a thick blanket of dread that settled over the huddled people and the seasoned team members alike. Jim's voice cut through the tense silence, a hushed whisper that carried the weight of their desperate situation.

"You two," he said, gesturing to a pair of women near the back of the group. "Go to Dodger and retrieve a Vendor each. Quickly, but quietly, I think we may need more."

The two women nodded, their faces etched with fear and determination. They knew the gravity of their task, the responsibility that now rested upon their shoulders. Without a word, they slipped away from the group, their footsteps muffled against the rocky terrain as they made their way towards the cloaked spacecraft.

Moments later, they emerged from Dodger's interior, each clutching one of the formidable Vendor devices in their trembling hands. Jim beckoned them closer, his movements slow and deliberate, mindful of the potential threat looming overhead.

"Listen carefully," he whispered, his voice barely audible over the ominous hum that permeated the air. "I'll show you how to fire these, but you must remain calm and focused."

With deft movements, Jim demonstrated the proper technique, his hands guiding theirs as he showed them how to aim and brace for the powerful recoil. The two women nodded, their eyes wide with a mixture of fear and steely resolve.

"When I give the order," Jim continued, "Aim for the centre of the craft. Hit it right in the middle, with everything you've got."

He turned to the rest of the team, his gaze sweeping over the huddled forms of those who had wielded the Vendors before. "This time, there will be no alternating fire. When I give the signal, we all fire simultaneously. Understood?"

A chorus of grim nods and murmured affirmations met his words, as the team steeled themselves for the confrontation to come.

The tension grew thicker by the second, the air heavy with anticipation and the knowledge that their very survival hinged on their ability to repel the alien threat.

Suddenly, without warning, a brilliant red bolt of energy lanced through the gloom, striking the protective dome that had been erected around the convoy. The ground shuddered violently, tremors rippling through the rocky terrain as the dome flickered and wavered under the onslaught.

Screams and cries of terror erupted from the civilian ranks as rocks and debris rained down, one particularly large chunk striking a woman squarely in the chest. She crumpled to the ground, her pained cries echoing through the chaos.

Within seconds, another searing bolt of energy struck the dome, the impact sending shock waves through the already battered barrier. Cracks spider-webbed across its shimmering surface, and the team braced themselves for the worst.

Jim's voice rang out, a bellowing roar that cut through the cacophony of chaos. "Everyone with a Vendor, on my mark! Five... four... three... two... one... FIRE!"

In a deafening chorus of thunderous reports, the Vendors unleashed their devastating payloads, streams of brilliant energy converging on the looming alien craft. The initial barrage impacted with a blinding flash, the craft's deflector shields flaring and buckling under the onslaught.

Clio, her face a mask of grim determination, maintained her position, her hands steady as she unleashed another salvo, pouring everything she had into the defence of her world. Clio now transfixed continued to fire every time Vendor charged. Clio now moving toward the alien craft and fired yet again. Everyone looked on in astonishment.

The alien craft reeled, its shields failing under the relentless assault. Explosions blossomed across its hull.

As Clio continued to fire her Vendor. Jim realised immediately she needed help and ordered everyone else to release the power of their Vendor's, "Fire!" He ordered.

The alien craft was spewing debris in all directions. Cries of triumph and relief mingled with the screams of the injured, as they celebrated their hard-won victory.

Yet, even in the midst of their elation, the cost of their struggle was laid bare. Clio lay crumpled on the ground, her body broken and battered by the shrapnel that had pierced the dome's weakened defences. Jessica rushed to her side, cradling her friend's head in her lap, tears streaming down her face.

As the smoke cleared and the alien craft's remains burned in the distance, everyone took stock of the aftermath. They had emerged victorious, but the battle had exacted a heavy toll.

Jessica's anguished screams now were piercing the eerie silence that had fallen over the battlefield. "Help my friend! Help her.. Please!" Her voice was raw with fear and desperation as she cradled Clio's broken body in her trembling arms.

Clio's pallid face was streaked with crimson, the once-vibrant hues of life rapidly draining from her features. A tangle of twisted metal shrapnel protruded from her abdomen, the jagged edges slick with her life's blood. Each shallow, rattling breath seemed to sap what little strength remained within her.

Jessica's screams echoed throughout the land, "There's so much blood... Oh God No, There's Blood Everywhere!" Jessica's words dissolved into a keening wail, her anguish reverberating through the still night air. She continued screaming. "Please, Someone Help Her! Get her on Dodger, quickly!"

Her frantic cries spurred people from everywhere into action, snapping them from their momentary stupor. Jim was the first to reach her side, his face etched with grim determination as he surveyed the severity of Clio's wounds.

"Rick, Josh! Get the medical bay ready immediately," He barked, his voice cutting through the chaos like a blade. "We need to stabilise her and stop the bleeding."

The two androids moved with immense precision, their synthetic forms blurring into motion. Within seconds, they had retrieved a stretcher from the depths of Dodger's interior, their movements deft and efficient.

As they gently lifted Clio's broken form onto the stretcher, Jessica refused to relinquish her hold, her fingers tangled in the fabric of Clio's tattered clothing. "I'm not leaving her!" She pleaded, her eyes wild with desperation. "Please, let me stay with her."

Jim's expression softened, just for a moment, as he met Jessica's gaze. "Of course," he said, his voice low and reassuring. "But we need to move quickly. Every second counts."

With Jessica in tow, the grim procession made its way into the depths of Dodger, the echoes of their footfalls reverberating through the spacecraft's corridors. The medical bay awaited, its pristine white walls and state-of-the-art equipment a stark contrast to the chaos they had left behind.

"AI, initiate emergency medical protocols," Josh barked, his almost human synthetic voice ringing with authority. "Prepare for trauma care and stabilisation."

The medical bay's sophisticated systems hummed to life, diagnostic screens flickering with vital readouts as the nanite infused equipment whirred and calibrated itself.

A trio of advanced medical drones hovered into position, their sleek forms bristling with an array of specialised tools and instruments.

Gently, Clio was transferred from the stretcher to the central biobed, her battered form dwarfed by the gleaming medical apparatus that surrounded her. Jessica hovered nearby, her hands pressed to her mouth in a futile attempt to stifle her sobs.

The drones moved with robotic precision, their manipulator arms extending and retracting as they meticulously catalogued and assessed Clio's injuries. Suction cups and micro-forceps extracted shards of shrapnel, while advanced scanning beams probed the extent of her internal trauma.

"Initiating nanite infusion," AI's dispassionate voice rang out, its clinical tones at odds with the gravity of the situation. "Administering coagulants and analgesics."

AI reported that there was damage to the artery just below her heart and the Nanites are urgently required. A slender injector extended from the biobed, its needle piercing Clio's pale flesh with surgical precision. A glimmering cloud of Nanites flowed into her bloodstream, their microscopic forms carrying payloads of repair and clotting agents with pain-relieving compounds.

For long, agonizing moments, the medical bay was a flurry of activity, the drones and AI working in concert to stabilise Clio's rapidly deteriorating condition. Jessica remained rooted to the spot, her eyes never leaving her friend's face, silently willing her to cling to life.

Finally, after what seemed like an eternity, the frantic pace began to slow, the drones retracting their instruments as AI's voice rang out once more.

"Patient stabilised. Vital signs within acceptable parameters, Nanites have repaired the damage." There was a momentary pause, the weight of the next words hanging in the air like a pall. "Prognosis... guarded."

Jessica exhaled a shuddering breath, her knees nearly buckling with relief. Clio was alive, for now, her indomitable spirit clinging tenaciously to the fragile thread of life.

As the drones retreated and the medical bay fell into a watchful silence, Jessica approached the biobed, her fingers gently brushing the blood-soaked strands of hair from Clio's brow.

"You're going to be okay," she whispered, her voice thick with unshed tears. "You have to be okay. We need you, Clio. We all need you."

In that moment, as the echoes of battle faded into memory, the true cost of their struggle became all too apparent. They had emerged victorious, but the scars of their ordeal would linger long after the smoke had cleared. Another woman was brought into the medical area luckily her wounds to the chest were not serious.

The scene in the medical bay was one of solemn vigil and raw emotion. Jim stood back, observing as Jessica hovered over Clio's biobed, her body wracked with sobs.

The trauma of the recent battle had taken its toll, the adrenaline rush giving way to the stark reality of their narrowly avoided catastrophe. Clio's battered form, swathed in the medical bay's sterile dressings and tethered to a multitude of monitors and life-support systems, was a sobering reminder of the high stakes they faced.

Jessica's grief was intense, a tangible force that seemed to permeate the very air around her. Her shoulders shook with each ragged inhalation, her tears tracing glistening paths down her ashen cheeks. The anguish etched onto her features was almost too much for Jim to bear witness to.

He had seen his fair share of trauma and loss in his time, but the sight of Jessica's raw emotional vulnerability struck a chord deep within him. In that moment, she was not a hardened warrior or a stalwart member of their team – she was simply a woman confronted with the potential loss of someone she loved dearly.

Jim's heart ached for her, for the pain she was enduring, and for the gut-wrenching uncertainty that hung over Clio's fate. He wanted nothing more than to offer words of comfort, to reassure her that everything would be alright, but he knew that such platitudes would ring hollow in the face of such emotional turmoil.

Instead, he approached quietly, his footsteps muffled against the hard deck, and placed a gentle hand on Jessica's trembling shoulder. No words were spoken, but in that simple gesture, he conveyed a world of understanding and empathy.

Jessica turned towards him, her eyes red-rimmed and brimming with fresh tears. For a moment, their gazes locked, and an unspoken bond of shared anguish passed between them. Jim gave her shoulder a reassuring squeeze, a silent promise that he would be there for her, no matter what the future held.

As the moments ticked by, the sobs gradually subsided, replaced by a heavy, weighted silence that hung like a shroud over the medical bay. Jessica's grip on Clio's hand never wavered, her knuckles white with the intensity of her grasp, as if anchoring her friend to the mortal realm through sheer force of will.

Jim maintained a careful watch, a steadfast presence amidst the storm of emotion. He knew that the road ahead would be fraught with even greater challenges, but in that moment, his sole focus was on offering what solace he could to his grieving comrade.

For in the depths of such overwhelming sorrow, it was the bonds of friendship and camaraderie that would sustain them, a flickering of hope in the darkness that threatened to consume them all.

Jeremiah's booming voice cut through the heavy silence that had settled over the medical bay, his tone urgent and laced with grim determination. "We have to move on from here," he bellowed. "They know our position. It's too dangerous to linger."

His words hung in the air like a death knell, a sobering reminder that their ordeal was far from over. The battle may have been won, but the war still raged on and their respite would be fleeting at best.

Jim turned to Jessica, his expression a mixture of sympathy and steely resolve. "Jeremiah's right," he said, his voice low but firm. "We can't afford to stay here any longer. It's too great a risk."

Jessica's grip on Clio's hand tightened, her knuckles whitening as she fought back a fresh wave of tears. The thought of leaving her friend's side, of abandoning her to an uncertain fate, was almost too much to bear.

Sensing her anguish, Jim placed a reassuring hand on her shoulder once more. "You can stay aboard Dodger," he offered. "Keep watch over Clio, ensure she receives the care she needs."

A flicker of relief passed over Jessica's features, her shoulders sagging ever so slightly as the weight of that burden lifted. "Thank you," she whispered, her voice thick with emotion. "I won't leave her side, I promise."

Jim nodded, his gaze lingering on Clio's motionless form for a heartbeat longer before turning to join the others in the preparations for their departure.

Outside, the rest of the team was already in motion, their movements fuelled by a sense of urgency that bordered on panic. The ground vehicles were being readied, their engines rumbling to life as supplies and equipment were hastily loaded into their reinforced cargo bays.

Dodger, too, was undergoing its own preparations, its sleek hull thrumming with barely contained power as its systems cycled through pre-flight checks and diagnostics.

Jeremiah barked orders, his voice carrying over the din of the frantic activity, coordinating the team's efforts with an iron-clad sense of discipline. "Rick, Josh, you'll take point in Dodger. Maintain a slower pace."

The two androids acknowledged the orders with a crisp nod, already moving toward the spacecraft's boarding ramp.

"Everyone else, get ready," Jeremiah continued. "We move in five."

Now a renewed sense of urgency, their earlier triumph over the alien craft tempered by the knowledge that their ordeal was far from over. As the last of the supplies were secured and the final checks were completed, they began to file into their respective transports, their faces etched with grim determination.

Within minutes, the convoy was ready to move out, Dodger's powerful engines spooling up to full thrust as it now took to the air, a tiger vantage point to protect everyone below. The ground vehicles fell into formation with their headlights cutting through the gloom.

As the convoy pulled away, Jim cast one final glance back, his heart heavy with the knowledge of what had happened to Clio and that Jessica remained with her keeping a solitary vigil over her fallen comrade.

But even in the face of such heartache and uncertainty, he knew that they had no choice but to press on. The alien threat still loomed large, and their only hope of survival lay in outrunning and outwitting their otherworldly foes.

With a steely resolve that belied the weight of their circumstances, Jim turned his gaze forward, his eyes fixed on the path that lay ahead. The journey would be fraught with peril, but they were resolute in their determination to see it through, no matter the cost.

The convoy disappeared over the horizon, leaving their former battleground behind, the weight of their mission settled upon them like a mantle – a grim reminder that in the battle for their very survival, there could be no rest, no respite.

Just before dawn broke they came to a halt and started to secure the camp. Ben said he would check over the next hill, once at the top he surveyed the devastated town that was once Hawthorne, it had been completely destroyed. Buildings lay in ruins, debris scattered across the once-bustling streets. However, in the distance, the fortified bunkers stood firm, their sturdy structures seemingly unscathed by the catastrophe that had befallen the town.

Ben relayed his findings to Jim and Jeremiah, with Jeremiah's pragmatic response highlighting the importance of securing those intact bunkers. Although Jim was understandably troubled by the destruction of Hawthorne, Jeremiah's focus remained steadfastly on their survival, prioritizing the need to establish a secure camp and make their way to the bunkers under the cover of night.

Meanwhile, Jim sought out Jessica, hoping to find good news about Clio. To his dismay, Jessica's distress only deepened his concern. She revealed that Clio, had undergone a procedure where her blood had been drained and replaced with a 'special fluid' intended to aid her well-being.

Sensing Jim's confusion of the situation. Jessica said, "I've been told by AI that this special fluid, is not an experimental treatment but tried and tested. I'm not so sure maybe it's a last-resort measure to sustain Clio's life in the face of dire circumstances. I just hope they know what they are doing. I'm just not sure what to think anymore." The severe life threatening condition of Clio worried Jim. The introduction of this special fluid raises numerous questions about its nature, purpose, and potential risks or side effects. It could be a cutting-edge medical intervention or a dangerous and untested procedure. Regardless, the grave situation is real, and the decision to undertake such a drastic measure underscores the dire straits Clio is in.

Jim upon hearing the explanation that Clio was in a state of limbo, neither alive nor dead, he asked AI for an explanation. AI responded with a measured tone, shedding light on the intricate procedure underway. "The 'special fluid' you speak of is a preservation solution, designed to prevent death and safeguard Clio's memories and vital organs," AI explained.

AI further elaborated, "The amount of blood we extracted from Clio is relatively small, merely two pints. However, this sample is crucial, as our technology is currently replicating and synthesizing an identical blood supply from those two pints. Once the full volume has been recreated, we will gradually reintroduce this invigorated blood into Clio's body, carefully removing the preservation fluid in the process."

AI's voice carried a solemn weight as it acknowledged the danger she would be in. "Without this intervention, Clio would have been clinically dead. Her blood volume was simply too low, and infusing a substantial amount of artificial blood directly could have been catastrophic."

Jim's expression was one of sheer shock, the revelations leaving him visibly shaken. Jessica, on the other hand, wore a mask of terror, her mind undoubtedly racing with fear for Clio's well-being and the implications of such an unconventional procedure.

Sensing their trepidation, AI sought to reassure them. "We are confident in our ability to restore Clio's vital functions," it stated with conviction. "The preservation solution has maintained her biological integrity, and the new replacement blood will breathe new life into her circulatory system. Though the road ahead is uncertain, we remain optimistic about her prospects for recovery."

AI's words offered a glimmer of hope amidst the harrowing circumstances she faced. The delicate balance between life and death was laid bare and one could only cling to the promise of AI's reassurance.

Elsewhere Jeremiah had been putting off the repeated requests for more updates of what and where was going to happen but now he was cornered by both Jim and Barbara. They wouldn't let him go until he gave them more information. Jeremiah took a deep breath, steeling himself for the difficult conversation. Jim and Barbara looked at him expectantly.

"I'll start with the bombshell," Jeremiah began. "Planet Earth is not your planet of origin."

A heavy silence fell over them both as the words sank in. Jim and Barbara exchanged bewildered glances, their expressions a mix of disbelief and shock.

"What do you mean?" Jim asked, his voice strained. "How is that even possible?"

Jeremiah held up a hand, signalling for patience. "I know it sounds unbelievable, but it's the truth. You originated from a different planet."

Barbara shook her head, her eyes wide with confusion. "But... how? We have no history of that. We've lived our entire lives here as have billions of others."

"I understand your scepticism," Jeremiah said, his tone gentle but firm. "But the evidence is undeniable. Your genetic makeup is unlike anything found on Earth."

As Jeremiah continued to explain the details, Jim and Barbara listened with rapt attention, their expressions flickering between shock and disbelief. The revelation challenged everything they knew about themselves and their world.

Suddenly, Jessica burst into the room, her face flushed with urgency. "I just heard from the AI that Clio is in good hands!" She said breathlessly. "Now what's going on here?"

Jeremiah quickly filled her in on the stunning revelation about their extraterrestrial origins. Jessica's eyes widened, her mouth agape.

"Jim, Barbara," Jeremiah continued, "You are not alone in this. Every adult on the camp needs to hear this. however now is not the time."

Jim and Barbara exchanged a long, pensive look, silently weighing what they had been told. Finally, Jim nodded resolutely.

He said. "Okay everyone needs to know."

Then the silence was broken by AI requesting their presence in the medical bay onboard Dodger.

Jessica, Jim, Barbara, and Jeremiah rushed towards Dodger's location. They found Clio lying motionless, her condition appeared lifeless.

The AI medical tech from the future, with futuristic technology at their disposal, wasted no time. They were inserting a probe through Clio's ribs, guiding it directly into her heart.

"They're not shocking her?" Jessica exclaimed, her voice laced with concern.

Jeremiah gently pulled Jessica aside, understanding the need to reassure her. "Listen," he said, in a calm and reassuring manner. "This is future medical tech, far beyond what you're familiar with. The probe isn't meant to shock her heart, it has a different purpose and AI thought you three should be present for this."

As Jeremiah explained, the AI medical tech prepared to initiate the life-saving procedure. First, they carefully switched off Clio's life support, allowing the future technology to take over.

Suddenly, the probe inside Clio's heart began to glow with a bright blue light, visible through her skin from the outside of her chest. Jeremiah turned to Jessica, his expression resolute.

"We have to trust them," he said. "The AI is making sure everything is okay. The probe is pushing pure, oxygenated new blood around Clio's body, focusing primarily on her brain first."

True to Jeremiah's words, the glowing probe pulsed rhythmically, simulating the action of a beating heart and propelling the oxygenated blood throughout Clio's body. They watched in awe as Clio's once-pale, lifeless face began to regain its natural colour, the hue of health slowly returning.

"Another probe is now entering the brain," Jeremiah explained, his voice tense with anticipation. "It will send an artificial shock, simulating the brain's actions to start a stopped heart. This will restart Clio's heart, its tried and tested well into the future."

As the second probe slid into position and entered the brain, little drops of blood started coming from the incision. The probe into the brain started and suddenly, Clio's body jolted and contorted as the artificial shock coursed through her brain, triggering a cascade of natural neural impulses, heading toward the heart.

For a moment, time seemed to stand still, and then, miraculously, Clio's chest rose and fell in a shallow breath. The medical tech monitoring her vitals, then confirmed that her heart had begun beating once more, faint but steady.

The group watched in stunned silence as the future technology worked its magic, coaxing Clio's body back to life, one intricate step at a time. Jeremiah's unwavering faith in the AI's capabilities had been justified, and a newfound sense of hope filled the room.

The chest probe continued its rhythmic pulsations, gradually increasing the strength and regularity of Clio's heartbeat. For nearly twenty minutes, the room was filled with a tense silence, punctuated only by the soft beeps of the medical equipment monitoring her vitals.

Suddenly after what seemed a lifetime, Clio's eyelids fluttered, and a deep, gasping breath escaped her lips. "Where... am I?" she murmured, her voice faint and raspy.

Immediately, the AI medical tech responded, its synthesised voice calm and reassuring. "You're safe, Clio. You're in our medical facility, receiving treatment."

Clio confusion etched on her face whispered, "Treatment? What... happened?" Her words were laboured, more of a whisper and each syllable an effort.

"You suffered a severe medical emergency," the AI explained patiently. "But we were able to stabilise you. Your vital signs are improving, and you're on the path to recovery."

Clio's eyes darted around the room, taking in the unfamiliar surroundings and the concerned faces of those gathered around her. "Future... technology?" she again whispered, her voice searching for answers amongst her apprehension.

The AI recognized the need to alleviate her fears. "Yes, Clio. The technology we used to treat you comes from a highly advanced civilisation in the future and may I add you are one of us. It may seem strange and unfamiliar, trust us."

A flicker of some sort of understanding crossed Clio's face, and she nodded weakly. "I... I trust you," she murmured, her eyelids growing heavy once more.

"Rest now, Clio," the AI soothed. "Your body has been through an incredible ordeal, and it needs time to heal. We'll be monitoring you closely, and we'll be here to answer any questions you might have when you wake up properly."

With a soft sigh, Clio's eyes drifted shut, her body surrendering to the restorative embrace of sleep. The AI medical tech continued its meticulous work, adjusting the probes and monitoring her vitals with unwavering precision.

As the AI medical tech had reassured confused Clio, Jessica watched the scene unfold with a whirlwind of emotions. Seeing Clio's eyelids flutter and hearing her utter those first few words. It was a profound moment, a reminder that even in the direst of circumstances, hope remained.

Yet, Jessica's relief was tempered by a deep sense of disquiet. The unfamiliar technology, so advanced and foreign, filled her with a mixture of awe and trepidation. She had witnessed the raw power of the future medical devices first-hand, their ability to manipulate the very essence of life itself. It was both miraculous and unsettling.

Clio now in a restful slumber, Jessica found herself torn between gratitude and uncertainty. She approached the AI medical tech, her eyes searching for reassurance.

"She's going to be okay, right?" Jessica asked, her voice laced with concern. "This technology... it's safe?"

The AI responded with its usual calm and measured tone. "Clio's vital signs are stabilising, and she is on the path to recovery. The technology we used is far beyond what you're accustomed to. It has been rigorously tested and proven effective."

Jessica nodded slowly, her mind trying to process the information. She glanced back at Clio's sleeping form, her chest rising and falling with each breath, the gentle glow of the probes pulsing in rhythm.

"It's just... so different," Jessica murmured. "But it's saved her life, I am forever grateful."

The AI acknowledged Jessica's mixed emotions. "It is natural to feel apprehensive about the unknown. This technology may seem alien to you, but its purpose is to heal and preserve life. We will continue to monitor Clio closely and ensure her full recovery."

Jessica took a deep breath, steadying herself. She knew that she would need to put her faith in the AI's capabilities, no matter how unfamiliar or unsettling they might seem. Clio's life depended on it.

With a newfound resolve, Jessica stepped closer to Clio's bedside, gently taking her hand in her own. A silent promise passed between them – Jessica would remain by her side, offering unwavering support and drawing strength from the extraordinary measures that had brought her friend back from the brink.

***

Attention now switched to the task that Jim had convinced Jeremiah he needs to do without delay, although not happy Jeremiah agreed.

Everyone now assembled together and Jeremiah started his explanation, "Your ancestors and my ancestors were left on Earth thousands of years ago to see how a small colony would manage on a planet similar to our home planet," Jeremiah continued, his voice carrying the weight of ages. "My ancestors, forgot that you were here. At that time they had put Sanctuary in place with Dave, Zeena, Rick, and Josh – androids designed to protect and guide you if you were ever in danger of extinction."

Barbara's looking totally bewildered, her mind really struggling with the implications. "But... Why were we just left here? How could they abandon us like that?" Was Barbara's penetrating question.

Jeremiah's expression was solemn as he continued. "Our ancestors became distracted by another violent alien species, and you were... overlooked, left to fend for yourselves on this planet."

A sardonic chuckle escaped Jim's lips, tinged with dark amusement. "Well, that's just great. Abandoned by our own kind."

"There was already prehistoric cavemen and prehistoric cavewomen inhabiting the planet," Jeremiah pressed on. "One of our female ancestors fell in love with one of these caveman, and it sparked a new hybrid species – the ancestors of modern humans."

Jessica's eyes widened, her mouth parting in surprise. "You mean... we're part caveman?"

Jeremiah nodded with a slight smile to Jessica saying exactly what she thought. He carried on, "With that came the diseases and ailments that plagued the primitive humans. It's the reason for so many illnesses and genetic defects that have persisted throughout your lineage."

Silence as Jeremiah's words sank in. Finally, Barbara spoke up, her voice laced with a mixture of wonder and bemusement.

"So, let me get this straight," she said, shaking her head. "We were abandoned by our alien ancestors, bred with cavemen, and now there are six billion of us... hybrids, roaming the planet?"

Jim let out a bark of laughter, his shoulders shaking with mirth. "Well, when you put it like that, it does sound pretty absurd."

Jessica, however, found little humour in the situation. Her brow creased with concern as she considered the implications. "What about diseases, Jeremiah."

Jeremiah nodded solemnly. "Yes, we'll need to discuss the ongoing health challenges that the breeding with the caveman species brought. However for now this is enough information to process."

His gaze steady and resolute. "Talk amongst yourselves about this and I am sure you will have plenty of questions in the days that come. You all deserve to know the truth about your origins and history."

Barbara exchanged a glance with Jim, a silent conversation passing between them. Finally, she let out a resigned sigh. "Well, I suppose it's better than living a lie."

Jim, ever the pragmatist, simply shrugged. “Might as well embrace our caveman roots, right?”

As they prepared to venture out and discuss this extraordinary revelation with everyone, a sense of trepidation mingled with a newfound sense of purpose. The truth, no matter how bizarre or unsettling, was a burden they would shoulder together.

Jessica said, “Well Jim and Barbara since you stopped on that cold bleak road to rescue myself and Clio, I can only say I am now totally bewildered.” Jim and Barbara now laughed and hugged Jessica’s with her totally honest response.

Chapter 17

HAWTHORNE AND BEYOND

There had been many revelations in the last few hours, everyone had been told about where we came from. Some laughed at the thought but others said it started to make some sort of sense.

The convoy had moved on, away from the encounter with the alien craft and they had arrived on 10th Street a road on the very outskirts of Hawthorne. What was once a very nice peaceful neighbourhood was now a mass of rubble and completely deserted. Everyone had oxygen masks on owing to the lack of oxygen in the atmosphere and there was now the first signs of plant life dying around them.

It was decided that vehicles and Dodger would squeeze in between the rubble because it was doubtful that the Aliens would come back into an area they had already destroyed. Amazingly Jake and Dot had continued to grow stronger since the treatment of their DNA and now they had a slightly younger appearance to each other, although no one else seemed to notice.

The group mainly made up of women had adapted amazingly and the small number of children had been well looked after. Only a few men had survived the onslaught of the aliens as if they wanted to just eradicate them entirely but Jeremiah knew it was something to do with reproduction. He decided not to mention this because he honestly thought that these survivors of the human race had processed enough. There would be plenty of time for detailed explanations once they had reached safety.

Jeremiah longed for a return to his own time line but he hid it well from everyone else. The next part of the journey was to make it to the bunkers just to the north of Hawthorne. He was disturbed as Ben and Henry arrived and started asking about these bunkers.

Ben looking puzzled. "What are these bunkers for?"

Jeremiah explained, "These bunkers have been used for many years to safely store ordnance and ammunition."

"But if there's ordnance being kept in those bunkers surely that is going to be extremely dangerous?" Ben asked and then he continued, "Explosives stored for years could become unstable over time."

Henry nodded in agreement. "Yeah, having a bunch of old explosives and ammunition just sitting around seems like an accident waiting to happen. Shouldn't that stuff be disposed of properly?"

Jeremiah held up his hands in a placating gesture. "Don't worry, these bunkers were specially constructed for long-term ordnance storage. They're heavily reinforced and have rigorous safety protocols in place." He went on, "The ordnance is carefully monitored and maintained to ensure it remains stable."

Ben said sceptically, "If you say so. Just seems risky to me."

"I have to agree with Ben," Henry said. "Well, if ordnance is being stored there, it won't exactly be the safest place to be hanging around, especially now that there is no one around to monitor it."

They both looked at Jeremiah with serious expressions, clearly still concerned about the potential dangers despite his reassurances.

Ben and Henry exchanged worried glances as Jeremiah continued speaking.

"In fact," Jeremiah said with a casual chuckle, "We'll have to go right through several of the bunkers to get to our destination. No way around it."

Ben's eyes went wide. "Wait, you're saying we have to actually enter and pass through a bunker filled with unstable, old dangerous explosives?"

Henry shook his head adamantly. "Absolutely not. I am not setting foot anywhere near those death traps."

Jeremiah waved a dismissive hand. "Oh, it'll be perfectly fine. These bunkers were built to last." He chuckled again, though the laugh sounded a bit nervous.

"This is insane!" Ben protested in a raised voice. "There's no way I'm risking my life, it sounds madness!"

Henry agreed, "Yes, let's find another route, even if it's out of the way. Cutting through an ordnance bunker is where I draw the line."

Jeremiah opened his mouth, perhaps to try reassuring them again, but Ben and Henry had made up their minds. They stood resolute, fuelled by self-preservation to avoid setting foot in a potential blast radius.

Jeremiah gave a flippant response about leaving Ben and Henry behind if they refused to go through the ordnance bunker but it landed like a lead weight. The two men exchanged an incredulous look, momentarily stunned into silence.

Ben was the first to find his voice, sputtering indignantly. "Leave us behind? Are you out of your mind?" His face flushed with a mix of anger and disbelief. "We're not going through that deathtrap of a bunker, but that doesn't give you the right to just abandon us here!"

Henry nodded vigorously in agreement, his jaw clenched. "Exactly! We're part of this team, this mission, whatever it is. You can't just ditch us in the middle of nowhere because we have reasonable safety concerns." He jabbed an accusing finger at Jeremiah. "That's the kind of reckless crap that gets people killed."

Ben paced in an agitated circle, running his hands through his hair. "I can't believe this. We finally make it to this secret base or whatever and you're threatening to maroon us? For trying to avoid an unnecessary suicide run?" He whirled on Jeremiah again, eyes blazing. "Well screw you man, we're not pawns for you to sacrifice!"

"Yeah, screw you!" Henry echoed heatedly. "We're not expendable! If you think you can just write us off like that..." His voice trailed off as he struggled for words, shaking his head in disgust.

The two men fell into a tense, fuming silence, glaring at Jeremiah as if they could scarcely believe his cavalier willingness to ditch them over this. Their postures were stiff with anger, daring him to double down on his reckless bluff.

A tense silence fell after Jeremiah's blunt words stating his responsibility was to the larger group, not just Ben and Henry. The two men looked taken aback, their anger momentarily deflated.

Ben recovered first, shaking his head adamantly. "You can't be serious. Sacrificing us isn't going to save anyone else! That's just twisted logic."

"Yeah, there has to be another way," Henry insisted. "Some compromise where we don't have to basically commit suicide."

Jeremiah levelled them with a grave look. "I'm deadly serious. If we try going around those bunkers, we'll run straight into heavy resistance. Too many lives will be lost pushing through."

He paused, letting that grim scenario hang in the air. When he continued, his voice took on a harder edge.

"But going through the ordnance bunker is a clear, undefended path. Yes it's risky as hell, but at least it gives everyone else a fighting chance. I won't let fear jeopardize this entire operation when there's a viable, if dangerous, option available."

Ben opened his mouth to protest, but Jeremiah raised his hand to silence him.

Then Jeremiah continued, "Don't try to argue self-preservation with me. I've sent better men than you two to their deaths for the greater good. If you want to back out, be my guest. But I will not let your cowardice endanger the lives of my other soldiers because thats what we are now, soldiers."

With those comments Henry and Ben exchanged apprehensive looks, their bravado faltering under Jeremiah's unnervingly ruthless resolve.

"Just think about it," Jeremiah said, his tone becoming more measured. "Are you really going to insist we take the bloodier path, just to save your own skins? When the ordnance bunker is right there?"

No one spoke for a long moment. Ben and Henry avoided each other's eyes, weighing their options in heavy silence.

Ben exhaled a frustrated sigh. After a tense moment, he levelled Jeremiah with a resigned look.

"Alright, fine," Ben said through gritted teeth. "We'll go through the damn ordnance bunker. But I want it noted that we're doing this under vehement protest."

Henry nodded stiffly in agreement. "Yeah, we're not sacrificial lambs. We have a right to voice our objections to this insanity."

Jeremiah arched an eyebrow coolly. "Your objections are noted but this is the route we're taking, end of discussion."

He turned on his heel, seemingly preparing to leave the confrontation, when Ben called out heatedly.

"Hang on a second!" Ben's hands clenched into fists at his sides as he glared at Jeremiah's back. "At least have the decency to acknowledge you're putting everyone's lives at incredible risk here!"

Jeremiah paused and slowly turned back to face them, his expression unreadable.

"You're right," he said. "Going through that ordnance bunker exponentially increases the chances, so you two along with everyone else and that includes me could end up dead."

Henry swallowed hard, his bravado deflating.

Jeremiah continued in that same measured tone. "I'm well aware I could be sending you two men and everyone else to their deaths. But I've weighed the costs and this is an acceptable risk for the potential pay-off of securing our main objective."

Ben recoiled, appalled. "Oh is that all we are to you? Acceptable risks? Expendable?"

"In this operation, Yes, everyone is." Jeremiah's voice was devoid of emotion. "So wrap your heads around that reality. Listen you two I need you clear-minded and focused if we're going to get through that bunker alive."

An uncomfortable silence stretched out.

Finally, Ben gave a stiff nod of resignation. "Yeah...we're clear. Lead the way."

As Jeremiah turned once more, Ben shared one last look with Henry, a million unspoken words passing between them about the sacrifice they may be about to make.

After some thought and reflection Jeremiah called everyone to gather around, his expression emotion free. All people were present but not the kids or Clio who was still recovering from her serious injuries. A hush fell over the group as they awaited Jeremiah's words.

"Listen up," he began, his voice carrying an air of solemn authority. "We've got a tough decision to make regarding our path forward."

He paused, surveying the expectant faces before continuing. "There's a series of ordnance bunkers we need to go through. They contain a stockpile of old unpredictable explosives and ammunition."

A murmur of concern rippled amongst them. Jeremiah held up a hand so he could proceed.

"Now, I won't lie to you - going through those bunkers carries extreme risk. One stray spark and we could all end up scattered across the landscape." His gaze was steely. "But here's the reality - if we try to circumvent the bunkers, we'll be exposed. Intel suggests we'd face heavy bombardment after being spotted by the aliens."

Worried looks were exchanged between many as Jeremiah laid out the two options starkly.

"So it comes down to this - do we take the risk and go through the bunkers? Or do we attempt to go around in the wide open space, sacrificing our presence and likely taking heavy casualties if spotted?"

The gravity of the choice put directly to them. Peter, who had worked with munitions, spoke up hesitantly.

"Sir, any idea what kind of ordnance we're talking about in those bunkers? Because if it's the real unstable stuff..."

Jeremiah shook his head. "Honestly, no way to know for sure. Could be absolutely nothing unstable. Could be enough conventional explosives to bury us all. We could be rolling the dice."

A tense silence as they digested the hazardous unknown. Finally, Ben raised his hand.

"For the record, Henry and I already stated our objections about going through the bunkers to Jeremiah. We think it's insanely risky."

Jeremiah gave a curt nod of acknowledgment. "Their objections have been noted. Now I need to hear from the rest of you." His gaze swept across the grim faces. "What's it going to be - the devil we know or the devil we don't?"

There was intense murmuring as they weighed the two risky options laid out clearly before them. Questions and concerns ping-ponged back and forth as they grappled with the life-or-death decision.

Then, Marina, a wiry woman with a mane of braided hair, abruptly stood up from where she was crouched. All eyes turned towards her as she swept her gaze across her comrades.

"We go through the bunkers," she stated firmly. A hush fell over the group at her definitive tone.

Marina squared her shoulders, then continued in a voice that carried conviction.

"Look, there's no sugar-coating it - going near all that decaying ordnance is like dangling over the jaws of death. But Jeremiah's right that alternative path around promises only slaughter."

She paused, letting that grim reality sink in before pressing on with intensity.

"At least with the bunkers there's a chance, however slim, that we make it through unscathed. It's a risk, yeah, but one with potentially zero casualties as the payoff."

Her eyes burned with the profound truth of her next words. "Because anywhere else we go, people will die. That's a guarantee."

One by one, heads started nodding slowly in grim agreement with Marina's logic. She looked around, making eye contact with all of them.

Marina saw the response and continued with her address to them all, "We knew this operation would be high risk when we signed up. Well, here's our next big gamble, people. It's a bad bet, sure, but therein lies the small hope of all making it out alive."

With that, Marina raised a defiant fist into the air. "I say we put our faith in our skills, in our luck and in Jeremiah's lead! We go through those bunkers and we stay steadfast in our resolve!"

For a beat, there was silence. Then Jonas, the stalwart field medic, pushed himself to his feet.

"She's right," he rumbled in his thick accent. "Through the bunkers! We trust you, Jeremiah!"

One by one, the rest followed suit, rising and adding their voices to a growing chant.

"Through the bunkers! Through the bunkers! We trust Jeremiah!"

Fists pumped the air as the last humans on Earth found their resolve, defiance replacing trepidation. Jeremiah watched impassively as his soldiers, yes soldiers because that's what they had become and were now committed to the devil they knew and placed their fate in his hands once more.

The chanting died down as Jeremiah held up his hand for silence. His gaze landed squarely on Ben and Henry, the two who had vocally objected to going through the ordnance bunkers.

"It's decided then," Jeremiah stated, his voice carrying clearly. "We move out for the bunkers in two hours. Final checks on masks and oxygen reserves need to take place."

He fixed Ben and Henry with an appraising look. "But I want your blessings too. This is a unity operation - are you two with us or not?"

Ben and Henry remained stone-faced, avoiding each other's eyes. The rest of the team wasn't so reticent.

"We want you in, man!" Jim, said fervently. "We need you both!"

"Definitely, you're part of this family," Barbara stated with a nod.

But it was Jessica, the unit's youngest adult, who spoke up most insistently.

"Come on, Ben, Henry!" She looked between them imploringly. "We're all in this hell scape together. Don't back out now!" Her passionate plea struck a cord with both Ben and Henry, you could see it in their eyes.

A general murmur of assent circulated as others added their voices, encouraging the two holdouts. Ben finally met Henry's gaze and some unspoken communication passed between them.

Taking a breath, Ben turned back to Jeremiah. "You're asking us to risk our necks on a one-way trip to oblivion. Can't say I love those odds."

Henry cut in grimly. "Or that death plan, to be honest."

Despite the words, their expressions had shifted to resignations. Ben gave a slow nod.

"But you're right - we're a team and we pedal or get left behind together." He managed a wry smile. "I guess we'll just have to get blessed and a little prayer to face those bunkers."

A chorus of cheers and relieved laughter went around the group. Even Jeremiah's stony mien cracked into the faintest ghost of a smile.

"Then I'll see you masked up in two hours," he said simply. "We've got a hot patch of real estate to cross."

As the team began prepping, Ben and Henry shared one last look that spoke volumes - a thousand unvoiced reservations but a commitment to seeing this insanity through to its end, together with their brothers and sisters in arms because those brothers and sisters needed them. It was then that both Ben and Henry approached Jessica and both hugged her, much to her embarrassment.

***

Everyone now preparing, when all of a sudden, Josh ran toward Jeremiah and he was in a hurry. "Everyone, listen up!" Josh shouted, his voice carrying a sense of extreme urgency. "Josh, what's the situation, what's wrong?" Asked Jeremiah, the reply was instant.

"Jeremiah, the crafts we encountered are landing about ten miles from here. But the bad news is, loads of these mechanical sentinels are leaving the ships and get this, they're heading our way."

Jeremiah pondered for a moment in deep thought. "They're trying to swamp us," he said grimly. "Our defences won't cope with this sort of onslaught."

"How many are we talking about?" Jeremiah asked, his voice tense.

"Around thirty ships," Josh replied, "but literally hundreds, maybe thousands of sentinels coming towards us."

Jeremiah's expression hardened. "We need to move and we need to move now!" he barked. "Darkness will come soon enough and offer us some protection, but we can't wait for nightfall. We have to move now!"

People scrambled to gather their belongings, their faces etched with fear.

"How far is the bunker?" someone shouted.

"Six miles," came the reply. "The terrain is okay and Dodger will lead the way."

"But what about the sentinels?" another voice cried out. "How will we defend ourselves?"

Jeremiah gazed and pondered his answer. "We'll have to move swiftly and stay ahead of them. Our priority is reaching the bunker. Once we're there, we'll have a better chance of holding them off, better still we have a good chance of losing them."

"What if they catch up to us?" a woman asked, her voice trembling.

"Then we fight," Jeremiah said resolutely. "We fight with everything we've got. But for now, we move. Everyone listen, you must grab what you can carry and follow Dodger. Stay together and keep your eyes peeled."

"Jeremiah, wait!" Jessica rushed towards him, her shout was frantic, Jeremiah was talking to Jim and Barbara he immediately turned to face Jessica thus halting his conversation with Jim and Barbara.

"We can't beat them," she said breathlessly. "Me and Clio encountered just one of those mechanical sentinels and it took everything Vendor had to destroy it. Jeremiah you must listen to me in what I say, we struggling against just one."

Jeremiah's expression hardened as he took in Jessica's words. Jim and Barbara exchanged worried glances.

"I know I remember your encounter?" Jeremiah said, his voice grave. "Hundreds, maybe thousands of them are heading our way."

Jessica nodded grimly. "I'm sure. These things are powerful and we're not equipped to take on that many."

Jeremiah cursed under his breath, "We have just one option and it is as I have already stated we must move out now and we have to outrun them."

"Maybe we can find a way to divert them or slow them down?" Barbara suggested, her eyes darting between Jeremiah and Jessica.

Jim shook his head. "With that many? It would only buy us a little time."

"So, what then?" Barbara asked, her voice barely above a whisper. "We can't fight them and we can't outrun them because they are so quick."

Jeremiah's jaw tightened and he looked at each of them in turn. "Then we have to find a way to outsmart them. We'll keep moving towards the bunkers, but we need to come up with a plan and fast. If anyone has any ideas now's the time?" Jeremiah turned away to hasten the departure.

Jessica seeing Jeremiah turn away, rushed over to him because he was moving quite fast.

"Jeremiah, how far can Dodger shoot?" she asked pointedly.

Jeremiah regarded her with a furrowed brow. "Not far, but we have a couple of missiles on board, purely defensive."

Jessica's eyes lit up and she pressed on. "Could we not fire them somewhere else?" she proposed. "Make the sentinels think it was us when they exploded?"

The others exchanged puzzled looks, trying to grasp Jessica's idea.

"You mean use the missiles as a decoy?" Jim clarified, stroking his chin thoughtfully.

Jessica nodded eagerly. "Exactly. If we can make them think we're in a different location, it might buy us enough time to reach the bunkers before they realise their mistake."

Barbara looked uncertain. "It's risky," she cautioned, "but it might be our best shot."

Jessica turned her gaze to Jeremiah. "What do you think? Could it work?"

Jeremiah considered the proposal, his mind weighing the potential outcomes. After a tense moment, he met Jessica's eyes with a determined nod.

"Alright," he said resolutely. "Let's do it, so Jessica, you and the onboard AI work on prepping those missiles. Jim, Barbara, coordinate with the others and make sure everyone is ready to move as soon as the decoy is in place."

Jessica felt a surge of relief, her plan gaining traction. She turned to Jeremiah once more. "What's our window? How much time will the decoy buy us?"

"Once the missiles are fired, we'll have a narrow window to put as much distance between us and those sentinels as possible," Jeremiah explained. "No heroics, no stragglers. We move together and we don't stop until we reach the bunkers."

Jeremiah walked away muttering and chuckling to himself, "Can't believe she's only nineteen."

With a collective nod, they set to work, Jessica's ingenious plan offering a way to get to the bunkers.

Jessica instructed the onboard AI what was required then she left Dodger, she forgot her oxygen mask and had to dart back onboard to retrieve it after she found it difficult to breath.

The onboard AI system sprang into action as soon as Jessica was clear and had retrieved her oxygen mask. AI carefully calculating the optimal trajectory for the decoy missiles. With surgical precision, the AI initiated the launch sequence.

Dodger's powerful, almost silent engines came to life, propelling the craft skyward. The sleek vessel ascended smoothly, rising just 100 feet into the air, its metallic hull gleaming against the fading sunlight. Once at the desired altitude, Dodger hovered steadily, its stabilisers compensating for the slightest fluctuations in the gentle wind.

Inside the craft, the AI ran a final systems check, ensuring that the missiles were primed and ready for launch. Intricate displays flickered with data streams, as the AI meticulously aligned the targeting coordinates for the eastern horizon.

"Missiles cleared for firing," the AI's synthetic voice echoed through the almost empty cabin. "Commencing launch sequence in three, two, one..."

With a deafening roar, the missiles erupted from their launch tubes, hugging the ground like brilliant orange comets. Their contrails etched vibrant paths across the twilight canvas, carrying the hopes of the fleeing group on their fiery tails.

As the missiles hurtled towards their predetermined coordinates, Clio stirred in her bed, the rumbling vibrations jolting her from her slumber. Her eyes fluttered open, disoriented and still weak from her recent ordeal.

"Wha...what's happening?" she mumbled groggily, her voice thick with sleep.

The AI's calm tones filtered through the cabin's speakers, offering reassurance. "Do not be alarmed, Clio. I have initiated a decoy to divert the approaching sentinels. You are safe aboard Dodger."

Clio's vacant look trying to make sense of the AI's explanation, her mind still foggy. Before she could inquire further, a brilliant flash of light erupted on the eastern horizon, casting dancing shadows within the cabin.

The missiles had found their mark, detonating in a spectacular display of sound and fury. The shock waves rippled through the air, reaching Dodger moments later with a thunderous boom that rattled the craft's frame.

"The decoy has been successfully deployed," the AI stated as a matter-of-fact. "We will now pickup everyone that needs to come back on board then we will proceed on our intended course towards the bunkers."

Clio nodded weakly, her eyes wide with a mixture of awe and trepidation as she witnessed the aftermath of the explosive diversion unfold before her. With the AI's reassuring presence guiding them, she allowed herself to sink back into the bunk, her exhaustion temporarily overriding her curiosity.

After returning to the ground to pickup the last remnants of the human race Dodger banked northward, leaving the fiery spectacle behind, the group's hopes hung in the balance, their fate inextricably linked to the success of Jessica's ingenious plan.

The tense moments ticked by as Dodger moved northward, hopes pinned on Jessica's daring plan. Suddenly, Josh's voice crackled over the comm system, his tone laced with a mixture of relief and disbelief.

"It's working!" he exclaimed, his words cutting through the static. "The sentinels are falling for it. All of them are moving toward the explosions!"

A collective sigh of relief rippled through the convoy, the uncertainty lifting from their shoulders. The onboard AI informed all on board and Clio, still groggy from her recent ordeal, managed a weak smile, the news buoying her spirits.

The AI's synthetic voice chimed in, its calm tones offering reassurance. "Excellent. We now have a window of opportunity to reach the bunkers unimpeded. Increasing speed and adjusting course accordingly."

Dodger's engines now roared, no longer silent and they had renewed vigour, propelling the sleek craft forward at an accelerated pace. The landscape below blurred into a tapestry of greens and browns, as the vessel carved a path through the darkening sky.

Within the cabin, the mood had shifted palpably. Nervous glances were replaced by determined expressions.

Josh's voice crackled over the comm once more, a hint of awe lacing his words. "The sentinels are swarming the blast site, searching for any trace of us. It's like a scene straight out of a nightmare, but..." He paused, letting out a disbelieving chuckle. "They've completely fallen for the decoy."

The AI's synthetic tones echoed through the cabin, offering a clinical analysis of the situation. "The sentinels' programming appears to prioritise pursuit and elimination over strategic assessment. While their single-mindedness has worked in our favour this time, we cannot rely on such tactics indefinitely."

Jeremiah's voice cut through the chatter, "Agreed. We need to make the most of this opportunity. Everyone, stay sharp and be ready for anything. We're not out of the woods yet."

Dodger hurtled northward, going on ahead to make sure the area where the entrance to the bunkers is safe. The sentinels, though diverted for now, would undoubtedly resume their relentless pursuit once the deception was uncovered.

But for the moment, they allowed themselves a fleeting sense of triumph, their path to the bunkers illuminated by the fiery decoy that had so brilliantly captured the attention of their mechanical pursuers.

After what seemed like an eternity, the looming silhouettes of the bunkers finally emerged on the horizon, nestled in the arid expanse of Nevada's high desert. As Dodger drew nearer, the structures came into sharper focus, revealing their imposing yet fortified design.

The bunkers, a cluster of squat, concrete monoliths, stood defiantly against the rugged backdrop of the surrounding landscape. Their angular forms were interrupted by the occasional protrusion of ventilation ducts and reinforced entry hatches, lending an air of utilitarian resilience.

Dodger banked toward the largest of the bunkers, its hulking form casting long shadows across the barren earth. As the craft touched down, a cloud of dust swirled in its wake, momentarily obscuring the view.

Jeremiah surveyed the surrounding area, his gaze sweeping across the desolate terrain before coming to rest on the nearby Walker Lake.

The lake's placid waters now a frozen surface but still reflected the fading hues of the evening sky, its glassy surface punctuated by the occasional ripple where the ice had not yet taken hold. The shoreline, a patchwork of sand and scrubby vegetation, extended outward like a weathered embrace, offering a stark contrast to the rigid lines of the bunkers. The vegetation now obviously dying. A child touched a plant but it crumbled in her hands frozen and looking like pure crystal.

"This is it," Jeremiah muttered, his voice tinged with a mixture of resignation and determination. "Our last hope."

One by one, the others emerged from Dodger, their expressions a myriad of emotions – fear, hope and a steely resolve. They gathered around Jeremiah, their eyes drawn to the imposing structures that would serve as their sanctuary at least for now. Then the following vehicles arrived, everyone had made it to the entrance.

Barbara's gaze lingered on the lake, her brow furrowed with concern. "What about water, it's now frozen over? Can we access the lake if we need to?"

Jeremiah nodded, his jaw set. "The bunkers have purification systems that we can hear working so the ice is just on the surface."

Everyone walked swiftly toward the nearest bunker entrance. These stark, utilitarian shelters would become their fortresses, their last bastions against the relentless onslaught of the sentinels, or so they thought.

Yet, as they passed through the reinforced hatches and descended into the depths of the bunkers, a glimmer of hope flickered within them. For now, at least, they had found some sort of sanctuary – a place to regroup, not as grand as the Sanctuary they had left but nevertheless it was a sort of sanctuary.

Jeremiah instructed everyone off Dodger once everyone disembarked, Dodger would head to the North of Walker Lake and go into a cloaking period and then hopefully meet us at our destination. It was too dangerous to remain on Dodger as it would attempt to break through the ice further North. Clio was took off on a stretcher as she needed to be carried into the bunkers. Leaving her on Dodger could be an issue if Dodger was overwhelmed by the lake.

Approaching the reinforced hatches, the heavy door swung open with surprising ease, granting them entry into the fortified complex of several tunnels branching off. Jeremiah said, "Its this particular tunnel everyone now keep close and follow me." Everyone shuffling along the tunnel but suddenly the tunnel came to a dead end with several saying this is the wrong tunnel, we need to go back and try another. Jeremiah chuckled to himself.

Then he started tapping the wall as he hummed a song, with each beat in the song he tapped the wall in a different place. This now was becoming obvious that this was a special sequence of taps and then in the dim light, lit only by the odd torch, a little six inch hole appeared in the wall where Jeremiah put his hand in and pushed. A big door around six feet wide opened and Jeremiah ushered everyone in. Once inside Jeremiah pulled on whatever it was in the hole, suddenly the door began to close very slowly. This gave Jeremiah time to slip through the opening. The door closed and sealed with a sound of air being expelled from somewhere. Masks now no longer needed as oxygen at normal levels.

However, their progress was soon impeded by a second, even more formidable barrier.

"Hold up," Jeremiah called out, his voice echoing off the concrete walls. He stepped forward, eyeing the imposing door with a mix of familiarity and trepidation.

A small panel, adorned with an array of peculiar symbols had caught his attention. Jeremiah's lips curved into a wry smile as he turned to Jim. "What's your phone number, Jim?" he quipped, a mischievous glint in his eye.

Jim's brow furrowed momentarily before it dawned on him and a hearty chuckle escaped his lips. "You sly dog," he shot back, recalling the light hearted banter they had shared during their first encounter back there in Tonopah when everything was more normal.

Jeremiah's gaze returned to the panel, he asked for silence because he needs to do this carefully because he will only get three attempts at this, his calloused fingers tracing over the symbols with practised ease. First, he tapped a sequence of hieroglyphic-like shapes, their intricate lines and curves seeming to hold some cryptic meaning.

Next, his fingers danced across a series of Roman numerals, their ancient forms belying the advanced security measures they concealed.

Finally, Jeremiah's digits found the more familiar Arabic numerals, punching in a sequence that seemed to defy any logical pattern.

Jim watched the process unfold, his curiosity piqued. "How very strange," he mused aloud, his eyes narrowing as he studied the eclectic mix of symbols.

With a resounding clank and a hiss of pressurised air, the second door lurched open, revealing the dimly lit depths of the bunker beyond. Tread carefully everyone, ordnance is everywhere in this one.

Jeremiah shot Jim a knowing glance, his expression of amusement and a grim determination. "You ain't seen nothing yet," he remarked, his voice laced with a hint of foreboding.

One by one, the group stepped across the threshold venturing into the unknown that lay within the bunker's fortified walls. As the heavy door sealed shut behind them, they couldn't help but wonder what other secrets and challenges awaited them in this subterranean sanctuary. Jeremiah said we have just one more door and it will open as we approach. With trepidation they approached and as they stepped through the door a brilliant light illuminated everything – they were in a massive cavern.

Everything hummed with a frenetic energy as what seemed like swarms of robots diligently tending to the colossal spacecraft before them. Jeremiah's booming voice echoed through the vast chamber, introducing the awe-inspiring vessel as the IS Archimedes.

Robots of varying shapes and sizes scurried across the ship's hull, welding and riveting metal plates with some sort of advanced tools. Recalibrating intricate machinery and carrying out meticulous maintenance tasks. Some were armed with cutting torches which precisely cut protruding panels, while others methodically inspected every nook and cranny, their robotic appendages probing and adjusting components with surgical precision.

The ship itself was a marvel of engineering, a true behemoth of the stars. Its sleek, angular form stretched hundreds of feet in length, with multiple decks visible through the illuminated viewports that adorned its flanks. The main hatch yawned open, revealing Rick and Josh, as they stood alongside Dodger. Dodger had successfully smashed through the ice and entered the cavern from Lake Walker.

The bright lights that had flooded the cavern were so bright they could hardly see. As their eyes adjusted to the bright lights there were stunned faces of the rescued individuals that reflected a kaleidoscope of emotions. The children's eyes sparkled with unbridled wonder, their mouths agape as they took in the otherworldly scene unfolding before them. Their gaze darted from the bustling robots to the towering spacecraft.

However, the adults wore expressions tinged with trepidation, their brows furrowed as whispers of uncertainty rippled through the crowd. "Where are we going?" One woman murmured, her voice trembling with a blend of hope and fear. Others echoed her sentiment, their eyes searching for answers amidst the controlled chaos.

Jeremiah's commanding presence momentarily quelled the rising tide of confusion. "My good people," he bellowed, his voice resonating with authority, "You are going home!" A hush fell over the assembly as they processed his words, their faces a tapestry of disbelief, relief and newfound anxiety.

Despite Jeremiah's reassurance, a palpable reluctance gripped some of the individuals. They exchanged furtive glances, their bodies tense as they contemplated the prospect of boarding this extraordinary craft. Whispered concerns drifted through the air, fuelled by the unknown.

With Jeremiah's declaration that they were going home, a palpable unease rippled through the crowd. Jim, Barbara and Jessica attempted to soothe the rising tensions, their voices carrying over the cacophony of robotic activity.

Jim stepped forward, his hands raised in a placating gesture. "Everyone, please, let's remain calm," he implored, his words struggling to pierce the din of murmurs and whispers that enveloped the cavern. Barbara joined him, her gentle eyes sweeping over the sea of worried faces.

"I understand your concerns," she called out, her voice laced with empathy. "This is all overwhelming, but Jeremiah has proven himself trustworthy time and again. We must have faith."

Jessica nodded, her gaze resolute as she addressed the uncertain individuals. "We've come too far to turn back now and there is nothing to go back to."

Their reassurances, however, seemed to fall on deaf ears. The whispers grew louder, fuelled by the innate human fear of the unknown. Some individuals clutched their loved ones tightly, as if seeking solace in familiar embraces, while others shifted uneasily, their eyes darting between the towering spacecraft and the open cavern behind them.

The robots continued their methodical work, oblivious to the emotional turmoil that gripped the human contingent. Their metallic limbs moved with precision, unwavering efficiency, tending to the gleaming hull of the IS Archimedes as if beckoning the reluctant souls to embark .

Despite Jim, Barbara and Jessica's best efforts, the arguments and objections persisted, voices rising in a discordant chorus of fear and uncertainty. The prospect of boarding the craft to them an alien spacecraft, or surrendering to forces chasing after them, proved too daunting for some, their trepidation growing.

The cavern was a crucible of conflicting emotions, with hope and doubt vying for dominance in the hearts and minds of those gathered. As the robotic symphony played on, they were faced with a decision to embrace the promise of what Jeremiah called home or cling to staying on Earth, but this was an Earth with no oxygen and no hope. This was a growing concern.

The atmosphere in the cavernous chamber was thick with tension, a dissonant symphony of raised voices and mounting concerns. Amid the clamour, a solitary figure emerged, her footsteps echoing with a deliberate cadence that demanded attention. As she approached the crowd, an eerie hush descended upon the assembly, their cries fading into a watchful silence.

IT WAS CLIO.

Her presence commanded an air of authority that transcended the chaos surrounding her. With a stoic expression etched upon her features, she surveyed the sea of apprehensive faces before her, their emotions laid bare in the flickering lights of the immense spacecraft.

Clio's gaze swept over the crowd, her eyes meeting those of the uncertain individuals one by one. In that moment, an unspoken connection seemed to form, as if she could sense the turmoil that churned within their hearts. Her lips parted and her voice resonated with a clarity that cut through the charged atmosphere like a beacon in the night.

"My friends," she began, her tone measured and unwavering. "I understand the trepidation that grips you. The path before us is shrouded in uncertainty, a journey into the unknown that would test the mettle of even the bravest souls."

A stillness enveloped the cavern, as if the very air held its breath in anticipation of her words. The robots continued their tireless ministrations, their mechanical whirs and clanks providing a rhythmic backdrop to Clio's address.

"But we must not allow fear to shackle us," she proclaimed, her voice rising with conviction. "For too long, we have wandered in the shadows, bereft of the light of hope. This spacecraft, this marvel of engineering, represents our deliverance – a chance to reclaim our rightful place in the world we once called home!"

Clio her eyes alight with a fervent resolve that seemed to ignite a spark within those who met her stare as she went on, "I cannot promise that the journey will be easy, nor can I guarantee what awaits us at its end. But I can assure you that remaining here, trapped in this subterranean purgatory, as our planet is slowly destroyed, is not the way. If you stay here then it becomes a fate far crueller than any trial we may face aboard the IS Archimedes."

A hushed murmur, as if her words had struck a chord within the depths of their collective consciousness. Clio paused, allowing her message to resonate before delivering her final, impassioned plea.

"So I implore you, my friends, to cast aside your doubts and embrace the promise of a new beginning. Let us board this vessel with resolute hearts and unwavering spirits, for it is only through courage in the face of the unknown that we can truly reclaim our destiny!"

With those words, Clio fell silent. Her message was resolute, a direct challenge to those who wavered, a rallying cry to those who yearned for the possibility of a life beyond the confines of their underground existence or to face the wrath and certain death on Earth.

A heavy silence blanketed the cavern in the wake of Clio's impassioned words, every soul present hanging on the precipice of a momentous decision. Then, with a quiet resolve that seemed to command the attention of all, Clio began to move through the crowd, her gaze meant everything to the faces it fell upon. It was left to Jake and Dot as Clio approached the eldest among them. There was purpose to Clio's steps, as if she carried the hopes and fears of those around her with every measured stride. She approached the elderly couple, their wizened features etched with a lifetime of hardship and longing and extended her hands in a wordless invitation.

Jake and Dot exchanged a quick glance with each other, a silent conversation passing between them in that fractional moment. Now they looked into the eyes of Clio. Their eyes glistened with tears that had been held at bay for far too long, a dam of emotion threatening to burst forth. With trembling hands, they reached out and clasped Clio's proffered hands, their gnarled fingers intertwining with hers in a gesture of absolute trust.

"Trust me," Clio whispered, her voice suffused with a tenderness that seemed to embrace the couple, enveloping them in a profound sense of solace.

A charged stillness was everywhere now, as if the entire cavern had drawn a collective breath, awaiting the response that would resonate through the depths of their shared uncertainty.

Then, in a moment that seemed to transcend the confines of time and space, Jake and Dot found their voices, their words ringing out with a clarity and conviction that belied their advanced years.

"We do trust you, Clio!" they exclaimed in unison, their voices loud and trembling with a raw, unbridled emotion that tore at the heartstrings of all who bore witness.

Dot's cheeks glistened with the trails of tears she could no longer contain, a lifetime of hopes and dreams crystallized in those saline rivulets. Her grip on Clio's hand tightened, as if drawing strength from the woman who had become a beacon of fortitude in their darkest hour.

Jake, his face etched with the wisdom of countless battles fought and sacrifices made, met Clio's gaze with an unwavering resolve that defied his age. His hand, calloused and weathered by the tribulations of their journey, clasped Clio's with a fervour that spoke volumes of the trust he had placed in her guidance.

In that profound moment, a shift rippled through the crowd, as if the uncertainty that had gripped them only moments before had been shattered by the raw emotion and unflinching faith displayed by Jake and Dot.

Clio, her eyes shimmering with a mixture of pride and determination, turned and led the elderly couple towards the waiting spacecraft, their footsteps echoing through the cavern like a drumbeat heralding a new era.

As they approached the towering vessel, the robotic symphony that had accompanied their passage seemed to swell in a triumphant crescendo, as if the machines themselves were paying homage to the indomitable spirit of those who had chosen to embrace the unknown. With each step, the weight of doubt seemed to lift, replaced by a burgeoning sense of hope that threaded its way through the hearts and minds of those who watched in awe.

In that defining moment, the path forward was illuminated not by the harsh glare of artificial light, but by the flickering flame of human resilience – a beacon burning brightly, guiding them towards the promise of a future beyond the boundaries of their subterranean existence and conquered world.

A profound hush settled over the cavernous chamber as Clio, Jake and Dot made their way towards the towering spacecraft. Their footsteps echoed like a reverberant heartbeat.

As they approached the yawning open hatch of the IS Archimedes, a murmur rippled through the crowd, a tide of whispered affirmations and renewed faith.

"Clio is amazing," one small child's voice muttered, the words carrying the weight of awe and newfound trust. "We trust her," an adult echoed, as if giving voice to the sentiment that had taken root in the hearts of those assembled.

One by one, the individuals began to follow, their hesitant shuffles evolving into a steady stream of humanity drawn to the promise of a future. With each person who stepped forward, the murmurs grew louder, a chorus of shared determination that seemed to swell in resonance with the robotic symphony that surrounded them.

Jim and Barbara stood transfixed, their expressions a tapestry of astonishment and pride as they watched Clio's unwavering leadership catalyse the transformation unfolding before their eyes. This young woman, whose strength of character had been forged in the crucible of their harrowing journey, had emerged as a bright light, her unwavering resolve inspiring even the most doubtful among them.

As the last of the individuals crossed the threshold and stepped aboard the spacecraft, Jessica lingered behind, her gaze fixed upon Clio with a mixture of admiration and gratitude. In that moment, the two women shared a profound connection, a silent acknowledgment of the extraordinary bond that had been forged through the trials they had endured together.

Without a word, Jessica boarded the craft smiling as she walked past Clio.

In that moment, the echoes of doubt and trepidation that had once reverberated through the cavern were silenced, replaced by a collective resonance of hope and fortitude. As the hatch began to close, sealing them within the embrace of the IS Archimedes, a sense of unity permeated the air – a shared understanding that whatever lay ahead, they would face it together, bound by the unbreakable bonds forged in the fires of their desperate struggle.

Chapter 18

WALKER LAKE

The weariness that had settled upon the souls of the rescued individuals seemed to momentarily lift as the robots ushered them through the corridors of the IS Archimedes, ushering them towards the promise of respite. The hum of activity echoed all around them, a reminder of the tireless efforts underway to prepare the vessel for its impending voyage.

Navigating the labyrinthine of passages, Ben and Olivia found themselves standing before the entrance to their assigned quarters, their eyes wide with a mixture of disbelief and cautious hope. Cradled in Olivia's arms, their infant child slumbered peacefully, blissfully unaware of the profound journey they had already undertaken.

With trembling hands, Ben reached out and activated the door mechanism, the portal like door sliding open with a soft hiss to reveal a space that defied their wildest imaginings. Before them lay a stunning apartment, a home of comfort and warmth that seemed worlds apart from the awful reality they had endured for so long.

Olivia gasped, her free hand rising to her lips as she took in the tastefully appointed living area, the plush furnishings beckoning them to sink into their welcoming embrace. A sense of overwhelmed emotion erupted within her, she turned to Ben as she struggled to find the words to express the tumult of feelings that coursed through her.

Without a word, Ben hugged his wife and child in a tender embrace, his own cheeks damp with the tears of relief and gratitude that he had fought so hard to contain. In that moment, their ordeal seemed to lift, replaced by hope and the promise of a future where they could raise their child in safety and comfort.

Ben and Olivia lost themselves in this home aboard a spaceship a real newfound haven, the corridors beyond echoed with the muted sounds of similar discoveries. Doors slid open to reveal breathtaking living quarters, each one a testament to the care and consideration that had gone into providing a sense of home for those who had endured so much.

In one apartment, Jake and Dot stood in silent awe, their not so aged hands now clasping together as they took in the opulent surroundings. A lifetime of hardship making every penny count no longer applied, now rewarded with the comfort and luxury they had only dared to dream about.

Down the hall, a young family marvelled at the spacious accommodations, their children darting from room to room, their laughter and squeals of delight echoing like music in the corridors. The parents exchanged a glance, their eyes shining with a newfound sense of hope, knowing that their children would now have a chance.

As the minutes ticked by and the weariness that had once threatened to overwhelm them began to dissipate, replaced by a buoyant sense of optimism. The robots continued their ceaseless efforts, preparing for the journey, a journey that would carry them all towards the promise of a new beginning.

As the preparations continued, the echoes of laughter and hushed conversations filled the corridors of the IS Archimedes.

Then a disembodied voice reverberated through the vessel's intercom system. The rich, modulated tones carried a warmth and familiarity that seemed to cut through the lingering apprehension that had hung in the air.

"Hi, I am Dave, your onboard AI," the voice announced, its melodic cadence inviting and reassuring. "Could you all please make your way to the Bridge where Jeremiah Jacks needs to address you and answer all your questions."

Murmurs swept through the apartments, the rescued individuals emerged from their temporary havens, their expressions a tapestry of curiosity and anticipation. Doors slid open, and families, couples, and solitary souls alike began to converge in the corridors, their footsteps echoing in a cacophony of purposeful strides.

As they navigated the winding passages everyone realised they didn't know the way, whispers of speculation and excitement drifted through the air, punctuated by the occasional exclamation of wonder by children tugging at their parents' hands, their eyes wide with unbridled curiosity, while the more aged ones leaned on their loved ones for support, their faces etched with a mixture of trepidation and hope.

The robots, ever-present and tireless, continued their duties, occasionally stepping aside to allow the human throng to pass, their metallic appendages moving with a fluid grace that belied their mechanical nature.

Rick came to greet them with instructions explaining to them. "Hi everyone from time to time everyone will come across a green button on the wall," he explained further. "Just press the green button and a door will open thus allowing you to step into what we would call a pod, it's different to an elevator, it goes horizontal not just vertical. Once inside, simply ask the pod where you want to go and the pod will take you there." He further advised them, by saying, "For example you could say 'take me to the Bridge' then that journey will commence."

Gradually, after following the instructions and going in numerous pods the people converged on the Bridge. The Bridge was a vast chamber that seemed to radiate an aura of authority and purpose. Rows of consoles and displays lined the walls, their surfaces flickering with inscrutable data and readouts. A towering view screen dominated the far end of the Bridge, promising tantalising glimpses of what was to come.

As the last of the individuals filed in, Jeremiah Jacks, a commanding presence, exuded an air of quiet confidence and leadership, his uniform crisp and adorned with intricate insignia that hinted at a lifetime of service and sacrifice, albeit from another time.

Jeremiah Jacks looked at the faces before him. A warm smile spread across his weathered features, and raised a hand in a gesture of welcome and reassurance.

"Welcome my friends," he began, his voice with a deep tone and depth but with clarity. "I can only imagine the whirlwind of emotions that must be coursing through you all at this moment. But fear not, for you have embarked upon a journey that will carry you home."

Anticipation coursed through the crowd, as if his words had ignited a spark of hope within each and every soul present.

"I know you must have countless questions," he continued, "I promise, in due time, all will be answered. But for now, let us bask in the knowledge that the darkest chapter of our shared ordeal has come to a close and a new era of hope and possibility awaits us on the horizon."

With that, the view screen flickered to life and outside the robots had ceased their work and were now moving on board.

In that moment, the true magnitude of their impending journey seemed to crystallize, a realization that they stood poised on the precipice of a journey that would transcend the boundaries of their wildest dreams.

Jeremiah Jacks now asked for questions and some answers would shock everyone to the core. He first told them that what they already had been told in snippets and he confirmed that these snippets were true. He went on to confirm about the prehistoric race already here on Earth when twelve humans were left here by our ancestors. Eventually they were absorbed into the population. He told them that the human genes in the end won the battle and it was from those initial humans that billions of hybrid humans had been born, He then told them of the mistake that resulted in the ancestors not returning for those fellow human pioneers, leaving them stranded. He then stated, "You are the remnants of those human hybrids."

His words echoed throughout, a revelation that seemed to defy the very foundations of their understanding. The assembled crowd listened with rapt attention, his voice bringing grim knowledge, each syllable chipping away at the preconceived notions they had clung to for so long.

Jacks continued, "Earth was never our planet first," he declared, his expression grave. "It had been under the rule of an evil race known as the shadows – a shadow-like people who wield robotic sentinels to carry out their malevolent bidding."

A shudder rippled through the crowd, as if a collective chill was shared at the mere mention of these enigmatic beings. Jacks paused, allowing his words to sink in before continuing his grim narrative.

"These sentinels are but the lackeys of the Shadows, tasked with conquering, killing and using the parts of their victims as sustenance, decorations, and subjects for their twisted experiments." His voice grew sombre, laced with a restrained fury that hinted at the horrors he had witnessed first hand.

"They spare no one," he emphasized, his gaze sweeping over the assembled faces, etched with varying degrees of disbelief and dawning comprehension. "Their methods are systematic, beginning with the reduction of temperatures and the systematic destruction of all life, culminating in the removal of oxygen from the atmosphere, leaving nothing but a barren husk of a world in their wake, but its considered by them to be part of their empire. Somehow those prehistoric caveman creatures survived mainly underground and in caves."

The silence that followed was deafening, punctuated only by the occasional sharp intake of breath. Families huddled closer together, seeking hope in each other's embrace, while solitary individuals stood rooted to the spot, their faces masks of horror and disbelief.

"The sentinels are merely the vanguard," he continued, his voice taking on a sombre cadence. "Once a world has been secured its terraformed to meet their twisted specifications. Centuries later the Shadows themselves arrive, now terraformed for them, their very presence a blight upon all that is good and pure. Later when they have tired of the conquered planet they return it to a barren landscape. Devoid of all surface life."

He paused once more, struggled but managed to continue, "It is their insatiable hunger for conquest, their utter disregard for life, that has brought them to our doorstep time and again, leaving a trail of decimated worlds and shattered civilisations in their wake."

The message with all its revelations settled in, dread permeated the air, tempered only by the flickering embers of hope that burned within each heart – a desperate yearning for deliverance from the nightmare that had been unveiled.

A hush fell over the assembled crowd as an inquisitive voice rose from their midst, posing a question. "What about Area 51?"

Jacks paused. A knowing smile tugged at the corner of his lips as if he had been anticipating this very inquiry.

He answered, "Area 51, I know most have you have lived close by this infamous place." His voice carrying a hint of wry amusement. "That was nothing more than a carefully crafted smokescreen, a diversion to draw attention away from the true heart of our operations, operations that one day would save you."

A ripple of murmurs coursed through the crowd, individuals exchanged incredulous glances, their preconceptions about the infamous military installation being systematically dismantled by Jacks' revelations.

"Everything," he continued, "I mean everything, took place hundreds of feet below the Walker Lake, right here, where you now stand."

His voice now still and a profound silence had descended, punctuated only by the occasional sharp intake of breath or the shuffling of feet as individuals shifted their weight, struggling to comprehend the magnitude of what they had just been told.

For years, decades and even more, the enigmatic Area 51 had captured the collective imagination of humanity, shrouded in a veil of mystery and speculation that seemed impenetrable. Countless theories and conspiracies had been woven around its very existence, fuelling a global fascination with the unknown that had permeated every aspect of popular culture.

Yet, in a single, matter-of-fact declaration, Jacks had torn away that veil, revealing the truth that lay beneath, a truth far more profound and unsettling than any conspiracy theorist could have ever imagined.

Expressions of disbelief gave way to a dawning comprehension. The pieces of the puzzle began to fall into place, shedding light on the myriad of unanswered questions that had plagued mankind for so long.

Some nodded slowly, their eyes alight with newfound understanding, while others leaned in closer, this was indeed a staggering revelation.

Jacks allowed a momentary pause. Then, with a resolute nod, he continued with their undivided attention.

"The truth has been hidden from you my friends, shrouded in layers of misdirection and obfuscation for your own protection," he declared. "But now, as we stand poised on the precipice of a journey that will challenge everything you thought you knew, it is time to cast aside the veil of secrecy and embrace the reality that has been kept from you for far too long."

Captain Jacks' next revelation seemed to defy the very boundaries of plausibility, casting a newfound light on the enigmatic phenomena that had captivated the world for decades. As his word now had full attention, he delved into the truth behind the infamous UFO sightings that had fuelled countless theories and speculations.

"The UFOs that were encountered," he began, his voice carrying a certainty that commanded their complete attention, "I repeat the UFO's that were encountered, the small saucer-shaped craft, along with a few other configurations, were all designed for a singular purpose – to gather the resources and materials needed to construct this very vessel, These smaller vessels are now on board The Archimedes, the very ship they helped build."

Ripple's of astonishment coursed through the crowd, as the implications of his words took root. The very objects that had ignited the imaginations of generations, the subject of countless conspiracy theories and heated debates, had been nothing more than tools in a far grander scheme, a means to an end that had remained shrouded in secrecy until this very moment.

Jacks paused, his piercing gaze looking at a sea of stunned faces before him, gauging their reactions. Some wore expressions of disbelief, their minds struggling to reconcile the fantastical notion with the reality they had known. Others however seemed to embrace the revelation with a sense of dawning comprehension, as if the puzzle pieces were finally falling into place.

"This ship you now stand upon," he continued, his voice resonating with a newfound sense of gravitas, "Is the culmination of a plan that spans eons, a blueprint for your survival that has been sent back through the very fabric of time itself. So yes the blueprint for Archimedes came from the future.

The words sent a shock wave at the souls stood before him, then a stunned silence. In that moment, the boundaries of what they had deemed possible had been shattered, their perceptions of reality irreversibly altered by the revelations that had been laid bare before them.

Some exchanged furtive glances, their eyes alight with a mixture of awe, while others stood transfixed, their minds really struggling with the implications of a reality that transcended the confines of their understanding.

Yet, amid the tumult of emotions and the upheaval of preconceived notions, a glimmer of hope began to take root – a realization that, in the face of an existential threat that had spanned eons, they had been granted a lifeline, a chance to defy the inexorable march of fate and chart a new course toward survival.

Their leaders words had sunk in, a shift seemed to move throughout the crowd. Indeed a momentous revelation. For in that moment they had been anointed with a purpose that transcended the boundaries of their individual existences, a mission that would echo through the annals of time itself.

Jeremiah Jacks' expression grew sombre as he delved into the darker aspects of the revelations he was unveiling. A hush fell over the assembled crowd once more, their breaths seemingly held in anticipation of the grim knowledge he was about to impart.

"While the UFO's you encountered were tools in our grand endeavour," he began, his voice carrying regret, "There were others, yes other alien vessels with far more wicked intentions towards humanity."

Unease coursed through everyone present, at the mere mention of such malevolent forces.

"These craft," he continued, his brow furrowing as he recalled the harrowing encounters, "Harboured ill intent towards you, their motives shrouded in the darkness of cosmic indifference."

Each syllable of his words a chilling reminder of the ever-present threats that lurked beyond the veil of humanity's understanding. For many in the crowd, the notion of hostile alien presences had been relegated to the realm of science fiction, a fanciful concept that existed only in the pages of speculative literature or the flickering images of Hollywood blockbusters.

Yet, here they stood, confronted with the reality that such forces were not mere figments of imagination, but tangible entities that had cast their malign shadows upon the very world they had called home.

He continued "But you were not defenceless," he declared, his voice carrying a steely determination that seemed to cut through the pall of trepidation that had settled upon the assembly. "The UFO craft already mentioned to you and as already stated, are now present deep within this very vessel, they possessed the means to neutralise any threat that dared encroach upon our solar domain, you call it the Solar System."

Shoulders straightened, and expressions shifted from apprehension to cautious hope, buoyed by the knowledge that they had been shielded from these cosmic harbingers of malice, their safety secured by the very craft that are within this ship.

"Mankind never knew," Jacks continued, his voice tinged with a hint of regret. "The battles that raged in the void, the incursions that were thwarted before they could ever breach the veil of this atmosphere, remained shrouded in secrecy, hidden from the very souls we sought to protect." Jacks added, "Presidents, Prime Ministers, Kings and Queens knew nothing."

A profound silence now, punctuated only by the occasional rustle of fabric or the muted shuffle of feet as the assembled individuals processed Jeremiah Jacks' words. For many, the revelation that they had not been privy to a cosmic conflict of unimaginable proportions was a sobering realization, a reminder of the fragility of their existence and the ever-present threats that loomed beyond the boundaries of their perception.

For until that moment, no human had been granted a glimpse behind the veil of secrecy, a glimpse that had both humbled and emboldened them in equal measure. They were no longer mere passengers on a journey into the unknown, but warriors anointed with the knowledge of the battles that had been fought in their name, a stark reminder of the sacrifices that had paved the way for their deliverance. He went on to tell them that the aliens often depicted in movies called the greys did get into the atmosphere and were indeed bad apples and these had to be defeated because they were abducting humans at an alarming rate.

There was a sharp intake of breath from several over these revelations. Jacks added, "A long time ago we laid the foundations that should there come a time that this realm was threatened, there would be hope that some of our descendants left on this planet would have a chance. It was a measure put in place all that time ago as already explained. Yes you were forgotten and left to fend for yourselves and that was a terrible mistake. However the Androids we left behind helped create the Sanctuary that we recently left and it provided for you very recently with just that...Protection."

Everyone was now transfixed in the revelations. Jacks went on, "When that activation happened I travelled through time to oversee it all as did certain elements that we have just spoken about. I know you have many questions but hopefully today I have tried to cover most of them."

Jeremiah Jacks now changed his tone "I am now announcing my officers," he declared. "The position of Captain will be held by Jim, a man whom I trust implicitly, as I take up the mantle of Admiral Of The Fleet."

A ripple of murmurs swept through the assembly, punctuated by nods of approval and whispered acknowledgments of Jim's unwavering dedication and fortitude, the man that believed when most would not have done so. The man himself stood tall, his expression a portrait of humble acceptance tinged with a newfound sense of responsibility, his gritty Yorkshire resolve had indeed been tested..

Captain Jacks' gaze swept over the crowd, his eyes alight with a mixture of pride and resolve. "For their extraordinary bravery and unwavering courage in the face of adversity," he continued, The roles of Executive Officers shall be bestowed upon Clio and Jessica."

A chorus of approving exclamations erupted from the gathered individuals, as they recognized the selfless acts and resolute spirits that had earned these two women such a prestigious honour. Clio and Jessica exchanged a quick glance, their eyes shimmering with a mixture of humility and determination, a silent vow passing between them to uphold the sacred trust that had been placed upon their shoulders.

But Captain Jacks was not yet done, his voice carrying a note of profound admiration as he turned his gaze towards Clio & Jessica . "And it would be a remiss on my part if I did not offer a special mention to the new Executive Officers, firstly Jessica a young nineteen year old from New York City who just wanted a good time, well she had to endure what she saw on that Alien Craft. Most people twice her age would have been destroyed by what she had seen but no not Jessica a tenacious lady who became stronger and has shown great leadership many times. She deserves this position." Everyone applauded some even whistled their approval much to Jessica's embarrassment.

Captain Jacks then turned his attention to Clio, "Despite being critically injured, this young Arizona woman, this remarkable lady stood her ground and continued firing her Vendor at an alien craft, a display of valour and steadfast resolve that humbles me to my core." Admiral Jacks paused, his expression one of reverent awe as he met Clio's gaze and said. "It is an honour to have her presence among us."

A thunderous ovation erupted from the crowd, a cacophony of cheers and applause that seemed to shake the very foundations of the Bridge. Clio's eyes widened, her cheeks flushed with a mixture of pride and humility as the weight of Admiral Jacks' accolades.

In that moment, she stood as a living embodiment of the indomitable spirit that had carried them through the darkest of trials, courage and resilience that inspired all who bore witness to her unwavering resolve.

Yet, even as the adulation swirled around her, Clio remained grounded, her gaze steady and her demeanour radiating a quiet strength that transcended the need for fanfare or accolades. For in her heart, she knew that her actions had been borne not of a desire for glory, but of an unwavering commitment to protect those she held dear, a selfless devotion that had been forged in the crucible of their shared ordeal.

As the thunderous applause gradually subsided, Admiral Jacks turned his attention to another figure, his expression one of reverent respect. “And finally,” he proclaimed, his voice carrying a note of solemn pride, “The role of Weapons Officer shall be entrusted to the capable hands of the dead shot, Barbara."

A collective murmur of approval rippled through the crowd, as they acknowledged the unwavering marksmanship and tactical acumen that had earned Barbara such a vital role. She stood tall, her eyes alight with a steely glare that spoke volumes of her readiness to wield the awesome power that had now been placed in her hands.

As the echoes of Admiral Jacks’ finished by saying that Rick and Josh our most human androids will guide all our officers through their tasks, as the pronouncements faded into the charged stillness of the Bridge, a unity had taken root within the hearts and minds of those gathered. For in that singular moment, they had been anointed not merely as passengers on a journey into the unknown, but as a cohesive unit, bound by the unbreakable bonds of shared adversity and unwavering resolve.

The officers that had been chosen were living embodiments of the qualities that had carried them through the darkest of trials – courage, resilience, selflessness, and an unwavering commitment to the greater good.

They would face the challenges that lay ahead as a unified force, drawing strength from the unbreakable bonds that had been forged in the fires of their shared struggle. And though the path ahead remained shrouded in uncertainty, they carried within them the spirit that had guided them thus far.

The charged stillness that had enveloped the Bridge was shattered by Captain Jim's commanding voice, his words carrying the weight of authority that befitted his newly bestowed role. "Prepare for our exit," he bellowed, his gaze sweeping over the assembled crew with a steely resolve. "All of Archimedes doors must be sealed before the outer doors to Walker Lake start to open."

On his command a flurry of activity erupted in the wake of this order. The robots that had been standing by in silent vigil sprang into action, their metallic limbs moving with a well-choreographed precision. Within moments, the echoes of clanking doors and the hiss of airtight seals reverberated through the corridors, each sound a testament to the meticulous preparation that was underway.

The new crew watched with bated breath, the reports began to filter in, a steady stream of confirmations that cascaded through the ship's communications systems. Executive Officer Clio, now known as Commander, her keen senses attuned to the ebb and flow of activity, compiled the incoming data with an efficiency that belied her youth.

"The ship is secured, Captain," she announced, her voice carrying a note of crisp professionalism that seemed to belie the moment.

Captain Jim's gaze found Clio's, and for a fleeting instant, a warm smile tugged at the corners of his lips, a gesture that spoke volumes of the newfound respect and admiration he held for this remarkable young woman. "Thank you, Commander," he replied, his tone gentler than the circumstances might have warranted, a bond that had been forged between them some time ago.

In that moment, unity rippled through the assembled crew, all understood that they stood poised on the precipice of a journey that would forever alter the course of their destinies. All eyes now turned towards the towering view screen, its surface flickering with a kaleidoscope of readouts and telemetry data.

Captain Jim stepped forward, his gaze fixed upon the display, his expression a mask of steely determination. With a single, resolute nod, he uttered the words that would set in motion the next phase of their extraordinary odyssey.

"Initiate Walker Lake outer door sequence," he commanded, his voice carrying a weight that reverberated throughout the ship. Everyone heard him wherever they were in the ship. Some adults saying this is like a movie.

A low rumble emanated from deep within the cavern, a vibration that grew in intensity with each passing second. The view screen flickered, and a series of external cameras flickered to life, offering a breathtaking panorama of the vast cavern that had been this ships sanctuary.

The immense outer doors began to grind open, very slowly as first a trickle of water then the trickle became more of a flood as the waters of Walker Lake flooded in.

A smaller side tunnel could be seen and Admiral Jacks advised Jim that this was how Dodger had gained access to the cavern whilst acting like a submarine.

The ancient mechanisms of the underground cavern straining against the weight of the water. A dark gloom spread over the ship as the water rose past the Bridge level, it was now a torrent of water, quickly the chamber completely flooded leaving the Archimedes totally under water.

Gasps of awe could be heard as the spaceships floodlights came on and the true majesty of their surroundings was revealed – a vast, cavernous expanse that stretched out before them, its walls shimmering with a kaleidoscope of natural hues that defied description under the water.

Without sound the giant spaceship edged forward through the flooded chamber toward the expanse that is Walker Lake.

Chapter 19

BATTLE STATIONS

The spacecraft Archimedes slowly disengaged from the rocky alcove. Her powerful thrusters kicked up clouds of dust and debris from the underwater floor as she backed away from the cavern's mouth, freeing herself from the underground grotto's embrace.

Bright external lights from the cavern and the ship pierced the deep blue atmosphere of Walker Lake, illuminating the underwater landscape around the craft. The AI pilot expertly guided Archimedes through a series of narrow canyons formed from ancient lava flows. Her sensors pinged constantly, mapping the topography.

She moved farther from the cavern's entrance, now the light quickly fading until as only the craft's floodlights cut through the darkness. Archimedes felt her way deeper into the flooded calder (rough waters).

The silence was broken. Jim spoke up urgently, "Josh has just reported we're picking up a lone distress signal. As soon as we break through to the surface, pinpoint that location and get coordinates locked in."

The massive spacecraft 'The Archimedes' continued pressing through Walker Lake.

"Almost to the surface," the AI pilot called out. "Initiating vertical ascent in three, two, one..."

Archimedes shot up through the water like a bullet, smashing through the icy surface to rest magnificently on the surface of the frozen lake.

"Surface reached, re-establishing signal lock," Josh intoned. "Plotting vector...got it! The distress beacon is coming from bearing 216 by 334, approximately 14 miles from our current position."

Jim nodded firmly. "Lock in those coordinates. Let's go see who needs our help out here."

The craft rose silently into the air and to everyone's amazement its advanced propulsion making no noise whatsoever. Admiral Jacks ordered them to proceed at a steady, slow speed while they prepared for the 'Clean Sweep' operation.

After several crew members asked about the mysterious clean sweep and Admiral Jacks explained grimly. "We are carrying ten hypersonic missiles with a very important payload. This payload represents our hope of one day driving the alien invaders off this planet."

He paused, seeming to weigh his next words carefully. "Each missile has been armed with a thriving ecosystem of genetically engineered bacteria and viruses. They have been specifically modified to be able to survive and propagate in the alien atmosphere in which the invaders have seeded across Earth. We believe the shadows, over time will have little resistance to them."

Admiral Jacks said, "Its over to you Jim."

Captain Jim looked up to Barbara and Josh as he said calmly, "Fire The Missile." Within an instant of the missiles being discharged the Hypersonic missiles were on their way to different parts of planet Earth.

The world outside appeared serene yet frigid. A blanket of pristine snow covered the landscape as far as the eye could see. The sunlight reflected brilliantly off the unbroken white expanse, almost blinding in its intensity. Not a single footprint or any other sign of life marred the frozen tundra's surface.

No breeze to disturb the silence. Bare tree branches were encased in thick layers of glittering ice. Now and then a branch would fall with the sheer weight of the ice, their skeletal forms etched starkly against the gray sky, certainly not natural. In the distance, a range of mountains, their craggy peaks adorned with clinging deep snow.

An aura of profound cold emanated from this crystalline world. Every object, seemed to radiate a biting chill that the sensors picked up.

An almost supernatural hush blanketed the frozen domain. Occasionally, a delicate chime would ring out as a branch shed a layer of brittle ice. But the eerie stillness would quickly reassert itself, the world locked in an unworldly winter's frozen embrace, beautiful yet utterly inhospitable to anything but the hardiest of life forms. It was a place of austere, unwavering tranquillity.

The barren, frozen landscape stretched out in all directions, utterly devoid of oxygen or any other gases that could sustain life. It was a world of perpetual winter, locked in an icy grip.

The ground itself was a vast expanse of solid ice, cracked into rigid sheets and glazed with a dusting of frost crystals. No soil or vegetation could be seen - the entire surface consisted of frigid, bluish-white ice as far as the eye could perceive.

Overhead, the blue sky started to form an inky blackness, the atmosphere was starting to slip away now and the normality of colour was no longer there. Thousands upon thousands of stars burned brilliantly against the empty void.

Earth was now a cold, dead world - losing any ability to hold warmth or support respiration. An eerie silence blanketed this now alien geography, with no gaseous medium to propagate even the faintest sound. Even the breeze detected earlier by the ships sensors, was gone.

Josh was reporting back that all the cannisters were now exposed to the planet. The last one being detonated over Australia.

As the ship approached the coordinates of the distress signal, Captain Jacks and the crew braced themselves, unsure of what they might find. But what they witnessed made their blood run cold.

In the distance, the unmistakable silhouette of an alien craft hung ominously in the void. Its bizarre, non-humanoid angles and protrusions marked it as clearly extraterrestrial in origin.

But it wasn't the mere presence of the alien ship that shocked them. It was the appalling act it seemed to be in the process of committing.

The two humans in a sort of snow buggy with space suits on obviously protecting them from the hostile world. As the Archimedes crew watched in horror, the two humans began to visibly crumple and contort under incredible forces.

Jacks' face drained of colour as he realized what was transpiring. "They're...crushing them. Compacting them down to a dense mass." The two human beings were now being processed their lifeless bodies being held in mid air by the power of the alien craft. Exactly what had been described so horrifyingly by Jessica on board that craft and now it was being carried out right here and right now. The humans were now encased in the same description that Jessica gave, they were crushed and sealed into a sheet of plastic.

"Why?" someone whispered, aghast. "What possible reason could they have?"

Admiral Jacks shook his head grimly. "Who knows the motivations of such beings. But one thing is clear - they have no regard for life whatsoever."

Jessica couldn't look away she was riveted, her eyes could not move from the horrific scene unfolding on the ships screen. Her hands trembled as she watched the alien ship crush and compact the men.

Revulsion and disbelief warred within her. What manner of beings could be so utterly devoid of empathy or mercy? To snuff out lives with such calculated indifference - it beggared comprehension. She thought, were they men or women or a married couple, her mind racing. A lump formed in her throat as the implications sank in. If the aliens showed no compassion whatsoever, what hope do we ever have, her blood ran cold.

Jessica felt bile rise up, fought down the urge to be sick right there on the bridge. Flashes of the gruesome compaction sequence replayed in her mind's eye, searing themselves onto her psyche. The cold, clinical way the craft had simply erased these people from existence.

"Inhuman..." she whispered, voice scarcely audible over the pounding of blood in her ears. "Monstrous..."

She shuddered violently, feeling a pit of revulsion and despair open up inside her. If these were the sort of beings they faced, this implacable void of empathy...did they even stand a chance?

Jessica hugged herself tightly, trying in vain to stop her body's panicked shaking. Of all the scenarios she had braced for, nothing could have prepared her for the bone-chilling callousness they had just witnessed. She knew that sight would haunt her nightmares for a long time to come.

Admiral Jacks' face was steely with resolve as he witnessed the alien ship's cold-blooded act. Jaw clenched, he whirled to face his crew.

"Shields up, maximum deflection!" he barked.

"All hands to battle stations, now!!!"

The crew scrambled to their positions, fear and adrenaline coursing through them after seeing that chilling display of alien malice.

"You have seen what they're capable of," Jacks said grimly. "Prepare for any eventuality."

He turned back to the viewscreen, watching intently as the alien craft began to move away from where the victims had been brutally destroyed.

"Ensign, plot an intercept course. Ahead full! We're going after them."

There were a few gasps from the crew at this daring order. To purposefully engage such remorseless beings...

"Sir?" someone questioned hesitantly. "Are you certain?"

"That's an order!" Admiral Jacks roared. "We can't let them just carry on unmolested after that atrocity. Lock plasma cannons and arm deterrence missiles!"

The klaxons began blaring as the ship powered up its weapon systems. Jacks gripped his chair tightly, a fire burning in his eyes.

"If it's a fight they want, we'll give it to them tenfold. Strap in tight - we're about to show these bastards what we're made of!"

With a lurch, the ship accelerated in pursuit of the alien craft, determined to bring its merciless crews to justice - or avenge their victims in a blaze of fury.

All this time Captain Jacks had been cool calm but not now he had witnessed many things but these two people that had been begging for help had been murdered. Now everything had changed.

The ship's interior took on an urgent intensity. Klaxon alarms blared, their harsh wailing cutting through the controlled chaos. Emergency light strobes in pulsing crimson across bulkheads and consoles. Emergency battle station lights flashed throughout the ship, as people hurried to secure themselves and others.

On the bridge, crew members' faces were bathed in the flashing red glare as they worked their stations feverishly. Fingers flew over control surfaces, bringing weapon systems online and rerouteing auxiliary power to defensive shields.

The overhead lighting flickered and dimmed as the ship shunted energy to vital systems. A constant thrum of built-up power vibrated through the deck plating beneath their feet.

Sharp orders and terse status reports echoed through the intercom, adding to the rising cacophony. Crewmen urgently consulted damage control maps, preparing countermovement actions before the first shot was even fired.

On the main gun decks, weapons specialists fed armour-piercing munitions into autoloaders as targeting sensors swivelled into alignment. Capacitor banks began cycling with a rising electrical whine as they built up for staggering discharges of plasma energy.

The air was thick with tension, drowning the crew in an atmosphere of controlled panic and fierce determination. Every soul braced for the unavoidable violence to come, minds focused with laser-like intensity.

"Captain!" Clio shouted urgently from her sensor station. "This ship...it's different. Not like the android sentinel ships we've encountered."

Admiral Jacks' expression hardened as he turned towards her. "I know, Commander. I've seen the telemetry."

He straightened, squaring his shoulders as if bracing himself. "That's no mere robotic probe out there. It's the real thing." His voice took on a grim tone. "The Shadow Race...and they've arrived ahead of schedule."

Murmurs of dread rippled through the bridge crew at those ominous words. Jacks looked out at them, his eye blazing.

"Let there be no illusions, people! We're staring true evil in the eye this time. The Shadow Race makes the Sentinels look like children's toys."

He stabbed a finger at the view screen, where the alien monolith cut an imposing figure amid the backdrop of stars.

"Those twisted wretches live only to subjugate and destroy. If they defeat us here, not just our worlds - but our entire species faces extinction..."

Jacks' fist clenched violently. "Slavery and brutality on a cosmic scale, at the hands of monsters who know no mercy, no remorse. Who just executed two humans before our eyes!"

He slammed it down on his armrest, the impact ringing through the tense bridge.

"So I'll ask you one last time, crew. Are you ready to face the darkness head on? To slam the door shut on these soulless conquerors before we leave on our journey?"

The Captain's piercing gaze passed over each of them in turn.

He added, "We are the bright line between the light and the abyss. So say it with me now - let the Shadow Race be introduced...to the fury of the Human Race!"

A primal roar of defiance and determination answered him, shaking the bridge deck underfoot. It was a cry from the depths of their collective souls - put voice to the singular, a will to live free or die on their feet.

No matter the odds, mankind would not meekly accept the lash of tyranny this day. As one, they turned to face the eternally ravenous darkness, ready to give their all to keep its hunger at bay.

Jacks focused on the instruments and glancing toward Barbara saying, "On my mark Barbara, now lock weapons onto this craft," she acknowledged him as she struggled to get a lock there was a computer warning.

"Warning! Incoming hostile attack vector four !" The computer's toneless voice boomed over the intercom.

"Brace for impact!" Jacks roared, gripping the arm of his chair. "All crews brace!"

On the main viewer, blazing lances of coruscating energy lashed out from the Shadow Race dreadnought. The potent beams of annihilation crossed the void in an instant, forcing the Archimedes shields to flare brilliantly.

The entire bridge shuddered violently as the impacts slammed home. Crewmen grappled for hand-holds, teeth gritted against the violent juddering. Displays flickered and overloaded from the onslaught of electromagnetic interference.

"Deflector output at maximum!" someone called out, voice straining. "They're hammering us with gamma lasers and what appear to be some kind of unknown energy!"

Jacks clutched his restraints with white knuckles, riding out each bone-jarring volley.

"Remember this ship of ours has technology way above theirs so send it back to them double!" he roared. "Fire every countermeasure battery at their bow!"

At his command, the ship's entire arsenal joined the blinding crossfire. Directed energy, charged particle beams and smart munition missile salvos lashed back at the alien juggernaut.

"You want to storm the gates of hell, you black-souled monsters?" he snarled at the alien craft. "Over my dead body you will!"

"Damage report!" he barked over the cacophony of battle.

"Forward shields holding, we can't keep taking these proton lances head-on!" His weapons officer responded, sweat beading on her brow. "Return fire is diminishing and not penetrating their armour!"

Jacks gaze hardened. It was time to go unto the breach.

"Then we punch through a new way," he said grimly. "Prepare to deploy the Vendor system!"

The bridge crew snapped to attention at those words, they knew what a hand held Vendor can do but what can a massive ships Vendor do, all faces tense. The Ships Vendor was their ship's ultimate contingency armament - never before utilized in combat in this time zone .

He stabbed a finger at the view screen, where the alien dreadnought's nightmarish silhouette loomed implacably.

"That's the face of extinction out there. So make your choice - obliteration at their hands? Or a fighting back with the Vendor?"

A grim pause lingered on the bridge as the choice sank in, he looked right at Jim. Jim gave a resolute nod.

"Vendor Systems confirmed, Captain. All crew...brace for very severe shockwaves in thirty seconds!"

Technicians began initiating the complex firing sequence, sending commands that would prepare the Vendor technology.

Jacks allowed himself a feral grin as the system built its power.

"Alright you Soulless Shadows...let's see how you like being introduced to human creativity from the future!"

With a deafening thunder, the Vendor discharged its fire. You could see the target clearly.

As the Vendor system discharged, reality itself seemed to groan and distort around Archimedes.

Captain Jacks held on with grim determination, his teeth gritted against the torrential cacophony threatening to overwhelm his senses.

All he could see through the madness was a roiling vortex of distortion surrounding them - a bizarre dimension of fractured geometries.

Just then for an instant there was total silence, the energetic maelstrom outside found its horrific purpose. Like a collapsing star, the frenzied spatial distortions contracted with an apocalyptic implosion directly ahead of them.

Where the Shadow Race's dreadnought had hung defiant just moments before, an all-consuming singularity of ultra-dense gravimetric force replaced it. The monstrous alien craft's seemingly impregnable defences proved appallingly insufficient against the Vendor's localized folding of space-time itself.

In the span of a mortal heartbeat, the aliens' mighty warship was subsumed, its unimaginable mass captured, compressed and crushed down into an infinitely dense point of no-return by the awesome energies unleashed.

The vortex anomaly collapsed in on itself with a silent implosion that created a profound, transient void and then, like a perverse second Big Bang eruption... detonation forces propagated outward in a universe-shattering shock wave.

Jacks shouted, "All power to the shields!"

The detonation shock wave unleashed by the Vendor's catastrophic implosion of the alien dreadnought was of truly cosmic proportions.

At its fever bright, searing wavefront the energy released defied comprehension like a roiling hell storm of gamma radiation, subatomic fallout, and rippling gravitational tsunami powerful enough to tear anything in its path asunder.

Like an ocean of annihilation hurtling across the void, the cataclysmic blast engulfed everything in its path. Matter itself was ionized into its fundamental particles by the sheer ferocity of the advancing front.

The maelstrom crashed against them in an unrelenting cosmic tide, almost shearing away at their protective cocoon. Thunderous impacts resonated through the ship as exotic particles slammed home.

The bridge crew watched in breathless horror through displays gone static as the wavefront's nightmarish leading edge loomed ever larger like a searing light devouring oblivion, seething with the primal violence of an entire star going nova.

Then it was upon them, subsuming them utterly in a single fleeting instant of scouring, apocalyptic bedlam that strained the very bonds of physics itself.

But guttered by desperation and sheer force of will, the stalwart shields held - barely. The ship rode out the cosmic battering like a battered wraith lashed by the fires of creation.

As the last of the the fallout and shock wave passed, Jacks let out the breath he didn't realize he'd been holding. Sparks rained down around the bridge as fail safes re-engaged with resetting klaxons.

An eerie silence hung over the battered bridge as the crew slowly came back to their senses in the aftermath of that cataclysmic event. Wisps of smoke and the acrid tang of ozone filled the air.

Jacks shakily pulled himself upright in his command chair, surveying the devastation around him through ghost-light emergency illumination. Crewmen groaned and staggered to their feet, disoriented but miraculously alive.

Sparks showered from shattered consoles as a few chuckled weakly at the sheer improbability of their survival. Tension bled away into nervous laughter at having defied oblivion itself.

Jim hauled himself up from where he'd been flung across the deck, coughing through a pained grin. "Well...I don't know about the rest of you...but I think I soiled my suit just a tad back there."

Jacks replied, “If I ever fire the Ships Vendor again can someone please remind me to get more distance from the target.” Jim smiled at the comment.

That broke the strained silence, laughter rippling through the bridge crew at the masterful understatement. Jacks smiling back wiped a trickle of blood from his brow.

“Hey now,” he called out in a joking tone, forcing levity into his voice. “Next time I order Vendor to fire ...Can I add to what I said. Let’s be sure to get a few hundred thousand miles away first, shall we?”

The attempted humour released a wave of anxious mirth yet again from the crew. They clung to Jacks’ words like a lifeline, allowing the worst of the tension to disperse as they revelled in being improbably, impossibly alive.

“Sure thing, Admiral,” Jim wheezed through a half-sob, half-laugh. “We’ll just warp right over to the next damn system first!”

Guffaws and snorts of hysterical relief echoed through the ruined bridge at that. For an endless moment, the profound absurdity of their near-obliteration overwhelmed them all in a cacophony of breathless, giddy laughter.

Jacks watched his crew with fierce pride as they surrendered to the need to purge the stark terror from their souls with humour. They had stared into the eye of oblivion fearlessly - and it had blinked first.

Then a voice, heard ship wide, "Dave here, no serious injuries reported just cuts and bruises and some broken bones. Everyone is being looked after."

Jacks felt a feral grin spread across his battered face. “Well then...didn't we like to give those Shadow bastards an encore, eh?”

A ragged cheer answered him as the indomitable human spirit rallied once more. They have survived to keep on fighting in the future.

Now it was time to leave Earth and head to wherever Jeremiah Jacks needed us to go. He says we are heading home.

***

Later when the crew were stood down and the ship was in space, Clio and Jessica sat huddled together in a quiet corner of the ship's observation lounge. Through the battered viewports, the endless star field stretched out before them, a tapestry of brilliant pinpricks sewn across the cosmic blackness.

They had barely caught their breath after the cataclysmic battle, the memory of those apocalyptic forces still fresh enough to make them shudder. For a few stolen moments, they could simply be two friends sharing a quiet conversation amidst the aftermath.

"Can you believe we actually pulled that off?" Clio asked, shaking her head in disbelief. "Using the Vendor like that...we're lucky we didn't rupture into our component atoms."

Jessica let out a tremulous breath. "I know. When that shock wave hit...I really thought that was it for us." She managed a wan smile. "Leave it to Jeremiah Jacks to gamble everything on some crazy, futuristic experimental tech."

"Heh, yeah...just another day at the office for him, I guess," Clio chuckled ruefully.

A contemplative silence fell between them as they watched the stars continue their stately celestial processes, untouched by the furies of battle raging amongst the motes of life.

"So..." Jessica ventured after a moment. "What do you think is next? After a showdown like that with the Shadow Race's force?"

Clio pursed her lips, pondering. "Well...unless I miss my guess, we'll be high tailing it towards the rendezvous coordinates as fast as we can push the engines. We're going to need all the allied ships we can muster."

"Seven months," Jessica mused. "Just seven months until we can find more ships like ours then make a concerted push for the true home world, wherever that is."

Her gaze grew distant, seemingly seeing past the infinite star fields before them towards something longed-for but indefinable.

"Can you imagine it, Clio? Finding the mythical cradle of humanity at long last? Our real home among the stars!" Remarked Jessica.

Clio matched her friend's wistful expression with one of her own. "I've dreamed about it since I was a little girl, hearing constant Sci-Fi stories." She shook her head slowly. "I can scarcely picture what it will be like. A world of our own, safe from the threats of alien domination and subjugation at last and where humans don't fight each other."

For a moment, their war-wearied souls dared to look beyond the perpetual crisis towards a different destiny - one of reclamation, rebirth, rediscovered unity.

"We're so close, Jess," Clio whispered. "Seven more months of fighting the good fight, and our entire race may be reborn amongst the stars."

Jessica's hand found hers and squeezed it tightly.

"Then let's make sure we get there," she replied with fierce resolution. "No matter what bastards like the Shadow Race, gets thrown at us next."

Together, bathed in starlight, they wordlessly redoubled their commitment to the trials ahead. The dream of their ancestral home world among the heavens beckoned - and they would stop at nothing to deliver humanity to its cosmic door.

The journey continues.......

Epilogue

NEW HORIZONS

The story of Jim, Barbara, Clio & Jessica will continue as they reach for new Horizons in the void of space. New encounters and new hope as their journey continues and I would like you all to come along.

Printed in Great Britain
by Amazon

45190621R00238